Also by Beth Webb

Star Dancer

FiRe dReAmeR

THE BOOK OF FIRE

BETH WEBB

MACMILLAN CHILDREN'S BOOKS

First published 2007 by Macmillan Children's Books
a division of Macmillan Publishers Limited
20 New Wharf Road, London N1 9RR
Basingstoke and Oxford
www.panmacmillan.com

Associated companies throughout the world

ISBN: 978-0-330-45411-7

1 3 5 7 9 8 6 4 2

A CIP catalogue record for this book is available from
the British Library.

Typeset by Intype Libra Ltd
Printed and bound in Great Britain by Mackays of Chatham plc, Kent

For Gabriel, my own Fire Dreamer, and for Jenny.
May you always have Fire in your heads.

Acknowledgements

My thanks, as always, to my friends
and family for all their love and support,

especially Bruce Johnstone-Lowe
of the British Druid Order,

Yeoman Raven Master Derrick Coyle R.V.M. at the
Tower of London, for his patient advice about ravens,

Pete Knight for his expertise on fire and the Romans,

Andy for Iron Age forensics, and Chloe
and the Kilvites for their untiring help with
plotting and criticism.

Contents

LUGHNASADH

SAMHAIN

The story so far . . .

At the end of the Iron Age the Romans are on the verge of invading Britain. The druids have prophesised the birth of the Star Dancer, who will bring hope in the midst of despair. Desperate to find the boy, to train him in war-craft and druidry, they ignore the birth of Tegen, an insignificant girl who weilds a wild, untutored magic and who believes she a has a destiny to fulfil.

Eventually the druids begin to accept her, but she has two arch-enemies: the scheming Gorgans,who longs to be the Star Dancer himself, and Derowen, a malicious witch whose dark powers are pitched against Tegen.

With the help of Griff, Tegen's foster-brother, she at last begins her training as the Star Dancer and a druid of the Winter Seas, but she is tricked into accidently killing Gilda, the kindly midwife who believed in her from the moment of her birth.

Tegen's confidence is further crushed when the green silk shawl that she believes holds her magical powers is stolen. Derowen and Gorgans raise a demon, believing that it will destroy Tegen.

Instead it destroys them and becomes the catalyst for Tegen to grow into her full inheritance . . .

BELTANE

. . . A time when spirits move between the worlds.

. . . A time for lighting cleansing fires
to banish winter's sickness and to protect from magic.

. . . A time for the Shadow Walker to reach his hand into the
darkness to summon a new familiar from the land of the
unblessed.

1. Admidios

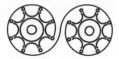

He shivered in the desolate remains of his great hall. Only two blackened walls still stood where once he had feasted with his warriors. No thatch clung to the twisted remains of the charcoal beams.

Rain lashed on Admidios's face as he nursed his malice and resentment. He had always been denied the power and honour he deserved.

Bitter memories flashed through his head: his noble father, his slave mother, his younger brothers who took turns to wear his crown; the great Emperor Caligula who befriended him, but who was murdered; then the new lords of Rome who sneered at him.

The relentless winds flung a fresh blast of rain into Admidios's face. He tried to light a fire, but the kindling was soaked. Feeble trails of wet smoke faded with the evening light.

His fingers dug under the chin of the newborn lamb as he jerked its head right back. The creature gave a strangled bleat, but was bound too tightly to struggle. Admidios drove his knife into its throat. Air and blood gushed and bubbled as the creature fell limp.

Admidios's warm, slippery fingers dropped the blade. He spread his hands to the skies and screeched above the storm's whine: 'Come to me, spirits of hate. Give me the power to defeat all who despise me.'

There were other memories too: a baby boy, screaming and kicking inside a cloak, then hidden in a basket and taken from Britain to Rome. There, Admidios had been the boy's guardian. Those years had been good. He had been greeted as 'Magistrate' in the street. But the obedient child had grown into a rebellious youth.

Admidios snapped a twig and wished it was his nephew's neck. 'If I cannot have his obedience, I shall have his title! Power *will* be mine!'

He stood. It was almost dark and the hall's ruined beams groaned and swayed, threatening to fall on him. He wiped the animal's blood across his face and threw back his head. The wind flapped and tugged at his cloak. 'Spirits of anger and loathing, take my body for your own!' he called.

*

☀ 4 ☀

The storm sighed away. Silence echoed in the empty ruin.

A demon had heard him. A demon that longed for vengeance as much as he did. A demon who had recently been defeated . . . by a mere girl.

Will you give me your soul? it whispered.

Admidios lowered his arms and looked around as the darkness swallowed the ruins. 'If you give me my desires, I will serve you through this life and all my lives to come!' he swore.

In return, you must do something for me.

The voice thrilled him as it trickled like warm sand into his mind. 'Anything, Lord!'

Find the raven-haired one. Harness her power into my service.

Admidios fell to his knees. 'Just show me how!'

When the time comes, the voice came again. *Meanwhile, you must walk in the shadows and wait for me there. I will send you a servant of mine you can trust. For now, I give you a gift. Use it wisely.*

The presence had gone, as had the wind and rain, leaving only night.

Shaking, Admidios groped around for the unlit pile of wood. He struck flints together once more. 'Obey me and bring fire!' he hissed. A spark caught in the damp kindling. A flame leaped. He cried out in pain for the light seared his eyes.

He stamped at the orange and gold tongues until they died.

In that moment of light, he caught sight of his gift.

It was a shrunken human head.

2. First Flight

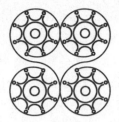

The uneasy spirit shifted inside the unfamiliar body. She wasn't used to her new form yet – in fact, she didn't even realize she had been reborn. She only knew she was a young raven peering over the edge of the nest and looking down on a world that seemed . . . *wrong.*

The early summer spread before her in a mist of tiny foliage sprayed with frothy white and pink blossoms. Warm sun made her feathers feel good. She yawned and stretched her wings. Just then, her mother landed on the edge of the nest and, seeing a wide-open beak, she pushed a strip of flesh into the waiting throat. The young bird swallowed and eyed her hungry siblings with beady malevolence, daring them to complain.

They squawked with jealousy, but she didn't care. She swallowed and rearranged her feathers as she continued to watch the world below. She didn't know what she was looking for . . . a grub maybe, a chick fallen from a nest?

. . . Or a human in a blue dress, long black hair spreading out behind her as she ran, chasing a giggling child and a large mud-coloured dog.

Suddenly the raven knew she had to do something important. *Now.* She scrabbled up the nest until she swayed unsteadily on the twiggy rim. The breeze teased and lifted her rainbow-black plumage as she stretched her wings to their fullest. She relished the cooling air under her flight feathers as she surveyed the world below. She wasn't frightened. She knew that was where she must be: down there with the dogs and cats and rats and all the other terrors her parents warned her of.

She fanned her tail and *quorked* to the sky. Delight. Delight. Now. She must do it *now*!

At that moment her father landed shrieking behind her. 'Stop! You are too young. Your tail is scarcely grown . . .'

But the spirit was not fond of waiting and good counsel. She had been created from resentment, self-will and the desire to rule. She let the wind catch under her outstretched pinions and launched herself into the air.

But a long branch of crab apple loomed in front of her. It caught in her left wing, she lost her trim and tumbled in an ignominious ball, next to the human in blue.

The girl put out her hand. 'Are you all right? Let me look – I won't hurt you . . .'

The raven jabbed her beak at the five fat worm-shapes thrust towards her, grabbed the middle one and tried to snap it.

'Ouch!' the girl yelled, shaking her off. 'Let go, you beast, I was only trying to help!' She jumped to her feet and sucked at the blood that beaded from the cut.

But the raven lifted her head and spread her ruff of neck feathers. She liked the taste of that blood. What was more, now she was on the ground things began to look 'right' again. She recognized the world from this angle. Trees were *meant* to be seen from this way up, as was the human girl.

The bird braced her feet as a band tightened around her puffed-out chest.

That was familiar too.

It was hate.

3. Rumours of War

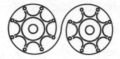

The moon had waxed and waned four times since that day. Now the sun was hot and high.

Tegen had come to the marshy village in Sul's Land just after Imbolg. She was thin, weary and looking for work. At the first house within the palisade she found a woman in agony with a difficult birth. Tegen delivered the child, then stayed to help.

Snowdrops had been in flower the day she had left her childhood home at the foot of the Mendip hills by the Winter Seas. Now the harvest was as tall and golden as the spears of the god Lugh, and almost ready to cut. Small, hard beans and crisp, sweet peas were bulging in their pods, the neatly hoed fields swelled with vegetables, and the geese were laying more eggs than anyone could eat.

Tegen was fifteen summers old and turned the heads of the local lads with her raven's-wing hair and green eyes, but she showed no interest in them. She spent her days weeding the fields, drying herbs and keeping the family's two older children away from the stores of honey. But she knew she could not stay. Her path lay towards Mona, the druids' island in the land of the Ceangli people. There she longed to finish her training as a bard, then become an ovate, and one day a full druid.

After work Tegen took her dog, Wolf, and went to sit on a steep, treeless hill overlooking the early-evening village. She loved the sight of the small patchwork fields edged by ditches and hedges, buzzing with children yelling to scare the birds away. Beyond the dark green late-summer trees, low mist hung around the valley, for it was there the Goddess, in her guise of Sul the Healer, bubbled endless hot water into muddy pools.

As she sat alone, Tegen remembered her old home and wept for Griff, her beloved foster-brother and hand-fasted man, who'd been killed in the cave demon's maelstrom. That same torrent also swept away Derowen the witch and Gorgans the White One, who together had schemed to destroy her. Tegen still had Griff's strong ash staff, and Wolf had been his dog. Both comforted her when she felt lonely and lost.

She had been the Star Dancer, born to avert a great evil in her home village. That task had been achieved when she defeated the demon; now she was on her own in the world.

Nearly every evening she danced for the Goddess under

the Watching Woman constellation. If the night was dry, she told the owls and glow-worms the old bardic stories her dear friend Gilda had taught her. Sometimes she just sat and scratched Wolf behind his ears. But mostly she came to wait for a sign that she must leave.

No one she met knew where Mona was. 'It's a place of dreams and spirits, not where a pretty young girl should be thinking of going!' was all they said.

One evening, heavy rain clouds scudded across the skies and Tegen climbed the hill as usual. Wolf ran away to find his supper, but Tegen took her ash staff and drew a circle around herself, making a sacred space. Shaking off her cloak and kicking aside her clogs, she stood barefoot and bareheaded so the warm summer rain streamed down her hair and back. Raising her arms, she greeted the spirits of the East with a few steps of dance, then she bowed to the spirits of the South and brought them the nodding waves of red poppies that shivered across the valley. To the West she opened her hands wide. 'Thank you for the rain that makes our crops grow,' she said. Then she looked up into the dark clouds, '. . . although perhaps we've had enough for now!'

But it was when she turned to the spirits of the North that she forgot what she was doing.

For coming down the road on a fat little moorland pony was an old man huddled under a cloak. Her heart started to pound. An instinct told her this traveller was important. But why?

Tegen watched until the man entered the village palisade. Swiftly she bowed to the spirits of the North. 'Sorry, I will give you double greetings tomorrow,' she promised. Then she whistled for Wolf, picked up her things and trudged home through the mud. As she reached her roundhouse, cheerful voices within told her the old man had knocked at the first door he came to and been given hearth-room inside.

She didn't want to meet him in case he was perfectly ordinary . . . She didn't want to be wrong.

Tegen walked around the back of the house to where the family tethered their own little brown mare. The traveller's pony was a beauty, about thirteen hands, cream-coloured and iron-shod. Rain poured off the springy, well-groomed coat. The long mane was the colour of milk and hung across her soft brown eyes. Despite the wet, Tegen pulled a handful of fresh grass and stroked the pony's velvet nose while she munched contentedly. 'My Griff would have loved you,' she whispered.

'She's called Heather,' said a warm voice behind her, 'and I am Owein.'

Tegen turned and saw a youth only one or two years older than herself. He leaned heavily on a crutch as he hobbled towards her, his left leg hanging twisted and useless.

'I'm Tegen.' She turned back to stroke the pony,

embarrassed that she had not come into the roundhouse to welcome him properly.

'I don't suppose you'd help me and fetch her water, would you?' he asked, holding out a leather bucket. 'I tend to end up on my backside in this mud!'

'Of course.' She smiled. 'I won't be long.' She took the bucket and ran to the stream beyond the gate. Why did I think he was old? she wondered. Perhaps it was because of his leg – that must make him sit awkwardly in the saddle, and he'd been huddled under that cloak . . . But she was getting too cold for speculation. She hurried back, watered the pony, then led the guest inside.

The roundhouse was dark but warm, and scented with wood smoke. High above, the conical thatched roof was sooty, and cluttered with pots, baskets, herbs, meat and clothes, all hung up to keep dry and rat-free. The family were sitting on stools around the central hearth while Alawn, the father, spooned a stew of goat-flesh, barley and turnips into wooden bowls. In the shadows on the far side, his woman was sitting on the bed feeding the baby. The two older children squabbled over a hot loaf.

Owein hobbled to his panniers and after a few moments of rummaging, pulled out a chunk of cheese. 'May I contribute to the feast?'

'Thank you.' Alawn nodded and swapped it for a bowl of stew. 'Will you say the blessing, stranger?' he asked.

Owein put his food down and raised his hands to the

South. 'Blessed be Lugh, for his spears of light that bring long arrows of golden grain. Blessed be the spirits of the North for the good earth, and the Lady Goddess for its fruitfulness. Thanks to the spirits of the East for their wind, and the West for their rain.' Then he bowed to all four quarters and sat down again.

Tegen sat up straight. He's a *druid*, she thought. Villagers don't pray like that! She was wet through but didn't want to miss a word, so she let her sodden clothes steam on her back as she ate by the fire.

The young man intrigued her. His hair was long and chestnut red, waving halfway down his back. His chin had only a light beard, but his thin face was bright with intelligence. He ate heartily, chatting of barley harvests and tribal fisticuffs.

And what of the druids? She longed to ask, but dared not, for as the evening drew in, the neighbours were gathering inside the smoky roundhouse. Travellers brought news and, in these days of the Romans coming ever closer from the south-east, everyone was on edge to know more.

Tegen tucked the older children into bed, but all the while her ears were wide open for every hint of who this stranger might be and where he was going. But his talk was only of troop movements, burned crops and ruin.

The room was deadly silent as Owein spoke. 'The invaders are winning almost every battle,' he said as he met the eyes of his listeners in turn. 'The Romans fight as one.

Our tactics cannot match that. What makes matters so much worse is we Britons are forever squabbling amongst ourselves. We *must* unite.

'As soon as the harvest is gathered, druids and chieftains will gather east of here, on the Sinodun hills by the River Tamesis. There will be delegates from the Silures, Ordovices, Atrebates, Catuvellauni and our own Dobunni. They are gathering to swear to a peace treaty. It is our only hope.'

He put down his bowl and leaned forward so his bright eyes gleamed in the firelight. 'Many are urging to keep going as we are, but the price will be too high.'

'What sort of price?' Alawn asked, anxiously glancing towards his sleeping children.

Owein followed his look. 'Defeat comes with slaves' chains, foreign laws and strange gods.' He sat straight and lifted his chin. 'We are children of the blood of the Morrigan, the Battle Goddess who fills men's veins with molten iron instead of blood. This is *our* land! We will trade with any that bring well-crafted goods, we'll gladly marry a stranger, but these – these *barbarians* with their roads that slice in straight lines through our fields and sacred places – they are *raping* the Land!'

The small crowd of listeners stirred uncomfortably as Owein spoke, his eyes alive with passion. At last he picked up his bowl and finished his almost cold stew.

Tegen's chest tightened – but was it from fear of the

Romans and possible war or the thrill of a world beyond the certainties of village life?

Talk of politics was lubricated with beer until the rain passed and the low moon rose bright below the Watching Woman's stars.

The roundhouse became very stuffy. Tegen slipped out into the night air and ran up her hill. Alone at last, she pulled a linen shawl from around her waist and began to dance. At first she moved nervously, like a silver birch in a breeze, uncertain of what she wanted to say to the Goddess that night. Could it be something about needing to move on, but being uncertain of when or where to go?

Was she asking for protection from these Roman warriors who melded into one enormous giant in combat?

At last a drum rhythm came. It was steady and made Tegen think of walking a long time through wind and rain. She closed her eyes as she swayed her hips and hands in time to the beat of the invisible musician in her head.

Soon images crept into her mind. There was a fire . . . She raised her hands to feel its warmth. The flames parted, and between them she saw a pale chalk road stretching onward, through valleys and woodlands. Ahead there was a white horse, and green hills crowned with towering lime-washed walls. There was darkness and light, and a black shape that flapped and hovered and made her afraid.

Then there was fire again, this time encircling her. She turned and turned, arms outstretched towards it, but there was no gap in the flames. Fear fought with excitement. Was this for good – or evil? Tegen did not understand what she saw, but she sensed the Goddess weaving her presence through the steps and images.

She was so deep in her seeings that she did not open her eyes at all as her feet rustled and swished through the long wet grass.

Suddenly she stumbled over something that grunted and moved.

Tegen gasped and opened her eyes as strong hands prevented her from falling. 'Owein, I'm sorry,' she panted, out of breath. 'Did I hurt you?'

'Don't worry,' he laughed. 'I can't move out of the way, so I often get trodden on. I wear thick boots and I'm used to it. Anyway, it was worth it to see you dance. Are you a bard? I'm not much good at magic, but I could tell your steps were full of it.'

Tegen's cheeks burned as she wound her shawl around her hair and twisted it into a knot. Dare she discuss her powers with a stranger? Even if he was a druid? Ignoring him, she turned away. But her mind was spinning with thoughts. Could he be the guide I've been waiting for? Do I really trust him? I ought to go alone . . . Too many people have died because of who I am.

Owein took her silence as an invitation to follow. His crutch thumped and shuffled behind her as she marched down the hill and across the field towards the village palisade. He *had* to know more about her. Her right cheek carried the star-pattern tattoo of the Goddess's Watching Woman. Who was she? *What* was she? The family she lived with said she knew herb lore. As he had ridden towards the village that afternoon, he was sure he had glimpsed her making her prayers to the spirits of the four quarters.

He managed to keep pace and tried again. 'I am an ovate. I want to study politics and law. Did you hear me telling the others I am on my way to Sinodun to meet with the druids and the chieftains?'

'Yes.' Tegen stopped and stared up at the night sky, her heart thumping hard. She bit her lip. Dare I believe the Goddess has sent him? If she has, I mustn't let this opportunity pass.

'When are you going?' she asked out loud.

'Soon. I'll be making for the Stone Forest in the east, then I will join the Ridgeway path and be at the tribal meeting place by the time the grain harvest is gathered.' He hesitated and glanced at her profile in the silvery light, 'Do you want to come?' he ventured.

Tegen closed her eyes and summoned back the image of the white road. 'Tell me – these Sinodun hills – are they anywhere near the island of Mona?'

'No.' He laughed. 'That's a long way in the other direction.'

She did not let her disappointment show. She just nodded and walked on.

Owein stopped and leaned on his crutch. His warm voice called out in the dark. 'So you *are* a druid! Someone is bound to be going home to Cymru when the talks are over. They'll take you.'

Tegen hesitated and stared back at Owein's starlit figure. 'What's Cymru?'

'The land that is crowned by the island of Mona. The meeting at Sinodun is important. There might even be some arch-druids there from the Isle of the Blessed,' he added.

Tegen didn't want to show her ignorance again by asking where that was. 'I can pay for a guide. I have gold.'

Owein caught up with her. 'Keep quiet about that. Even druids might be thieves. But there is bound to be someone going that way, yes.'

Tegen could not help looking down at Owein's twisted leg. 'Why are *you* going? It can't be easy for you to travel . . .'

He swung his weak foot forward so the toe of his boot touched the ground. 'I'm going because all druids must. Anyway, travelling isn't too bad – I have Heather, and the rest of me is healthy. I wasn't born like this. I broke my ankle a couple of years ago, it never mended properly and then my whole leg withered. In a way I am glad. It did me a favour.'

'How?'

'Because by birth I should be a war leader, but I'm not interested in battles or how many heads I can impale on spikes. I love the law. I want to be a full druid: helping kings and queens rule with fairness and common sense. We Britons hold death too lightly and our tribes fight too easily.' He waved his right arm northward. 'Even now there are two villages scarcely a day's walk from here who are threatening to wipe each other out over a herd of pigs that both side say the other stole!'

He shrugged. 'They are mad! We don't have *time* to fight each other. I know we will all be born again when we die, but that doesn't help the widows who are trying to feed their children *now*.'

They passed through the gate in the palisade. The moon shone on a cluster of low roundhouses. Warm light seeped from cracks and wind-eyes. In Alawn's house, the wattle door-panels stood ajar, letting in the cool night air.

Owein looked back over his shoulder. 'I won't be staying here long; my pony has a swollen fetlock and needs to rest for a few days.'

Tegen followed him inside and pulled the doors closed behind her. The neighbours had gone. She looked around in the soft firelight. To her right, the older children slept, plump as pigeons on a hay-filled sack. Beyond that, Alawn and his woman lay on a bed of sheepskins, the baby snuggled between them.

Her own mattress was a pile of straw next to the quern, and more had been left near the hearth for Owein. The fire was low, a glowing heart in the darkness.

I love this place . . . this is my new family . . . I am safe here, she thought.

But she knew it was time to move on.

While Owein patted his bed into shape, Tegen combed her hair and watched him from behind its dark curtain. There is more to him than meets the eye, she thought.

Tegen pulled back her blankets and whispered aloud: 'Owein, will you let me know . . . before you go? I . . . I might want to come.'

'Of course,' came his muffled reply.

As sleep wrapped her in deep brown oblivion, she was aware that her finger throbbed, and from somewhere in the darkness there came a harsh raven's cry.

4. Words That Stay

A quarter-moon later, the grain harvest was almost ready and Owein announced he was leaving. All morning he fussed over packing his panniers and grooming Heather.

Tegen watched him tighten the pony's girths. 'Why do you have to go *today*?'

'Once the harvest is in, everyone will be on the move. There'll be warriors on the roads with scores to settle with neighbours, hundreds of traders after business at the Lughnasadh fairs, and of course the druids and chieftains causing mayhem by demanding precedence on the thoroughfares as they make their way to Sinodun. There might even be Roman troop movements if we're really unlucky.'

Tegen looked around at the damp fields. 'Can't you stay a little longer? If this showery weather keeps up, the harvest will have to be kiln-dried. It'll be hard work – I ought to stay . . .'

'Why? I've watched you – you're always helping. You've more than paid for your keep since you arrived. If you don't want to come, that's up to you, but I *thought* you wanted to find someone to take you to Mona . . .'

That was the magic word. 'All right, I'm coming! Give me a few moments,' she called as she ran inside the round-house to pack.

Over the last few days Owein and Tegen had talked a great deal. She found she could tell him something – but not all – of her struggle to become a druid, of Gilda's death and of her decision to leave the village by the Winter Seas. Owein had said very little about his past, but Tegen instinctively liked him and respected his good sense. A nagging thought at the back of her head told her if she didn't go with him, there might not be another trustworthy travelling companion for a while . . . even if he *was* going in the wrong direction.

She hugged and kissed the family. Without glancing back, she whistled for Wolf as she pulled her pig-leg bag on to her shoulder and followed Owein along the muddy path and away from the village.

Once more, Owein was huddled like an old man against the rain under his shabby green cloak. Heather's milky tail swayed as her round rump moved steadily along the stony road and into the woods beyond the fields. Beside him, Tegen walked bright-eyed with excitement, her ash staff in her hand as her long black plaits swung over her cloak. Wolf twisted his thin tail into a tight curl and loped after them.

At the last bend in the road before they lost sight of the village, Tegen turned and sent back a blessing and a prayer for fine harvest weather.

They walked all morning. The path was steep, rough and heavily wooded, full of potholes and loose rocks. The night's rain soon passed, but the whole world looked grey and bedraggled. Tegen's feet dragged heavily in her mud-caked clogs. She found herself stumbling and twisting her ankles. She watched Owein's sure-footed mount enviously.

Owein had not talked much all morning, but Tegen wasn't bothered. Her early bounce dissolved in the damp chill, and her mind kept wandering back to her parents and Griff. At noon they rested under an old oak in dark leaf. Raised, gnarled roots made good stools. Owein slipped from his pony's back and steadied himself with his crutch as he pulled smoked ham and a beer-loaf from a pannier. 'Hungry?'

'I must have a drink first.' Tegen followed her ears and soon came to a stream, where she refilled the water skins.

When she returned, Owein was silently holding a long strip of creamy parchment stretched between two spindles. He didn't hear Tegen for he was engrossed, staring intently at lines of dark marks that crawled like spiders in procession along the skin.

She stood behind him and peered over his shoulder. 'What's that?' she asked.

He jumped, rolled the spindles together and stuffed them back into his basket. 'It's nothing.'

'You're reading, aren't you?' she challenged. 'My old mentor Witton told me about that. He said it's words that stay. He said it's evil because it traps the meaning of thoughts. Is it evil?'

Owein blushed. 'You read the Ogham, don't you?'

'Yes, but they are a few simple signs that say many deep things. They aren't the same at all. How come you can read?'

'I was *made* to learn.'

'Who by?'

'I don't want to talk about it,' he said.

Tegen sat on the tree root next to him and snatched the object back out of the pannier. 'What's this called?' she demanded.

'A scroll.'

She untwisted the spindles awkwardly. One slipped from her hand and rolled across the mud.

Irritated, Owein grabbed it back. 'You've got it all mucky

now,' he snapped, wiping at the dirty smears with his sleeve.

'Stop fussing. You're such an old woman!' Tegen wet the hem of her skirt and wiped the mess away carefully. Owein started to roll it up, but she stopped him. 'Leave it open to dry or it'll go mouldy.'

He sighed and spread the parchment across his knees.

Tegen leaned over and examined the writing. 'Will you teach me to read?'

'Druids don't read. They *learn*!'

'Don't be such a misery. At least tell me what it says!'

Owein read: *'His rebus adducti et auctoritate Orgetorigis permoti constituerunt ea quae ad proficiscendum pertinerent comparare, iumentorum et carrorum quam maximum numerum coemere, sementes quam maximas facere, ut in itinere copia frumenti suppeteret, cum proximis civitatibus pacem et amicitiam confirmare.'*

Tegen stared wide-eyed. 'Was that a spell?'

'What, being able to read? No, it's a skill.'

'No, I meant those sounds you made. It sounded like some awful incantation.'

At last Owein laughed. 'No, that's Latin – Roman speech, describing their "peaceful and friendly" invasion of another land almost a hundred years ago.'

'It sounds so eerie. The shapes look like the words they are making.'

Owein twisted the wooden spindles together. 'It's dry

now . . . Maybe I'll teach you, if we have time.' Then he slipped the scroll into a linen bag and stowed it at the very bottom of his pack.

As he rearranged his belongings Tegen saw him pull aside the soft folds of a rich cloak, bright with greens and blues and yellows. There seemed to be six or even seven colours in the weave, but she couldn't be sure.

But that meant . . . he couldn't be . . . *could* he?

Owein sat up again. His face was drawn and pale. 'If anyone asks, I can't read and I don't speak their language, right?'

Tegen scowled. 'Why won't you trust me and tell me about yourself?'

His face clouded. 'This is a time of war, and there are some things it's safer not to know. Anyway, I really don't want to talk about it. I shouldn't have shown you.' Then he tore off a piece of bread, sliced some ham and chewed without saying another word.

Tegen took her share and ate alone on the other side of the tree.

At last Owein whistled for Heather. After a few moments, she came trotting obediently, followed by Wolf. The great hound leaped up to Tegen and shook himself vigorously, splattering water everywhere.

Once on the road again, Owein relaxed a little. 'I am sorry

I was rude. My life has been . . . unsettled. I have many painful memories. It was my uncle who taught me to read and speak Latin,' he said. 'He is convinced that the Romans are good for our land. More importantly, he hopes for a high government position for himself one day. I lived with a foster-father for a few years, a good man. He and I believe that if the Romans came in peace, we would welcome them as visitors and merchants. But they have a compulsion to fight and conquer wherever they go. They are vicious and brutal and they don't respect our laws or our religion.'

Owein pulled himself tall and opened his arms to the landscape. 'We see our land as sacred – it is the body of the Goddess married to the Green Man – you know all about that. But these invaders treat it as if it was just – well, *land* – something people can *own* and use and do what they like with – like a slave.'

Tegen shuddered at the thought and reverently touched a young hazel bough that hung low across the path.

Owein was warming to his subject. 'And have you seen their houses? They are impossibly huge and square-cornered. How can the spirits move when there are no circles for them to dance in?'

'The house I grew up in had corners, although the hearth was circular,' Tegen said, remembering the stone longhouse with its turf roof and three wind-eyes. She felt a lump swell in her throat. I must let the past go, she told herself.

They followed the twisting road, until in the late

afternoon they heard the sounds of many heavy feet tramping behind them. Tegen turned to smile and give the travellers' blessing, but the sight that met her eyes made her go cold.

From around a bend, ten armoured men were marching straight towards them in pounding rhythm. The soldiers were stony-faced under their iron helmets and cheekpieces. Their arms swung high and their armoured plates clanked.

Tegen stood in the path, her eyes and mouth wide, as the men bore down on her.

Owein swore. He grabbed Tegen's shoulder and tugged her into the bushes as the men marched past. 'Mind out, they'll mow you down!' Heather whinnied and shifted nervously. Owein held her reins firmly and whispered reassuring words in her ear. All the time he kept his back straight and his bad leg pressed out of sight in the undergrowth.

After the soldiers came two men on horseback. Their animals were taller than any Tegen had ever seen before, beautiful, sleek creatures with neatly plaited manes and tails. Their riders were no less strange, clean-shaven with gleaming decorated armour, white kilts and red cloaks fastened at the shoulder.

Wolf slunk to his mistress's side and growled as the smaller man yelled down at them harshly. Tegen didn't understand the words, but his meaning was clear enough.

She yelled back and waved her fist.

'Don't be a fool!' Owein hissed, pulling her back and trying to hide his own face at the same time.

The taller rider turned back to stare down his chiselled nose at Owein. He looked as if he wanted to slow, but his companion urged him on, leaving the road to its old quietness.

Owein sighed and coaxed Heather back on to the track. 'That's bad. Very bad,' he muttered quietly.

'Are they Romans?' Tegen asked, picking up a stone and throwing it ineffectually after them. 'What bastards! Did you understand what they said?'

'Unfortunately, yes.' He was pale. 'Can you climb up something and look along the road to see if there are any more coming?'

A little further to the right was a fallen beech tree, leaning at an angle against an ash. It would be easy to climb. Tegen hitched up her skirt and pulled herself along the trunk until she had a good view all around.

To the east, she could see the retreating backs of the Romans. To the west, there were three people with a cart and a couple of horses, but apart from that, the way was too sheltered by trees to be certain.

She went back with her news.

Owein glanced around nervously. 'They have their own roads to march along – why desecrate ours?' He spat at one of the horses' hoof prints.

'Were they spies?'

'No. Spies are usually British-born and bribed with gold or promises of power. You wouldn't know if you met one.' His face tightened and she asked no more.

Heather was glad to be back on the path and trotted happily. Tegen had to walk hard to keep up.

'How far back was the cart?' Owein asked.

'Not far. Although they won't go fast on this road. In fact, I'm surprised the wheels are still on it.' She sprang lightly over a pothole.

'Traders?'

'Could be.'

'Good. We'll see if we can join them. Safety in numbers. I stick out like a sore thumb on my own – I am too easy to spot.' He patted his withered left leg.

'Why should the Romans care about *you*?' She narrowed her eyes. Then she rounded on him. 'I saw a seven-coloured cloak in your basket. Only kings and royal children wear those. Who are you *really*?'

Owein reddened. 'How do you know about my cloak? Have you been snooping in my things?'

Tegen shook her head indignantly. 'You half pulled it out when you put your scroll away. It was difficult *not* to see it.'

'Of course. I'm sorry.' Owein sighed. 'My father is a prisoner of the Romans, and I am the foster-son of a man called Eiser who lives by the rearing river in the west,' he replied tersely.

After a tense moment Tegen realized Owein would say

no more for now. She changed the subject. 'When I was up the tree, I saw something strange,' she said. 'A very long way off, there was a hill. It was steep-sided and stuck up like a single bare breast from the forest. Where I come from, we had a similar hill, called the Tor. The druids used it for ceremonies and secret rituals, although I never went up there. Our Tor was surrounded by water in the winter and green meadows in the summer. It was beautiful. It made you feel good to look at it. This wasn't the same; it felt eerie but I don't know why.'

'Where was it?'

'Straight ahead.' Tegen pointed along the road. 'East and a little bit north.'

'Good,' Owein replied. 'That's the Hill of the King. It means we are well on the way.'

'Why is it called the Hill of the King? Does a powerful chieftain live there?'

Owein laughed for the second time that morning. 'No, it's ancient. It's said that an evil king summoned dark forces to do his bidding. He was put to death by good men who wanted to keep the world safe. But his spirit walked. The only thing the king truly loved in life was gold, so they made him a tomb of it: not just a thin covering – they heaped unbelievable treasures over his corpse. He has so many exquisite grave goods it'll take forever for his avaricious spirit to admire and count everything, so he'll forget to torment the living.'

'Is that why there is such a huge mound? To keep out grave robbers?'

'Yes. If the treasure is ever taken, his spirit will walk again.'

As they talked they came into a clearing and Tegen climbed a fallen monolith to try to see the hill once more.

'Get off!' Owein grabbed her arm urgently. 'That belongs to the Old Ones – they still roam these parts!'

Tegen jumped down, picked a sprig of meadowsweet and laid it on the lumpy rock as a conciliatory gift. 'Who are the Old Ones?'

'Nomads. They aren't evil, but they don't abide by our laws either. It's said –' here he leaned over and whispered with awe – 'they can summon the Stone Forest to *dance*!'

Tegen felt her skin tingle with fear and delight at the thought.

That night they camped in a stick-and-moss shelter like Griff used to make for himself. The traders caught up with them and they talked around the fire. There were two women and a boy of about thirteen, also going to the meeting at Sinodun. They were carrying cloth and salt and were happy to travel with new companions. A larger group was less likely to be robbed.

Their leader, Caja, was a small wiry woman with a

vicious tongue. Her name meant 'daisy', but Tegen thought she was more like an adder.

Two days passed. Then late one afternoon the party climbed out of a shallow, boggy valley that wound north between undulating hills. To their left, the strange, steep-sided hill had suddenly become very close.

But the slopes were alive with small, dark figures climbing and crossing in a businesslike way. On top, a small wooden frame had been erected.

The Romans had claimed the Hill of the King for their own.

5. Calleva's Reward

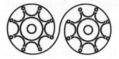

The Sun God was riding towards the western horizon when Caja called everyone together.

'There is a village just beyond these trees,' she said. 'We will ask for hospitality for the night there. They have a roundhouse they rent to travellers. *Wynne . . .!*' she yelled at her sister. 'Find that piece of yellow wool that's got moth holes. Offer them that.'

Everyone cheered up at the thought of a proper bed for the night, but when the path climbed out of the wood a terrible sight met their eyes.

There was no village. Only a wide, well-laid road that crossed the old path from east to west. It was straight as a spear-shaft and newly ditched. On each side, the trees and bushes were shaved back for at least a stone's throw. To their left, the road led directly to the Hill of the King, as if it was the wicked old ghost's royal parade. To their right, it ran in a diminishing line until the distance claimed it.

'Have they taken the treasure?' Tegen whispered.

'If they have, we're all in big trouble!' Owein replied.

'Turn about!' roared Caja. 'We'll find somewhere to camp. *Kieran!*' she yelled at her sister's boy. 'Follow that track into the woods. See where it goes.'

Moments later he was back, out of breath and pale. 'You'd better come and see,' he panted, '*quickly.*'

Caja coaxed the cart between the trees. Tegen winced every time the iron-shod wheels cracked against a stone. Very soon they came to a newly cut clearing, where a small huddle of miserable-looking huts had been thrown up on the bank of a stream. A tall man with unkempt hair and moustaches blocked the path to the hamlet. His chest was deep, and his eyes blue and steady. A worn five-coloured cloak flapped around his shoulders, announcing he was a warrior of repute. But the look in his eyes showed defeat.

He watched the travellers with arms folded and chin held high.

'Something bad has happened here,' Tegen whispered to Owein. He nodded, urged his pony forward until he faced the man, then, steadying himself on his saddle-horn, he slid to the ground. He did not want to antagonize this man by riding into his village. They had left Dobunni lands the day before, and the Atrebates were warlike and known to favour the Romans.

'I am Owein, foster-son of Eiser of the Dobunni lands, by the rearing river,' he began. 'We are travellers to the meeting of the tribes at Sinodun. May we have shelter in your village for a night or two?'

The warrior scowled. After a few moments he replied, 'Are you blind as well as crippled? You can see we don't have enough shelter for ourselves, and what harvest is still standing is ours. Nothing to give you. Go away.'

Caja put her hands on her hips and began a foul-mouthed tirade. But Owein interrupted her. 'We are tired and hungry. We need to stop. We will find our own food. We simply want your permission to share your riverside for a night or two.'

'*Look, damn you!*' the man roared, opening his arms to the hovels that surrounded him. 'A moon ago we were a thriving community, an old and well-respected village, giving hospitality to passers-by. We welcomed the bastard Romans, showed them where to find stone and water. As a reward they came at dawn and threw us out of our own homes at sword-point.'

He turned his face away and rubbed his eyes on his arm. 'I am Calleva, son of Verica, chieftain warrior to Kings and Gods since I could hold a spear and father to ten children. But now everything has been destroyed and I lead a group of hovel dwellers. Go. We don't need witnesses to our shame.' He started to walk away, his head held high.

Owein was not going to be defeated. 'If you let us stay, we could help you start to raise a good roundhouse . . .'

'We're not staying long enough to *need* a roundhouse,' Calleva replied, without turning around. 'We have sickness here. As soon as we have gathered our harvest and the dying have left us for the Otherworld, we'll be on our way.'

Tegen took a deep breath. 'I have some skill with herbs,' she ventured.

'We don't trust strangers,' Calleva snapped.

A thin, whey-faced woman came and stood by him. 'Ask them if they have salt . . . You could let them stay on the other side of the stream. We can watch them from here.'

The man looked over his shoulder and raised an eyebrow. 'Well?'

'We have salt,' Caja replied, taking a small grey slab from a wicker basket, 'and we will throw in this as well.' She beckoned to Wynne, who jumped down from the cart and smiled shyly as she held the yellow cloth at arm's length. The woman fingered it hesitantly, then looked at her man. 'Let them stay. They look all in.'

The warrior grunted and jerked his head in the direction of a small rise on the far side of the water.

Caja took it as permission to camp. She put her fingers in her mouth and gave a shrill whistle. 'Get back here!' she screeched at Kieran, who had started to explore.

The horses hauled the creaking cart across the stream and then up the bank on the other side. Caja cast an eye over their allotted site. She pointed to a flat, bramble-free space. 'There.'

'*Kieran!*' she yelled. 'Go and hobble the horses so they can graze.'

'We'll camp here too,' Owein said. 'We'd rather wait with you than go on alone. But our food has almost run out. Can we barter for a share in yours?'

Caja turned on him. 'Can't stop you camping where you want, but we've enough problems feeding ourselves without looking after a cripple as well!' She poked Owein in the chest. 'And as for you offering *our* services to build *them* a roundhouse – how *dare* you? Who do you think you are? Bloody King Caractacus? I don't think so! Get out of my way!' She pushed Owein aside and stormed past.

Tegen took a deep breath to leap after the woman and strangle her, but she caught sight of Owein glowering a warning. He turned away and started to unpack. Livid, Tegen whispered loudly, '*Why* can't I tell her what I think of her? Put your royal cloak on; *then* she'd shut up! I'm going to give that woman a piece of my mind!'

Owein grabbed her arm. 'Keep your mouth shut, Tegen. We don't trust *anyone*. Not totally. Sleep with one eye open and your hand on your dagger, right? Now get some wadding for our shelter. I'll cut the poles,' and he stumped towards a hazel copse.

Tegen seethed as she drew her knife and hacked chunks from the velvet mosses under the trees. She calmed as she worked. The colour and texture reminded her of her lost green silk shawl. It made her remember dancing, learning to do magic, and dear Gilda.

'May she be born again soon,' Tegen whispered to herself.

But there was no time for feeling sad. Owein had bent a silver-birch sapling into an arch and was tying smaller branches along it in an upside-down boat-like framework. Together they wove ferns and grass between the supports and roofed it with the mosses.

A little distance away, Caja and Wynne flung a length of oil-soaked linen over a rope tied between two trees. They spread the fabric edges wide and pegged them down with wooden spikes. Lastly they lay horse hides on the ground to keep the sleepers dry.

Kieran went to gather firewood. Tegen glimpsed him crouched behind a fallen elm, glad of a few moments' peace. He scowled when he realized she had seen him, but Tegen said nothing and kept working.

Once the camp was ready Owein untied his bow from his pack and brought down a fat pigeon. He flung himself on the ground next to where Tegen was helping Wynne to light a fire. Drawing his knife, he cut the off the bird's head, pulled the guts, then began to pluck, sending feathers everywhere. Finally he skewered the body with green sticks, ready to roast it.

The firewood was wet. Tegen watched nervously as the

flames smouldered and struggled to catch. 'Won't the Romans see all this smoke?'

Owein shrugged. 'It'll be getting dark soon. They'll think we are part of the village – what's left of it anyway.' Then he added very quietly, 'I don't think they'll expect to find me right under their noses.'

'Why can't you tell me why they are after you?' Tegen whispered back.

Owein sucked his lips. 'The same reason you haven't told me everything about *you* – it's too dangerous.'

A harsh cry from the top of a dead elder tree made everyone turn. There flapped a raven. Bright black eyes glinted from under a heavy brow-ridge as it snapped its vicious beak twice and spread its wings. Rose-sheened black plumage scooped the air as it swooped silently down and tugged at the pigeon's spilled intestines.

Owein threw a stone, but missed.

Screeching *kek-kek-kek,* the bird flew away into the dark.

'If I didn't know better, I'd say it was cursing us,' Wynne said, nervously pulling her cloak around herself.

'I am certain it *was* cursing us,' Tegen said quietly to Owein. 'I know ravens are supposed to be birds of wisdom and good omen, but –' she rubbed the white scar on her finger and shivered – 'sometimes I think they are following me, and I don't like it.'

'Why should they?' Owein laughed as he turned the spitted pigeon.

Tegen shrugged and used some of their meagre supplies to make flatbread, which she baked on a hot stone at the edge of the fire.

After the meal Owein nudged Tegen. 'You're a bard – you should be telling everyone a story.'

'I'm better at dancing stories than telling them.'

'But you won't improve if you don't practise!'

Tegen sighed and began the ancient tale of the hunt for the magical boar, Twrch Trwyth, and the wonderful comb and scissors he kept between his ears.

But even though the story followed noble heroes through great dangers in distant lands, Tegen could not get the image of the raven out of her head.

6. The Stone Forest

Tegen awoke with a start. The light was scarcely showing the difference between path and tree. Wolf lay
snoring at her side, warm and comfortingly heavy.

There it was again, a small sound.

Someone was moving outside her shelter. A pale shape
shifted. A twig cracked. Tegen held her breath as she
watched the figure turn and walk away. Somewhere in the
woods the horses stamped and whinnied. Then there was
silence.

Tegen whispered for Owein, but he was not there. I bet
he's gone to read his silly scroll in private, she thought. No,
it's too dark. Maybe that was him going to the privy.

But the tread had been even; it could not be Owein. Tegen
pushed back her cloak and eased herself out from under
Wolf's bulk. He snorted and twitched as he dreamed of

chasing hares. She pulled on her clothes and shook the dog, warning him to be quiet.

Together they stepped out into the cool morning air. Tegen stood absolutely still, listening for the tiniest noises. Wolf pricked his ears and waited beside her. Then they picked their way across the dewy ground between the travellers' tent and their cart. Down at the water's edge the faint light showed a scattering of footprints from boots, clogs and bare feet – but there was another shape, a large print with heavy stud-marks.

The stream was shallow and fast. Tegen jumped across the wet pebbles to the gravel bank on the other side. There again were the same studded prints, both coming and going. Wolf lowered his head and ran this way and that, sniffing the ground, then curled his tail and loped off between the trees. Tegen lifted her skirts free of the whortleberry plants that carpeted the wood and followed. The trees parted.

She stopped.

Standing dead ahead on the new Roman road were two figures, grey and indistinct in the half-light. One was dressed in a long, pale-coloured robe, the other in breeches and shirt. Both were clean-shaven and had short hair. Despite the noise of the dawn chorus, Tegen could hear them speaking in harsh, clipped tones. *Latin,* she remembered.

Suddenly she realized both men were looking her way.

She grabbed the scruff of Wolf's neck and slunk back between the trees, cursing her carelessness. Had they seen her? Maybe not. She watched as they walked into the woods on the far side of the road.

It must have been one of those men in our camp just now, she thought. What did they want? The one in the long robe must be Roman, and the other one . . . was he a spy? Owein said they paid Britons . . .

When Tegen was sure they had gone she crept forward, her hand on Wolf's back for comfort. Once she had reached the stony surface, the growing light showed traces of dark mud.

She glanced around. All seemed quiet.

If Owein won't tell me what is going on, she thought, I'll just have to find out for myself.

Tegen took a deep breath and ran. She leaped the first ditch, sprinted across the road, then jumped the second ditch before diving between the trees on the northern side. She aimed to the right of the gap where the men had disappeared.

There was less light under the canopy of trees. Wolf put his head down and led the way and Tegen followed, wincing every time her foot snapped a twig. A wren swooped across their path, making them both jump. Wolf nuzzled Tegen's hand and gave her a small reassuring lick.

She stopped and listened; Wolf's ears pricked. The woods were full of sounds, but which were human and which were not? The dog moved to the left. Tegen followed. Very soon she could see a tall grey stone, standing like a warrior sentinel . . . then another . . . and another.

'The Stone Forest of the Old Ones,' she murmured to herself. 'I wonder if the stones really do dance? Do they need a spell to make it happen?' She stepped forward and placed her hand reverently on the cool rock. It loomed above her, although it was difficult to judge how high, as brambles and hazel crowded its true shape and size.

'I wish I knew more about the Old Ones,' she sighed. 'I can feel magic here. Owein seemed nervous about it, but I am sure this isn't an evil place. It feels *earthy* . . .'

Beneath her feet, trampled grass and hacked-back brambles revealed a clear track northward. As Tegen followed it, more and more stones crowded around her, some standing, others fallen. One or two were smooth, others looked as if they had been hacked in anger, and a few flowed and rippled like water in rock form. High above, a strident bird cry seared across the melodious calls of thrush, blackbird and robin. Tegen shivered and pulled her cloak more tightly around her shoulders.

She breathed deeply and felt a strong, earthy rhythm pulsing through her veins, just as she had at the Beltane fair as a child.

Forgetting the men she was following and ignoring any danger, Tegen closed her eyes and began to dance, weaving between the stones, honouring the Lady Goddess in her summer finery. As she moved, Tegen's fingers trailed on the rock and her hair brushed the swaying ivy strands. Then the stones started to move . . . they *wanted* to dance, they *were* dancing in their rocky hearts, feeling the same earth music through their cold and ancient roots.

At last, Tegen stopped and leaned against a giant stone to catch her breath. She turned towards the first glimmers of the Sun God steering his golden chariot into the heavens. She raised her arms to the early-morning breeze and laughed. 'I greet you, spirits of the East, and celebrate your power of life and inspiration-bringing Awen. Bless this new day. I have no incense, but I welcome you.'

Then she turned to the South. Just above her head the canopy of leaves was heavy with a myriad of shimmering greens. High in the branches the birds were singing for the joy of being alive as the early sky washed itself in cornflower blue. 'Blessed be the new day, a day to fill with hope . . .' She paused as she thought of the thin, angry villagers who had been thrown from their homes to make way for the road. They said there was sickness there. I will go and see them as soon as I get back, she promised. Her stomach rumbled – after breakfast, that is.

Then she turned to the West. 'Come spirits of rest and healing,' she said aloud. 'May those poor people find new lives in a good place where they can start again. I wish I could help more, but I can't. I must be on my way.'

Then she closed her eyes and leaned her forehead against

the cool roughness of the nearest rocky slab. 'And spirits of the North, I greet you too. Thank you for allowing me to dance with your warriors of stone—'

But the strong hand that clamped around her mouth allowed her to say no more.

7. Driven by Darkness

The raven closed her wings and peered down through the foliage. Day after day she had been compelled to follow this sloe-haired human and her dog in their tedious, ground-hugging meanderings.

What had driven her? It was more than a longing for the taste of blood again. It was . . . it was a darkness inside . . . or was it *behind* her? The raven turned and looked nervously at her tail. No, the rainbow sheen on her own midnight plumage pleased and delighted her. It was a darkness of *absence* that terrified and bullied her onward.

She feared and loved it at the same time. She devoured it when she tore at carrion. It devoured *her* whether she played on the tossing air or sat still as a rock.

Now she had to get closer to her quarry. She hopped on to a lower branch. Something was happening, something that threatened her prize. Other humans had surrounded her, had captured her . . . perhaps they were going to put her in a cage.

She snapped her beak at a flying beetle. I have heard of such things. That would be good; then she will stay in one place and I will be free to fly and tumble on the winds. The raven preened her breast feathers. I am already in a cage, she grumbled. Although I can stretch my wings, I cannot go where I like.

Rebellious for a moment, the raven launched herself into the summer air, rolling over and over in delight, chortling and gurgling as she flew.

But heavy as lead came the command from the back of her head:

This is no time for tomfoolery! Follow!

8. Capture!

Tegen's arms were yanked behind her and tied. Then she was lifted into the air and flung over an iron-clad shoulder. The man stank of sweat. She kicked and screamed, but her captor only tightened his grip.

'Keep still and you won't get hurt!' snapped a voice in British.

Tegen tried to lift her head, but she could only make out the lower half of a second figure walking alongside, wearing green breeches and an undyed linen shirt.

'Let me go!' she demanded.

The man's hand pulled a dagger from its sheath. 'I *said*, shut up and stop wriggling.' His other hand grabbed a fistful of her hair and jerked her neck back. She tried not to howl at the pain. A pale, flabby face lowered to her level, then smiled, showing immaculate teeth. The dagger pricked under her chin.

Tegen glared venomously.

He laughed, let her go and stepped back from her vision. Her chin banged against her captor's armour. Metal plates slid across each other, pinching the skin at her stomach as he marched.

Tegen felt like a sack of flour. She lifted her head again. The path they were following retreated between the rows of giant stones. She was going further and further away from Owein.

Suddenly her heart flipped. *Wolf!* She couldn't see him . . . She looked around urgently. Where is he? Better not whistle. There's no point in us *both* being caught. I hope he finds his way back to camp. Suddenly an awful thought struck her – if Wolf does go back, he might lead Owein to me. Then he would be caught as well! Miserably she realized there was nothing she could do to help herself or Owein, so she let her head bounce up and down as she watched her captor's bare hairy legs carry her through the undergrowth.

As they walked, Tegen noticed the soldier wore thick-soled sandal-boots that left heavily studded footprints. Had it been him snooping around in their camp? This man was wearing a short red tunic under his armour, and he didn't look like either of the figures she had seen on the road earlier.

Why wasn't I more careful? Tegen berated herself, but there was no point getting agitated . . . I just need to think.

Once more she tried to look around, but overhanging branches knocked her head and tangled in her plaits.

'Ouch!' she howled.

Feeling the tug, her captor put her down, pulled out his knife and cut her hair free.

'Walk! It's not far,' snapped the man in breeches.

Now Tegen could see him properly her heart missed a beat. It *had* been him on the road. Was he a spy?

He was a large man and wore the same strapped boots as her captor. She tried to look back to see if he too left the studded footprints she had noticed by the stream, but the soldier's heavy hand shoved her forward.

Soon they were in a clearing. On each side, the tall stones marched away in a curved sweep to right and left until they disappeared between the trees beyond.

Straight ahead was a rough wooden hut with a thatched straw roof. In front was a fire, and sat at a table were two men draped in lengths of white woollen cloth. One was short and grey-haired, the other tall and dark. Tegen recognized them both; they were the Roman riders who had passed Owein and herself on the road three days earlier.

The smaller man smiled, showing bad teeth, and spoke in Latin. *'You've brought a pigeon for us to roast, I see, Gaius Admidios.'*

The man in breeches laughed and replied as he dragged Tegen towards the table by her hair. 'Stand there by the fire,' he snapped in British. 'Don't worry. I have just told my friends Tribune Quintus Caelius and Legate Suetonius Paulinus here' – he gestured to the two men – 'that we're not going to eat you. My name is Admidios.' He leaned over and added in a low, oily tone, 'And however things might appear at the moment, you can trust me. I have to keep up appearances of being on their side.'

Tegen shuddered at the sound of his voice.

Quintus slammed his fist on the table. *'Stop talking and question her!'*

'They want to know what you were doing spying in these woods,' Admidios demanded, shaking her roughly.

Tegen glared up at him. So this is what a spy looks like, she thought. She didn't want to admit she had been following *him,* and she knew he wouldn't believe the stones had woken and had been dancing with her. 'I was looking for whortleberries,' she said.

He translated. The tribune replied.

'He wants to know what whortleberries are,' Admidios said, 'and so do I. I've never heard of them.'

Tegen nodded towards the trees. 'Over there. Dark blue berries that grow on small bushes. I was hungry. I got lost.'

Admidios scowled. *'Bilberries?* Why didn't you say so?' He leaned close to Tegen, his face only a hand's breadth from her own. 'Whortleberries must be a dialect word – which means you're not from round here! What tribe are you?'

Tegen scowled back into his pale, ice-cold blue eyes. 'I'm of the Dobunni.'

'Clan?'

'The clan of Witton the druid. He was our chief as well.'

Admidios took a few moments to turn all Tegen had said into Latin. Then he turned back to her. 'You're a long way from home. Are you alone?'

She sensed danger. She must avoid mentioning Owein at all costs, glad for once she knew little about him. 'No, I'm travelling with salt traders. We're going to some fairs.'

'Where?'

'Lots of them, all along the Ridgeway.'

Admidios slapped her face. His touch chilled her. 'You'll have to lie better than that.' He gestured to the Romans. 'These gentlemen saw you walking along the road only a couple of days ago in the company of a young man.' He smiled. 'We want to find him. He is a thief. He stole the pony he rides and must be punished according to the law.' Admidios stood to his full height, smiled and laid a heavy hand on Tegen's shoulder. 'Tell us where he is and we will let you go.'

Tegen shrugged as well as she could with her hands so tightly tied. She knew very little about Owein, but she would swear he was no thief. 'I did walk with him for a bit, but he was arrogant and kept trying to kiss me. I didn't like him. I'm hungry. Can I have something to eat?'

Admidios ignored her and turned to talk to the Romans.

Quintus clicked his fingers. The soldier who had carried Tegen poured wine into red pottery cups from a thin-necked jar with an impossibly pointed base.

Tegen's stomach rumbled as she watched and listened hard for any clues as to what was going on.

The tall Roman, Suetonius, spoke at last. He snapped a few sharp words and his eyes flashed. He seemed irritated.

Then Admidios replied. His sibilant tones sounded deferential and persuasive, and the Roman's temper subsided.

Strange, thought Tegen. It's almost as if he had some sort of power over these men . . .

Suetonius beckoned for more wine. Again he drank, then leaned on the table, staring hard at Tegen. His long hooked nose gave him a predatory air. He nodded to the soldier and said something as he pointed to the edge of the clearing.

Tegen found herself hauled over a metallic shoulder once more and dumped at the base of a tall, grey monolith with her cloak dropped next to her. The three men kept talking and arguing, but they ignored her. She watched the Sun God's chariot climb higher into the sky, and the day began to get hot. Her throat was unbearably dry and ants crawled inside her dress, tickling her unmercifully. She longed for Wolf; she missed Owein.

What was worse, something sharp was sticking into her back. Tegen eased herself into a sitting position and felt around with her fingertips until she discovered a stone blade fashioned from flint. She grasped it point upward, then gritted her teeth as she tried to saw across the ropes that bound her. But it was too small and she kept dropping it.

'*Damn!*' she muttered. 'Now I've gone and cut myself!' She glanced up through the trees. The Sun God was at his zenith, and the huge black raven that had been standing atop one of the tallest stones to her left was staring down at her.

She tried to spit to avert the evil eye, but her mouth was too dry.

Admidios suddenly looked at her and came across, a beaker in his hand. He crouched down at her side and let her sip water as he spoke in his silky-smooth voice. 'I am sure you think this is all very strange, my dear, but you have stumbled on something rather sensitive. I am negotiating a truce that will, in the end, save many lives. There are too many ears in an army camp, so we hold our secret discussions amongst these ancient stones, knowing the pagan British are afraid to come here. The lesser ranks of the Romans are daunted by these ancient spirits as well, so it is an excellent place to hide secrets. Then *you* turn up, bold as a magpie, doing witchcraft amongst the stones at dawn – oh yes, I saw you . . .' He lowered his voice to barely a whisper. 'Now, what *are* you doing here?'

As he spoke, she found her mind was lulled into muddled softness. She pulled herself together. 'Looking for whortleberries,' she replied sullenly, opening her mouth to drink again.

'Don't lie!' he spat, pulling the beaker away. 'We also

observed that last night you camped with the cripple. You know where he is headed and why.'

Tegen tried not to think of water and looked hard at an ant crawling over Admidios's sandal-boot. She could see heavy conical studs pressing into the loamy soil below. A chill crept up her spine. It *was* him at our camp before dawn! How am I going to get out of this? Goddess help me!

'Do you want more?' He put the water to her lips. She leaned forward, but he snatched it back. Then he stood, towering over her, held the cup at arm's length and poured the contents on to the ground. 'Can't waste good water on a liar,' he said.

Tegen watched the dark patch bloom. She licked her lips and said nothing.

'Well, as it happens,' he said, smiling, 'your turning up here is most fortuitous. We have decided to keep you until the young man in question comes to rescue you, which, if I know him at all, he will be unable to resist.'

Tegen squinted against the sun as she glanced up at Admidios. He *knew* Owein? *How?*

The man smiled. 'You will come to trust me, I promise,' he said and walked back to his companions at the table.

'I'd rather die!' Tegen whispered as she curled up and tried once more to get comfortable.

*

Now! said the voice inside the raven's head. *Go! It is him you must serve. He knows my will.*

The wind stirred the trees and the raven spread her wings, sweeping down into the clearing in a glorious arc. She landed on the wooden table, scattering cups and tipping a platter of bread and meat. Carefully, as if she had been trained since fledging, the bird chose a fat green olive from a dish, picked it up in her beak and hopped forward to drop the prize meekly on the table in front of Admidios. Then, spreading her wings a little, she lowered her head.

The men in togas stopped talking and stared openmouthed at the huge bird. Admidios smiled, picked up the fruit and popped it into his own mouth. He chewed, then spat out the stone.

'So, the gods have sent me a helper at last,' he said to the raven. 'Who sent you? Tyrannis the Thunderer? Not the Dagda, the Good God – I can't see *him* helping me. Maybe Mars in Rome . . .' He leaned forward and whispered, 'Or was it *him*?' He broke off a crumb of bread and tossed it to the bird. 'Are you the one he promised? What's your name?'

The raven swallowed the morsel, opened her mouth and screeched, 'Krake-krake . . .'

'Krake? Good. Stay close by.' He raised his left arm and whistled. The bird flew from the table and landed on the improvised perch, staring at her new master with first one, then the other shining eye.

'I really don't care who sent you,' he said quietly, stroking her gleaming black head with the tips of his fingers, 'but you'll do very nicely. Very nicely indeed.'

9. Night Shadows

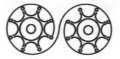

Tegen drifted in and out of a daze. Her throat hurt and she felt light-headed with thirst. In the clearing, the men walked this way and that, arguing, spreading scrolls and parchments on the table, then thumping at them with their fingers.

It was a while before she realized Admidios had a *raven* on his shoulder. Ugh! He's got it as a *pet*. Tegen shuddered and turned her face away.

The afternoon became cooler. She tried not to think of Wolf or Owein, but she couldn't help worrying whether they too had been captured.

When it gets dark, she decided, I'll have another go at getting free. She looked around carefully. The standing stone at her back had a definite sharp edge a little higher up. If I can stand, she thought, I might be able to cut the ropes on that. Meanwhile I'll lie still so I don't get any thirstier.

The smell of cooking made Tegen's stomach twist. Admidios came and stood over her, gnawing on a pork bone. He didn't say anything, just chewed and looked. She pretended she was asleep.

'We'll leave you here tonight,' he said. 'It might help you remember about the cripple.'

Tegen opened one eye. 'If you know so much about this young man, why don't you just go and get him?'

Admidios crouched by her head, his flabby face looming upside down into her vision. He tore at another mouthful of meat and chewed. 'Because he's not there.' Then he stood and tossed the bone at Tegen's face. 'My good friend Sergius over there will keep you company. See you in the morning. Sleep well.' Then he strode away.

Relieved that Owein had managed to get away, Tegen lifted her head to see who Sergius might be. Next to the hut a tall, broad-shouldered soldier in full armour stood smartly to attention. Under his red-crested helmet, the wide cheekpieces made his face narrow and sinister. The setting sun glinted on each curved plate of iron wrapped around his body. He didn't look like a man who'd be frightened of the dark.

But luckily for Tegen, he was.

Once his masters had gone and night had fallen, Sergius built up the fire and sat by it. But he was never still. He jumped at every tiny sound, drawing his short sword and moving nervously, always keeping very near the light.

After a while he chose a dry stick and plunged it into the flames. Every time a twig cracked or a bird rustled in the trees, he grabbed the firebrand and waved it at the dark.

The flickering red and orange flames fascinated Tegen – she was certain they held a message for her, if only she could get a closer look . . .

Once or twice he came and inspected her, holding his torch high and stepping as if the ground itself was deadly. Then he scurried back to the safety of the fireside, but he was gone too quickly for Tegen to be sure of what she saw in the flames.

Eventually Sergius perched on a stool and sprawled over the table as he picked at the remains of the meal. At last he dozed off.

He did not hear the shadows as they crept out of the forest.

Blackness oozing out of blackness, and darkness seeping from darkness. Slowly the shadows took solid form. Pale skin with dark swirling patterns; wild, spiked hair and huge white eyes. One by one they emerged . . .

Sergius awoke with a start and gulped back a scream. He leaped to his feet. Trembling, he fumbled for his sword. He didn't know which figure to fight first.

Tegen, who was wide awake, watched with bated breath. Could these be the Old Ones? she wondered with awe.

When a cool hand slid over her mouth she did not resist. More hands lifted and carried her into the forest.

Behind her, she heard Sergius scream. It was a strangled cry, cut short.

At last she was allowed to stand. She felt a sharp edge sawing at her bonds. Her hands were numb, yet aching at the same time. Her legs wobbled and she felt faint.

'Run with us!' a soft voice whispered. 'Silent.'

Soft leaf-fall sounds of many feet surrounded her. She could not see where she was going, but kept her head low and moved left or right at the light touch of guiding hands.

Lady Goddess, I don't know if these are friends, but they don't feel like foes. Help me know what to do next, she prayed.

The night was pitch-black. A thick covering of cloud blanked both stars and moon. At last Tegen sensed cool air moving around her, and the texture of the ground underfoot changed from loam to gravel. They were out of the woods. Hands guided her down into the ditch, up on to the tightly tamped surface, down again, and once more on to soft, friendly ground to the south, leaving the Stone Forest behind them, and the Hill of the King to their right.

Then she heard water. 'I must have a drink,' she whispered. 'I've had almost nothing all day.'

'Keep running!' a voice urged in the dark.

'Can't run if she don't drink,' said another.

Tegen followed the sound of the water, ducking and weaving between the crowding trees until she felt the soft squishyness of mud under her clogs and her feet were cold and wet. She knelt on the stony stream bed, not caring that her clothes got soaked as she put her face right under the water and drank and drank.

Bliss.

A hand grabbed at the back of her dress and pulled her up. 'Not too much. You be sick.'

'We go!' urged another voice. '*Now!*'

'Quick-quick, no wait for iron-men.'

Once more Tegen ran, guided by hands and whispers, across the stream and up a hill. She guessed it was near the clearing where she had camped and Calleva's people clung to survival. They seemed to be taking her back to Owein, but would he be there? With twists and turns they ran past the camp until the wind told her she was beyond the trees. Almost ripe barley hissed and whipped around her thighs. Straight ahead in the darkness she could just make out the brow of a long, low hill, deep jet against the lighter black of the first hint of dawn in the sky.

In the middle of the slope was a low rise, like a sleeping giant.

'Not far now' a voice whispered.

At the top of the hill, Tegen was led on to a long, close-cropped grassy hillock. She gulped . . . It was a wight-barrow, a place where the spirits of the long dead were put so they didn't walk.

'You hide, yes? You not afraid?'

Tegen felt a cold terror clutching at her shoulders. 'Can't . . . Can't I just go back to my friend? We passed our camp, back there . . .'

'No-no. Too dangerous. You stay here. Man with pony come get you tomorrow dark-time. Iron-men think you far away. Safer.'

In the darkness, Tegen could hear puffing and panting and grinding noises as a heavy stone was shifted. Once more, hands guided her forward.

'Stay here. Hide. Stay quiet. Iron-men don't like spirit places. They not come here.'

A hand touched Tegen's right cheek where her Star Dancer tattoo marked the nine-pointed pattern of the Watching Woman, the Goddess's stars. 'You druid-girl, yes?'

'Yes,' Tegen replied.

'You love our stones? You dance with them. You heard stones' hearts morning-time?'

For a moment Tegen remembered the beauty and excitement of the stony pulse under her fingertips as she leaned against the stone warriors in the dawn light. 'Yes, I love the stones. I hope I didn't offend you.'

'No,' came the voice again. 'Druids fear and hate our

stones. They love only trees. But you different. You gave flower offering to old stone. We see.'

'But that was days ago. Have you been following me?'

'Old Ones see everything,' the voice laughed. 'If you love stones, you safe here. Hide druid-girl. We come back when dark wings cover sun-face.'

Then firm hands pushed her on to her knees and guided her forward. Tegen reached out and felt a hole edged by cut rock and damp earth.

'Feet first,' another voice warned.

Tegen swivelled around and let her feet reach into nothingness below.

'Thank you!' she said. 'Can I repay you in some way? I have gold.'

She heard the sound of spitting. One shape leaned closer above her head. 'Gold destroys. Hill King drowned in gold. Gold belongs to Sun God. Sacred to him. No, we take your dog. Big dog. Strong dog. We like him.'

'No . . .' Tegen gasped. 'Not Wolf, not him, he's all I've got . . .'

'Hurry, iron-men voices!' someone else urged.

Tegen was firmly pushed forward. Her stomach flipped as she slid downward, rocks and earth scraping her back. The drop was not deep and she landed on a stone floor. She looked up and saw, against the slightly lighter sky, vague silhouettes of spiky-haired figures peering down at her.

The shapes pulled back. Once more there came the sound

of rock grating against rock, leaving her in blackness deeper than she could ever have imagined.

Then there was silence.

10. Owein

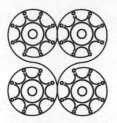

The night before Tegen was captured, Owein had not slept well. He had cramp, so at first light he had dressed and gone down to the stream. Sometimes rubbing his bad leg with cold water helped to ease the pain. But as he sat to untie his boot he heard whispers and a voice he had hoped never to hear again.

His uncle was *here* . . . and he was talking with Caja!

Owein shuddered. Romans he could cope with – he was good at playing the ignorant British peasant – but Admidios's hushed, persuasive tones in the blue-grey light of early-morning were enough to make him flatten himself behind a bramble bush, not daring to breathe.

He could not hear what Admidios and Caja were saying, but the soft reasonableness of that voice took Owein back to his childhood in Rome – growing up in his uncle's care and going to school with the sons of senators. Admidios trained Owein to obey his every word. There was no gain-saying him – when he spoke, he melted the listener's will to absolute compliance.

Liberation had come when Owein had been sent back home without his uncle to complete his British education, so eventually, when the time came for him to be made into a puppet governor, he would be acceptable to both sides. Admidios had followed him to Britain, but Owein's new foster-family had sent him away.

Now, lying on the stream bank in the dark, Owein strained to make out what his uncle was saying, but he spoke too quietly. Owein dared not move closer, lest a rustle or a snapped twig betray his presence.

At last, heavy footsteps hinted that Admidios was walking away. The sounds paused, then moved on and faded into silence.

Owein crept back to the shelter he and Tegen had shared. But it was empty. Her pig-leg bag and ash staff were still there, but that was all. She must have gone to the privy. He sat at the entrance and waited for her. His head swam with the sound of Admidios's voice layered with memories and fears from his childhood.

Suddenly he realized it was almost light and Tegen had not come back. A strong instinct told him she was in danger. Did Admidios have her? Swearing roundly, he dragged his panniers outside and loaded them on to Heather's back. He had to take everything; he had much that was too danger-ous to leave around for snooping eyes.

From the other side of the stream came the sound of wood being cut for early-morning fires. Owein mounted and made his way to the makeshift village, where Calleva and his men were stripped to their waists as they worked. 'Good morning!' he called out. 'Have you seen my friend, the girl with the dark hair?'

Calleva rested his axe and stroked his long moustaches. 'The girl who promised healing help but never turned up? No.' He turned and lifted his axe for another swing.

'She's disappeared,' Owein said. 'I'm worried.'

Calleva shrugged, but his pale wife put down the bread she was kneading and walked across to Owein. She stroked Heather's creamy mane timidly. 'I did see her, very early this morning,' she said. She pointed towards the Roman road. 'I . . . I think she was following someone, although I'm not sure.' She hesitated and glanced nervously towards Calleva, who was hacking at a log as if it was a Roman skull.

'Did you see who it was?' Owein asked.

'A stranger came before it was light. He woke us and wanted to know if we had seen a young man with a bad leg on a pony. He offered us gold . . .' She smiled. 'We didn't say anything. Since . . . since *this* happened we've been wary of strangers.'

'Could you see what he looked like?' Owein asked.

'He came into our hut, so I saw him clearly. He wore

British clothes with Roman boots. His hair was short, and he was clean-shaven like one of *them*. He was as tall as my man, and he talked with a slight "hiss". He had an air of expecting to be obeyed, if you know what I mean?'

Owein rummaged in his pouch and found a silver piece. 'I am sorry it isn't gold, but I hope this helps you and your family a little. If the girl comes back, can you ask her to stay nearby until I return?'

'If I see her,' the woman said. But Calleva was yelling for water so, clutching the coin, she hurried away.

Owein coaxed Heather along the northward path. He halted on the edge of the cleared land by the Roman road and looked around from the safety of the trees.

To his left the first streaks of sun touched the wooden structure at the top of the Hill of the King. Owein guessed it was a surveying platform. He could just about make out a couple of guards on sentry duty at the top. On the northern side of the road the trees were still in darkness and seemed deserted, apart from the cacophonous calls of the dawn chorus.

Owein looked around carefully for any clues as to which way Tegen might have gone. Why had she left without saying anything? Surely she hadn't wandered into the Stone Forest? Owein knew that if this half-British, half-Roman man was Admidios, he would be staying in comfort at the nearest army camp.

Plumes of cooking smoke were rising from behind the

hill. That must be the garrison. Owein didn't want to risk going inside unless he knew for certain that Tegen was there. Calleva's woman had said Tegen seemed to be *following* the man, not *with* him . . . Had she been captured since then?

Owein decided to make his way towards the camp. He might meet British slaves cutting timber or fetching water. He could ask for news discreetly.

He urged Heather forward, across the first drainage ditch on to the new, well-tamped surface. Gravel, not paving stones, Owein noticed. Well, I suppose it was built in a hurry. He let his mind drift back to the noonday heat shimmering on a wide, stone-paved road in Rome.

Shouted orders in the distance warned of soldiers approaching. Owein shook himself and urged Heather across the next ditch and between the hazel, birch and hawthorn on the far side. To his left, he could see the first huge, grey monoliths at the entrance to the ancient Stone Forest. A clear path ran between them. He made the sign against evil and picked another route through the trees.

Easing the pony onward was a struggle. Not only was she wide, but her mane and tail were long and kept catching on twigs and briars. Owein dismounted, drew his dagger and hacked a path through the tangle of branches and ivy. But it was too dense. He could make little headway. If he was going to get anywhere, he would have to wait until dark and risk taking the main path between the stones. He knew the words of spells to keep the ancient spirits from harming him, but he never managed to make *real* magic work . . .

At last he tied Heather to an ash sapling and went ahead to see if he could find an easier way.

As the sun climbed high in the sky he wished he had the skills to read signs and divinations; he might be able to cast bones to see where Tegen was. He had, of course, learned *how* to do it as part of his ovate's training, but he could never get the knack of interpretation. The law was his metier, and that was useless to him now. Miserably he sat on a fallen oak, leaned back and tried to think.

11. The Hunter to the Prey

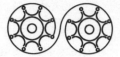

Not far away, Caja bit into a gold quarter-stater the stranger had given her. It was solid. She smiled as she rolled the gleaming coin between her fingers. Such good pay for so little work. What use was a cripple anyway? Defectives should be left to die at birth.

She glanced across at her lanky, dun-haired nephew, Kieran. He could chop wood and mend the cart. He was a child worth having. Pity he was her sister's boy, not her own, but she managed to get good work out him all the same, and that meant more time to drink beer.

Caja checked everything one last time. The cart was fully laden: tent, salt, cloth, sister and nephew. She flicked the reins across the horses' backs and the wheels lurched forward. They made their way across the Roman road and left it well behind as they followed the ancient white chalk Ridgeway to the north-east. It was rutted and narrow, but it was the quickest route. 'We'll be at Sinodun in a few days,' Caja remarked to Wynne. 'Then we'll get selling our stock and go home rich.'

Her sister looked nervously behind. 'We shouldn't have done that . . . not selling the boy to the Romans. No good will come of it.'

Caja snarled at her. 'Nonsense. You're pathetic!' She held up the golden coin to the light. 'Have you ever seen so much wealth in your life? It's more than *you* ever made!'

Wynne spat, jumped down from the cart and walked. She had kept well out of the way when the man with British breeches and Roman boots had come asking if they had seen a cripple on a pony. But, as Caja had said, what harm had been done? The man hadn't hurt the boy, just looked at his hut and gone away. But in her heart she knew it was wrong to betray someone who had done them no harm.

Wynne wished she had had the courage to stand up to Caja. She yelled for Kieran.

But the boy was as nimble as a fox. He leaped away and disappeared amongst the trees at the side of the road. He kept pace with the cart, but well out of sight, hacking with his dagger at trees as he walked. When his Mam screeched like that, it meant his aunt was cross with her. Soon one of them would take the horsewhip to his back, whether he'd misbehaved or not.

He hated Caja, and his Mam too at times. It had occurred to Kieran that sending his aunt to the place of shadows in

Tir na nÓg might be a blessing for them all. He toyed with the shiny pommel of his dagger. But then, he thought, if I do that, I'll be pursued by her spirit for the rest of my life. What's worse, he asked himself, horsewhip or haunting?

He kicked at a large stone, wishing it was Caja's head.

High above, Krake flapped lazily, circling the travellers, screeching *kek-kek-kek* harshly in the air. Round and round she flew. She could not understand why she could find no trace of the girl in the blue dress nor the boy on the pony.

Once or twice, she swooped low over the cart. The humans ignored her. There were many packs on the wagon, but the raven's senses told her that her quarries were not hidden amongst them.

She spread her wings and leaped for the sky. Higher and higher she flew, then twisted back, dropping, spinning and tumbling back towards the earth.

From the middle of the Stone Forest, there came a piercing whistle.

Give me one more tumble, one more play! Rebellion swelled in her chest. She wouldn't go back just yet; the air was too good.

Then the ghastly emptiness dragged her back to earth. There was her master. He held out his left arm and Krake landed obediently on the rag-bound wrist.

'Well, have you found either of them? The boy or the

girl?' Admidios held out a morsel of meat. Krake snapped her beak on the prize and tugged at it.

'You're a superstitious fool,' sneered Quintus Caelius from where he lay on a wooden bench. 'How can you expect a *bird* to tell you where your prey has escaped to?'

Admidios fed the raven another strip of flesh. 'My dear tribune, I am sure you've heard that these intelligent creatures are well known for leading the hunter to their prey. I just need to train her to know whom to look for. They can't be far. It's just a pity that the guard was a coward. He shouldn't have let them slip through his fingers like that.'

Admidios walked across to the legionary's corpse, which lay exactly where the Old Ones had left him the night before. The blood had blackened where his throat had been slashed. 'Mind you, the boy is stronger than I would have given him credit for,' Admidios said. 'I didn't know he was capable of killing a trained soldier, especially one the size of this moron.' He lifted his arm and Krake fluttered down to peck at the corpse's eyes and nibble at shreds from the edge of the flyblown throat wound.

Quintus shuddered and clicked his fingers for more wine. A slave appeared and filled cups for both men, then disappeared back into the hut. The Roman glared at Admidios. 'When we were in Rome, you promised me that you had trained the boy to obey you. I sent him back to Britain so he could learn British ways. You recommended he be fostered with that fool of a Dobunni king, who then reneged on our treaty. What was his name? Eiser? Now you wonder why the boy has escaped!'

Quintus laughed cynically as he leaned on his elbow and drank. 'In the palm of our hands we had such a gift: a bloodline acceptable to both sides in this wretched war. But now we've lost him, thanks to you. Foolish Caligula's greater fool!' Quintus waved his finely boned hand dismissively. 'Go and catch him, for Jupiter's sake, and bring him back alive.'

The tribune pulled a scroll from a basket by his side and began to read.

Red-faced from the abrupt dismissal, Admidios whistled for Krake and strode towards the garrison. He knew this was his only chance to get his own position of favour back. He needed to capture Owein quickly and make him fall in with the plans so meticulously prepared for him. The Romans were good masters when one was getting results, but if not . . . Their gods and their laws made no allowances.

Admidios quickened his pace as he thought of the comforting routine of work within the barracks at the northern foot of the Hill of the King, well away from the ranks of eerie stones. That pathetic little man Quintus had insisted on making the clearing the headquarters for his undercover operations so no one would come snooping. It worked. Even with *his* powers, Admidios couldn't think, even less weave spells, with the ancient Stone Magic pressing in all around him.

Admidios promised himself that when he came into his power the tribune would quickly meet a fatal accident.

Meanwhile, once more, Owein had given Admidios the slip. The British girl had said she was travelling along the Ridgeway, and spies had certainly mentioned a big meeting of druids and chieftains at Sinodun, by the River Tamesis, after the festival of Lughnasadh. Owein was unlikely to miss such a meeting. Maybe that turncoat King Eiser would be there too? Perhaps a little pressure, a little blackmail, might persuade him to hand Owein over? Furthermore, the old king had a daughter, Sabrina. She might prove useful if all else failed – as a wife or a hostage. It didn't much matter which.

Admidios smiled. Sinodun was close to the garrison town of Dorcic. It might be worth a visit . . . he had heard a new bathhouse was being built there.

The day was clouding over. He preferred dull days. He didn't dread the sun like he did fire, but he was more comfortable with less light. Admidios pulled his cloak around his shoulders as he strode towards the army encampment. He'd paid the salt-woman too much for the information she'd given. And the girl – how did she escape? Owein must have had help to rescue her – but who? That sulky old warrior in his makeshift village?

Admidios glared sideways at Krake who sat heavily on his shoulder, her black eye just a hand's breadth away from his own.

'Why can't you find them?' Admidios went on. 'Useless bird! I should have let you starve this morning!'

The raven turned her gleaming blue-black brow and her thick, flesh-ripping beak towards her master. Beauty and cruelty in one look.

Admidios shivered with dread and delight. 'Are you the raven-haired one I must press to serve the master?' He whispered, stroking her breast with the back of a finger.

The bird shook herself and stretched her neck, fluffing out her ear-feathers. Then she lowered her head and pulled from under her talon one long black hair.

'Is that from the girl? Then I forgive you this time. Well done, my beauty!' He took the hair and wrapped it around his finger.

Admidios gave a sullen and silent '*Ave*' to the guard on duty at the gate in the palisade around the barracks, then made his way past the ordered rows of leather tents. At last he reached his little room in the long wooden ranks of officers' quarters and slammed the door behind him. It was almost dark inside. He refused to have a brazier for either light or heat. He had dreaded fire since the night of his pact.

He knelt on the hard earth floor and opened one of his baskets. 'A map,' he said. 'That is what I need.'

He took out a gourd of fine sand, unstoppered it and shook the contents evenly across the ground. Then, with his finger, he drew the Roman road, running east to west. The British track that joined the road from the south-west and became the chalky Ridgeway to the north-east he marked with strips of uncured leather. Carefully he placed a few glass beads to represent the great stones, his wine cup upside down for the Hill of the King and a pebble for the shanty village. He clicked his fingers for Krake, who immediately came to his shoulder. Grabbing her, he plucked a tail feather.

Furious, the bird screamed and flew frantically around the hut, flinging herself uselessly at the door and roof. At last she perched on the edge of the bed, panting with her beak open and neck plumage raised.

Admidios ignored her and placed the feather on the sand to represent the Roman camp. Now his map was complete, he reached into his basket and pulled out a small bundle of scarlet silk. He unwrapped the shrunken human head, no bigger than his fist, and placed it at the crossroads. 'You'll be able to look all ways from there,' he said softly, smiling to himself as he edged his map with human teeth. Then he began to chant under his breath.

Finally he tied a tiny finger bone to the black hair Krake had given him. 'Now where are they?' he asked as he let it sway freely above the shrunken head.

He put a few tiny, shrivelled toadstools into his mouth and chewed until his head began to swim. The bone-and-hair pendulum began to swing wildly, refusing to settle.

Livid, he lifted the desiccated head, shook it and spat into its sewn-up eyes. 'Tell me, All-seeing One, where *are* they?'

Suddenly Krake screamed and flew at Admidios's face, digging her talons into his scalp.

'Get off, you idiot!' Admidios raised his arm to beat her off, but dropped the head. It smashed. Cursing wildly, Admidios snatched his dagger and tried to pin the bird, sliding across the floor, shattering the wine cup and destroying the map of sand all in one motion.

Krake flapped and fought back, feathers flying, talons and beak snatching and snapping, hate mingled with obedience to the demon that drove her. His fiery fingers worked her beak into meaningless shapes and sounds, making her screech:

'*Leave!*'

Admidios froze. All around, night-black feathers floated softly to the ground in the semi-dark. He panted for breath and sucked at blood from a cut on his wrist.

'*What did you say?*'

Krake jumped on to the camp bed and spread her wings, put her head back and screamed as the demon twisted her beak and tongue once more. She recomposed herself and turned her head to look Admidios in the eye.

'*Leave!* Now! Catch them on the road,' she said.

12. Wight-barrow

Deep in the wight-barrow Tegen felt cool air on her face, but the blackness was complete.

At first, she stood quite still, afraid to move in case the ground fell away beneath her feet. But she was tired. Carefully she leaned back against the wall, stretching her fingers right and left as far as they would go. Cool, rough stone met her touch. Granite slabs were stacked like cheeses, interlocking neatly to make walls, and above was a roof, but it was too high to feel all the way across.

Tegen slid her right foot forward. She kicked something that rolled and rattled. She shifted her weight. Something snapped underneath her clog. It didn't sound like a twig; it was thicker, dryer and stronger. If only she could *see* . . . She stooped and groped blindly until she touched something broken. She picked it up and ran her fingers across it. One end was sharp and shattered, the other knobbly and about the size of her own knuckle. In between ran a short, thin shaft.

She gasped and threw it away. It clattered and rattled against something hollow.

Her heart pounded in her chest. Once more she felt around in the dark, until her fingers met a smooth domed shape. She picked it up. One side was like a plain bowl, the other was curved into two ridges, each above a deep hollow – or were they round gaps? Then came a triangular space with a fine, sharp division in the middle. From either side of this rose wide, sweeping wings that curved back to meet the bowl. Trembling, Tegen made her fingers explore along the bottom edge for a row of neat, smooth, matching pegs.

They were there.

She put the shape down carefully, then stood, clasped her hands in front of her face and breathed deeply. 'Forgive me,' she said out loud. 'I did not mean to disturb your rest, friend. I am hiding from men who want to destroy our land – yours and mine, to enslave our people. Please, may I have sanctuary here until your children come to let me out tonight?'

Her voice sounded lonely and lost in the void, although she could hear the space was not big. Gingerly she cleared other parts of the skeleton aside until there was enough space to sit.

And wait.

*

Owein snapped his eyes wide open. He had been stupid enough to doze off. Now he was surrounded by a silent circle of the Old Ones. What would they do?

He sat up and spread his hands to show he held no weapon. 'My name is Owein. I am looking for a friend, a girl with long dark hair. Have you seen her?'

The Old Ones stepped a little closer and eyed him carefully. There were three young men and an older woman, all clothed in rawhide breeches and plain linen shirts. Their hair was moulded into stiff spikes with white chalky paste, and their faces plastered with the same, then decorated with blue spirals so they looked continually surprised.

The woman nodded. 'Your spirit good. You follow. Pony safe.'

The Old Ones slipped into the forest shadows, flickers of light that went out one by one. Owein was left alone with a young man about his own age who raised his right hand, fingers spread wide, and smiled. 'I am Donal. We seen your friend. We will get her in dark time. Then you both go. Yes?' He turned and walked away.

Owein swung his crutch and tried hard to keep up. 'You've found Tegen?' he asked breathlessly. 'Where is she? Why can't I fetch her now?'

Donal shook his head. 'Now not good. Come.'

Owein followed the tiny glimmers that betrayed Donal's movements. Sometimes the boy disappeared completely in the dappled shade. When he stood still he could have been a hazel coppice or a young oak. When he moved he was a fox. Once or twice Owein thought he'd been deserted, but then Donal was back at his side, the rims of his eyes red against his white face. 'Hurry!' he urged.

Here and there, great looming shapes appeared on their left, but their path did not go between the stones. Owein dared not show his fear of the ancient gods. Slowly they made their way north, the sun rising hot and bright above the trees to their right.

Suddenly a loud rustling made the travellers freeze. Then Donal chuckled, put his fingers to his lips and gave a call like a song-thrush.

Wolf came bounding gleefully towards Owein and knocked him over with delighted enthusiasm. Donal crouched and put his hand firmly over the dog's muzzle. He spoke one or two words softly. Wolf immediately calmed and sat, looking up at the boy with adoration, his tongue lolling out.

'Hush. No play now!' Donal warned.

Owein struggled to his feet as Wolf sprang across and licked his face all over. 'Good to see you too.' He smiled.

They left the tall trees behind and wove their way between scrubby tangles of hazel and honeysuckle.

Eventually Donal led Owein to a deep, chalky ditch, thickly coated in brambles and tall ash trees. Owein found it difficult to make his way down; his clothes snagged as he moved and several times he almost lost his footing. At the bottom at last, he saw Heather grazing on a patch of long grass. She nickered and nuzzled him. Gently he ran his hands across her withers and rubbed her ears.

'Thank you for looking after her. Where was she?'

The boy shrugged. 'She loose in the forest. You slept. Too dangerous. We help. That yours too.' He pointed to Owein's saddle, hanging on a low branch, and the pannier baskets alongside.

Owein put his free hand on the boy's shoulder. 'Why are you helping? You Old Ones have never had much to do with our tribes and our ways. We have never done you any favours.'

Again the boy shrugged. 'Now time for everybody change. We need help too. We help each other and make iron-skin-men go away. They do not love our stones, the earth-bones. Land is angry. We are angry. They do not love your trees. You are angry. If we are angry together, we have strong anger, yes?'

As darkness fell, slight rustlings and almost imperceptible movements brought the rest of the clan. They gathered in the small bramble-free space next to Owein. A toothless woman in a leather cap produced what looked like a large rock. She laid it on the ground, hit it twice smartly with the butt of her knife and the clod fell apart to show a clay-baked trout, cold but mouth-watering. Others brought barley bread and leather bottles of water. All sat and ate in silence.

Owein chewed on his food. When he asked where Tegen

was, his new friends whispered, 'She safe. Next dark-time we get her. Now, too dangerous. Iron-men look for her. Hide for one sun's path. They think you gone already. Better later.'

Owein was not in a position to argue: lost in impassable woodland, with no idea of where Tegen was, he might just be able to get himself out, but he would need help to find a way through for Heather. Without the Old Ones there was no hope for any of them. But at least they were safe. For now.

That night the Old Ones slipped away, leaving him alone in the camp with dire warnings not to move. When they returned, they were whispering excitedly. The following morning, as the sun rose, Donal tapped Owein lightly on the shoulder and beckoned to him to follow. 'Leave pony. Come softly.' Donal had dried blood on his hands and down the front of his clothes.

The young man led the way back towards the stones: some straight, tall, warrior-like, others squat and crouching – all forbidding, even in the broad daylight.

They could hear men shouting long before they came to the clearing. Ahead, the huge monoliths swept to left and right, beginning a stone circle that disappeared into the trees beyond. Donal crouched behind a slab half hidden by bryony. Owein did the same, careful not to touch the cool surface. 'See, they spit on sacred places,' the boy whispered.

Straight ahead was a small wooden army hut. In front

were a table and stools. Red dishes and wine cups were scattered, some smashed on the ground. A short, grey-haired man in a toga was waving his fist at a tall man in breeches, who did not seem at all daunted. He simply crossed his arms and stared at something by his feet. Owein went cold as he let his eyes drift to the same spot.

There lay a Roman soldier. His throat was a dry mass of black blood. A raven pecked at what had been eyes.

The grey-haired Roman went silent, picked up a scroll and began to read. The man in breeches called to the bird, which flew to his shoulder. Then he walked away.

Owen went very pale and tried to stop himself from shaking. 'It *is* him! And he has a familiar!' he whispered. 'This is dangerous!'

Once more he peered into the clearing. Now the Roman was also walking away. Soon everything was silent, except for the hum of thousands of flies shimmering turquoise-blue as they laid their eggs on the dead man's wounds.

Donal walked forward and beckoned Owein to follow. Together they stood by the corpse. Slivers of white bone were beginning to show where the raven had feasted around the neck.

'They dishonour him. No rites, no sacred death-walk to Otherworld. He let your girl go.'

Owein was puzzled. 'He *let* Tegen go?'

'Didn't mean to.' Donal laughed quietly. 'We are swift,

we are sure!' The boy raised his blood-stained arm and clenched his fist.

'You did this?'

'Me, and friends, last dark-time,' the boy replied with a grin of self-satisfaction.

'You are the noblest of warriors.' Owein touched his forehead and bowed to show respect. 'Next time I have mead in my horn I will raise it and shout to all men that you are a hero. I will write a song about you to be sung in feast halls.'

The boy's smile broadened, showing two lost teeth, his tongue and gums startlingly red against his white-painted face. Then he pointed to Tegen's cloak on the ground. 'Take. She need later.'

Owein pushed his crutch under his left arm as he folded the thick white wool into a clumsy bundle.

'Come,' the boy said again. Then, with movement as light as a stag, he bounded away through the forest.

As the sun rose, Tegen was aware of pale chinks in the blackness that had swallowed her all night. Soon the grey turned to streaks of light. She stretched and yawned. She was cold, stiff and beyond hunger. She stared up at the tiny cracks and wondered if she dared make a hole bigger and try to escape. If she did and the Romans found her, they might torture or even kill her! There was no way they'd believe she didn't know where Owein was. They might even think *she'd* killed the soldier.

If the Old Ones don't come by the time it's dark I will escape, she promised herself. She tried not to think about whether her bony companions had died imprisoned, or if their dead bodies had been placed there with ceremony. She rubbed her arms and shoulders. I wish I had been able to grab my cloak. That would have been some comfort, she thought. It had all happened so quickly. She made herself comfortable, but her head churned with questions and worries about Owein and Wolf.

She closed her eyes and imagined the night stars with the constellation of the Watching Woman gleaming at their heart. It might help if I could dance in here, she thought . . . She stirred a foot slightly and a bone rattled across a stony slab.

She licked her lips. They were dry and sore. She was finding it hard to concentrate. She stood, and with her fingers and the little light available she searched the tomb. It had a long central chamber and five smaller ones splayed off it, like an oak leaf. Most of the bones were in the side chambers. The middle passage was fairly clear, but treacherous with mud and loose pebbles. Soon she reached a wider, higher area, which seemed to be the main entrance. Her fingers told her it was blocked with a huge boulder. Every gap was sealed with turf and smaller rocks. Some were loose – she might be able to pull them away and slip through . . .

But she had been warned to stay put. She kicked the blocking stone and sat in the mud with her chin in her hands. She cursed her helplessness.

As the few tiny streaks of growing light caught on the bones around her feet, thoughts of death began to prey on her mind.

Tir na nÓg is simply a resting place before rebirth, she told herself firmly. Some of these bones might have belonged to people who are alive again now – maybe even friends of mine. Tegen groped her way to one of the dry side chambers and reverently cleared the central slab of bones. She had a raging headache and felt sick, but at last she shivered herself to sleep.

Her head filled with whirling images of stars, all looking to the north and moving in that direction. Usually the constellations moved from east to west, following the moon, but these stars were different.

They all had faces.

13. Star Dancing

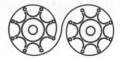

As darkness fell on the second night, Donal led Owein up, out of the ditch. Heather scrambled behind them, the chalky surface loose under her hoofs. At the top they stood once more between the ancient uprights of the Stone Forest: a sweeping curve of towering teeth set in the earth's jaw.

Owein breathed deeply. He must show no dread. He whispered a greeting to the spirits of the North. After all, they too were of rock and stone. They would protect him from other ancient gods who might be angry at his trespass.

Hazel, oak and rowan were dark and wet in the fading evening light. Their friendly boughs embraced the uncanny stones. Owein let his fingers trail against rough bark and smiled at his stupidity. All gods and goddesses were, in the end, great spirits of earth, air, fire and water – and they were One Spirit. There was nothing to fear.

Slowly Donal led Owein south. Every few steps the boy stopped and listened. 'Horse too noisy,' he whispered at last. He motioned Owein to wait as he slipped ahead through the deep-blue forest. Somewhere a blackbird cackled a warning, but nothing else stirred.

Owein held his breath. At last Donal returned. 'Guards,' he whispered. 'Tie horse. We come back here with your friend. You walk, yes?'

Owein wanted to groan, his back and arm hurt from so much walking, but he had no choice. He nodded, pushed Tegen's cloak into a pannier, tied Heather to a sapling and leaned on his crutch. 'I'm ready!'

There was no moon when they reached the Roman road, so they crossed without fear of being seen. On the far side they kept going south, leaving the Hill of the King behind on their right. Soon they were splashing in shallow water, then wading through hissing barley as they made their way up a hillside. At the top a long, low shape hugged the horizon, pitch black against the starry dark of the evening sky.

Donal stopped . . . and pointed.

'She's not in *there*, is she?' Owein asked, horrified.

'No, she not,' Donal replied. 'Look.'

Beside the wight-barrow, a slim, dark figure was moving and swaying in the starlight. Owein gave a low whistle. The dancer froze.

Donal hurried forward. Owein struggled to keep pace behind. 'Tegen!' he called softly.

'How long you out?' Donal demanded. 'Dangerous. You get seen!'

Tegen ran towards her friends. 'No one saw me. I waited until it was dark. I pulled the loose stones from around the large boulder at the entrance. I put them all back. I *had* to get out. Has anyone got any food? I haven't eaten for two days.'

Suddenly she stopped and stared at Donal's white face and white spiky hair. 'I had a dream, in there,' she said, pointing back to the wight-barrow. 'It was about stars . . . that had *faces*. I didn't realize it at the time, but it was about you – and the other Old Ones.'

Donal looked hard at Tegen. 'You dance with stones, now you dream with ancestors. You strange druid-girl! What your dream?'

Tegen thought for a moment. 'I can't tell it. I can *dance* it though.'

Owein looked around nervously. 'We need to get on the road, Tegen. We can't afford to get caught . . .'

Donal put his head on one side and listened. Somewhere an owl called and a nightjar replied. 'No one here, but us,' he said, and gave a throaty sound like a bullfrog. From out of the trees, six or seven more of the Old Ones slid eerily into view, their chalky hair and faces stark in the soft light. Their white heads seemed to float disembodied towards the wight-barrow. Silent as wraiths, they gathered.

Donal whispered a few words to his people, then turned to Tegen. 'Now, dance us your dream,' he said.

Tegen took a deep breath, closed her eyes and held her arms out wide. She did not long for her old green silk shawl or for the jangling golden bands she sometimes wore on her ankles. This was a story that had to be told in the silence of the night.

As she tried to dance what she had seen, Tegen realized she needed the others to take part as well. She beckoned to the white-faced figures around her and placed them in a pattern. Each one stood in for one of the stars of the Wyvern, the mighty dragon who always points the way north.

Surrounded by the constellation of astral faces against the night sky, Tegen closed her eyes and listened to the soft, distant music of the wind in the trees as she began to move in a gentle, walking rhythm. At first she led the Wyvern, sweeping east, then to the north through the woods, towards the Roman road and the Stone Forest and beyond. She found her dance *telling* the Old Ones to go that way.

'*Stop!*' Donal hissed.

The dancers froze. 'Stranger?' whispered a woman's voice.

'Maybe bird,' answered another. 'Time to go. The gods have answered us. Enough.' And with that, they melted into the night. Tegen, Owein and Donal were left standing on the edge of the trees facing the clear expanse of the new road. Beyond, in the silvery starlight, was the first of the ancient stones standing guard between the oak, ash and thorn, all that was left of what had been.

Donal pushed Tegen's pig-leg bag and her ash staff into her hands. 'My brothers fetch these for you. We hurry now. Silver Lady rise in sky soon. Light makes danger here.' He checked all was clear, then beckoned for Tegen to follow. Once she was safe amongst the trees on the other side, Owein set off on his too-slow journey across the expanse of road.

Suddenly a harsh screeching shattered the silence of the night and a vicious black shape separated itself from the rest of the darkness, knocking Owein off balance. He fell on to the gravel surface and swiped at the creature with his crutch. The bird attacked again. Tegen did not hesitate. She sprang on to the road and lashed out with her staff. Wings and talons flapped and clawed at her face, but at last the bird swept away.

'Evil creature!' she muttered as she helped Owein up. 'Why did it come from nowhere and attack us like that?'

Donal hissed between his teeth. 'Beware, that omen-bird got demon eyes!'

Owein made the sign against evil and scrambled after the others towards the northern side. A short walk through the woods took them to the clearing where Heather waited. The little pony nickered with pleasure at the feel of her master's kind hands again. 'Thank you, Donal – for every-thing,' Owein said as he pulled himself on to her back.

'All well,' the boy replied out of the darkness. 'Cross-roads watched by iron-men. Go north, turn towards the Sun God's hand at dawn, come to Ridgeway. Miss guards. Stones will keep your feet on the path. Yes.'

Tegen reached out and squeezed his hand in the dark. 'Thank you. May the Stones guard your people on their journey too.'

'No more talk.' Donal turned the pony's head towards a clear track between the trees. 'No ditches. Easy.'

Owein drew a small knife with a mother-of-pearl handle from his pouch. 'Please let me say thank you.' He held the offering in the flat of his palm.

Donal took it. 'Is good. I like.' Then he grasped Owein's free arm. 'Stones guard you both,' he said.

'Goodbye!' Owein kicked Heather's flanks gently and she swung into her old, steady rhythm.

Tegen followed, her head hung low and a lump in her throat at the thought of leaving Wolf behind. But she could not argue. The Old Ones had saved them.

Just then, a crashing of branches and wildly scuffling leaves made them both jump. Tegen gripped her staff, but the huge paws on her shoulders and hot breath on her cheek told her it was no wild beast, only a large and over-excited dog. She dropped everything and hugged him as he licked her face and hair joyfully. 'I can't take you with me.

☀ 100 ☀

You must stay with new friends now. Go back!' She pushed him firmly away, trying not to let tears sting her eyes.

'No,' came Donal's voice from the darkness. 'Keep hound. You sleep not afraid with ancestors. They bless you with prayer-answers. You tell us north is safe. We go there soon. We are paid. Keep dog.'

Then, with the slightest rustle between the trees, the Old Ones were gone and Tegen and Owein were alone.

Tegen shuddered as she picked up her things and wiped the dog-slobber from her face with her cloak. 'Yuck!' she laughed as she turned on to the path. Ahead, Owein slowed so she could join him.

'Oh, I forgot,' he said, and rummaged in his bag. He pulled out half a barley loaf sliced open and stuffed with fish. 'Hungry?'

Tegen pounced on the food and ate so fast she gave herself painful hiccoughs.

In the Roman garrison, Admidios tossed and turned on his camp bed. He had ignored Krake's words. Ravens don't speak – not like that, anyway . . . his mind must have been befuddled by the magical fungi he had chewed.

Sleep claimed him at last and he dreamed he was following Owein, intending to make him obey – or to kill him – but he found his way blocked by the girl with the tattooed face. Her hair turned to ravens' wings and he knew he had to recapture her. Then he was running after her with a rope made of fire that burned him and terrified him, yet he could not put it down.

Suddenly Krake landed in the open wind-eye and screamed at him. Admidios swore, but did not move. She opened her beak and screeched more loudly. He had to get up. He *had* to. The empty space behind her *demanded* he woke, *now!* She flew down and landed on his exposed shoulder, gripping his bare flesh with her talons and drawing blood. Her master howled, flailing his arms. Where was the wretched bird? The soft 'tic' of her talons on the stool by his side betrayed her. Admidios picked up a boot and threw it hard. It caught her on the beak.

Angry and afraid, Krake flapped away into the forest and sat on the highest branches of a beech tree. There was nothing she could do. Her master would not listen, so she hunched her wings around her head and tried to shut out the demonic torments that failure always brought.

14. The White Road

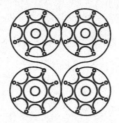

'It's the white road I dreamed of in Sul's Land – it's beautiful!' whispered Tegen. The pale ribbon of the chalky track gleamed in the moonlit darkness. 'Do we travel along this all the way to Sinodun?'

'Mostly,' Owein replied. 'We turn off towards the end, but that won't be for several days. Are you up to walking for a while? I want to be as far away from the Stone Forest as I can by dawn.'

'I can walk, but why are we in so much danger? Isn't it time you told me the whole truth?'

Owein said nothing as he slumped in the saddle like an old man once more. The only sound was the steady trudge of Heather's hoofs against the stony path.

Tegen was livid. She ran after Heather and thumped Owein on the back. 'You can't treat me like this! A British man in league with the Romans captured me as bait for *you*

– not that you came – and I have been shut in a wight-barrow with the skeletons of generations of ancestors for two nights. For *what*? I have a right to know!'

Owein just shook his head. 'Honestly, the less you know the better.'

'And where were you the other morning?' she persisted, running ahead and staring Owein in the face. 'I woke when I heard someone snooping around the camp. You weren't there. What were you doing? Are *you* a spy for the Romans? I wouldn't put it past you! You are so secretive!'

'I did come looking for you,' he replied quietly. 'If you give me a chance, I'll answer some of your questions. I woke with cramp while it was still dark . . .'

For a while Tegen listened, but he still offered no explanations as to why he was wanted by Admidios and his friends. Tegen sighed. She was too exhausted to push for more answers. She would have to wait.

As they travelled, the moonlight showed half-harvested fields and palisaded villages. Dogs barked and geese hissed as they passed by. As the east began to lighten they found a couple of deserted roundhouses near a few squares of overgrown farmland. They freed the pony of her burdens and hobbled her by a stream in a grassy hollow.

'We'll sleep in the goose house.' Owein pointed to a heavily leaning hut on short stilts.

Wolf was sniffing around the back of the compound.

Tegen called him to her side. 'But there might be beds, even clean straw in the houses. Wouldn't that be nicer?'

'Too obvious if any one is following us,' Owein replied as he pulled himself up the ramp and pushed back the remnants of the door. 'This looks so rickety, it could fall down any moment. It's not the sort of place people hide. If we hear anyone searching the houses, it'll give us a few moments to get away.'

Tegen crawled in behind him, followed by Wolf. The whole structure swayed as they tried to make themselves comfortable on rancid straw. I will *make* him tell me in the morning, she promised herself.

They slept until the sun was past the mid-haven. The day was sultry and hot. Tegen woke first and walked down to the stream where Heather was nibbling grass. Tegen bathed and washed her clothes. Being wet was better than stinking of stale goose dung. Feeling brighter, she greeted the spirits and wandered through the deserted fields. Over the years, the crops had re-seeded themselves. She gathered late broad beans and bolted leeks in her skirt. There were peas too, but most of the pods had sprung open, making their contents difficult to glean. She found turnips and the rather mucky remains of a honeycomb in an abandoned skep. She had no means of storing this, so she blissfully licked at the thick, waxy sweetness. Soon Heather's panniers were bulging with provisions for several days and she sat on a log to comb her hair and think.

Should I be travelling with Owein? she wondered. I'm sure he's not a criminal, but he's got dangerous enemies.

Suddenly, in the tree canopy above, birds flapped and squawked in a cacophony of hate. Tegen looked up. A large raven was jumping from branch to branch above her head, calling *pruk pruk* at her.

Tegen clapped her hands. '*GO AWAY!*' she yelled, 'I don't *like* ravens – go and peck someone else's eyes out!'

The bird screeched and soared into the sky, circling, then turning south-west.

Was this the omen-bird the Old Ones had warned them about? Unnerved and shaking, Tegen picked up a stick and rattled it against the shed walls to wake Owein. With curses and mutterings he emerged, yawning and squinting up at the sun. 'Is it really this late?'

'Yes, and I've been busy.' She showed him the food and told him about the raven.

Owein paled. 'A raven *again*? That's very bad. We must get going quickly.'

Deep down she had needed Owein to reassure her and to laugh it off. Instead, he too seemed afraid. Once more he was hiding things from her.

'I didn't think a high-minded lawyer would be discon-certed by a *mere bird*!' she snapped.

Owein said nothing as he went towards the stream to

wash, leaving her staring after him, angry and afraid. Why couldn't he just *talk* to her? She untied Heather and led her back up to the goose house, stamping and cursing all the way. Fumbling and snatching at the straps and girths, Tegen readied the pony.

'That's *it*!' Tegen said to herself. 'It's time to leave Owein to his own problems. I won't go to Sinodun at all!' Hurriedly she packed a share of the food into her own bag. But as she looked along the road her heart sank. Where was she? Which way was Mona? Did it *matter*, as long as she left Owein? Gritting her teeth, she hauled her bag on to her shoulder. She could ask the way later. Right now, she needed to *leave*.

At that moment Owein returned. He was still silent, but he looked pale and upset as well. In her heart Tegen knew he needed a friend as much as she did. Her resolve faded. I'll give him one more chance, she decided. Scowling, she whistled for Wolf. The great mud-coloured hound bounded out of the woods, his thin tail curled in excitement. He jumped at Tegen to give her an extra wash, then turned his attention to Owein, who shoved him away.

'Why are you in such a foul mood?' Tegen challenged. 'In the name of all that's sacred, tell me what's wrong!'

Owein looked up at the hot, white sky. 'It's that raven. They are known for leading the hunter to the prey. Usually the predator is a larger animal that can bring down the victim and rip it open. Then the bird can feast as a reward.

In this case, I think it is the same creature that attacked us on the road last night.'

Tegen glanced at her finger, which throbbed. 'How *could* it be?'

'Do you remember saying you thought ravens were following you? I think you're right. I think it's *one* bird, a familiar for someone whom I strongly suspect is a Shadow Walker.'

'A Shadow Walker?' she whispered. 'What's that?'

Owein looked around carefully. The chalk road stretched ahead through the dappled woods. All was quiet except for the hedgerow birds and the rustle of the undergrowth as Wolf leaped around.

'It's a man – or a woman – who does magic, but with evil intent. He literally walks in the shadows. He does nothing in the open daylight. He usually has an animal that is a physical host for a demon who is guiding him.'

Tegen shivered as she remembered that Admidios had a pet bird. It couldn't be him, could it? 'How do you know about this man?' she asked.

Owein sat up in the saddle and clenched his jaw. 'I have said too much as it is. Please . . .' he said more gently, 'tell me what happened to you yesterday.'

Tegen didn't want to talk; she was too angry with him for not trusting her with the whole truth. She kicked a stone, but she knew sulking would not help. If I open up first, she reasoned, he might begin to trust me. She took a deep breath and began with hearing the footsteps in the camp before dawn. As she talked, Owein listened intently and he asked a few questions. When she had finished, they both fell silent again.

'You know this man Admidios, with the porridgy-face, don't you?' she asked after a while.

Owein nodded. 'I'll tell you all about him, I promise. I just need a clearer picture of what he is up to first.' He pulled Heather to a halt and looked at Tegen. 'I need your trust a little longer. It might be safer for you to travel on alone soon. If . . . If anything happens to me, keep following this road until you come to a very wide river flowing south. Don't ford it, but take the track that follows it northward on this side until you come to twin hills. That's Sinodun. You'll be safe there. Someone will help you.'

Tegen caught his eye for a moment and knew he was telling the truth.

Owein looked away and they walked on without speaking.

The white chalk road ran north-east along a ridge of heavily wooded uplands. On the left, the land fell into flat, well-farmed plains. The road was busy with carts and pannier-laden ponies carrying the grain harvest from fields to villages, sheep and cattle being moved between pastures, and children chasing flocks of geese.

They passed two small cohorts of soldiers patrolling the road, but they took no notice of Owein and Tegen.

As the warm sun sank slowly at their backs, the road swung to their right and climbed towards a hilltop stronghold circled with three rings of concentric ditches. The rising tiers of white chalk ramparts gleamed pink in the evening light. The lower ramparts were built up with huge sarsen stones, making daunting walls. On the topmost level, a strong wooden palisade with intermittent guardhouses looked defiant and impregnable.

At the highest point, the chief's thatched longhouse billowed rich-scented cooking smoke into the evening air.

Owein kicked Heather into a little more of a trot. 'They'll be closing the gates soon. If I carry your bag, can you run a bit?' Tegen handed her things across and tried to keep up, but her feet hurt and she wished she could just lie on the cool grass by the roadside and let Owein go on ahead. She was too tired to care about a bed – or even food.

From inside the palisade a horn blew for sunset. The gates started to swing together. The guards shouted and waved to the travellers to hurry. Weary and hot, they kept running and passed breathless through the steep-banked first defences. Wolf loped behind, his tongue lolling. Just inside the heavy lower gate, a long shed sheltered a blacksmith as he hammered out a white-hot bar of iron, sending red and yellow sparks flying. Two boys were struggling with huge bellows. For a moment Tegen felt homesick as she remembered the hours she and her foster-brother, Griff, had worked the bellows for her father as he poured lead and silver in their Mendip home.

The smith paused and watched them pass. Then he turned and yelled at the boys for letting the fire cool. They both bent their backs to the wheezing leather sacks, making the heart of the fire burn white.

Mosquitoes buzzed and worried as Tegen hauled herself up the cobbled zigzag path between the ramparts. At last she reached the upper gateway – two huge grey stones carrying massive wooden doors on pivot hinges. Braziers burned on each side, casting eerie shadows at rotting heads impaled on spikes atop the almost closed gates.

As Owein and Tegen slipped inside, the gates slammed shut and were barred. Tegen spat to avert the evil eye and blessed the dead warriors' spirits who now guarded the place. Owein glanced up, then looked away quickly. Tegen fought nausea as a large bird perched on one of the heads and ripped a strip of flesh from behind the nose. The head rocked, and the bird jumped off, letting the whole thing list to one side with a dreadful leer in the firelight.

Ahead, the path split into three. Behind the walls to the left, large cauldrons of water were bubbling over fires, piles of stones nearby ready to heat so they could be catapulted at any oncoming enemies. Leaning against the palisade was a stockpile of spears.

Behind the right-hand wall heaps of stinking rubbish and

rotting flesh made Tegen's stomach turn. In the waning light it looked like the defeated warriors had been cut up and left flyblown as ready ammunition. Wolf slunk to Tegen's side. The hot summer night stank.

'It looks like they are expecting a battle,' Owein whispered. 'I want to get out of here as soon as possible.'

They took the central path to the chieftain's longhouse at the top of the hill. A heavy oak door stood wide. Owein dismounted, left his name and Heather with a guard, then taking his crutch he followed Tegen inside. Two rings of tall tree trunks supported the thatched roof, making a wide chamber. In the centre a fire burned fiercely in a stone-lined pit. Cauldrons of pork sizzled, and bread baked in clay ovens. Trestle tables were set around the fire, and women bustled about with jugs of ale, avoiding a knot of fighting dogs.

A shout went up at the far end of the hall and a tall, heavy man with long plaits and a badly scarred face came and crushed Owein in a bear hug. 'Welcome to my hall. I am Baras, chieftain of the foremost clan of the Atrebates.' Then he turned to Tegen and kissed her rather too warmly on the mouth. Embarrassed, she discreetly wiped the spit away.

Baras smiled broadly as he drew Owein aside and whispered, 'Your uncle is here and he's expecting you. He's told me who you are, my boy. Make sure no one else knows. You can't be sure who you can trust these days . . .' Then he stood and roared, 'Ale! Meat! Salt! Bring it now!' He turned back to his guests. 'Will you wash first? My slaves are notoriously slow and will take until tomorrow unless I whip them.' He put two fingers in his mouth and gave an ear-piercing whistle.

A pretty girl with dimples led them towards a round-house behind the great hall. 'This is where guests sleep,' she said. 'I'll bring you water and clean clothes.' She smiled flirtatiously at Owein, giggled and left them to go inside alone.

The last of the daylight showed the roundhouse was spacious and clean, with six or seven fur-covered beds placed around the walls. No fire was lit, but the evening was sticky. Tegen scratched at her bites.

'I don't like this place, Owein. Those heads . . . Something is seriously wrong here, but I don't know what . . .'

Owein leaned against the doorpost and looked out at the bustling stronghold. It was the same as any other British enclosure in the evening. People were cooking, eating, swigging ale and sitting around talking. All seemed calm enough.

'I know one thing that's wrong,' he said. 'My uncle is here, and he is someone I do not want to meet again. The gates are shut and there is no way out until morning – unless you want to leap the ramparts, that is. I suspect the heads belong to people who wished they had tried.' Then he stomped out into the night to use the privy.

Tegen's heart sank, but before she could worry about

who Owein's uncle might be, the slave-girl brought water, a towel and fresh linen tunics. Behind her, a small boy carried half a dozen rushlights, which he pushed into a pot of sand on the table. When they had gone, Tegen washed and changed. She rummaged in her bag for a pouch of lavender, then crushed the fragrant flowers between her fingers and rubbed the oil on her ragingly itchy bites.

The last hints of day had faded and Tegen found the darkness overwhelmed her. It wasn't just night – it was a swallowing emptiness that she didn't know how to counter. Despite the heat she found she longed for fire. Lately she seemed to be able to see pictures in flames. She ached for some sort of clarity and if Owein wasn't going to tell her what was going on, she'd glean it herself. She had been taught little about divination, but she had to do *something*. She picked up one of the rushlights and went to the hearth. The logs were laid, but there was no kindling. Using the straw from her mattress, she tried to coax a fire in the hearth. Flames rose, then died under the logs.

In that brief moment she knew she had glimpsed something, but what? It had been too quick. She rummaged in her bag and found her Ogham sticks, then, chanting a spell for summoning wisdom, she tossed them on to her bed, but the rushlights were too weak to see the marks clearly. Her fingers tingled with knowledge she could not reach. The old druid Witton would have been able to read them by touch, she thought.

Tegen went to the door of the roundhouse and looked for the stars. The night was cloudy, but smoke from the stronghold's numerous hearths would have obscured them anyway. 'Lady Goddess,' she prayed, 'show me what I need to know. What are the shadows I feel?' The scent of lavender soothed her mind. Perhaps if I could eat some hazelnuts they'd bring me insight . . . I wish I still had my old green silk scarf. I would love to sneak out of the gates to dance for the Goddess in the dark.

But her thoughts were interrupted by Owein returning. 'Is that the washing water?' He threw down his crutch and knelt by the bowl. He splashed his face and rubbed his wet skin vigorously on the towel. Then he stopped and sniffed. 'What's that smell? Lavender? Are you doing magic?'

'It's for mosquito bites.' She paused. 'And I tried some divination, but I can't get it to work. If you aren't ready to tell me the truth, perhaps you could teach me, to make up for it?'

Owein snorted. '*Me?* Teach divination? I'm hopeless at magic. I told you, I want to be a lawyer.'

There was a firm knock on the doorpost. '*I'd* be delighted to teach you,' said a soft voice.

The sound sent shivers down Tegen's spine. 'Who's that?' she asked, but she knew exactly who she would see, as a tall figure entered the shadowy roundhouse.

15. Shadow Secrets

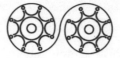

Owein swung himself forward and stood squarely in front of the speaker. 'Uncle,' he said firmly, 'go away. You aren't wanted here.'

'I didn't come to see *you*, Sextus,' Admidios replied, striding past him. He smiled at Tegen, showing a set of perfect teeth. 'So, you arrived safely. Now, why would a girl with a tattoo on her face even *think* of learning divination?' With his left hand he cupped her chin and with his right he stroked her cheek. 'It seems the little snooper who likes wild berries is a *druid*, and a powerful one at that!'

Tegen twisted her head and bit his thumb. 'Get off me, you bastard! Leave us alone!' and with her fingers she spun a web of protection in the air between them. Wolf slunk to her side and bared his teeth while Owein picked up a rush-light and held it high.

Admidios squirmed away, shielding his eyes, then forced

himself to relax. He snarled at the dog, who sank to his belly, hackles raised.

'I told you to *go away*,' Owein repeated.

'Or you will do *what*?' Admidios asked, as he rubbed the bite mark. 'Haven't you missed me, Sextus? I've missed you. I'm intrigued to know how you sprang this little vixen from our grasp at the Stone Forest. I didn't know you had it in you to kill a fully armed legionary. I must admit I was impressed.'

'I didn't kill him,' Owein replied, 'and my name isn't Sextus.'

Admidios turned to his nephew, lowered his voice and purred, 'Oh, but it *is*, dear nephew. You cannot deny *everything* about your past. I bet you haven't even told your charming companion who you really are. Shall I?'

Owein grabbed another rushlight and walked forward. Tegen could see his hands were shaking in the dancing flames.

Admidios moved back towards the door. 'Well, druid girl, I'm surprised you lowered yourself to biting, like a slave whelp. You have far more magic in you than that. You'll be coming to me for training yet – I have plenty you will want to learn. When you are ready, just call. I won't be far away . . .'

He stepped outside, then turned back. 'By the way, you are both expected in the hall. Food is ready.'

Tegen hugged herself and scowled. 'I'm not hungry!'

'Suit yourself!' Admidios sneered and walked across the courtyard towards Baras's longhouse.

Owein picked up his crutch and stood behind her. 'You've got to eat,' he said quietly. 'We have a long road ahead; you will need strength, especially if *he* is around.'

'That's the man with the raven, the one who I saw skulking around our camp and who questioned me in the Stone Forest,' she said, then added vehemently, 'and I *hate* him.'

'I guessed.'

'And he's your uncle, the one who made you learn to read Latin?'

'Yes.'

'The Shadow Walker?'

'Yes.'

'And you led him right to us?'

'I haven't seen him for over a year. I had no idea he was nearby until the other morning – and you had already gone; it was too late to warn you. I did my best to help free you, I really did. Now I'm just trying to get you as far as possible on the road to Sinodun . . . I had no way of knowing he would be *here* either. He must have overtaken us while we slept in the goose hut.'

He pulled her cloak around her shoulders. 'Now it's getting chilly outside and we are expected at Baras's table. I will tell you everything as soon as I can – I swear. For now, say nothing and try to look as if you are enjoying yourself.' And with that, he led her towards the sound of feasting.

Owein was given a seat at the high table with the chieftains and important guests. Tegen was glad to be ignored and left to eat in the shadows with the lesser warriors and children. Owein was right, she was hungry. She devoured thick slices of boiled pork served on a red earthenware dish like the ones she had seen the Romans using. She sopped up the salty juices with spelt bread, drank her first wine and watched Admidios carefully.

He sat as far from the fire as he could, his face shielded from the dancing flames by one of the roof supports. To the eye, Admidios seemed nothing more than an overweight, overbearing man of about fifty . . . But Tegen sensed the unseen secrets of the shadows dancing around him.

Her cheeks flushed. How *dare* he suggest that she would ever learn from *him*! She shuddered, but to her horror she realized she was oddly flattered at the same time. This man, who had explored the depths of spells she didn't even know existed, had noticed her – and thought she was worth training.

16. Fire Magic

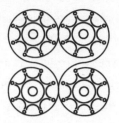

That night Owein snored. Loudly.

Tegen was glad when it was light enough to get up. She slipped out of her bed, pulled on her clothes, greeted the spirits and went for a walk.

She made her way to the main gate and stood staring at the array of impaled heads. Some were almost picked clean, hanging by the dome of the skull, their jaws fallen off long ago. Others looked as if they hadn't been dead long. What was it about them that made her feel so edgy? She had seen heads on spikes before.

She turned at the sound of heavy footsteps on the cobbles behind her. It was the blacksmith, taller even than Admidios, bearded and strong. 'Come with me,' he said in a surprisingly gentle voice. 'Your knife needs sharpening.'

Instinctively Tegen trusted the sad but kind look in his eyes, and her knife was indeed very blunt. She followed his leather-clad back down the path, twisting between the ramparts to the forge. The man clapped his huge hands as he approached. Two boys who had been sleeping by the hearth jumped up and rubbed their eyes. 'You've let my fire go out, you good-for-nothings!' he roared. 'Wash and eat or you'll be useless!'

They ran off as their master sat on a split-log bench in the smoky shed. The smith smiled. 'Draw up a stool. They are good lads, but it wouldn't do to show I was fond of them. They would take advantage.' Then he rested his chin in his blackened palm as he looked at Tegen.

'Now what can I do for you?'

Tegen shrugged. 'You said my knife needed sharpening. I don't know how you knew, but it does . . .' She passed it across.

The antler-hilted blade nestled like a child's plaything in his hand. 'Come for it later. But first you need a powerful spell, I think. Last night you came in with a shadow at your shoulder, and it has deepened dangerously since then. You need protection. You are strong in spirit, but not in learning. Now, what could I give you?'

'Do you know the way to Mona?' she ventured. 'If I could get there quickly, instead of going to Sinodun first, that would help me a lot . . .'

The smith scratched his thick beard and shook his head. 'Not yet,' he said. Then he rummaged in a wooden box. 'You will go there later. Ah! This will do.' He pulled out an iron finger-ring, walked over to his fire pit and blew. Suddenly the whole shed roared with a rushing wind. Smoke and cinders whirled into the air then sank, leaving a pall of dull grey ash, but the fire was leaping high and bright. The smith tossed the ring into the centre and watched as the iron began to glow red, yellow, then white-hot.

'Enough!' he roared, and the fire went out as if doused by water. He leaned forward and picked up the white-hot metal with his bare fingers. Then, taking Tegen's right hand, he slipped the ring on to her middle finger. It was cool.

She turned her hand and examined the gift. It had faded back to almost black, highly polished and quite plain except for a narrow line cut all the way around. Along it, six Ogham were incised: oak, ash, hazel, hawthorn, holly and rowan.

'You will be protected by fire as long as you wear that,' said the smith. 'Iron is hard earth-blood. Fire plucks it from stone, and fire can send it back. If you ever need an answer, look for it in fire. Remember, fire protects from magic, but it also leads you into the deepest part of a mystery. Fire will lead you to your innermost soul and bring you out into the world again.' He very gently held her hand in his. 'Fire creates and destroys, cleanses and leaves soot. What you put into a furnace, and how long you leave it there, will determine what comes out: be it gold, charcoal or bone ash.

He looked into her eyes. 'But be careful – always use fire to drive shadows away, *never* to summon them.'

The smith picked up a small shovel and began to scrape the useless clinker from the hearth. He found a few red coals, still hot and alive. He stacked them into a small heap, then covered them with handfuls of twigs and straw to rekindle the flames.

Tegen watched in silent awe. She could feel the cool magic of the ring rippling and swirling around her. 'Thank you,' she said at last. 'How did you know I needed help?'

He ignored her question, as he dusted his anvil with his sleeve and began inspecting a pair of red-enamelled terret rings. 'Come back for your knife after mid-haven sun,' he said without looking up.

Tegen walked back up the slope to the main gate, twisting the iron ring on her finger, wondering at its simplicity and strength.

At the top she paused once more to look at the impaled heads.

'Traitors all. No need to feel sorry for them,' a smooth voice whispered by her left ear.

Tegen jumped. 'Good morning, Admidios,' she said icily and tried to walk past him.

He placed a strong hand on her shoulder. She shrugged him away and spat.

'I was wondering why you were up so early,' he went on.

'Has the blacksmith been bothering you? I wouldn't trust him, if I were you.'

Tegen closed her hand over her ring. 'My knife was blunt. I took it to be sharpened.'

'If you allowed *me* to teach you, your knife need never be blunt again . . .' He leaned forward and whispered in her ear, 'You have no idea of the *power* I can offer you . . .'

Tegen reeled. The sound of the Shadow Walker's voice both thrilled and horrified her. She turned, and his pale eyes compelled her to look back into his. Her breath caught in her throat.

At that moment Wolf came bounding up to her. He growled a threatening note at Admidios, who turned on his heel and strode away.

17. The Truth About Owein

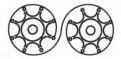

Tegen wanted to leave Baras's stronghold then and there, but Heather needed re-shoeing. Even though Owein also wanted to escape Admidios, he would not risk taking the heavily laden pony along the stony road in her current state. Tegen knew that despite her fears there was nothing she could do, unless she went on alone and without her knife.

As she passed Baras's longhouse she saw the Shadow Walker in deep discussion with the chieftain, who seemed to be an old friend. So at least he was out of her way for a while.

She found Owein quietly reading his scroll at the back of the roundhouse, where light seeped in through a break in the wall. She sat next to him. 'Well?' she asked.

Slowly he rolled his parchment up and put it down. He sighed. 'I owe you an apology for putting you in danger.

I honestly had no idea that we'd meet Admidios, or I wouldn't have brought you from Sul's Land. If you want to travel on your own from now on, I won't blame you, but please remember me as a friend.'

Tegen raised an eyebrow. 'A lot depends on what you have to say,' she replied tersely.

'Admidios is my father's half-brother by a slave-woman. He is a minor king, but he capitulated to the Emperor Caligula about sixteen years ago, when he thought there was more to be gained by "going Roman" than by fighting. I was born in Britain, but Admidios kidnapped me when I was a baby and took me to Rome as a "gift" for his new masters.' He paused and took a deep breath. 'I am the only living son of King Cara of the Catuvellauni, although most people know him as Caractacus. In Rome I was called Sextus Caractacus Catuvellaunius, but Owein is my real name.'

Tegen gasped, 'Caractacus? The great rebel leader who was betrayed by that queen in the north? Cartiman-something?'

'Cartimandua, Queen of the Brigantes. After my father was captured, my parents and the whole family were sent to Rome as "prizes" from the heathen world. They should have been put to death, but my father is a brilliant man and learned Latin quickly. He went to the senate – a meeting of their chieftains. There he spoke with such eloquence that he was freed and made a Roman citizen. However, he still remains a "guest" and cannot return home.

'For a while we were reunited. I grew up with Roman citizenship and education, but my parents taught me as much as they could about our land and our ways. In fact, they were encouraged to, under Admidios's supervision. It was decreed I should be "groomed" to be taken back to Britain to become a high king–governor of a province, or even of the whole land. Being the son of a legendary hero and brought up in Rome made me, at least in theory, acceptable to both sides. I was the perfect choice.'

Tegen's mouth and eyes were as wide as a carp's as she listened.

'As I grew up, our overlords suspected I was learning too many "unstable" ideas from my parents. I was sent to Britain to be fostered with a Roman-allied family to finish my British education.

'The Dobunni king, Eiser, was delighted to have me in his care. All five of his sons had been killed in battle and he had one daughter left, Sabrina. He planned for us to marry, although she is older than me. He wanted us to rule the land together and raise a rebellion. With my oath of allegiance, he adopted me and broke all ties with Rome.

'Admidios came to Eiser's home to remove me, but he was tied up, put backwards on an old nag and sent on his way!

'Then I had my accident. I was useless to Eiser. As you

know, no tribe in the land will accept a deformed king. It's against the law. Eiser sent me away, but I was relieved. At last I could do what I had always longed for. I went to study law and druidry under a very wise old Silure, just across the river in the land of the Cymry. I was coming back from there when you met me.

'I suspected Admidios was in Britain, but I wasn't sure. I had hoped to escape his notice a little longer.'

Tegen leaned forward and whispered, 'So you want to get rid of the Romans? You'll help us?'

'Oh yes, but I am not sure how. Once they have a hold in a country they rarely let go.'

A knock at the doorpost heralded the arrival of Admidios once more. Dressed in an immaculate white tunic and freshly shaved, his smile sent a chill down Tegen's spine.

'*Ave!* I am pleased to see you *both*. I'll be leaving soon, and it's not safe for two young things to be travelling alone. How about I accompany you on your road?'

Tegen and Owein exchanged looks. Owein stood. 'We are doing very well, thank you, uncle. We wouldn't wish to keep you from more important business.'

'No trouble at all. I have a few days free and it would be my pleasure to be your escort. After all, you are almost my own son and a very *important* one at that.'

He glanced towards Tegen and was about to say something when a loud swishing noise announced the arrival of the huge black raven. Admidios raised a gauntleted wrist so the bird could perch.

The empty voice screeched inside the raven-skull, *That's her! That's danger!* and Krake clacked her thick beak and hissed.

Tegen waved her right hand across her face to create a spirit shield. She tried to make the gesture look as if she was pushing her hair back from her face, but a flicker in Admidios's eyes showed he knew what she had done.

He lifted one corner of his mouth in a cold smile.

After the midday meal was served, a servant brought the newly shod Heather to Owein and he began to get her ready.

'Let's go *now*,' Tegen urged, 'before that ghastly uncle of yours notices we're gone. I don't want to see him again *ever*.'

Owein shook his head. 'I fear it won't be as easy as that. He'll have a good horse and will overtake us without any problem.'

'Can't we use back roads? Are there no other paths to Sinodun?'

'Plenty of farm tracks, but I don't know them. It could take us forever to get there, and the druid meeting will start in half a moon.' Owein struggled with a twisted girth strap, then pulled himself straight and looked at Tegen. 'Listen, I know you won't like this, but I think we had better leave *with* Admidios. Now he's found us I want to keep him in my sight. I am certain he is planning something, and I want to know what.'

Tegen was horrified. 'You can't mean it! He gives me the creeps. You yourself said he was dangerous! I would rather be in Tir na nÓg than here with him . . .'

'Don't speak too lightly of Tir na nÓg,' Owein warned. 'Help me with these panniers, will you? If you would rather, *I* will go with him. That'll give you a chance to slip away on your own.'

'Thanks a *lot*!' Tegen yelled as she kicked the baskets and stormed across the courtyard and through the skull-topped gates. She ran back down to the smithy, hoping to ask the advice of the huge man with the blackened hands. She knew nothing about him, but his magic felt honest and clean, not like Admidios's . . .

But the forge was deserted. The fire was cold and the boys were gone. Tegen's knife lay polished and oiled on the anvil. She picked it up and slipped it into the sheath on her belt. In its place she left a small silver piece, and she danced a short blessing on the spirit of the smith. 'Thank you,' she whispered and went out into the sunshine.

In the courtyard Admidios was waiting, saddled and mounted on a gentle white mare. He looked more Roman than British, in a wide toga that flapped in the wind.

The sight made Tegen seethe with anger.

Owein sat quietly on his fat little hill pony. His long auburn hair was combed and flowing over his broad shoulders. A dark moustache smudged his top lip. In his plain green cloak, blue tunic and green plaid breeches, he looked every inch the young British nobleman.

Tegen knew she did not want to travel without Owein, however irritating he could be, and there was something about Admidios that, despite her loathing, made her want to know more . . .

'I'm coming!' she called as she ran for her bag and her staff.

18. Shadow Walker

Admidios's smooth, sibilant voice droned on and on as they followed the endless white chalk road. 'I have been so worried about you, dear boy,' he said. 'When you left the house of that awful man Eiser I searched high and low for you. You can't imagine how devastated I was to hear of your accident . . . How did it happen, by the way?'

'My horse slipped and rolled. I was caught underneath and broke my ankle.'

'Oh, the gods be praised that you weren't more badly hurt – I just wish, dear boy, that I had been around to help you at the time. I am quite a healer, you know.' He patted a leather bag sticking out of the top of a pannier. 'I have all sorts of magical things in here.' He smiled and Tegen's stomach lurched. Owein just stared straight ahead.

Admidios was undaunted by their silence. 'Well, when I heard King Eiser had not only turned against the Romans but had thrown you out, Legate Suetonius Paulinus – that's the tall gentleman you met, Tegen, the one with the rather large nose – well, he was all for sending troops in then and there. He'd have destroyed Eiser's stronghold, but it was *I* who dissuaded him and saved everyone. Suetonius is a powerful man, tipped to be Emperor one day – he likes to make a firm impression . . .' Admidios leaned forward in his saddle and spoke in a conspiratorial whisper. 'As you know, I have convinced the Romans that I am working for *them*, but I use the *favour* they have for me to benefit the people of Britain . . .' He drew himself tall and stuck out his chest. 'I have, I pride myself, saved many innocent lives by my intervention.' He waggled a finger at Tegen. 'If it hadn't been for me, things would have gone *much* worse for you when you were caught snooping around. They wouldn't have given you *anything* to eat or drink. I saved your life, my dear.'

She pulled back her lips in a snarl. 'When I was thirsty you poured water on the ground in front of me; then you threw a gnawed bone at my head. You call *that* saving my life?'

Admidios laughed. 'My dear, if I had done any more, my cover would have been blown, and that wouldn't have done *anyone* any good – now, would it?' He ducked as low-hanging hazel boughs scraped against his close-cropped head.

Tegen wished the twigs would poke his eyes out. She let

herself fall behind a little and stuck out her tongue as she tried to remember how to send an ill wish without it bouncing back on herself.

All the while the raven stared, her black, glass-bright eyes gleaming beneath her heavy brows.

'Did you hand-raise your bird?' Tegen asked aloud to cover the long silence.

'No,' Admidios replied, 'she sort of *found* me. But she's very tame. I think someone must have trained her. She is a beauty, isn't she? Her name is Krake.'

Beauty? thought Tegen. She is *evil*. She glanced at Owein, who rolled his eyes.

Admidios took no notice and went on, 'Ravens are birds of good omen, of course. Do you believe in *omens*, Tegen?'

She closed her eyes for a moment and stroked her iron ring. It was hot. 'Yes,' she said.

'Good,' Admidios said very quietly. 'Very good.'

As the day wore on, Admidios dismounted and walked behind. He said it was to give his mare a rest, but in reality he wanted to watch Tegen. As he did so, his certainty grew that true vengeance would be to harness the powers of this extraordinary young woman and to turn her against Owein.

Murder was too good for his wayward nephew. Despair lingered longer and was more painful than a slit throat.

As he walked he watched Tegen's raven hair unravel from its plait and blow free in the summer wind.

Yes, whispered the demon in his head, *it is her you must bring to me.*

'Of course, Lord,' Admidios whispered, but in his heart he added, *after she has served me first . . .*

By the evening of the following day, more white ramparts were well in sight. But there was no cooking smoke. A dark feeling hung over the place. As they came closer, Tegen realized that the chalk-faced ditches were streaked with soot. The palisades were burned and the place was deserted. Admidios made no effort to slow. 'There'll be nothing to see. This is what happens when stupid peasants resist the inevitability of having new masters.'

Owein glared at him. 'Have you no conscience, uncle? I bet this betrayal was *your* doing.'

Admidios looked away.

Tegen turned towards the rising slope. 'I'm going to see if there is anyone left alive who needs help.' Wolf loped behind her, sniffing the air, his long skinny tail hanging limp and nervous as he followed his mistress.

'Please yourself,' Admidios said as he dismounted and stretched out on the grass. 'I'll wait.'

'For once, uncle is right,' Owein said, 'There is no smell of smoke in the air. It's long over.'

Tegen ignored him as she trudged towards the shattered remains of the lower gates. 'I've got to know what happened . . .' She glared back at Admidios, who was cleaning his fingernails with his knife tip.

'Wait!' called Owein, turning his pony's head to follow. 'Slow down . . . I am coming. It might not be safe!'

Together they made their way up the zigzagging pathway. Sling pebbles, broken spears, knives, swords and bits and pieces of discarded armour made the way treacherous.

High above, red kites swung in wide swoops, sometimes diving down, then climbing in graceful swirls back up into the evening sky. Owein coaxed Heather up the slope until, at the top, he stopped by the great oak gate. The left-hand leaf was blackened and burned through, and the right one hung lopsided on its bottom pivot. The summer wind blew, and the heavy wood swayed and creaked.

What had once been a bustling community like Baras's stronghold was now a desolate place of burned homes, emptiness and silence.

Nothing smouldered; nothing moved. They made their way around the enclosure. Owein spoke quietly, 'Everyone is dead or gone.'

A sickly sweet stench pervaded everywhere. Tegen peered around the blackened end of the chieftain's longhouse and her stomach twisted and she vomited. In the cobbled courtyard beyond was a heap of smashed furniture piled with torsos. Rotting arms, legs and heads intermingled with chair seats and stretchers, table tops and benches. All half-burned. Blackened. Defeated. The low sun behind their backs spilled a blood-red light on the failed cremation. At the very top, a ribcage was silhouetted against the darkening sky.

There was a flap of sooty wings and Krake glided smoothly on to the cold pyre for her supper.

The wind was getting stronger and an empty metallic sound rattled across the ground. Owein urged Heather forward, and with the tip of his crutch he scooped up a shattered helmet with a red crest.

'Romans!' he said.

Tegen twisted her iron ring around her finger. It was very hot. Again her stomach heaved and she wiped the sick away with the back of her hand.

They camped once the wrecked stronghold was well behind them. Tegen and Owein lit a fire, then rolled themselves in their cloaks. They were too tired to build a shelter. Admidios insisted on putting up a small tent for himself, with a bent hazel tree and a spare cloak.

Wolf slunk away to hunt in the darkness, followed by Krake who was hoping to steal from his prey.

The firelight was cheering, but Admidios stayed in his

tent and stared as smoky figures and shapes wound and twisted their way from the flames to torment him.

From the glowing heart grinned a blackened, shrivelled shrunken face.

19. Sleeping with the Ancestors

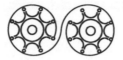

The following day neither Tegen nor Owein spoke to Admidios. He changed into his British clothes and rode ahead, straight-backed and silent.

'Do you think he had something to do with the destruction we saw last night?' Tegen whispered.

Owein glared at his uncle's back. 'I'm certain of it.' Then he added, 'Can't you do some magic to get rid of him permanently?'

Tegen laughed.

'No, really, I mean it,' Owein said.

She narrowed her eyes and thought. 'He's surrounded by powerful protection spells, There's a sort of hot prickliness in the air whenever he's close. Can't you feel it?'

'We'll be at Sinodun in a few days' time, and I don't want him around when we get there. What's going on will be too sensitive for his spying ears.'

'I'm not sure that using magic to hurt people is exactly *right*. Cursing is a dangerous business; whatever you send out always comes back to you – although,' Tegen added, 'I must admit I have been tempted, this last day or so!'

'Don't you think that there are times when ethics become situational?'

Tegen wrinkled her nose. *'Pardon?'*

Owein laughed. 'You look pretty when you do that – I mean, there are times when the ends justify the means.'

Admidios turned in his saddle and raised an eyebrow. Owein called out, 'We are discussing politics, uncle. Just as you taught me.' Then Owein went back to his whispering. 'Can't you put the spirit of an adder in his breeches so he dies in agony?'

Tegen was shocked. 'You're serious, aren't you?'

'I am sure the Goddess would approve – in this case!'

Just then Tegen spotted a dark, raised shape between the trees to her left. 'What's that?' she asked out loud.

Owein shrugged. 'Just a wight-barrow.'

Admidios turned in his saddle once more. 'It's a very special place. It was built by the Wise Ones in the times of the beginning. It was a place for dreaming the future.'

Tegen was intrigued. 'But I thought the barrows were tombs?' In her mind she could still hear the *snap* of bone under her clog.

'Some ignorant people think that,' Admidios sneered.

'In reality, the dead were allowed to rot, then the bones were placed there so the living could sleep with the ancestors. The dead dreamed whispers from the shadows of the Otherworld. Secrets only the wisest sleepers could hear.'

'I slept in a barrow once, and I dreamed of the future . . .' Tegen said wistfully.

'*Where?*' Admidios reined his horse so Tegen would catch up with him.

'Shh!' Owein hissed.

Tegen blushed and shook her head. 'It doesn't matter.'

By now they were almost alongside the long, low mound to their left. Tegen turned off the road and walked up to the tall sentinel stones that guarded the entrance.

'Aren't you frightened?' Admidios asked, keeping back a little. The white mare danced, feeling her rider's nerves.

Tegen dropped her bag, stepped forward and laid her face against the cool rock. 'Why should I be? They were born of the earth, like trees and water.'

Admidios slid from his horse and stood beside Tegen. He longed to reach out and touch the stones as she did, but he knew the great monoliths hated him and his kind.

Tegen turned to Owein. 'I would like to sleep here tonight,' she said. 'I have questions I need to ask.'

Owein dismounted. 'Suits me.'

Admidios was nervous. He looked around as if he expected an attack from between the trees. 'The sun is scarcely setting. There is a stronghold only a little further on. There will be a warm welcome for us there – good food and red wine . . .' His fingers caressed his belly.

But Owein was already spreading their cooking gear on the grass, and Tegen was gathering firewood. Owein looked up. 'Feel free to go ahead and find a soft bed if you want. I'm staying with Tegen.'

Admidios stood with his arms folded and his brows low over his shadowed eyes. 'You don't get rid of me that easily. I'm sleeping here too.'

Tegen and Owein exchanged glances. Wolf slipped between them and raised his hackles. At that moment Krake, who had been blessedly absent for a while, wheeled in from overhead and fluttered a silent landing on the tallest guardian stone at the entrance. There she spread her wings, balancing against the wind, then hopped on to Admidios's shoulder.

'It looks like we're all staying,' Owein muttered as he tossed Tegen a pouch of kindling. She said nothing as she struck flint against iron, sending sparks into the hay and shavings. She blew, and a thin trail of smoke smouldered into a burst of flame.

The smith told me my soul is protected by fire, she reminded herself. Then she chanted out loud:

Spirits of fire and hearth and light,
let these flames burn bright tonight.

Lighten up our way ahead,
so we may always safely tread.

She looked up to see Admidios hugging himself and staring into the shadows as if afraid. 'Are you cold?' she asked sweetly. 'Break up some wood – that'll help get the fire going.'

Admidios swore, got to his feet and snapped dry branches violently with his boot.

Night fell, and Wolf hunted down a small hare. Krake tried to steal his food by tugging at his tail and distracting him, but the huge dog only snarled. Admidios kicked Wolf away, split open the hare's belly and tossed the guts at his pet. Suspicious, Krake jumped backwards and forwards, coming closer, then leaping away, as if nervous that the offal might suddenly attack.

At last Wolf, having filled his belly, left a few half-chewed remains and stretched out contentedly by the fire, toasting his rough brown hide. Soon he was snoring.

Owein stirred a vegetable broth in his small cauldron. 'Wouldn't you rather be feasting on boiled pig up at the stronghold, uncle?' he asked hopefully.

Admidios shook his head, 'No, it'll be dark soon. I feel it is my duty to be looking after you two. You might need a strong magic to protect you in such a –' he looked around and shuddered – 'a *sacred* place.' Then he produced a wooden spoon and bowl from his bag and, keeping his face turned from the fire, he helped himself generously.

Tegen looked at the wight-barrow, dark and eerie in the gloom. She swatted a few mosquitoes and picked some pink yarrow to put in her pouch, then taking her cloak and her food she scrambled up the mound. 'Forgive me for climbing on your bones,' she whispered to the spirits. 'I need a place to think.' Low on the southern horizon she could see the first pale light of the moon glimmering through the trees. She turned her back and looked up at the stars of the Watching Woman. Tonight, as she ventured towards the ancient gateway of Tir na nÓg, she needed the Lady's protection. She had to dream in order to know what to do about Admidios – should they escape him? Or was he their companion for a reason?

Tegen ate her food and pulled off her clogs and stockings. Tonight I will dance for you, Lady . . . She closed her eyes and in her mind she saw a fire, but as she watched it became smaller and more distant until at last it was just a tiny pin-prick of light – a star within the Watching Woman.

Tegen unbound her hair and flicked it loose so it would move like black flames. She held her arms high and let her body become one with the fire of the stars.

Suddenly she heard uneven footsteps on the grass. She spun around. 'Don't move,' Owein whispered. 'Admidios is making a spell down there. If you are going to sleep with the ancestors, you must go in *now*, before he puts something nasty in there to wait for you. I really have *no* magic – I can't help you.' He hauled himself further up the mound until he was next to her.

She swept her fingers over her head and handed him a couple of hairs. 'Hold these tightly and think of me well and happy in the morning. It's a very simple spell – anyone can do it.'

Owein twisted the silk around his finger and glanced nervously over his shoulder.

'Can he see what I'm doing from down there?' Tegen asked.

'Very clearly,' he replied. 'Where's the moon?'

'Just rising,' Tegen pointed at the pale, half-faced glow that shone between the treetops to the south.

'That's good. It's within the constellation of the hunter's bow. That is the sign of lawyers and priests and is ruled by fire. We will be safe . . . if you are friendly with the spirits of fire, that is.'

'Yes,' she said quietly, 'I am.' And she folded her fingers over her iron ring. It was hot.

Just then the harsh voice of the raven scolded in the night and a blue glow came from between Admidios's hands.

'What's he doing?' Tegen whispered.

'I don't know, but I don't like it,' Owein hissed back.

Tegen swallowed her dread as she grabbed her cloak and slithered down the slope on the far side and into the barrow through a gap between the stones. She paused for a moment to leave the sprigs of yarrow at the opening. 'A gift for the stones . . . and to protect myself as well,' she said softly as she made the sign against the evil eye and slipped into the darkness.

She was alone with the ancestors. Her feet were bare and she could feel her toes touching bones.

Stooping low, she gently moved a few ribs and leg shanks to one side. 'Forgive me if I disturb you, my Mothers and Fathers. I need your wisdom to fight against the enemies of our land. Please may I share your dreams and knowledge?' Then she wrapped herself in her cloak, curled up on the damp earth floor and closed her eyes.

Outside, Owein watched helplessly as Admidios stepped slowly towards the entrance. The eerie blue glow from his fingers showed his lips pulled back in a snarl. Under his breath he whispered, 'You aren't going to escape me . . . Your dreams must serve *me* before I surrender you to your new Lord.'

The Shadow Walker spread his glowing hands, steadied his fears and stepped towards the stones. His spell was almost ready to send inside, but he had to be certain it touched the *girl*, not the stones she crouched between.

He had to get close enough to see her at least . . .

As Admidios reached the opening, he stopped. His blue wyr-light reflected two huge eyes peering back at him. Wolf was crouched between the guardian stones at the entrance to the barrow, growling a low warning note.

Admidios hesitated.

The dog-eyes in the night widened, and the growl dropped a tone.

Admidios gave a soft whistle and Krake swooped through the darkness to land on his shoulder. 'Kill the dog,' he whispered. The raven opened her beak and made a coughing noise. The emptiness behind her drove her on, but starlight burned the bird's eyes and the yarrow filled her with dread.

Admidios flicked his fingers and sent a spell that turned each of Krake's feathers into a stabbing dart in her back, driving her forwards. But Tegen's yarrow magic was too strong. Torn between pain and fear, Krake lifted her wings and floated towards the trees and the dark.

Wolf lifted his head and barked, just once, but it was enough to send Admidios stumbling backwards. He swore as his spell crumbled. Then he too bolted for the safety of the trees.

Owein sat huddled in his cloak, sweating and holding his breath as he cursed his inability to do more than the simple spell Tegen had taught him. With every heartbeat he held the image of her running across the grass in sunlight. 'You *will* come out, all will be well . . .' he muttered.

Although he was sure that Admidios had given up, Owein kept Tegen's hair wound tightly around his finger until the first hint of dawn, when he allowed himself to sleep. Wolf and the earth spirits would keep the Star Dancer safe.

20. The White Horse

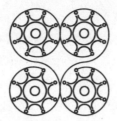

When the cacophony of birds woke him, Owein stretched, rolled over and stared up at the grey sky that threatened rain.

A loud snoring assured him that his uncle was still fast asleep. Owein sat up. Where was Tegen? With a shiver he remembered. Was she all right? He knew *he* wouldn't have the courage to sleep alone in a wight-barrow!

He eased himself upright, took the leather water carrier and went in search of a stream. It was his turn to get breakfast – it was the least he could do. As he came struggling back up the hill, spilling more than he was saving, he heard a shout from between the trees above him.

Tegen ran pell-mell down the slope, waving her arms frantically. 'Owein! Wait! Let me help!' She was rosy-faced, her black hair streaming wildly in the wind.

He handed her the bucket gladly. 'Well, it looks as if you had a good night. Did you dream well?'

'Oh, I slept like a log.' She examined the bucket. 'Not much left, is there?'

'I kept slopping it.'

'Never mind!' She grabbed Owein's arm with her free hand and shook him. Her green eyes were round with excitement. 'We haven't got time for breakfast anyway. We've got to move, *now!*'

'Steady on!' Owein groaned. 'Why the hurry?'

Tegen stopped and pointed to her left, along the path of the Ridgeway. 'I don't remember my dream, but when I woke I had a very strong image of the white road and the white horse. Just like last time.'

Owein shrugged. 'So?'

Tegen pushed on through the long grass. 'It was light, so I decided to go for a walk so I could listen to what the Lady was saying without Admidios and that wretched raven hanging around. I went along the road for a while and, just as Admidios said, there is another stronghold ahead. But it's been abandoned.'

Owein winced. 'Like the last one?'

'No. It looks as if everyone just went. Maybe they surrendered. There were no piles of corpses or any signs of fighting, although all the houses had been burned.'

'That's standard Roman practice, so people are discouraged from going back.'

'Well, I was walking around and I felt sort of *pushed* onward . . .'

'And?'

'I left the stronghold, and the ground to my left fell away steeply. I saw a shape cut in the grass and filled in with white chalk. I couldn't see what it was from above, so I went down the hill and looked up at it, and do you know what I saw?'

'A white horse?'

'Yes . . . How do you know?'

'I have been along here before. The white horse is the Atrebatian badge! This stronghold is one of their border markers with the Catuvellauni.'

'More than that!' Tegen's voice was urgent. 'You must know it's one of the forms of the Goddess?'

'Epona,' Owein replied. 'The white mare that symbolizes the whole of Britain.'

'Exactly. Ever since I first saw Admidios riding a white mare I've felt a nagging anger. Now I know why. It's because by law only a king or a servant of the Goddess may ride one. It's sacred, and he's no right to her. He's desecrating the Lady's name!'

They were almost at the top of the slope and, ahead, the long, low shape of the wight-barrow lay like a great giant's bed between the trees.

'So what we are going to do,' she said, smiling, 'is take the horse.'

Owein shook his head. 'Don't. I *know* Admidios. He'll send an evil curse after us. No good will come of it.'

'No, he won't, because I'll pay for her fairly. Anyway, we are only taking back our birthright. *He* doesn't deserve her!' And she flounced ahead.

Owein struggled behind. 'But he'll wake. What if he catches us?'

Tegen's eyes twinkled with merriment. 'He won't. Remember I said I didn't think it was right to use magic for harm, even if the ends did justify the means?'

Owein nodded.

'Well, I thought Admidios looked a little tired and decided to give him a little *herbal* help. He was awake when I came back from my walk and I gave him a nice warm cup of beer – mixed with valerian. He'll be sound asleep for quite a while yet.'

Owein looked down at his uncle's jowls, wobbling with every snore. 'He *fell* for that?'

'You know how much your uncle likes his drink!' Tegen smiled as she looked down at him. 'Even Derowen would have been proud of me.'

'Who's Derowen?'

'An old witch who lived in my village. She was a brilliant herbalist, but evil. Thank the Lady she's dead now. I pity the poor woman who gives her rebirth. Now come on, we need to pack.'

*

Tegen fitted the saddle and tightened the front and rear girths, talking softly to the mare all the time. Soon the white horse stood proud and ready in the morning sunlight. 'She is lovely,' Tegen said, stroking her mane. 'I shall call her Epona.' With that, she led her to a fallen tree and mounted. 'I've never ridden with a saddle before. It feels very secure, with its horns at each corner.'

'*We* taught the Romans how to make them like that,' Owein said bitterly as he swung on to Heather's back. 'Ready?'

'Just a moment,' Tegen replied, pulling a solid-gold armband from her bag. It had belonged to her enemy, Gorgans, and she had used it to dance Star Magic at the funeral of her beloved Gilda. The gold gleamed with a finely crafted horse cantering around the curve. How appropriate! She tossed it neatly atop one of Admidios's panniers.

'Payment for the horse,' she said softly. Then, with one last gesture, she sent a curse towards the black raven that swung and tumbled high in the skies above them.

21. Sinodun

Tegen guided Epona on a lower path, allowing a good view of the beautiful white chalk horse with its flowing mane and tail, galloping forever across the towering hillside above. To the great creature's right were the desolate, soot-streaked ramparts of the deserted stronghold.

Neither Tegen nor Owein wanted to look any closer. They had seen enough of what the Romans could do.

In the plains that spread across the landscape to their left, the far-flung patterns of little patchwork fields were slowly being shaved of their harvest. 'It won't be long until the Lughnasadh fairs,' Owein said. 'Once the crops are in and the people have given thanks to Lugh's bright spear, the leaders will be arriving at Sinodun. We need to be there first. I want to talk with the druids and learn what I can about the alliance the tribes have forged.

'And I must warn them that Admidios cannot be trusted.

He always wanted to be a druid, but was refused. He was hopeless as a king as well. Bitterness turned him from being merely unpleasant to being downright evil.'

Tegen turned and surveyed the road behind her. The sleeping draught would not hold forever. She glanced up at the sky and squinted for a glimpse of a black bird with a wedge-shaped tail. But apart from a cloud of starlings rising from a field of stubble, there was nothing.

They rode their mounts as fast as they could without tiring them. Wolf trotted happily alongside, enjoying the adventure and catching small animals when he was hungry.

The road was busy with travellers. The news was always the same; the Romans were swiftly and surely taking over. Strongholds were being destroyed and the land was no longer held as sacred. There were temples to strange gods, and new laws with magistrates to enforce them.

The old shook their heads in despair. The young carried their spears and knives well sharpened.

Mid-afternoon of the second day they came down a steep slope into a wide-bottomed valley. Owein gave a shout. Ahead lay a broad river. Tegen and Owein did not need to urge their mounts forward. The animals smelled fresh water and were soon trotting towards the silvery, rushing flow.

On either side, the flood meadows were bejewelled with summer wild flowers. A ford was clearly marked with way-stones. Between them, two horse-drawn wagons were

making their way across while a scattering of coracles carried fishermen with nets.

On the far side, two Roman guards were talking, leaning
on their spears. The sun glinted on their armour as they
moved.

Tegen's heart sank. 'Do we cross?' she asked. It wasn't
just the Romans that filled her with dread: she had never
seen such a river before. The Winter Seas at home were
much wider and muddier, but the water there was almost
still, with only shallow tides.

This river was rushing and wild.

Owein pointed north. 'No, we go that way. If we crossed,
we'd end up in Iceni lands within a few days – then there'd
be action! They are so pro-Roman you'd think they invented
the toga!'

Tegen laughed and dismounted so Epona could drink
and bathe her hoofs. Owein bought hot bannocks from an
old woman cooking on an iron griddle. Tegen was stiff and
sore from riding and was grateful for a chance to walk. She
took off her clogs and stockings, sat on a way-stone and
dangled her feet in the water.

For the rest of the afternoon they meandered their way
northward along the river bank in the cool purple shade of
the overhanging willow and ash trees. The hot harvest sun
burned down and Tegen stripped to her linen underdress.
Heather rolled her fat, easy way under the boughs as Owein

wove rushes into two green hats to keep off the burning heat.

By early evening the road had swung west and the sun was in Tegen's eyes, despite the new hat. A small cloud of dust ahead heralded the thundering hoofs of two spirited chestnut ponies. Harnessed together with shining brass fittings, they pulled a war chariot carrying two fully armed men wearing green and crimson plaid cloaks.

The chariot slowed as it approached the travellers. One of the men jumped down and ran forward, pointing a spear at Tegen's chest. 'You ride a Roman horse with Roman fittings. Who are you? Who is your servant here?' He gestured at Owein with his spear tip.

Tegen let go the reins and spread her hands. 'I am unarmed. I am Tegen, daughter of Nessa and of Clesek, silver worker from the Dobunni people of the Mendip hills. I am a bard of the druid company of the Winter Seas. I bought the horse with gold, for it was an insult to see a man who was no servant of the Goddess riding a white mare.'

The man scowled under his long, fair moustaches. 'And you?' He laid the spear at Owein's throat.

Owein held his head high, but spoke softly. 'Tell your lord that the youngest son of his friend in Rome has come.'

The man looked askance at Owein, then swung himself lightly back into the chariot. 'Go!' he snapped. His companion flicked the reins and wheeled the chariot back along the way they had come. As the ponies galloped the wind caught in the men's red and green plaids and twisted their long brown hair. Tegen thought they were so much more handsome than the shaved Romans. She smiled a little as she urged Epona to follow at her finest pace.

Owein and Heather trotted behind as the road continued north-west, almost head-on into the setting sun. On both sides, the flat land was cleared and farmed, with small clusters of roundhouses dotted here and there. All looked prosperous and peaceful. Ahead were two hills, the left one wooded and high, the other lower and ringed with white-faced ramparts and palisades encircling the stronghold. As they came closer Tegen could make out a fine central long-house with soft blue smoke seeping through the thatch.

Owein reined his pony to a halt and waved his hands expansively. 'Welcome to Sinodun. I'm relieved the Romans haven't harmed it. Connal, the high chieftain here, is the last man on earth to give in to the invaders. We'll feast well in a truly *British* house tonight.'

Tegen smiled at the thought, but as Owein moved off she called out, 'I'll catch you up,' before she dismounted and slipped between the trees. I am the Star Dancer coming to a meeting of druids; I must look like a bard. She slid her three remaining golden bands over her ankles, replaited her hair and pulled on her blue woollen robe.

Just at that moment she heard a clattering, throaty trumpet sound. Once more a dust cloud was rising along the road that came from the stronghold. This time there were more chariots – one in front coming at a tremendous speed, and at least three behind. On each side were outriders with tall war carnyxes: dog-headed, swan-necked trumpets that they winded repeatedly.

Tegen's blood ran cold. Were they coming *after* her? Was Owein wrong about Sinodun's lord? She grabbed the horns of Epona's saddle and swung herself up, coaxing her into a trot. Tegen sat very straight and tall. I am the child of the Goddess, she reminded herself. I have the right to wear blue and ride a white mare. I will face whatever – whoever – is coming.

The first chariot was well within sight now. It was pulled by a pair of fine black horses. Their charioteer was a stately woman with hair like a dark storm and a many-coloured cloak streaming out on both sides. In her right hand she clutched a war spear as well as the reins. The woman let out a bellowing command and stopped a few strides in front of Tegen.

Dust rose and settled. Epona took a few nervous paces sideways.

'Steady,' Tegen soothed her. 'We won't run away; we are British. We never leave the field of battle . . . even if I don't have any spears – not that I'd know how to use them.' Then, with one fluid gesture of her right hand, Tegen began a spell of protection, but she had hardly started when a voice yelled, 'Hey, don't turn us into toads!'

From behind the young woman a figure jumped down

and landed awkwardly. Owein, for the first time wearing his full seven-coloured cloak, was swinging himself along as fast as he could.

'Tegen!' he gasped as he caught his breath. 'I'd like to present my foster-sister, the Princess Sabrina of the Dobunni, daughter of King Eiser. Sabrina, this is my friend Tegen, bard of the Winter Seas.'

The young woman on the chariot dropped the reins and solemnly raised the spear in her right hand. As she did so, the men with the polished bronze carnyxes sounded their horns so loudly, Tegen's ears hurt. She wasn't sure how to greet a princess, but she remembered her old mentor Witton telling her that druids were equal to kings in rank. Tegen remained in the saddle and tossed her plaits over her shoulders. Taking a deep breath, she intoned a solemn blessing:

May your fight burn bright in Lugh's eyes.
May the Goddess of War bless your sword's edge.
May the cauldron of Bran serve those who fall by your side.

Tegen glanced nervously at Owein for approval – he was beaming with delight, as was Sabrina. Encouraged, Tegen added, '*May none of your enemies be reborn,*' and she raised her left hand and traced the shape of a curse in the air.

'Excellent! Well said!' Sabrina laughed, rattling her spear against a chariot wheel. She turned to Owein, 'You told me she was good, brother, but I didn't realize she was *this* good. A bard fit to sit beside a princess. You will tell us tales tonight, druid girl. Then I will serve you first cut of the roast meat!'

Tegen blushed. 'Er . . . thank you.'

'A druid lost for words! That's a fine show!' Sabrina threw back her head and laughed again, showing several missing teeth.

But she is still beautiful, Tegen thought.

The princess barked an order and Owein climbed back to his place behind her. The chariots were turned and they thundered off towards the stronghold.

Left alone, Tegen and Epona followed at a trot.

Just inside the lower gate by the bottom rampart there stood a blacksmith's forge. It was larger than the one at Baras's stronghold – a long, open-sided building with a fire pit at each end. Several men were hammering, sending bright sparks into the murky darkness behind them. Boys sweated over bellows or carried wooden buckets of water for tempering the metal.

Leaning against the central post was a huge man with shaggy black hair and a wild, unplaited beard. His shoulders were bare, but his chest was covered by a grimy leather apron. As Tegen passed, he beckoned and she guided Epona in his direction.

'Girl,' he said, in a surprisingly gentle voice, 'your horse is about to cast a shoe. Let me see to her.'

He stepped forward, his eyes kind with a pale blue

steady gaze. She thought of the other smith at Baras's stronghold. They looked so similar, but he couldn't be the same man . . . could he?

She swung herself out of the saddle. 'Which leg?' she asked, standing back to appraise Epona.

'Near-hind.' He moved around and lifted the hoof.

Tegen wiggled at the shoe. 'I didn't hear anything, and it feels firm enough,' she said.

'She'll have cast it within another day.' Then the smith spoke low and quick. 'Be careful. Put your gold away and don't ride into the stronghold on a white horse. It will inflame already hot tempers. Let me look after her.' Then he yelled at the nearest boy to take the mare to the shoeing stall.

'Don't I know you?' Tegen began, but he had turned away. The bellows were roaring and someone was hammering on an anvil. She shrugged, pulled off her armbands, then picking up her bag she trudged the steep path between the ramparts. She was cross; she had been looking forward to being someone special for once, to having everyone turn and say, 'Look, there goes a servant of the Goddess, she has a white horse!'

But as she walked, the iron ring on her finger became hotter.

22. Accusation

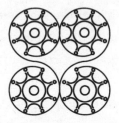

True to her word, that night Sabrina kept a place for Tegen by her side at dinner in the crowded longhouse. The great hall had ten tree-pillars supporting the roof beams. In the centre, slaves turned whole goats and pigs on spits, the sizzling meat gleaming with dripping fat. On all sides, tables were piled with bannocks, vegetables stewed in ale and large dishes of salt. The light from the fire made the brown darkness warm with golden red light.

The princess was gnawing on a pork bone. As soon as Tegen sat next to her on the bench, a servant loaded her plate with slices of steaming meat and filled her drinking cup with warm ale. Happily she pulled out her knife and began to feast. Sabrina nodded a welcome, but was too busy eating to talk. Tegen was content to be quiet and take in the atmosphere.

Chieftains, warriors and several druids were packed

around the tables, all deep in argument and conversation. After the meat was eaten and the bones thrown to the dogs, dishes of cherries were handed around, with bowls of warm scented water for washing greasy fingers. At the far end of the hall a bard began to sing and play a harp. When he finished, the listeners cheered and shouted. The man rose, bowed and passed the harp to a woman in the green of an ovate.

Tegen realized it would soon be her turn. Her heart sank. She was no songbird. Frantically she tried to think of a tune she could hold. Maybe she could dance a story?

When the harp came to Tegen at last, she spoke to the young man who offered it. 'Do you know "Rhiannon's Joy"?' she asked. He nodded and rippled his fingers over the opening chords. Tegen slid off the bench and ran into the clear space between the high table and the fire.

The young man played with gentle grace notes and some fine flourishes. Once she had the tempo of his version in her head, Tegen began to dance the story of Rhiannon and her love for the handsome Pwyll. She wished she had someone else to dance the part of the noble prince on the hill of madness. As she moved, her mind filled with the story of the young woman and her magical horse that could outrun everything. The tale blossomed alive and bright. In her mind she only needed to think of her own Epona's lovely shape and movement to became one with the story-horse in her dance. She was exhilarated and blissfully happy.

She stopped at Rhiannon's wedding. This feast in Sinodun was a night for celebration, not for tales of lies and false accusation.

The whole hall erupted in shouts and applause as Tegen stood triumphant and breathless. She thanked the harpist and slid back into her seat.

Then a voice spoke above the applause: 'A fine tale to be told by a *horse thief.*'

Everyone fell silent and looked from the speaker to Tegen.

Admidios stepped forward and stood where she had danced, his back to the fire. He was wearing his full British cloak and breeches, his raven perched on his shoulder, her beady eyes glinting malevolently in the soft light.

Only the spit and hiss of logs on the hearth disturbed the tension. Admidios's shadow fell across the dining table as he leaned forward on his knuckles, his jowls shaking with rage. 'I accuse this girl,' he said.

Tegen's heart thumped too loudly and her cheeks burned. How had he got here so soon without a horse?

Krake fluttered as she felt her balance go, and her master shoved her away. Her wings beat against the smoky air as she swept around the fire, at last perching on a rafter above his head. 'Thief!' the bird screamed and splashed Admidios's head with white. Furious, he wiped himself clean with his sleeve and cursed her.

A few of the guests tried to laugh, but Admidios stood to

his full height. He took a deep breath, and the air around him crackled. A suffocating silence filled the hall.

At last the chieftain of the stronghold stood and forced a smile, his golden torque glinting under his bushy grey beard. 'Welcome to my hall. My name is Connal.' He spread his hands expansively as he spoke. 'We are all friends here. This is a feast to greet you all, druids and warriors alike – even your servants and slaves are welcome.

'Come, sir – tell me your name and eat with me. I have some excellent mead. We will ask the druids to sort out this unpleasant matter in the morning.'

Admidios bowed his head respectfully. He was pleased. He had only just arrived, but this invitation immediately established him as a man of power and honour. The druids would listen to him, and in the morning he would make sure the wretched girl was found guilty. She would be openly discredited before she began to work her charm on anyone. If all went well, her punishment would be to become his slave. Then he would *make* her obey him.

Admidios sat, drew his knife and stabbed the steaming slab of pork placed in front of him. He licked his lips and complimented his host.

Tegen watched through narrowed eyes as a red-haired druid on the far side of the hall nodded to Admidios and raised his horn of ale in salute. So he had friends here. She picked at the cherries and arranged the pips in patterns as she told Sabrina the truth about Epona. Owein came and squeezed on to the bench on the other side of his foster-sister. 'What in the names of all the gods is *he* doing here? He should have been at least two, or maybe three days behind us.'

Sabrina smiled, her gapped teeth making her look mischievous. 'I will ask some of my spies what they know. They see everything.'

Tegen raised an eyebrow. 'You don't, by any chance, have the small hill people amongst your company, do you? Some call them "the Old Ones"?'

The princess was surprised. 'Yes . . . How did you know?'

Tegen shrugged. 'It just sounds like them.'

23. The Testimony of Gold

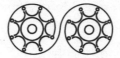

Tegen's straw bed on the eastern side of the hall was cool and comfortable. A door stood open, letting in air and early-morning sun. All the unmarried girls slept together behind a hurdle partition, giggling and chattering into the night. The best guest houses had been set aside for senior druids and chieftains.

Next morning Owein came to find her. 'Wake up! The druids have sent for you. Admidios is pressing his case.'

Her heart sank as she yawned. 'Give me a few moments,' she muttered as she groped for her comb.

Outside the door, Owein shifted his weight impatiently from his good leg to his crutch and back again. 'Hurry up!' he called.

When at last Tegen appeared, her waist pouch was bulging. She whistled for Wolf and pulled on her rush hat. Beyond the stronghold, the sacred hill rose green and majestic. Remnants of silver mist drifted between the flat plains to their left and the river valley on their right. She breathed deeply. Despite Admidios's presence, it was good to be here. Owein and she followed the cobbled path down between the lower ramparts. Each ditch had rows of sharp, fire-hardened stakes embedded in the ground to discourage any enemy foolhardy enough to try to find a way through.

As they climbed the green slope towards the meeting place Owein gave a low whistle and pointed to the north. 'By Tyrannis! I don't believe it!'

Tegen looked across the river that curved like a protective arm around the stronghold's two hills. There was no ford; instead it rushed past countless green wooded islets dotted along its course. On the far bank were flood plains and ancient earthwork defences, but beyond these a square, well-ditched palisade was being erected around a series of evenly spaced rectangular buildings.

The Romans were building a garrison scarcely ten arrow shots away.

The great earthworks that had once protected Connal and the Atrebates tribe had now become the *Romans'* outer defences – turned against the people they had once served.

Tegen's blood went cold. 'Are they about to attack? What can we do?' she gasped.

'If they were going to attack, they would have done so by now,' Owein said quietly. 'That is a permanent camp – there are no tents, and the wooden barracks are already being replaced with stone. They must be hoping to negotiate with Connal.' He sighed. 'There's nothing we can do, except try to prevent Admidios causing division between the tribes. I think that's what this accusation of horse theft is all about: he doesn't care about Epona; he just wants us all to argue as violently as possible, to wreck our alliance so our stand against the invaders collapses.' He glanced around and whispered, 'If you can, avoid saying anything about Admidios collaborating with the Romans, at least until we know the allegiances of those who are here. And for good- ness sake, don't admit you "helped" him sleep! I'll be sitting right next to you. If you are stuck, just look at me and I'll think of something to say.'

At the top of the hill she followed Owein into the cool shade of the ancient trees, mostly oak, ash, beech and thorn, heavy with late-summer foliage rustling gently in the heat. The dark-skinned giants ringed a clearing with a central altar – a storm-thrown oak buried trunk down, the roots left clawing at the sky.

Ten druids stood waiting, dressed, despite the heat, in their woollen robes of solemn white, blue and green. Owein went to greet some of the people he knew. With his striped breeches, white linen tunic and dark red hair blowing in the wind, he looked every inch a prince.

A bald old man with a wispy white beard and eyebrows gestured Tegen to enter the sacred grove.

The old druid turned to Tegen. 'My name is Dallel, chief

druid of the Atrebates clan.' He smiled through his sparse white whiskers. 'We all enjoyed your story-dance last night. But today you stand accused of the crime of horse theft.' He turned to the gathered assembly and raised his voice. 'Will this girl's accuser please state his case?'

Admidios stepped forward from behind the altar. Beside him walked the red-headed man who had raised his horn to him the night before. The man leaned on his staff, smiled and spoke clearly. 'As Admidios the mage is not of the company of druids, I, Medyr of the Atrebates, have the honour of speaking for him. Admidios accuses Tegen, bard of the Winter Seas, of taking of a valuable white mare whilst he, the true owner, slept.'

Dallel rubbed his chin as he considered the speaker and his client. Then he turned to Tegen. 'And how do you plead?' he asked.

Owein took a deep breath. 'I, Owein, son of Cara, known as Caractacus High King of the Catuvellauni, ovate and student of the druids of Siluria, have the honour of representing Tegen, bard of the Winter Seas.'

'Very commendable, I am sure,' sneered Medyr, 'but how does the girl *plead*?'

A flicker of a dark bird swooping overhead made Tegen hesitate. Then she spoke. 'I am not guilty,' she said. 'I paid for the horse fairly.'

The druids murmured as thoughtful eyes scrutinized Tegen and Admidios.

'Very well,' Dallel replied, turning to Tegen. 'Tell us what happened.'

She recounted briefly how Admidios had joined her and Owein uninvited. Then she went on: 'I learned in my first days of bardic training that only a king or a servant of the Goddess may ride a white mare,' she said. 'This man had no right to her.' Several of the druids nodded in agreement.

'But that does not condone *theft*!' Medyr's eyes flashed. 'I understand this girl has had hardly any training. She scarcely has the right to wear blue. She certainly hasn't the understanding to deal with a complex legal matter such as who may ride a white mare. That should have been referred to a druidic court.'

Dallel tapped his lips with his forefinger, then raised his arm. Medyr fell silent. 'We will discuss such issues later. First of all, let the girl continue with her story.'

Tegen took a deep breath and described how, when Admidios was asleep, she had thrown the golden armband into his pannier for payment.

Medyr crossed his arms, smiled and shook his head. 'That, ladies and gentlemen, is an out-and out *lie*. My client would never have brought the case if it were true.'

Dallel turned to Tegen. 'And can you prove this? Do you have witnesses?'

Before she could speak, Owein interrupted. 'I was there.'

Medyr sniffed and spread his hands. 'That's not *proof*!

That is simply a boy's say-so against the word of the *mage* Admidios.'

A woman in green stepped forward, exasperated. 'But this young man is an *ovate* and the son of *Caractacus*!'

'Again, we only have *his* word for it,' Medyr replied.

Owein was not perturbed. 'But what Tegen says *is* provable. Admidios, please push back your sleeves.'

His uncle's eyes narrowed and he shifted uncomfortably as he held out his arm to be inspected. He had dreaded something like this: his puffy flesh had swollen around the gold. He had tried everything to remove it – greasing his skin with pig fat and soaking it in cold stream water, but the bracelet had remained stuck fast.

Medyr thrust out his bottom lip and spread his hands. '*So*, my client wears a golden armband. Many of us do. That proves nothing.'

Tegen whispered to Owein. A slow grin spread across his face. 'But my client has the *matching pair* to it,' he answered slowly and clearly.

Tegen opened her waist pouch and pulled out the second golden band, which she placed in the hands of Dallel. An exquisitely crafted horse ran eternally around and around. The old druid smiled. 'And where did you get these, Tegen of the Winter Seas?'

She shivered at the memory. 'From the druid Gorgans, the White One from Tir na nÓg.' She recounted how Gorgans had taken off his gold to work evil magic in the burial caves. 'When he died, I was called upon to dance magic to put the demon back. I put the bracelets around my ankles to make music for my steps. It helped . . .'

Dallel stood and held the armband up. 'Look at this carefully, brothers and sisters. Admidios, step forward and let us see what you are wearing. We shall compare them.' When all present had inspected both pieces Dallel turned to his fellow druids. 'What is your judgement?'

'They are a pair,' everyone agreed. 'Tegen has paid for the horse.'

Dallel turned to Admidios and tapped the band with his finger. 'My judgement is that she has *overpaid*. You owe her change: five silver bands of good workmanship or one thin golden one.' With that, he grunted and shuffled to his seat. He clapped his hands and a servant brought him a drinking horn.

'Be content, Admidios. You have not done badly in this matter. We have the Romans at our gate. We can't afford to be fighting each other.'

Admidios was breathing hard, snorting fury from his nostrils. He clicked his fingers and Medyr ran to his side. The two men conferred for a few moments, then together they left the grove.

24. Scrying the Summons

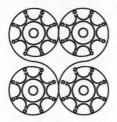

Tegen was delighted with the verdict. She hugged Owein and left him at the hill-top grove. 'Thank you so much,' she said. 'I must go and see Epona, now she is really mine!'

Glowing with pleasure, she ran down the hill, skirted the lower ramparts and entered the outer gate. Noise and smoke billowed from the long, open-sided forge. At both ends the pit fires were raging hot as the boys worked the huge bellows, sweat pouring down their backs. Tegen watched the smiths hammering sword blades and pouring white-hot liquid into arrow-tip moulds. Others were carrying pigs of raw iron and stacking them against the back wall, but the tall man with the black beard and the kind eyes was nowhere in sight.

Beyond the far end of the forge three horses were tied to a rail, waiting to be shod. Two were piebald, and the third was a fierce-eyed dapple grey. Tegen went to stroke their noses, hoping that Epona would be somewhere nearby.

But there were no other animals. Her heart sank.

A short, wiry man with an oily brown pigtail came around the corner. 'What do you want, miss?' he asked abruptly, untying the nearest animal.

'I was looking for my horse, a white mare,'

The man shrugged. 'Ain't seen one like that. Who did you leave it with?'

'A big man with black hair and a beard like a bush.'

''E don't work here,' he said, leading the piebald away. Then he called over his shoulder, 'Although if it's who I think it is, 'e'll come and find you when 'e's good and ready.'

'He's got my horse . . .' Tegen called after him, but the clamour of hammers drowned her voice. She swore, then trudged back up between the ramparts, muttering curses all the way.

She almost knocked Owein over at the top. 'What's the matter?' he asked. 'You look as if you could strangle someone!'

'I could – the smith,' she said, and told him the tale.

Owein laughed. 'Oh well, never mind.'

Tegen put her hands on her hips and glared at him. 'What do you *mean*, "never mind"? The man's a thief – he stole my horse! I'm going to take *him* to court!'

'Listen,' Owein put his hand on her arm. 'Remember

what you said – all white mares belong to the Goddess. What's more, the armband you gave to Admidios wasn't really yours; you found it when that druid died. Things come and they go. Epona served you well when you needed her. She's the Lady's horse, not yours, so why don't you just wait and see? And whatever you do, never curse a smith. It's unlucky.'

'I just did.' Tegen scratched her head, ashamed.

'Well, go and take it off again, then come into Connal's longhouse as soon as you can. You are needed.'

Tegen did as Owein had suggested. When she caught up with him in the shadowy coolness of the great hall he was seated at one of the long tables, drinking ale. His foster-sister, Sabrina, was dressed in breeches and tunic, pacing back and forth, talking loudly and gesticulating vigorously as she spoke. Her wild, black curly hair tumbled around her shoulders. Tegen was jealous – her own hair was always as straight as a reed.

When Sabrina saw Tegen she stopped and leaned on the table so her silver necklaces swung forward. Dark worry shadows encircled her blue eyes. 'Can you scry?' she demanded.

Tegen hesitated. 'Er . . . no . . . not really. You see, I haven't really been trained properly. I'm on my way to . . .'

But Sabrina wasn't listening. She resumed her pacing. 'I've had a summons to go and fight with a group of rebel Brigantes who are planning a major attack on the Romans in the north. They insist that I go and help. We Dobunni have a pact with them. I am obliged to go . . .'

'But there is something about it that doesn't ring true,' Owein put in. 'If Sabrina goes and it is a trap, she could be killed, but if she *doesn't* go and it *isn't* a trap—'

'My refusal will be seen as a slight,' Sabrina finished for him. 'Then the alliance will be broken and war will break out between the tribes when we need it least.'

'Why don't you ask one of the proper druids?' Tegen sat and picked a bean-cake from a dish on the table.

Sabrina paced up and down like a caged wild cat. 'Druids always ramble on and on. They are all old fogies. I need a simple, direct reply *now*, not weeks of deliberation and rituals.'

Tegen thought for a moment. 'But surely the Brigantes must realize that at a time like this you have to be careful?'

Sabrina shrugged and started to twist her hair nervously between her fingers. 'Politics is never that simple. Damn!' She spun around and began to pace again, her head down and her hands clasped behind her back. 'You two are *useless*!' She rolled her eyes and kept walking.

Owein looked at Tegen pleadingly. 'You can divine a *bit*, can't you? Couldn't you go and sleep in a wight-barrow or something?'

'Where's the nearest one?'

Sabrina laughed bitterly. 'Next to the new Roman garrison across the river. I'm sure they'll put a comfy bed in there for you if you asked them nicely . . .'

Tegen winced. 'Have you got a silver bowl?'

'I have no use for such things.'

'I do,' Owein chipped in.

Sabrina raised an eyebrow.

'Druids use them,' he replied as he went out of the door. Moments later he returned and handed Tegen a small silver dish.

'Where's the nearest spring?' she asked.

Sabrina shrugged. 'No need, there's a bucket of water by the door.'

Owein shook his head. 'It won't do. I think there's a spring above the pond on the western slope.' He picked up his crutch and led the way.

At the bottom of the hill, the ground became soggy. Tegen took off her clogs and stockings. Frogs hopped and croaked as she pushed between the giant bulrush stalks until she found where water bubbled up from the ground.

She filled the bowl and sat on the bank with Owein and Sabrina. 'You want to know whether to go to battle or not. Is that right?'

Sabrina nodded. 'I am not frightened of going. War is what I do best. It's just I didn't like the look of the messenger, and the place he mentioned isn't the sort of territory the Romans would be fighting over. If I go, I will take twenty warriors with me. That will weaken the defences here, and the meetings during the next half-moon are vital to the well-being of Britain.' Sabrina crouched down on the grass. 'I don't understand the Goddess's ways. I was born with a spear in my hand and that is the way I will die, but I need to be certain what I am doing is right.'

'I will do my best,' Tegen said. She stood and offered the bowl of water to the West. 'Spirits, I greet you and thank you for the gift of water.' Then she turned to the North: 'Spirits of earth, show the path Sabrina should tread.' She raised the offering to the East: 'Spirits of the East, fill me with your Awen, breath of inspiration.' Then lastly she looked towards the South: 'Spirits of fire and light, illuminate Sabrina's path.'

The hot noonday sun danced on the water. Tegen raised the bowl level with her chin and stared at the rippling surface. The brightness formed painful fiery shapes and images. She closed her eyes, and in the darkness greenish figures danced the same frenzied pattern. She remembered her dear friend Gilda telling her to listen to the Goddess in her heart.

I am listening, Tegen said in her mind, but I don't know what these shapes *mean* . . .

She tried again, but once more the light hurt her. She squeezed her eyelids tight shut, but the dark green images swirled and grotesqued madly until her head ached. 'I'm sorry. It hurts.' She poured the water on the ground. 'I have let you down.'

Soft footsteps approached across the dry grass. They turned. 'Look who's here,' groaned Owein.

Admidios shielded his eyes from the sun as he smiled at Tegen. 'I have offered to teach you divination, dear girl . . . Why don't you ask me for help?'

Sabrina shuddered, folded her arms and glared at Admidios. 'What do you want?'

Tegen rolled the gleaming silver bowl in her hands and watched a sunlit drip of water chase a fly around the smooth inside. It seemed important, but she couldn't be certain *why*.

'I have come to talk with Sabrina,' he said. 'With you all, in fact. I believe I haven't been, shall we say, quite *open* with you. If I explain myself, I might smooth matters between us a little.'

'Like why you accused me of theft?' Tegen glared up at him.

Admidios smiled and bowed his head. 'My apologies. I was, shall we say, a little taken aback to waken and find myself quite alone. If it hadn't been for a detachment of friendly Roman soldiers who had a spare mount, I would have struggled to arrive at Sinodun in time for the talks at all. May the gods be praised. All was well. I apologize if I offended your Goddess, I had no intention of—'

'*Uncle*,' Owein snapped, 'what do you *want*? We're busy.'

Admidios sighed and settled himself on the grass. 'Firstly I wish to say that I have betrayed no one to the Romans. I am as angry at their cultural insensitivities as anyone else . . .'

Sabrina rolled her eyes and Owein gave her a warning glance. He wanted to know what his uncle was thinking.

'As I expect you know, I rescued Owein when he was a baby. He was born in the midst of war. I saved his life by taking him to Rome. Since then he has seen at first-hand the benefits the Empire can bring to Britain, which is, at best, a rather backward country, for all its ancient wisdoms.'

Sabrina clenched and unclenched her fists. Tegen kept staring at the grass, trying to listen to the silent words beneath the spoken ones – what was he playing at?

Admidios, sensing he had an audience, kept speaking. 'So now the Romans are here, let us make the best of things. Let us form alliances and have heated houses, good roads, sanitation and writing . . .'

Owein scowled as he poked his crutch at an innocent molehill.

Admidios continued. 'Why fight when we could learn so *much* from these people? Now, as you know, with stealth and deceit I have wormed my way into the Empire's confidence. By my skill and character I have convinced them that I would be a suitable magistrate of a town, maybe even a province . . .'

Owein raised an eyebrow in his direction. Admidios spread his hands. 'Oh yes, Owein Sextus, they still want *you* as a governor. If only you would give them a chance, you could maybe even rule the whole country. They would much prefer a British nobleman like yourself to that pompous upstart Suetonius Paulinus, who is worming his way up the ladder of promotion . . . Think what you could achieve, making sure that the best of the old ways are adhered to but adopting the more *profitable* of the new . . . If only you would let me *help* you, dear boy.'

He ignored the dangerous glare in Sabrina's eyes and the dagger loose in her hand.

When Admidios turned to her, he lowered his voice, 'And Sabrina, *dear* lady, there is a place in the scheme of things for you too. War is no place for a fine girl. You shouldn't have to face the rigours of the battlefield – I couldn't help overhearing you discussing the call to war just now . . . forgive me.' He bowed. 'To be honest, I am not surprised that you are afraid to go and fight. I would be. There is no shame in that. None at all.'

He had gone too far. Sabrina leaped like a deer and landed with her knees in his chest, her dagger at his throat.

Tegen held her breath. How she wished that Sabrina would drive the gleaming iron home. Her fingers curled around her own weapon.

Admidios lay spreadeagled on the grass, a Fury at his throat and his jowls quivering with terror. 'I-I was only going to ask you to marry me and share my power . . . I-I do like a strong-minded woman . . .'

Sabrina spat in his face, got to her feet and flung her

dagger so it grazed his left cheek. 'I won't insult the earth by spilling the rest of your blood on it,' she said through tight lips. Then she retrieved her weapon and stalked away. Tegen and Owein followed as fast as they could, leaving Admidios holding his bleeding face and staring after them with poison in his eyes.

'Why didn't she just kill him?' Tegen whispered to Owein.

'I suspect because he has powerful friends. As long as he stays alive, this stronghold is safe. If he doesn't report in somewhere regularly – probably that dunghill the other side of the river – this place will be burned to the ground before sunset. At least until the druids' meeting is over and the alliance is sworn to by all, we must ensure that he remains unharmed.'

Sabrina strode back up the hill and stormed into the chieftain's longhouse, swearing and shouting orders.

Not far behind, Owein flung himself on a bench and called for ale. Tegen waited for a short break in Sabrina's tirade before daring to speak. 'I think, I *think*, that the call to war is a trap, and that Admidios is behind it.'

Sabrina spun around and glared at Tegen. 'So you suggest I stay here, accused of being scared to fight . . . by *that* . . .' she pointed with a shaking hand down the hill, 'that *slug* . . .'

'Er, yes . . . *no* . . .' Tegen knew both answers were wrong. She took a deep breath. The image of the droplet chasing the fly flashed into her head once more. Suddenly the meaning was clear. The real battle would be at Sinodun. 'I'm certain you are needed here. Admidios was nowhere nearby when we discussed your call to battle – so how did he know? He must have helped to plot it!'

Sabrina was too worked up to listen. War was in her blood, and war it must be. A man with a stern look came in carrying five or six long swords. She inspected them briefly. 'Good, put them in the luggage cart and be ready in one hand-span of the sun's course.' He bowed and left.

Sabrina drew her dagger and dragged it slowly and deliberately across the table. Her knuckles were white. 'No one – *no one* – calls me a coward,' she said.

Then grabbing the handle, she slammed the point deep into the wood.

25. Magic Tricks

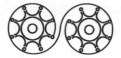

Sabrina's war band was a splendid sight. Chariots gleamed and jingled with crimson-enamelled bronze fittings and, despite the heat, the warriors all wore their cloaks, which spread like hawks' wings in the summer wind. The princess raised her heavy sword so it flashed in the sunlight, then brought it down sharply with a cry. The warriors shouted back, carnyxes sounded and the gates swung wide.

Tegen had a sinking feeling as she watched Sabrina riding between the ramparts and along the road. Turning south, the princess led her war band towards the ford where Tegen and Owein had watched the river only a few days before. Sabrina planned to travel eastward, then turn north and ride around the great salt marshes. She aimed to be in the northern Brigantes territory within a half-moon.

The chariot wheels sent up clouds of pale dust as they

disappeared along the road that wound between little hedged fields. A short while later, the ox-cart baggage train followed on behind them.

Owein sighed and turned away. 'May the Goddess guide her,' he said.

'And may Admidios's belly rot while he is still alive,' Tegen added, spitting. 'He didn't really think she'd marry him, did he?'

Owein shook his head. 'He was only trying to rile her. She and Admidios have met only once or twice, but each time he has managed to make her *really* angry. One day he will go too far and end up with her iron under his ribs.'

If she doesn't get killed rising to his bait first, Tegen thought. She turned her attention to fifty or sixty tents and booths that were being erected on the meadow to the west. 'What's going on there?'

Owein shrugged. 'Just a fair – vagabonds and musicians pretending to be traders. A load of money-making nonsense. They'll have heard there's a tribal meeting and in the next few days they'll be massing here like flies on a dead dog. Druids and kings mean followers and servants, all with money to waste.'

But Tegen wasn't listening. 'Did you say *musicians*?' she whispered, her eyes scanning the site with longing. Her feet were already tapping at the thought of a tune. Dancing for dancing's sake, not to do any seeing or healing, just for the delight of a jig or a reel . . .

'They'll probably be a few breathless old men whistling through broken teeth.' Owein turned back towards his lodgings. 'I'm going to lie down.'

'You're such an old misery!' Tegen's eyes were bright, 'Why don't you come to the fair? It'd cheer you up.'

'It's too hot and I don't *want* to be cheered up. My foster-sister is being sent to her certain death and my back and leg hurt.' And with that he stamped away.

The large meadow was well cropped by a herd of wiry cattle sheltering from the heat under a spread of dark green oak and ash trees.

All around the field, more and more booths were being erected, tents and benders were scattered here and there; the smell of cooking made Tegen's stomach rumble. As she walked, she listened hard for a flute or a tabor.

Maybe, she thought, those beautiful dark-skinned women might be dancing, like they did when I was thirteen, back at home. Maybe the man will dance with fire again . . . and just maybe they'll have silk for sale . . . She missed her green shawl. Although she no longer believed her magic depended on it, she still longed to swirl it around as she moved.

But there was not a note of music to be heard. The only sounds were shouting and hammering as traders set up their pitches. Then something unexpected caught her eye;

Admidios was sitting in the cool emerald shade of a large ash tree, surrounded by children. He was even letting the little ones sit on his knee.

Hoping he hadn't seen her, Tegen slipped behind an empty cart, crouched low and watched between the wheels. The traders' clatter and banter drowned out his words, but she could see he was laughing, and doing magic tricks. He made a cake appear behind a girl's ear. Then he swallowed it and brought it back from the pocket of a surprised little boy. The audience clapped with delight.

What's he up to? Tegen wondered.

Just then, Admidios gave a long, low whistle and rustling down from the trees swooped Krake, gleaming with exquisite, rainbowed blackness.

At the sight of the bird Tegen slid very slowly under the cart and lay face down in the purple-shadowed grass, listening as hard as she could. Even above the hubbub, the bird's harsh voice cracked and screeched so loudly it was plain to hear that, one by one, the raven was repeating the children's names. Then Admidios seemed to be talking to the children, and listening to their answers very intently.

Tegen brushed an ant off her nose and tried not to sneeze.

Then Admidios clapped his hands, sending a shower of dark red balls across the grass. The children squealed, collected them up and starting eating. He waved his hands and his audience scattered. A few passed quite close to

Tegen's hiding place. One of them dropped the remains of her prize. Tegen reached out and picked it up. She couldn't believe her eyes it was a *real* plum. Making something *look* like a plum was easy enough, but to conjure real food out of thin air was powerful magic.

Only one boy remained, a tall lad, scrabbling in the grass for any remaining fruit. Admidios clipped him around the ear and he fled, red-faced.

As Tegen watched him go she realized she knew him: it was Kieran, the salt traders' lad. Without thinking, she pulled herself from the shelter of the cart and turned to watch him running away.

A heavy hand landed on her shoulder. Fingernails dug viciously into her collarbone and a thumb pressed with agonizing pain against her spine, making her legs buckle. 'If you ever want to know what I am saying,' Admidios said softly, 'come and *ask* me.' He spun her around and smiled, showing his immaculate teeth. 'You are *special*, my dear. I will gladly tell you anything you want to know.'

Tegen squirmed and twisted free. The iron ring burned on her finger. 'Very well. What *were* you saying and why did you hit that boy?'

'I was simply giving the children a magic show,' he replied. 'Not up to druid standards, of course – I merely asked for a little information in return. That useless fool had nothing to tell me. An imbecile, of no concern.'

Tegen crossed her arms and glared at Admidios. 'What sort of information?'

'Like – what their parents think about the Romans, whether they will help the new masters build a strong country, or if they will fight like cockroaches who need to be crushed.' He rubbed his smooth chin and added, 'The problem with many great leaders is they fail to take note of what the little man in the country thinks. If they are on your side, then the world can be won, but if they are against you, they are as annoying as horseflies and need to be swatted.' He raised an eyebrow at Tegen. 'Do you follow me?'

He went on, not waiting for an answer. 'In short, I am destined to become great, but I am helping to secure my future by being sure of those around me.' He sighed. 'Over the years Sextus has turned down all his chances. But *you* . . .' he turned to Tegen and fixed her with his pale hooded eyes, 'you *also* have a powerful destiny. All you lack is training.'

Tegen took a breath. Training was what she wanted more than anything, but not from a Shadow Walker.

Admidios looked across the water to where the new garrison was rising day by day. He swept his arms wide. 'I shall have a villa built for me over there. It will have marble walls and a mosaic floor. I expect you don't know what one of those is, do you, my dear? You must come and visit when it's finished. The new town will be named Dorcic.'

Tegen's lips were pursed so tightly they hurt. 'Damn your

villa,' she hissed. 'You are *using* the children to spy on their parents!'

Admidios laughed. 'You do have a talent for the succinct.' Suddenly he put his hand into her ear and pulled out a ripe plum. 'A gift for you.' And he bowed.

'I'd rather *choke* . . .' Tegen knocked his hand aside. The fruit landed in the grass and was promptly squashed by a passer-by.

Just then the raven landed on her master's shoulder and fixed Tegen with a one-eyed stare.

She strode away through the crowds, head held high, trying to look a great deal calmer than she actually felt. She despised and loathed Admidios, yet his voice summoned her, weaving tempting tendrils through her mind.

Tegen dared not admit it even to herself, but she longed to know what he wanted to teach her.

LUGHNASADH

When Lugh's bright spears are gathered up,
Cut and stooked, then crushed and ground,
Some are brewed in malted cup,
The rest is baked in bread that's brown.

The Mother brings her Son to share
As wheat or oats, barley and rye,
He spreads his bounty everywhere,
But first, the sacred Son must die.

26. The Smith

In the first grey light of dawn, the rustle of leaves was the
only sound within the sacred grove.

Between the trees, there pressed an unmoving crowd of
three or four hundred silent people, all focused on the
centre, where Medyr stood holding a white bull's tether.
The great animal cropped the grass next to the spreading
upturned root. Around them, six silent druids waited like
ancient standing stones, their white robes glowing in the
half-light. Twm with the twisted back, dark-eyed Sean, twin
sisters Danaan and Gwynedd, both grey, but tall and slen-
der.

Between them they guarded the air, fire, water and earth,
while Dallel and his plump wife, Bronnen, stood either side
of the Gate of Lughnasadh in the south-west. Taking their
positions in between the druids were the ovates in green

and the bards in blue, almost melting into the dusty grey-brown shadows.

The spectators were villagers and farmers, as well as the merchants and traders who had come for the fair. Right at the back were the slaves, unable to see a thing, but commanded to attend – for all must give thanks to Lugh and the Goddess for harvest home.

The light swelled and birds began to chatter and sing, rustling and squabbling in the dawn chorus. The air was fresh and the last pale stars faded in the west. In the east, streaks of gold caught on the few tiny clouds near the horizon.

As the first brilliant spark of sunlight showed above the dark rim of the earth a ram's horn sounded – then another . . . and another. Dallel put a torch to a bonfire at his side, and the flames leaped. The druids at the four quarters greeted their spirits, offered incense, lit a candle, poured water, then blessed the grey stone that marked the north. Drums began to beat and women chanted a hymn in throaty chorus.

Tegen couldn't help swaying to the music, but she held her place. This was too solemn a moment to dance for pleasure. The golden armbands she wore on her ankles jingled a little and she contented herself with that.

Into the circle, through the Gate of Lughnasadh, came a white horse. On its back was a woman acting the part of the Goddess in her guise of Bera, Mother, and Lady of the Harvest. At her side walked a tall, broad-shouldered man with black hair and beard.

They were both dressed in long white robes and their heads were crowned with wreaths of wheat, barley and oats. Bera carried a sheaf of scarlet poppies that looked like blood spilled over her lap.

The music and singing fell silent.

'It's Epona, and the smith . . .' Tegen whispered.

Owein nodded. 'Of course it is. Who else would be fit to carry the Lady and play the part of her son?'

Tegen had never seen a full Lughnasadh festival before. Her heart leaped in her mouth. 'What's happening?'

Owein leaned closer so he could whisper. 'The Mother brings her son, the Mabon, who is the Harvest, so he may be cut down and fed to the people. It is the way.'

Tegen was shocked. 'But they not going to actually *kill* the smith? He's kind, and wise.'

'I thought you called him a horse thief and you wanted to take him to court?'

'I didn't mean it . . .'

One of the older druids glared at them to be quiet. Tegen felt sick. Surely they aren't really going to sacrifice a *man*. They're just going to act it out – *aren't they?*

Her hands felt clammy as she watched the woman who was Bera dismount and kiss the smith on the cheek. He in his turn bowed to her and returned the kiss. Then they walked hand in hand deosil, following the sun's path around the circle.

When they arrived back at the southwestern gate, where they had entered, Bera stood next to the fire, stretched out her hands to the smith and proclaimed, 'This is my son, the Mabon. I conceived him in darkness, gave birth to him at Beltane, now he is full grown. I bring him to you so you may eat and drink for another year.'

The smith turned and knelt at Bera's feet. She placed her hands on his head in blessing and stepped back. One by one, first Dallel, then Bronnen, laid their hands on him as well, followed by the rest of the druids.

'Now us,' whispered Owein, hobbling forward. Tegen followed, her heart in her mouth. Was she taking part in a ritual killing? She tried to breathe slowly. She knew that by placing her hands on the smith's head she would be acknowledging her part in his death. Could she? *Dare* she? If she didn't, would it mean the people would starve?

Owein was already standing in front of the kneeling man. Then he moved to the right, turned and watched Tegen as she approached. Her knees felt weak. 'Go on,' Owein whispered. 'It's all right.'

Tegen stepped up to the smith. His black bushy beard parted in a welcoming smile. Her iron ring felt cool as she placed a shaking hand on his oily hair. He smelled of smoke and the forge.

'Thank you for the harvest,' she managed to say. She felt

her eyes stinging as inside her head she screamed, How can we do this? It's not *right*!

She turned away, but strong fingers caught her wrist. The smith gently pulled her back towards him. She knelt on the dry grass so she could look into his face.

'Thank you for your compassion, Star Dancer. But death brings life and life brings death. Unless life is given out of love, it has no meaning. Always give lovingly and willingly, and all shall be well. Things aren't always what they seem. You will understand this one day. Remember me – my name is Goban.' He smiled, leaned forward and kissed her cheek. His beard prickled. Tegen wiped her eyes, nodded and kissed him back.

'May you be born again soon,' she whispered.

'Oh, I will be,' he said, smiling. Then he turned his eyes to the elderly ovate behind her.

Tegen walked back to her place, her head bowed, remembering when she had thought she was going to be sacrificed. There had been the voice in her head that had told her not to be afraid . . . And who else was it that used to say, 'All shall be well?' *Gilda*, who had always helped her to face fear. How could she forget?

But she had no more time to think about the past. The smith had stood and walked to the centre of the circle. There, next to the eternally stretching hand of the upturned root, he stood, his head held high. The bull was brought to his side, with five strong men holding ropes tied to its legs and neck.

Bera came and stood next to the smith. She raised her arms to the sky and wept. Then she turned to the crowd and said quietly but clearly, 'I give you my son, your Mabon.'

The bull let out a tremendous bellow, then kicked and thrashed as his throat was slit. The men with ropes pulled hard, and the animal's roars rose, then subsided. The great creature sank to its knees and fell with a thud to the earth. The men busied themselves making sure the creature was dead.

Then they stepped back.

Tegen saw with horror that the smith also lay dead, with blood blooming across his white gown like Bera's sheaf of poppies pouring from his throat. She watched, cold and numb, as his body was placed on a woven hurdle tied behind Epona. She rushed forward. 'Where are you taking him?' she demanded.

One of the men lashing the body smiled at the pale, crimson-soaked figure. 'Where he can sleep, so he can come back to us next year, strong and hearty as ever.' He straightened up. 'Ready?' he called out to his companions.

'Ready!' the others replied. Someone slapped Epona on the rump and the bier started to move away.

'Wait!' Tegen called, as she tugged off her ice-cold iron ring. She pushed it on to the tip of the smith's little finger. It stuck above the first joint. 'May the fire of the Goddess protect you on your way,' she said. His hand felt loose and warm. It was impossible to believe he was really dead, but his blank, staring eyes told her it was so.

Owein came and stood beside her. 'Don't you have this ceremony where you come from?'

Tegen pulled her long black hair over her stinging eyes. 'We used to kill a goat, then have a party.'

Owein put a comforting hand on her arm. 'He comes back.'

Tegen sat on the grass and hugged herself. 'How?' she demanded from the muffled depths of her arms.

'He just does. He always does and he always will. It's the way of things, as long as we respect the earth. But he won't live again if we destroy the ground.'

'Who would be so stupid as to do that?' She looked up, her eyes wet and wide.

'Who indeed?' Owein chewed his lip. 'I have heard that the Romans sometimes sow an enemy's land with salt so nothing will grow – and that some farmers are greedy and demand too many crops without letting the earth rest . . . There are all sorts of ways.' He patted her on the back. 'Our people still care for the Goddess and her son. Come, it's time for breakfast.'

Tegen walked towards the great upturned root, where slaves had put up trestle tables and were now unpacking bread and ale, pies, cresses, fat-hen and fruit. She glanced around to see if there was any sign of Admidios. Then she took a plum and bit into its soft yellow flesh, letting its sweet blood trickle down her chin.

Is it right to kill a *real man* to express even such a deep truth? Tegen wondered. Death brings life, and life, death. Sacrifice with love brings hope, she reasoned. So it goes.

Only a few strides away, Dallel and his fellow druids were standing around the ox's carcass talking earnestly to the ovates, explaining the sticky white and red mass of blood and guts that spewed across the ground.

Tegen was intrigued. Old Witton had taught her the very basics of augury from spilled intestines, but it was an art that wiser heads than hers spent whole lifetimes exploring. She knew the way the animal fell was also important. The men restraining the dying beast were instructed only to prevent it from dashing into the crowd, not stop it from landing as it would. This beast had twisted around at the last moment and its head was towards the north and the Roman encampment.

'This means,' Dallel's cracked voice announced, 'that there will be famine ahead. It is not good news, my friends. Also, look . . .' he prodded the slit belly with his staff, 'the gut has been cut, and the contents are spilled, do you see?'

'Isn't that the carelessness of the man who drew the knife?' someone asked.

'Nothing happens without a reason,' Dallel replied firmly. 'If a man was clumsy, the message might be that more care needs to be taken. If the blade was skilfully drawn, but the guts lay near the surface, that teaches us about situations that are delicate and need to be handled with extra care.' He paused, stooped down and lifted the edge of the ox's belly skin. 'I believe that is the case here.'

The druids murmured and discussed the finer points of slitting a sacrifice. Tegen's stomach churned and she turned on her heel, only to walk straight into Admidios. 'Of course, they don't know what they are talking about. They are *amateurs*.'

Tegen sidestepped him.

'Do you know what this *really* means?' he continued as he fell into step behind her.

She ignored him but he persisted: 'It means that we, the people of Britain, must look to the Romans for our future.'

Tegen turned and glared up at him. 'And have our guts spilled for the privilege!' She took a step towards Admidios and, amazed, he stumbled back. Finding courage she didn't know she had, Tegen poked the Shadow Walker in his ample belly. 'Furthermore,' she growled, 'the ox represented the Mabon, and *he* died to give life and hope to our land. It was a gift of love, and neither you nor your masters are going to cheapen that!'

27. Lughnasadh Fair

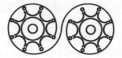

Later that morning, the sounds of music drifted up from the crowded meadows below. Tegen put on an ordinary dress, hid her gold and gathered up her coins. She combed and plaited her hair and ran outside. Wolf leaped around her in joyful circles, barking and jumping up to lick her face. 'I've washed already today,' she laughed as she pushed him away.

Owein was astride his fat little pony by the stronghold gates. Heather shifted restlessly. 'She hasn't had any exercise for days,' Owein said. 'Come on then, let's go and waste our money!'

Tegen was glad he was less cynical than the day before. The distant sound of music made it impossible for her to keep her feet still. She danced and spun as they made their way down the cobbled path between the ramparts to the road below.

As she passed the forge, she twinged with guilt for not mourning the smith. But he had given himself willingly and with love. Her job was to accept the gift and live to celebrate the life he gave. It was an insult to the Mabon to do otherwise.

Once they reached the meadow, they could hardly move for the crush of people. Children ran around playing tag or eating crumbly honey cakes. Mothers carried babies as pedlars pushed past, yelling their wares and balancing baskets on their head.

To the right, a square had been roped off. Two men were wrestling, to the roaring crowd's approval. Half a dozen others were waving their fists and yelling bets while a small boy stole coins from unwatched pouches.

Heather picked her way carefully through the press, undaunted by the noise and bustle.

Admidios was sitting in the same place as the day before, in the cool shade of the trees that edged the field. Once again youngsters surrounded him, squealing delight at his conjuring tricks.

Tegen pointed. 'Watch what he does next. He'll bribe the children to spy on their families.'

Sure enough, after a while Admidios bade the children sit. Once they were quiet and calm he began to talk.

Owein could see very clearly from his vantage point on Heather's back. When Admidios was pleased with an answer, the child was presented with a cake from a basket by his side. One by one, they drifted away. When Kieran stepped forward, Admidios yelled and waved his fists. The boy skulked out of sight behind a tree.

'Why did he do that?' Owein asked. 'That's the salt traders' boy, isn't it?'

'He's got no information. Probably all he hears from his mother and aunt are curses.'

At last Admidios stood, dusted himself down and made his way towards a table selling ale.

As soon as he had gone, Kieran returned and searched the grass for leftover food. Tegen and Owein made their way to where he scrabbled miserably in the shade. Wolf sniffed, then licked Kieran's face. The boy rubbed the dog's head and almost smiled.

Tegen found some nuts in her pouch and offered them. 'Can I sit here?' she asked.

His hungry eyes flickered from the cobs to Tegen; he grabbed them and sprang off into the crowds.

'Don't bother to say thank you,' Owein muttered as he watched him disappear.

'He looks famished and terrified.'

Owein shrugged. 'So would you be if you lived with that awful Caja woman. Come on, let's see what the fair has to offer.'

Tegen soon found a group of musicians. Three farmers in their grey workaday smocks had gathered with their instruments around a fire where chestnuts popped in an iron pan.

A tall girl stood behind them playing a slow air on a flute, while the old man by her side was beating a bodhran. One by one, the others joined in. Another droned an accompaniment on bladder-pipes. The third, with long moustaches, played a large bow pushed into a clay pot filled with sand. The result was plaintive, but added magical deep notes.

Tegen threw off her clogs, moved into an open space and began to dance. No spells, no magic, just movement for the joy of it, flowing with the music, letting her steps ripple like water over rocks.

Seeing the crowd Tegen was drawing, the moustachioed man nodded to the others and the music changed to a jig, then a wild cascade of songs and tunes that spun faster and faster, until Tegen was quite out of breath. At last she flopped down and accepted a cup of ale.

The crowd applauded and the girl flautist took round a basket for money.

The grass was cool against Tegen's back. Her hair had come undone and spread around her. She stared at the sky, feeling completely happy. The girl came and stood shyly in front of Tegen, holding out a handful of silver coins. 'We've never done so well.' She smiled. 'The grandfathers said, is this enough for your share?'

Tegen sat up, amazed. She hadn't expected to be *paid*! She took the coins. 'Thank you – that is very kind of you.' She put them in her pouch and waved to the old men. They were busy chewing on roast nuts and counting their share of the takings. 'Come back soon, lass,' called the one with the bodhran. 'We'll play for 'ee any day.' And he blew her a kiss.

Owein was sitting on the grass in the shade of a booth. He pulled himself up as she approached. 'You know what?' he said. 'I think you deserve a treat. You've earned it.'

'A treat?'

Owein pointed to a nearby stall. 'New shoes. Those clogs you wear are so broken and splintered they are scarcely on your feet. Throw them away or give them to a beggar!'

Tegen looked down at her clogs. True, they had splinters and the leather straps had broken long ago, but she had never worn anything else. In the marshy lands where she had grown up, shoes were an un-thought of luxury as well as impractical. She went to the stall and stroked the soft leather.

A fat little woman in a red dress was sitting on a stool behind the table, spinning wool on a stick. 'They is all two silver coins.' She smiled, showing pink gums and a half-chewed wad of herbs.

Tegen picked up a white pair made from a single piece of leather, drawn together with a thong woven around the top.

The woman screwed up her face and waved a chubby finger at Tegen. 'Too small, my ducks. Come here, let me look at your feet.'

A little while later Tegen stepped gingerly across the field wearing calfskin shoes. She was amazed at their lightness and suppleness. They gave her the ease of bare feet without the pain of treading on stones. She might even be able to dance in them!

As the sun began to sink in the sky Tegen and Owein made their way back up the sacred hill for the evening ceremony. They were both hot and tired, and the sight of a roaring cooking fire spitting sparks into the evening sky made them hotter, but the welcome smell of roasted ox promised a mouth-watering feast.

As they came between the trees of the sacred grove Owein stopped dead.

Tegen stared at him. He had gone deathly white. 'What's the matter?' she asked. 'Are you ill?'

Owein swallowed and shook his head. 'Tyrannus bring thunder . . . ! It's Eiser, my foster-father. He's *here*!' Owein slid from Heather's back, lifted his crutch from its loop in the pony's harness and walked forward, holding himself stiff and erect.

Two men were standing next to the great oak root. On the left was grey-bearded Connal, lord of the stronghold and the lands around. On the right was a tall man with strong features, dark moustaches and a mass of curly hair shot through with white.

They stopped talking and turned to look as Owein approached.

Tegen glanced from one to another. So this was King Eiser of the Dobunni? The man who had wanted to adopt this son of the great Caractacus, marry him to his last remaining child and bequeath him his crown . . . only to send him away because he had broken his ankle? She had expected a monster, but she saw a face that was tired and sad, but honest.

Owein stretched his withered left leg to rest as much as possible on the ground until he found his balance. He dropped his crutch. The two men silently surveyed each other.

King Eiser nodded. 'You look well. Join us.'

Tegen tactfully withdrew to the cooking fire beyond the sacred space. Owein would not want her company that night. But she did not mind. The flames fascinated her: they seemed so playful and warming in the evening light, but as she stared at the twisted dark shapes in the heart of the flames she shuddered. Something was wrong. What had Goban the smith taught her about fire?

By her side, Wolf was devouring discarded offal, and a small glint in the shadows beyond told Tegen that Krake was there too.

*

At the bottom of the hill, in the darkness between the trees at the water's edge, two voices whispered in Latin.

'The tribune is losing patience.'

'Tell him the boy is almost persuaded. I just need time.'

'We don't have time. Caractacus believes his son is missing and he is stirring up discontent amongst the Celts in Rome. Sextus must come forward as a faithful servant of the Empire before the start of winter. If necessary, we will attack the stronghold and take him by force.'

'If you do that, he'll never work for you.'

'I am sure he will. Legate Suetonius is to become Imperial Governor of the Britannic Isles on winter's eve. There will be a celebration for him in Corinium Dobunnorum. I expect Sextus will enjoy seeing Eiser and his warrior-daughter as the main attractions at the event. We can also arrange for him to have a trip back to Rome to watch his parents die the same way . . .'

There was a quiet thud as the speaker jumped into his boat. 'One last thing . . .'

'Yes?' Admidios stepped towards the river's edge.

'Remember, lions are always hungry . . . they aren't fussy about who they eat.'

With that, the sound of paddles faded into the rush of river water, leaving Admidios sitting on the bank snapping twigs between his fingers. 'You've let me down!' he hissed to his demon. 'You promised me power and vengeance! I have neither!'

'*You promised me the raven-haired-one . . .*' murmered a voice in his head.

'But that's not so easy,' Admidios began.

'*Nor is what* you *want . . .*'

'I need more power!'

'*You're incapable of controlling what you have.*'

'At least tell me how to achieve my ends!'

The wind sighed in the trees and the voice laughed as it said, '*I will tell* her *what you need to know . . .*'

28. Walking in the Shadows

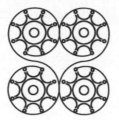

Dallel called the evening circle, then tables were once more erected in the clearing. Servants put benches around and the smell of roasting ox wafting from the cooking fire beyond the grove made Tegen's stomach rumble.

She looked around for Owein. He was seated between King Eiser and Connal, the chieftain of Sinodun, deep in conversation. She was beginning to feel a little lonely. Apart from Admidios, she knew no one. She sat at a table and chewed barley bread while she waited to be served with meat. The light was fading. Wild strokes of gold and crimson painted the skies.

Restless, she left the table to wander between the trees in the deepening dark. The sacrifice of Goban brought memories back of when she too had been dressed in white linen and led out to a circle of solemn druids by a ritual fire. She had thought she was going to be put to death, only to be proclaimed the Star Dancer. She took a deep breath and held her head high.

The Goddess helped me not to be afraid, she reminded herself. Perhaps the smith wasn't afraid either – he didn't seem to be. He was so certain of rebirth . . .

Then her heart did a flip. If Goban was born to avert the evil of drought and famine, will it be *my* end to die facing the evil I am born to prevent? Her hands touched her neck as she thought of the blood that had poured from the smith's throat.

'No,' she whispered. 'I have already fulfilled my destiny – in the caves by the Winter Seas. My only task now is to become a full druid and to serve a village.'

Tegen wandered around the wooded crown of the hill, then, leaning against a tree, she swatted mosquitoes as she watched the sky turn indigo, then black with a million brilliant stars. The moon was not up, but between the leaves above her head she glimpsed the jaws of the Wyvern constellation.

That meant that great things were pending. But what, and were they good or bad?

Tegen moved silently around the grove to the north-east, where the sign of the Goddess's own constellation, the Watching Woman, gleamed and twinkled. It is almost too bright tonight, she thought. 'I remember the stars looking like that before – when I needed extra strength . . .' she said aloud.

'There are *other ways* of gathering strength – and power,' came a low voice next to her ear.

Tegen's heart stopped. Admidios had been standing as still as a tree in the darkness. 'You've been following me! How *dare* you? Leave me alone. I don't want *anything* from you.'

Admidios spoke softly. 'I was here before you were. *You* came to *me*, as I always said you would.'

Tegen's instinct was to leave quickly, but at her back was a thicket of brambles and elder, and before her loomed this huge and dangerous man. She was trapped – almost. From just beyond the trees was the sound of merrymaking and the flickering glow of the fire. She tried to focus on these as she took a small, sideways step.

'I don't understand why you see me as *sinister* . . .' Admidios hissed with soft sibilance. 'I only wish to see you achieve your full potential.'

His words made Tegen hesitate. She tripped over a root and sprawled in the leaf mould.

Admidios came closer. She could feel the hairs on the back of her neck rise, but she could not move. 'You have so much power you haven't even *begun* to tap . . .' He helped her up. 'I suspect, for example, that you are a Fire Dreamer . . . Am I right?'

Tegen's scalp tingled. Her breath felt tight as Admidios's words wound their way inside her head. She knew she should run, but her legs would not obey.

'What's a Fire Dreamer?' Her voice was husky.

Admidios kept a hold of her hand as he led her back amongst the trees. 'Look,' he said. By her feet was a neatly laid but unlit pile of wood on the starlit grass. 'Stretch your hands over that, and think of fire.'

'Like this?' Tegen asked. Then she squealed as bright golden flames shot up, almost catching her skirt.

Admidios retreated into the shadows. 'Yes,' he said quietly. '*Exactly* like that.'

Tegen's heart thumped as she stared at the fire, then turned towards his shadow. 'How did you do that?'

'I didn't. *You* did. And you can do more . . . You can see the future and the past in fire. You will dream what needs to be dreamed and know what needs to be known.'

Despite her inner warnings, Tegen was intrigued. She pushed all thoughts of fleeing aside as she squatted and watched the flames carefully. 'I can see shapes and patterns, things that sort of make sense, but not quite . . .'

Another part of herself chided urgently: *You can't trust him . . .*

But his soft, reassuring words lulled and soothed her fears. 'You need to know how to ask a clear question, then how to interpret the answer. Haven't the druids taught you that?'

'I haven't been taught much,' she heard herself saying. 'I am on my way to Mona to study.' She was mesmerized by the flames and could not take her eyes away from them. A voice at the back of her mind screamed, *RUN! RUN!*

But to her horror she found she wanted to stay. She longed to know more . . .

Admidios's face was in darkness. 'You have great gifts, my dear. You must *use them* . . . make the fire higher, look more deeply. There must be something you have always longed to know the answer to?'

Tegen drew a deep breath and held it as her mind churned with thoughts, fears and memories. The flames spat and crackled as they rose higher. She shook her head. 'It's no good,' she said at last. 'It's just a jumble of whirling lights. I can't make one idea hold still.'

'That's because you aren't asking a simple enough question,' Admidios whispered from the shadows. 'Make yourself comfortable. Feel the warmth . . . sit . . . relax . . . try again . . .' Tegen was very sleepy. She knew she should get away, but all she could do was lie on the ground and stare into the flames.

MOVE! MOVE!

'I'm tired,' she whispered. 'Later.' And she stretched out her leaden limbs.

Admidios clicked his fingers and a wide-winged, noise-less shape glided down through the smoky darkness. Krake landed before her master, then lowering her head and spreading her wings slightly she made a rattling noise in her throat. 'That is her way of acknowledging me as her

lord,' Admidios said. 'Turn!' he ordered, and the bird presented her back to him. With one swift movement he
plucked a tail feather. The bird screeched indignantly and
hopped on to a low branch.

'She was heading for a moult anyway. Sit up,' Admidios
said, handing the quill to Tegen. 'Pass this through the
flames three times.'

Without thinking, she obeyed. The fire leaped and made
the edges of the feather glisten with red gold. The stench of
burning made Tegen want to retch. Admidios took the
scorched blade and drew it across her forehead, making a
blackened smudge.

'That is to give you the mind of a raven,' he said. 'As you
must be aware, they know both the past and the future.
They don't give this knowledge willingly. You have to *take*
it.'

He clicked his fingers. 'Fetch me a bone, Krake. A good
one. And it's got to be whole.' The bird flashed her white
inner eyelids, then swooped towards the sacred grove and
the sounds of feasting and laughter.

Tegen knelt by the fire, mesmerized by the orange, gold,
yellow and red. She felt dizzy and sick. I shouldn't be here,
she thought. Am I staying because I *want* to, or because I
have to?

Just then the bird returned and, with a light thud, she
dropped a short ox rib on the grass.

Admidios kicked it across to Tegen. 'Now, the essence of

divination is to read signs. I suspect that you have at least been taught astrology?'

Tegen glanced up at the Watching Woman and did not answer. At the sight of the stars, a flash of clarity glanced through her mind, but her captor's persuasive voice brushed it aside easily.

'The sound of wind in the trees, the flights of birds and all these natural things are fine for beginners – the ovates and the druids – but for *real* workers of magic, like you, *Star Dancer . . .*'

Her stomach went cold and she gasped as he paused and turned the faint outline of his pale face to the edge of the firelight.

'Oh yes, I know you are the Star Dancer we have all been waiting for . . . It isn't just the pretty tattoo on your face. I've been watching you. You carry magic around with you like a seven-coloured cloak. Did you realize you have only just begun what you were born to do? The fate of the whole of Britain is in your hands, yet the druids have left you entirely untaught and exposed to all the spirits. This is why you need me. To save Britain, we must work *together*.'

'Yes, of course,' she found herself saying; it all made so much sense now.

Admidios stretched out his left hand, casting a shadow that fell across Tegen's face – although from where he was standing, that was impossible. He lowered his voice. 'And after you have learned Fire Dreaming, and told me what I need to know, you can join me Walking in the Shadows, and we will become one with the gods. You'd like that, wouldn't you?'

'Yes.' Tegen smiled. 'I would.' Warm goose down smothered the protestations of her inner voice.

'Shadow Walking is nothing to be afraid of, my dear. It is quite simple. If you spend all your time in the bright sunlight, you become blinded. If you move to the shadows, your eyes are protected, you can see much further. I've seen you wear a hat against the glare of Bel's chariot. Doesn't it help to ease the sun-blindness and headache? Can't you see better with it?'

He leaned forward and spoke urgently. 'Join me and I will teach you the heights and depths of mage-craft, things the druids know nothing of.'

Tegen sat in a limp heap as his words spun her in an ever-tightening cocoon.

'I can see the longing in your heart to go to the sacred island of Mona. You will learn nothing there; you will arrive too late. Don't bother. Stay and be my apprentice. My dear nephew bears an old, but undeserved, grudge against me. You must persuade him to come to his senses and fulfil his duty as High King of Britain. Then together the three of us will become the *Romans'* masters.'

He stepped behind her and crouched down until she could feel his breath on the back of her neck. She shivered with delight and horror at the same time. He passed his hand in front of her eyes and images of knowledge and power whirled in her head . . . Images that did not include the night stars.

Tegen's eyes shifted towards the sky again. She could just see the edge of the Watching Woman. Her mind screamed, *What spell has he put on me?* Panic made her heart drum.

As if he could hear her fear, Admidios's voice went on smoothly. 'You are free to go, if you wish, just as Krake is free.' He held out his arm and the bird flew straight to his shoulder. She bowed her head and rubbed her blue-black crown under his chin. 'But . . .' he smiled over the bird's bobbing head, 'you won't go, because I have a great deal that you want.' He clicked his fingers and from the fire at her side the tongues of flame began to take shape and to make sense in Tegen's mind.

'Am I right?'

Tegen found herself whispering, 'Yes.'

NO! her mind howled. No! I don't want anything to do with your Shadow Walking! Let me go!

You can go when I have finished with you, came Admidios's cold voice inside her head. *And that won't be for a long time yet.*

Outwardly, Admidios acted as if nothing had been said. He picked up the bone Krake had brought and ran a finger along its length. 'See, this has been chewed by a hungry man, and there are shreds of flesh left on it, but the bone itself is whole. That is important. If there are any breaks, they will dictate the way it cracks in the fire, and what you see won't be true for *you*; it will belong to the man or beast who broke it. It is better if you clean the flesh from the bone yourself – then it will be your "seeing" from beginning to end. But this will do to demonstrate.'

Admidios tossed the rib into Tegen's lap. 'Put it into the flames.'

Her mind was completely numb as she picked up the bone and dropped it into the orange and red heart of the fire. The fragile pile of ashy sticks fell apart as the flames licked the new food. The savoury smell of cooking meat scraps gave way to a caramel sweetness, then the stench of burning.

'Ask the fire what I must do to fulfil my aims,' Admidios hissed, standing well back from the heat and light that seared him.

Tegen tried to close her mind to his voice, but she could not. Against her will she repeated the question into the fire, then watched transfixed as the bone blackened, cracked and twisted in the heat.

'No!' Tegen shouted, suddenly jumping to her feet. 'This is all wrong!'

The flames died. Everything went very dark. Tegen was panting and sweating.

'Pick it up,' Admidios's voice ordered tightly from the blackness. 'You must hold it in your hands and let it speak to your spirit. By all means consider the shape the thing takes, but you must also listen to the shadows that lurk in even *your* whiter-than-white soul, little Star Dancer. These will tell you things even your precious Goddess doesn't know.'

At the mention of the Goddess, Tegen's eyes slowly adjusted to the wholesome dark of the night. She could just make out Admidios. The few stars reflected no brightness on his skin. He swallowed light. She hated him. She took a deep breath. She *had* to find the strength to run away, but an overriding compulsion to know more made her lick her fingers.

She reached out . . .

'Hurry. Take the bone and answer my question.' Admidios leaned forward so his head was very close to Tegen's, his pale eyes glowing wide and urgent.

Go away! Go away! Let me go! her thoughts screamed. Why won't my legs and arms obey me?

The blackened bone was quite cold. A shudder ran through her as in her mind the twisted shape took the form of a man lying dead. She looked up, but the Shadow Walker's face dissolved into darkness. Over his shoulder, the Watching Woman constellation sparkled icy bright.

To give extra strength to her children who are in trouble.

The words were spoken loud and clear into Tegen's mind by a voice she had heard only once before. The Goddess had reassured her at a time when she had thought she was dying. Now she was speaking again.

'No!' Tegen shouted, flinging the bone away. 'I won't help you. I *hate* your Shadow Magic.' Goban's warning rang in her head. 'And I won't use the power of fire for *your* ends!'

She spat to ward off the evil eye and wove a spirit shield around herself. Then she rubbed the sooty feather-mark away. 'I don't want to have *anything* to do with you. Do you understand? You stink of rot in the presence of the Goddess. When you die, may you go to the lowest abyss of the Beyond – you and that foul raven of yours – and may neither of you ever find your way back to be reborn!'

And with that she stamped off through the trees towards the light of the sacred fire.

Admidios smiled and bowed slightly. 'Anything you say, *Star Dancer*. But you *will* tell me what you saw tonight, by one means or another.'

He turned to his familiar, who was scratching for insects in the grass by his side. He reached out and grabbed the bird by the neck. She fluttered and squawked in fear, then hung limp and submissive in his fist, making a rattling noise in her throat. He stroked her thick beak and brought her eye level with his own. 'And you, Krake – or whatever your real name once was – are going to help me. *Aren't* you?'

The captive spirit wriggled helplessly within the bird. Then the raven opened her beak, screeched and bit Admidios on the nose.

29. Night Visitor

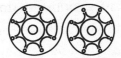

Tegen sat up all night on her straw bed behind the screen in the longhouse. The other girls dreamed as she scratched Wolf's ears and stared into the empty darkness. It was not fear of Admidios that kept her awake, but the 'bone vision' of the man lying dead – was he murdered? She sensed she knew who it was, but the image had been fleeting.

Thank you, Lady, for giving me the strength to get away, she prayed. What must I do about what I saw? If only I knew who it was, I could warn him . . .

A shadow moved near the wall of the longhouse. Tegen glanced up and saw Owein, silhouetted against the dying red light from the hearth. 'Can I join you? I can't sleep.'

Tegen pulled Wolf's long legs aside so Owein could sit. The dog half-woke and growled. 'Hush! Don't be silly!' she said.

'What happened to you this evening?' Owein asked. 'You disappeared straight after the ritual – there was so much food we were throwing it to the dogs in the end. Some musicians came up from the fair to play and everybody was dancing. It's not like you to miss that!'

'It was Admidios,' Tegen rubbed her fingers through Wolf's wiry pelt as she whispered the whole tale. 'Someone is going to die, but until I know who I can't do anything to prevent it.'

Owein settled himself down. Wolf snapped at him. Tegen slapped the dog lightly. 'Quiet, or I'll put you outside.'

'Why not try the ritual again?' Owein suggested. 'You can obviously do it. If you aren't frightened or in a hurry you might see more clearly.'

'And become a Shadow Walker myself?' she hissed. 'How could you even *think* such a thing?'

'Is it such a bad idea? *You* could control it.'

Tegen ignored the suggestion. 'I didn't tell Admidios what I saw. But he's going to try to find out. He has some sort of aim, and this man's death will help him achieve it . . . Whatever it is, it won't be good.' Then she added, 'He brags about how good he is at seeing and divination, so why did he need *me* for Fire Dreaming, or whatever he calls it? Why didn't he just do it himself?'

'However good you are at divination, it's always difficult to see your own path.' Owein picked at his teeth with an end of straw. 'Are you going to tell him?'

Tegen was shocked. 'Of course not! You're talking nonsense tonight. Go away – I need some sleep.' She tugged her cloak over her shoulders and lay down.

Owein got up, strode to the great door that stood ajar to let in the summer air and slipped outside.

Next morning, after the early rituals and breakfast, Tegen and Owein went down to the fair. The morning was warm and bright, and the crowds were up early, buying and selling, laughing, arguing and drinking.

In the middle of the meadow a long strip of cleared ground had its edges marked with bundles of straw. At the end nearest the stronghold, ten fine horses were waiting, some impatiently beating the ground. Each rider was resplendent in a brightly coloured shirt and ribbon-plaited hair.

Gleefully Tegen ran along the line-up inspecting the horses. 'They all look so splendid!'

'Are you going to bet on the winner?' Owein asked.

Tegen shook her head.

Owein chewed his lip. 'I like the look of that bay second from the right. The one with the pretty blonde girl as jockey.'

Tegen laughed. 'You mean you like the look of the *rider*!'

'No – well, yes.' He blushed. 'It's just that a smaller rider means that the horse can run faster. Less weight. Most people bet on the tall male warrior-types to win, even if they are riding a bag of washing on legs, but they too heavy and slow the animal down. They're looking at the outside without thinking!'

He slipped away and gave a few coins to a man with a money pouch balanced on his beer belly.

Tegen sat on a bundle of straw and waited for the off. Then her heart missed a beat. Admidios was standing on the other side of the racetrack. She resisted the urge to slip into the crowd. She knew she mustn't let his presence bully her, but she dreaded him all the same. He turned, caught her eye, smiled and bowed.

Tegen fixed her gaze on Owein's bay mare. The next rider was a tall man on a large stallion, who sneered down at the pretty jockey. She ignored him and stroked her mount's mane.

Good for you! thought Tegen. And she sent the girl a small, silent blessing, hoping that wasn't cheating.

Suddenly a horn sounded and the horses leaped away, eyes wild, plaited manes flowing. Tegen bit her lip. The girl was in the lead. The sneering man was just behind. He raised a cruel-looking whip and was about to lash out at her.

Furious, Tegen began a curse, but before she could move, Owein caught her wrist. 'Don't!' he shouted above the thundering hoofs and yelling crowd. 'Admidios is watching you. Any magic you use, he'll twist against you. Believe me – I know!'

Tegen glared at him. 'You've changed your tune,' she shouted back.

'What do you mean?'

Tegen yelled in his ear. 'Last night you were all for me recreating the bone vision with Fire Magic.'

'What bone? What magic?'

'I told you last night, in the longhouse.'

'What are you talking about? I didn't see you anywhere last night.'

The crowds roared. A dark-haired man was lifted shoulder high and proclaimed the winner to the sound of horns.

Owein took Tegen's arm. 'That's my money gone. Let's go somewhere quiet.' As they sat in the shade Tegen repeated the tale of the Fire Magic and the night visitor. Just as she finished, Wolf came bounding out of the crowd, a stolen flatbread in his mouth, his tail tightly curled in delight. He dropped the bread and gave Owein a hot lick across his face.

Tegen stared. 'That's funny. Wolf growled when you came in last night.' Then she went pale; 'And there's something else: you were *walking normally*. You strode out of the hall as if you had nothing wrong with you! I am sure I wasn't dreaming.'

Owein looked Tegen in the eye. 'It wasn't *me* who came

to you last night. I strongly suspect Admidios was using a shape-shift to look like me.'

Tegen took a deep breath. 'Ah . . . ! When he put the bone in the fire he wanted to know how to "achieve his aims". It seems he's tricked me into giving him his answer. Now he'll be planning to murder someone. What an idiot I have been! I didn't think of a shape-shift. It's like you said about the jockeys – I was looking at outside appearances and not thinking!'

Owein shook his head. 'Don't blame yourself. It was the middle of the night. You were tired and upset.'

Tegen pulled Wolf into a big hug and rubbed his nose. 'You tried to warn me, you wonderful mutt. I'll take more notice of you in future.' Then she stared towards the race-track. 'No wonder Admidios looked so smug just now. How could I be so *stupid*?!' She pulled out her knife and began to stab at the ground.

'That won't help; it will only dull the blade,' Owein said. 'Calm down. I will talk to Dallel. Do you know who you saw in the bone?'

'No, it was too quick.'

'I suspect if it was someone you knew well, you would have recognized him.' Owein leaned back in the grass, pulled at a squeaking stalk and chewed. 'I can't think whose death would help Admidios, unless . . .'

Tegen looked down at him. 'Yes?'

'Oh . . . it's nothing.'

30. Prophecy

Owein mounted Heather and slotted his crutch into its saddle-loop. 'Dallel will be preparing for the tax collecting. If we go *now*, we might be able to catch him before things start.'

As they approached the sacred grove, a village of tents was springing up across the lower slopes. 'Who are those for?' Tegen asked.

'Druids. They'll be arriving in droves to help their chieftains with tax collecting,' Owein replied. 'After that they'll hear legal disputes, then stay for the discussions.'

'Will there be anyone from the Winter Seas?'

'Possibly. In the old days a high chieftain like Connal would have expected about one hundred and fifty druids, each with fifty apprentices, and each of those with fifty more . . .'

Tegen's mind boggled.

'Plus servants, of course,' he added mischievously. 'They all demanded the finest hospitality and their every whim fulfilled. If they didn't get it, the bards would make up scathing songs about the chieftain's meanness. It'd soon be sung at every noble's hearth in the tribal lands! That was a fate worse than death itself!'

'But how could anyone feed so many people?'

Owein laughed. 'Come on, Tegen. A bard never lets little things like reality get in the way of a good story!'

Tegen didn't particularly want to be a bard at that moment. The sun was high and her woollen gown was hot and itchy. 'Where is Dallel?' she asked. 'We need to tell him about Admidios.'

'Over there, surrounded by friends he hasn't seen for ages. It'll be better to talk with him when we can have his full attention. Admidios won't move in broad daylight. Let's get some food.'

They had scarcely eaten when a horn summoned all present to the sacred space. Next to the giant upturned tree root was a wooden throne with a wide, leafy canopy. On both sides, stools and benches were arranged in a semicircle. A few of the white-robed druids were already settled near the throne, catching some of its shade. The ovates and bards were left to sit in the full glare of the sun.

'It looks like the old man is expecting a good haul.' Owein pointed to ten wicker baskets the size of barrels set out around the throne. 'Those are for collecting taxes from the grateful tribesmen. It pays for warriors and keeps the King in a comfortable lifestyle.'

Tegen frowned. 'Should I have brought something?'

Owein laughed. 'Druids are exempt, you goose. On Mona they collect their own taxes.'

Suddenly Tegen had a thought. 'When is the festival over?'

'Why? Aren't you enjoying yourself?'

'Yes, but I need to get there soon. Something Admidios said has worried me . . . He said when I got to Mona it would be too late.'

Owein could sense the fears that gnawed at her. He patted her on the shoulder. 'Don't worry, you should be on your way by the new moon. I have half a mind to come with you, as it happens.'

'Really? That would be wonderful.' And she flung her arms around him in a bear hug.

For a brief moment Owein held her tightly. Then he turned away. 'Look, there is Eiser. No one is with him. Come, I'll introduce you.'

Tegen ran her fingers through her hair and brushed the grass and creases from her robe.

'You look fine, come on.'

'But I have never met a king before.'

Owein smiled at her from one corner of his mouth and she blushed. Taking a deep breath, Tegen approached the throne. Eiser sat tall and straight, his dark curly hair was shot through with silver, his face was careworn and his eyes carried the weight of the sky.

Owein stood before his foster-father and bowed as well as he could. His green ovate's robe fluttered in the breeze. 'My lord,' he said formally, 'may I present my friend Tegen, from your people of the Winter Seas?'

Tegen copied Owein's bow. 'Hello,' she said nervously.

Eiser raised an eyebrow. 'Ah, the Winter Seas. Have you ever heard of a good druid by the name of Witton?'

'He is dead, my lord. He went to Tir na nÓg just after midwinter a year ago.'

'May he soon be reborn,' Eiser replied. He hesitated, glanced around, then leaned forward and whispered, 'Do you know who took his last breath?'

Tegen looked at Owein nervously. He nodded his encouragement. 'Er . . . I did, my lord.'

Eiser sat up straight. 'You?' he whispered. 'So the rumours are true – there is a female Star Dancer who will save us from the scourge of the Romans! We have waited a long time for you.'

Tegen drew a breath. Twice in the sun's turn she had been addressed by her title. How could people know of her beyond the Winter Seas? *Might* she have a role to play in defeating the invaders?

Just then a bellowing voice called, 'My lords and ladies, please take your seats. Those who have taxes to offer to

Eiser, King of the Dobunni, please wait by the trees to be summoned by your clan name.'

Tegen and Owein sat to Eiser's right. They could see everything clearly, but the sun beat down on them.

A skinny bard with a black beard and an ash-wood harp stepped forward, bowed to Eiser and made himself comfortable on a three-legged stool. A small boy shaded him with an oak branch and the crowd fell silent.

'This should be good,' Owein whispered. 'Cluan is one of the greatest song-makers between here and the lost lands of Logres in the far west. He's particularly good at reminding everyone of how much the King has done for them in the past year, so people put more than they had intended into the tax basket!'

Tegen giggled as the bard's long fingers rippled over the first notes of a melody. He began to sing and the richness of his voice sent a shiver of delight down Tegen's back.

> *I am a bard, I sing only the truth.*
> *Behold the lord seated by my side*
> *and know that his care for you*
> *is scarcely less than the Dagda's own.*
>
> *He, and he alone, stood naked*
> *nine days and nights*
> *in the heat of battle, raising his shield*
> *against those who came to rape his land.*

His sword cut your enemies' hearts
from their living chests,
he smote off their heads
and fed their eyes to ravens.

This mighty Oak, this lord of all Britain
bloodied his blade on the field of battle.
He turned his spear into a deadly viper
whose fangs pierced the throats of your foes.

He sent those we hate to beyond the shadows,
the place of eternal death . . .

Suddenly the bard stopped, let his fingers drop from the strings and began to chant in a tight, high voice:
'*And you, Eiser, will soon lie cold, your breath cut short. You will die from a blow from no man's hand . . .*' Then he made a strangled noise, his eyes stared and his mouth foamed beneath his beard. Shaking violently, he fell to the ground. His harp clanged beside him.

The druids all stood, 'The Awen,' they gasped. 'The Awen is possessing him!'

Tegen sprang forward, 'He's choking!'

Owein pulled her back. 'You can't do anything. The prophetic spirits have taken hold of his body! We must wait for them to leave!'

Cluan arched his back, went rigid, then he vomited and

became limp. His eyes rolled up and his face turned the colour of curdled milk.

The people crowded into the sacred space, straining their necks to see. Tegen elbowed her way through. 'Let me through!' she demanded. Then she knelt by Cluan's head and placed one hand on his chest. He was not breathing.

'Stand back!' Dallel ordered, spreading his arms. 'Give the spirits room to do their work.' Then he said, 'Tegen, you have dared to touch a possessed man. If you do not bring him back to life, you will have his spirit, *and* whatever is within him, take hold of *you*. No one, however great a druid, can live long like that.'

Tegen was sweating with fear and heat. She looked around at the awe-struck faces. 'What must I do?'

Dallel's wife, Bronnen, bustled in a little closer. 'Put your fingers into his mouth, dear, to make sure that all the large bits of vomit are gone. They might be blocking his windpipe.'

Taking a deep breath, Tegen ran her finger inside his mouth, but there was only slime that dribbled on to his beard.

Tentatively, Bronnen crouched by Tegen's side. 'I have seen a man give another his breath to save him from Tir na nÓg.'

'How?'

'You blow your air into his mouth.'

Tegen hesitated. Then she tried to place her lips over

Cluan's, but the angle was too awkward. She looked back at Bronnen in despair.

'Roll him over on to his back . . . and pinch his nose, or your breath will come back to you.'

Tegen took the bard's shoulders and pushed him over, took a deep breath and tried again. The stench of warm vomit made her want to retch. Ugh . . . must I do this? she thought. Can't *you* bring him back, Lady?

'Now let go of his nose and press the air back out of his chest,' Bronnen said. 'Hurry, he's going blue!'

Tegen obeyed, then gulped another breath and gave that to Cluan as well.

Again and again she worked, breathing and squeezing until suddenly he coughed, his nose bubbled and his lungs heaved. More sick flew over Tegen's robe. She winced. Someone handed her a beaker of water and she raised Cluan's head and dripped a little into his mouth. His throat worked to swallow and his eyes flickered open as he reached out a shaking hand for more.

Seeing the bard's spirit had returned, Bronnen dared to kneel on his other side. His head lolled against her white-robed lap. 'Someone take him into the shade,' she ordered. 'Lay him on his side and stay with him.' One man scooped Cluan under his arms and another took his knees.

The crowd drew back and let them pass. Some of the younger bards touched his robe, hoping to gain a little of the prophetic Awen that had possessed him.

Tegen wanted to follow, but Dallel caught her shoulder. Under his wide whiskers his face was serious. 'Why did you dare to touch a possessed man?'

Tegen shrugged and wiped her mouth. Her hand shook. 'I need a drink,' she said.

Dallel persisted. 'Why did you do it?' he demanded, tightening his grip.

'Because he was dying!' *Isn't it obvious?* she longed to snap.

'No ordinary druid would reach out when the spirits possess a bard. Even Bronnen risked too much.'

'Maybe the Goddess told me to do it – I really don't know, I just did it,' and she spat to try to get the taste of sick from her mouth.

'So you *are* the Star Dancer, the one who has come to turn evil aside . . .' Dallel whispered, and with his free hand, he traced the nine points of the tattoo on Tegen's face. 'Be careful. There will be many who will fear you and be jealous.'

'I am more worried about saving Eiser's life. I . . . I think I too had a prophecy,' and she told him briefly about the bone in the fire. 'I have a feeling that the dead body I saw was the King's. I can't tell you why – it's just an instinct.'

'That makes no sense.' Dallel smiled kindly. 'How could the King's death help to advance Admidios?'

Owein coughed politely. They had not seen him standing nearby. 'If I may?' he ventured, turning to Tegen. 'Do you remember he proposed to Sabrina?'

'Yes, but that was just to annoy her, surely?' Tegen replied.

Owein shook his head. 'What if he *meant* it? As I can't succeed Eiser, she is the only heir. If Admidios married her, with Eiser dead, he would become lord of the Dobunni.'

'But why trick her into going away?' Tegen asked. 'She might be killed, and then his plans would fall apart.'

'I'd guess she's being held safely somewhere, ready to be "persuaded" to become his woman. Meanwhile,' Owein added very quietly, 'I'll warn Eiser to be wary. I wish Sabrina had listened when you advised her not to leave. I will ask the Old Ones once more what they know.'

Dallel sighed as he listened. 'Whoever you saw in your vision, Tegen, there is nothing you can do. What has been prophesied must be. But sometimes a doom can be delayed. I will talk to Cluan to see what he can add – if, that is, he remembers speaking. He might not, for the spirits took him completely.'

Tegen turned and looked back at the King, who was once more on his carved chair, calm and erect, while the white-robes rearranged themselves in order of rank on either side of him.

'If he is to die "from a blow from no man's hand", then maybe he will fall ill,' she ventured.

'Who knows?' Dallel replied. At last a servant came with mead for Tegen. 'Drink this. Eiser will either die of sickness, or he'll be murdered by a woman.'

In either case, Admidios will be in the clear, Tegen thought as the honey sweetness chased away the bile.

Dallel went on: 'Star Dancer, you must go to Eiser after the collection of taxes and see if you can prevent him getting ill.'

'But if I treat him, might I be accused of his murder if he dies?'

'I will vouch for your innocence with my life,' the old druid replied, his eyes earnest under his wispy white brows. 'Please, see what you can do. From the way you saved Cluan's life, I can see you are a powerful healer.'

'I can't make any promises . . . I haven't been trained.'

'If Eiser dies, there will be mayhem unless his daughter returns quickly. I will send warriors to find her immediately. The alliance between the tribes is fragile and Eiser's tribesmen will be howling for vengeance before his body is cold. Now take your place. We must proceed as normal.'

And the old druid turned back to stand by the King's side.

31. The Collection of Taxes

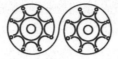

Eiser sat pale and straight on his throne. One by one the Dobunni clans came forward, each offering gold and silver coins, jewellery, fine pottery, drinking horns and cloth. Sometimes the clan-chief knelt and wept, begging exemption with tales of bad crops, Roman destruction or plague. When this happened, the druids huddled together and discussed the issue with much arguing and waving of hands.

Owein craned forward, fascinated and absorbing it all. Sometimes he tried to explain to Tegen what was going on.

But she was more interested in watching Eiser. He looked hot and ill. She chewed her fingers and remembered how Gilda had faded, and wondered if someone was slipping him a slow poison. But if he *was* dying of 'a blow from no man's hand' then Admidios *couldn't* be involved: it had to be a woman or natural causes . . . So it could not have been Eiser that Tegen had seen in the burned bone.

Yet a niggle at the back of her mind told her it *was* him – and that Admidios would be the murderer. It didn't make sense. I must do the ritual again without Admidios, she decided. I am sure he is planning a murder, whether it is Eiser's or not . . . I need to get a closer look at the body without panicking and dropping the bone, but is it wrong for me to do Shadow Magic?

I have got to know what Admidios is up to.

She was dragged back from her thoughts by Owein elbowing her in the ribs. 'Look!' he whispered urgently. 'Look who it is!'

Tegen's eyes opened wide. Kneeling before Eiser's throne was Caja the salt trader, offering a tatty stretch of undyed cloth and a small lump of salt for the collection baskets.

The king leaned on one hand and stared down at the woman. His face was wet with perspiration. Caja's scrawny, dirt-smeared figure grovelling at his feet was not improving things. 'Oh great lord,' she whined, 'our crops have failed, our village was burned by foul Atrebatian raiders, then Romans came and took my three sons as slaves. We have nothing . . . nothing left to honour you and the fine warriors who follow you! Please, I beg you, take this piece of salt and this – the cloak off my own back – as a gift.' Caja cocked her head to one side and simpered, 'The nights are warm, my lord. I can sleep without it.' She raised her tear-streaked face and smiled.

'I bet she's rubbed salt into her eyes to make them weep,' whispered Owein. 'That's an old trick.'

Eiser looked as if he felt too tired to care one way or the other. He nodded to the druids by his side.

'That means he wants a judgement,' whispered Owein.

A tall white-robe with a shock of white-grey curly hair leaned over and whispered to the King, who shrugged and waved his hand dismissively. The druid straightened and spoke: 'Take a slave from her clan in lieu of payment. And the salt. Give her back her cloak. She has a legal right to night covering.'

At this Caja really did look shocked. She opened her mouth to protest, but two men were already sweeping towards where Wynne was making for the trees. They pounced, grabbed a shabby figure and dragged it screaming and kicking to the feet of the King for inspection.

It was Kieran.

Eiser scarcely looked at him, but the druid nodded. 'He'll do.' Then the boy was bound and hauled, screeching and swearing down the hill.

Wynne ran after him, wailing, 'My baby, they've taken my baby . . . *Please, not my baby . . . !'*

Caja scowled, grabbed her sister's arm and dragged her away.

Tegen rose to her feet to protest, but Owein pulled her back. 'Be quiet. Judgement has been made.'

'But I have gold,' Tegen hissed urgently. 'I could pay their tax!'

Owein was adamant. 'You cannot question the judgement of a druid. His word is law. But it is *Caja's* problem, not yours. As head-woman of her clan she has to supply something for tax. If you paid it for her, you would have everyone else demanding you paid theirs too.'

'But he's not much more than a child . . .'

'He is old enough to work. I don't like it either, but you saw what Caja was carrying in her wagon. She had huge piles of cloth and slabs of salt. They were all dressed well when they arrived. I bet those rags are kept for special occasions. She is a cheat and Kieran is the price. Personally,' he added, 'I'd rather be a slave here than a nephew of Caja's.'

Tegen could see his point, but said nothing as she hugged herself and allowed her anger to simmer all afternoon. The sun was getting low in the sky before the last of the clan chiefs left, grumbling about paying taxes to a king who couldn't get rid of the invaders.

The brimming baskets were loaded on to a wagon and hauled away. Servants moved the carved seat to one side and dismantled the leafy canopy, while Owein and the older druids continued to argue happily.

Urgently Tegen pulled him to one side. 'Can't we help Kieran somehow? Slavery is wrong!'

Owein slapped her cheerfully on the back. 'Justice has been seen to be done within a holy oak grove. All is well in Britain. Ritual and tradition will keep the Romans at bay. Praise to the Goddess.'

Tegen saw red. 'And sarcasm doesn't help!'

Owein dropped his silly smile. 'I know, and I am as angry as you, but believing blindly in the way things have always been done is what keeps the druids from being an effective force against the Romans. There is nothing either of us can do about Kieran or anything else tonight. The horn is blowing and the circle is forming – it's time to greet the spirits.' Owein squeezed Tegen's hand. 'Come on, we must do the magic or the sun won't rise tomorrow.'

Tegen tugged her hand free and glowered as she took her place in the south of the circle, by the gate of fire.

The following morning the air was hot and sultry and heavy black storm clouds banked high on the western horizon.

Tegen avoided the fair and ignored Owein's suggestion to join the next tax gathering. She wanted to be alone. Most of the day she walked in the woods and chewed unripe cobnuts as she turned things over and over in her mind. What is the point of being given a gift like Fire Dreaming, if I don't use it? she reasoned. At last she made a decision – she *would* light a fire of her own, and this time she'd use a bone *she* had eaten from. Slightly guiltily she drew a rag from her pouch and unwrapped a roasted pigeon's thigh-bone she had saved from dinner the night before.

Moving deeper under the green canopy of ash and oak below the northern slopes of the sacred hill, Tegen came to a clearing. Making sure she could not be seen, she crouched out of sight between several cushion-shaped thickets of brambles and began to search around for kindling. She knew once the fire was alight, the smoke would betray her, but would anyone see, or care? She wouldn't need long. She had just started to lay the first sticks when a soft hush of wings overhead made her freeze.

A twig snapped close by. Tegen did not turn to see who it was. She did not need to. The skin on the back of her neck prickled as Admidios crouched at her side.

'I knew you couldn't resist,' he whispered in her ear.

She shuddered. Goddess get rid of him!

'What do you *want*?' she demanded as she fought the dulling, soporific wrappings of his voice.

Admidios stooped and began to lay bracken and small branches into a neat heap. 'I heard you are going to do some healing for Eiser as his life appears to be in danger.'

'How do you know? Are you poisoning him?'

Admidios laughed. 'Don't be ridiculous, child. How could I? He is surrounded by warriors and his food is tasted like a baby's. More to the point, why *would* I? I'm merely concerned, and I have some advice that might help you . . .'

Tegen stood and dusted the grass from her skirt. 'I told you the other night, I don't want anything to do with your sort of magic.' She kicked aside the unlit fire and turned to walk away.

Admidios caught her by the arm. 'But you *will* go to Eiser. He is ill and he needs help.'

Tegen twisted free. 'What do *you* care?'

Admidios smiled, showing his even white teeth. His eyes remained cold. 'He is an old friend.'

'You have *friends*?' Tegen sneered as she turned back towards the stronghold.

'Why is that so hard to believe?' Admidios called after her. 'Why do you find me so . . . *difficult*?'

'Because you are a slimy toad!'

He sighed. 'If you are suspicious of me interfering, I will keep well away – not that I would dream of meddling in a *druid's* work – but go to him . . . *please* . . .' he wheedled softly.

'I have already promised Dallel I will,' she called over her shoulder as she marched away.

'Thank you!' Admidios said. 'I am grateful.' He gave a low whistle and a swift, silent black shape swooped down from the trees to rest on the shoulder of his leather waist-coat. Admidios scratched the bird's blue-black head with something like affection. 'Yes, I'm very grateful.'

32. Eiser's Cure

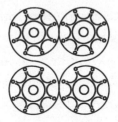

The air grew hotter and stickier. The King was staying in a roundhouse of his own on the shady side of Connal's hall. The door stood open to the east and the ageing warlord lay sprawled on a wooden bed near the doorway, his eyes closed against the setting sun. A faint recollection of a breeze stirred his greying hair.

The image made Tegen feel uneasy.

The guard leaning against the door nodded to her as she approached. She hesitated. 'Is he asleep?' she whispered.

A gravelly voice called out, 'Come here child. I am awake, and despite my reputation, I don't bite.' He took a deep breath and sat up.

Tegen swallowed hard. Now she was here she couldn't think of how to explain why she had come.

Eiser spoke first. 'You're Owein's friend; you brought the

possessed man back from the Otherworld. Who sent you to me? Dallel or my old nemesis Admidios?'

Before she could answer, the King sat upright. His face was gaunt. 'You know he's a Roman spy, don't you? He said he was going to send a healer to me.' Eiser half closed his eyes and examined Tegen from head to toe as he reeled out questions.

'It was Dallel who asked me to come,' she managed to say at last, 'although Admidios asked as well – he said he was worried about you because he was your friend . . .' She watched carefully to see what his reaction would be.

Eiser spat. 'Serpent under my table, more like!' He dismissed his guard with a flick of his hand, then glowered at Tegen under his dark eyebrows. 'Come closer! Now, tell me, why are you here, *really*?'

Tegen decided not to mention the bone as she took a deep breath. 'I came because of Cluan's prophecy. Dallel asked me to see if I could slow any illness that might be fatal. He is worried about you, but he is also concerned about what will happen to the tribes' alliance should you die. Would you like me to leave?'

'No,' Eiser replied. 'I would like some human company, someone who doesn't argue or want to discuss wars and politics. What sort of healing do you do, girl? Pull up a stool and have some mead.'

Tegen sat opposite the King and sipped sticky fermented honey from a silver cup, wishing it was ale or water. 'I do a little herbal healing,' she said, 'although I am only a bard-in-training.' She paused as she remembered the way she had healed old Witton. 'I do . . . *other* sorts of healing as well – sometimes, when the Goddess teaches me what to do and say.' Her eyes slid to the blackened hearth. She was glad it was cold. Fire Dreaming was Admidios's magic; she would never use it again.

Eiser leaned back on the rolled sheepskin pillows and closed his eyes. 'Is there a cure for heart weariness?'

'What's that?' Tegen asked.

'Old age and sorrow.'

Tegen hung her head and bit her lip. She knew death was a cure, allowing the sufferer to rest in Tir na nÓg before being reborn in the world, fresh and new again. But that wasn't what the King wanted. 'No, sir,' she said quietly. 'There is no cure. But . . .' she looked up and smiled, 'I will dance for you if you like.'

'Ah, yes.' Eiser stroked his beard. 'That would please me.'

Tegen unlaced her shoes and wriggled her toes on the bare earth. She moved to the entrance of the hut, where the evening sun spilled gold across the floor. She stretched her arms high and closed her eyes. In her mind she went back to the day when she had gone to the Beltane fair and danced her first magic, although she had not known what she was doing at the time. Once more Tegen could feel the steady rhythm of the little drummer boy who had taught her to dance when she was thirteen. The drumbeats welled from the soles of her feet up her spine and into her arms and hands.

As she threw back her head, her plait untwisted and fell free, spilling her long black hair over her shoulders in a silky cloak. In her head, the drumming changed subtly to match the warm air. The smell of the trees and the river floated up from the valley below. Tegen stamped her feet in tiny steps, wishing she was wearing her golden bangles to jingle as she moved. She kept her legs straight as she swayed like a tree in a breeze. Then in her mind the wind picked up, she loosened her elbows and knees and let the imaginary drum-music take her spinning like a sycamore key, her white skirt bell-like around her as she turned and turned.

For a heartbeat, Tegen stopped, lifted her face to the sky. In her head the music changed to a faster, brighter rhythm. She raised her hands and began to clap and stamp to the beat. Her head filled with colours of summer, warmth and excitement.

Then suddenly into her mind came a grey streak of cold. Then another, and another. Five in all, each ripping across the brightness of the imaginary landscape. Her steps slowed, her back twisted and her head drooped. The drumbeat slowed to a weak pulse. She let it lead her until her arms became too heavy to lift. The colours she was painting with her body faded into misty-dull oblivion.

But she could not stop dancing. She stretched her arms

around as if she was searching for something solid to hold on to. Her footsteps became uncertain. The ground became as soft and yielding as clouds beneath her heels. Spinning and swaying, lost and alone within her dance, Tegen began to feel afraid. This had never happened before. Lady, she prayed, what is happening? Am I in a trance? Where are you leading me?

Suddenly there came a wild tumble of dark curls, the colour of peat water, and her vision was marred by a black shape that swooped low and caught in her hair, tangling, dragging her down until she stumbled and fell head first.

Then nothing.

Tegen's head ached when she opened her eyes. She sat on the floor, panting. Owein was standing in the doorway. The day had darkened as a dead wind and leaden skies cut across the sun.

Eiser helped Tegen to a chair and wrapped her in a cloak. He leaned towards her, his thin face starkly outlined against the grey light from the door. 'What did you see in your trance, girl? What did the Goddess show you? How can I lead my people to victory once and for all?' He grabbed her wrist urgently and painfully.

She looked into his sad eyes and shook her head. 'You won't. There are five grey shadows that have taken all the colour from your life. But there is a wild darkness that will bring you comfort.' Tegen rubbed her chilly shoulders and looked at him. Her vision made no sense. 'I need time to think it through . . .'

Owein looked from one to the other. 'Come, Tegen, you need some beer and food. Cluan is well and will be singing in the longhouse tonight, and some travelling musicians will be there too.'

Tegen stood and bowed to the King. 'But there was something else, something important . . .'

'It will wait,' Eiser replied, staring at the cold hearth.

Outside, large drops of rain were splashing on the dry ground, making the earth smell tarry. Thunder rolled and lightening glanced across the slate-black clouds as they hurried to Connal's longhouse.

'Isn't it time for the evening ritual?' Tegen asked, staring across at the sacred hill.

'Yes, but you aren't fit to go. Trances take a great deal of energy.'

'Had you been watching long?'

'I'd only just arrived. Eiser said he felt as though you had danced his life story: all the triumphs, the glories, the deaths of his sons . . . Then something went wrong. You seemed to lose all the strength in your limbs and you collapsed in a heap. That was when I came in; you were burbling something about two darknesses!'

Tegen stood in the fire-lit doorway of Chieftain Connal's longhouse. On the far side servants were bringing in bread and vegetables from the kitchens, and by the central hearth Kieran and another male slave were turning a whole hog on a spit. Kieran nodded to Tegen, but a slap from the other slave made him turn back to his task.

Eiser and Connal were seated at high table, drinking while they waited for meat. Tegen sat on a bench and picked at a barley loaf. She took out her knife and spread the crumbly crust with butter, then dipped it in a bowl of crushed salt. The taste was heaven and too sharp, all at the same time. Owein poured cider into a beaker and passed it to her.

'I wish I could remember what else I saw. It was something important . . .' She finished the bread and took a handful of small purple plums from a basket. Near the fire, a band of musicians was tuning up. There were flautists, drummers, whistle players and a harpist.

Cluan was leaning against one of the roof-trees. He saw Tegen and bowed. 'My lady with power to raise the dead, are you dancing tonight?'

Tegen shuddered at being addressed in public like that. Spirits could be jealous and vindictive. 'Maybe,' she called back. 'And maybe not,' she added quietly to Owein. 'In fact,' she went on, 'I need to be alone. I am going to the sacred hill. I need to speak with the Goddess to try to understand what I saw.'

Owein shook his head. 'You can't go up there on your own on a night like this!'

'The storm has almost passed, and I'll take Wolf,' she said, whistling for him. Then helping herself to another barley loaf and butter, she walked into the rain and dark. The hard earth had become a sea of mud, but under her thin leather soles Tegen followed a cobbled pathway. Only the glow of the watchman's brazier ahead gave her any clue as to where the nearest gate lay.

A tall figure loomed in the dark. The firelight caught on a wet horse-skin cloak pulled over a miserable-looking face. 'Where do you think you are going, miss?' the guard demanded.

'To the sacred hill. I am Tegen the bard. I need to do a ritual.'

'Not tonight you don't,' he replied. 'When the night is too thick to see the difference between Romans and British, the gates are locked until dawn. Even to druids.'

Tegen could tell from his tone of voice that there would be no argument, so she turned and retraced her steps. In the dark she lost the pathway and found herself ankle deep in water. Lady, I wish I could see your stars, she prayed. I know something evil is happening. Show me what to do . . . please.

Then it came to her. She could make a strong spell of pro- tection and put it on Eiser's door until she could think of how to help him. She turned towards the roundhouse, sploshing and slithering her way across the compound. Cracks of light shone from the King's lodging. A man's figure was just leaving, letting the door swing and bang behind him. Distant lightening flashed. In that instant Tegen saw the cloaked figure was not Eiser, but it was impossible to tell who was making his way towards the merriment and warmth of the main hall.

Soft thunder rolled and echoed across the valley as Tegen crept around the dripping edge of the thatch, skirting the piles of stacked logs until she came to the doorway. There were no guards. She knocked. Silence. She pulled back the right-hand door and peeped inside. The room was just as before, the bed neatly made with brightly coloured blankets and sheepskins, and a small fire had been lit.

Across the floor was a trail of wet footprints. Just under the edge of the bed lay a carved, wide-backed bone comb, snapped in two.

Hearing the fragmented songs of drunken revellers coming in her direction, Tegen shut the door and slipped back into the night.

A sinking feeling told her whatever Admidios was up to had already begun! If only she could find somewhere to get away from him so she could think! Forgetting about the protective spell, she dived between the kitchen and the longhouse, slap into an angry cook, who pushed her aside. 'None of you lot belong in here tonight, lady. We got far too much work to do. Now, if you don't mind . . .'

'I've come to lend a hand,' she said, rolling up her sleeves. 'Shall I do some washing up?'

The cook shrugged and let Tegen pass. She picked up a small bundle of birch twigs and began to scrub at greasy bowls piled in a large wooden tub of cool water. The busy kitchen workers ignored her until a slim figure carrying a steaming bucket staggered in her direction. 'Out the way, miss. Hot!' And he began to pour.

Tegen looked up. 'Thank you, Kieran.'

The boy put the bucket down and looked at her. 'Listen . . . my aunt sold your mate to that Roman-looking bloke. She told where he was. That weren't right. I'm going to make it up to that cripple one day. Honest I am.'

33. Leeches

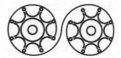

Later that night Tegen slipped away to the longhouse, where Cluan was still singing. Admidios was nowhere within sight. She poured herself a beaker of ale and sat well away from the central hearth. She dared not look into the flames although they called to her with all their magical potency. Fire made shadows, and that was Admidios's world. The evening was chilly and Tegen went to fetch her cloak rather than move nearer the summoning warmth.

When Cluan finished, a noisy game started up at the far end of the main table. Howls of laughter and the sight of Owein being clapped on the back made her curious. She went to sit where she could watch. A servant brought round a jug and refilled everyone's cups and horns. The ale began to warm Tegen's spirits and she found herself laughing. A small pile of silver and bronze coins by Owein's elbow showed he was winning hand over fist.

Tegen leaned forward and watched Owein throwing a white stone high in the air and scooping up handfuls of hares' knuckle bones before he caught it. The gaming pieces went around once more and Owein won again. A flagon of mead followed the ale, and the evening disintegrated into drunken sing-songs. Tegen threw off her cloak and began to dance. The crowd pulled back, clapping and stamping in time to the rhythm as her dance became wilder.

Eventually she flopped down on a bench and swigged at the nearest beaker. The alcohol warmed her head and she smiled when an ovate of her own age came and sat next to her.

'You are a wonderful dancer! I bet you're thirsty.' He laughed and filled up her beaker again. She guzzled the mead and wiped her mouth on her sleeve. The boy leaned across. 'My name's Angor, and I know an excellent game that will earn you a prize you'd like.'

Tegen tried to look at him, but he was swimming in and out of focus. She hiccoughed. 'I'm no good at knuckle bones.'

The boy put a small earthenware pot on the table. 'In here is something that will cure any illness in the world. Do you want it?'

Tegen eased herself upright. 'Depends what it is.'

'I'm not going to tell you. You must win first.'

'What's the game?' she picked up the mead jar and gulped down all that remained.

'Riddles.' The boy laughed again. 'I'll start, best of three. What goes out on a man's arm in the morning brightly painted, and comes back in the evening broken and smothered in blood?'

Tegen didn't hesitate – that was an old one. 'A shield!'

'Excellent, now it's your turn!'

She peered into the empty jug and said, 'Who goes to bed full of life and gets up needing a long sleep?'

'A drunk!' He slapped the table. 'One all! Now, if you get this the prize is yours. What is a road for birds, life for humans and death for fishes?'

'Air,' Tegen replied, amazed that she could make the drunken fuddle of her brain work at all.

'Well done! You win!' Angor put the cool, damp pot in her hands. She lifted the lid and peered inside. Something dark and glistening was wriggling around. She tipped it out on to the table and it split into a tangle of fat, black leeches, stretching, pulling and writhing in a dribble of muddy water.

'Ugh! Help!' Tegen yelped, jumping back and rocking the bench.

The drinkers at the other end of the table came crowding around. 'What you got there, Tegen?'

'Angor, this is one of your awful jokes!'

'What's that for?'

'Yuck! Squash them someone!'

Tegen stared down at her prize in horror. Suddenly she felt much more sober.

The young man sprawled across the table and grinned up at her. 'I told you, they heal everything! Don't you like 'em? I caught them myself this afternoon. After what old Twm was saying, I thought you'd be pleased – you being such a great healer and all.' He drank from his beaker, burped and winked. 'Just what you need. Trust old Angor – I won't let you down!'

'Who's Twm? What did he say?' Tegen asked.

Owein joined in. 'He's the old doctor who's almost bent double.'

'The one who looks as if he's lost a gold stater and can't find it!' someone shouted.

'That's him!' Owein laughed. 'He tried to teach me medicine when I lived in Siluria.'

'Well,' Angor went on, 'Twm says you can cure every-thing with these beauties!'

Tegen felt her stomach churn. 'Do you have to swallow them whole or chew them up?'

'Neither,' Angor replied. 'Twm reckons that illness is caused by poisonous spirits in the blood.'

'That goes without saying,' one or two voices agreed.

'So if the doctor puts leeches on to the patient, they suck the blood and that draws out the evil spirits as well, so the sick person gets better!'

'Oh, do change the subject,' Owein begged. 'You are making me feel ill!'

Angor yelled for more ale.

Tegen was beginning to feel queasy, but wasn't sure if it was the thought of leeches or too much drink. 'Where are you supposed to put them?'

'Near the part of the body that is sick,' Angor replied.

'Does that mean you have to put them on your bum if you have the runs?' a girl asked, wide-eyed in delighted horror.

Tegen ignored her. 'What did the other druids say? Did they agree with Twm?' she asked.

''Course they do!' Angor stood up and swayed a little. 'Give me the jar back when you are done. The potter loaned it to me.'

Tegen began to turn an idea over in her rapidly clearing mind. Tentatively she picked up the leeches and put them back in their prison. Surprisingly, they were bristly rather than slimy. She counted nine. One for each of the stars in the Watching Woman, the Goddess's constellation.

Next day the rain had started again, the fair was awash with mud and only the food stalls bothered to open. The Catuvellauni begged the use of Connal's great longhouse for their tax collection that afternoon. The druids, not enjoying getting wet, had agreed and were busy decorating the hall with greenery to ensure the correct spirits attended.

Tegen's head pounded with a hangover as she struggled to fix an oak bough to a beam. 'What do you think your foster-father will say when I present him with leeches?' she asked as the branch almost fell on her head.

Owein shrugged. 'I don't know. I'm expected at the tax collecting again this afternoon. I'm praying I won't be expected to sit on the Catuvellauni throne and receive everything. I can't face that. I'm *not* their king and never will be, but there is still no word of Sabrina.'

Tegen picked up a tendril of bryony and tossed it over the oak bough. 'Your foster-father wants me to help him, but there's no cure for grief and exhaustion.' Tegen chose a piece of holly to hang alongside the oak. 'Why doesn't Eiser send for Twm, as he is such a wise doctor?'

Owein sighed. 'Because Twm would want to wait until the skies cleared to chart the stars, then he'd consider how Eiser's stools rotted for a quarter of a moon . . .'

Tegen smothered a laugh as a slave approached. 'King Eiser is asking for you, lady.'

'I'm ready,' she said, picking up the pot of leeches. Then she looked Owein in the eye. 'Do you think these are safe? If your foster-father really *is* ill, will they save him? Or is he fated to die anyway?'

Owein drew Tegen aside and whispered, 'Eiser has lost heart and hope. Anything is worth trying, especially as

Admidios has taken no part in this. I was there when Twm was talking last night. What Angor said was true. May the Goddess guide your hand . . . and those *disgusting* creatures!'

Tegen found the King pacing to and fro in his hut, chewing his nails. 'Tegen, good to see you. Spread your cloak to dry. I have been thinking about your vision. That blackness that would comfort me . . . do you think it might be Sabrina? If only she would marry well and have children – not that she isn't a good warrior herself, but we need sons of our blood, giving rebirth to the ancient heroes we have lost, don't you think so?' He smiled, but gave Tegen no chance to reply.

'It's just that she has such wonderful hair, you know. I hoped it might have been this you saw in your trance . . .'

Tegen pulled up a stool, sat with her face away from the fire and closed her eyes, trying to recapture what she had seen the previous day. There were two darknesses in the vision in her head. One had frightened her, but the other had been strong and wild.

'Yes,' she said at last, when she could get a word in edgeways, 'it could be Sabrina's hair I saw. But—'

The King did not allow her to finish. He pulled a fine, looped plait from his pouch and stroked it. 'Oh, I am so relieved. I haven't felt at all hopeful lately, you know . . . She's all I have left in the world.' Then he noticed Tegen's jar. 'What's in there?'

She handed it to him. He lifted the lid and recoiled.

'Twm the healer thinks these can suck out the poisonous spirits that make people ill.'

Eiser sat on the edge of his bed. 'Yes, I've heard that too. Put them on to me. Let them feed on the spirits of despair that are sapping my strength. I need to keep on with this fight, at least until Sabrina returns.' He lowered his voice. 'Although I have nothing left to fight *with*. I fear we have already lost our country to these Roman infidels. In time our Goddess will be forgotten and our people will be enslaved. To think that I supported the Romans once, believing that they would bring peace between our ever-warring tribes.' He sighed. 'I was wrong. True, they have tried to unite us, but the price was slavery and the loss of our ways.'

Eiser laid back, his greying hair spread on the rolled pillows. He swung his legs on to the blankets and loosened the ties of his shirt. 'I don't know where the destroying spirits hide –' he put his hand on his sternum – 'but I ache in here.'

Tegen winced as she picked up the first leech. The bristly creature squirmed as she dropped it amongst the curly hairs of Eiser's chest. It wriggled around, stretching and contracting, then slipped and fell inside his shirt. The King jumped, groped around and retrieved the creature. 'You will need to prick my skin, maybe, to remind this little fellow what he is supposed to be doing.' Eiser pulled his knife from its sheath and passed it handle-first to Tegen.

She stared at it in horror. 'I can't . . . *cut* you . . . !'

He smiled. 'You don't need to stab me. Just make me bleed a little.'

Tegen took a deep breath and made nine small pricks in the pattern of the Watching Woman across the King's belly and ribs. Then, one by one, she laid the leeches to the swelling red-purple drops. At the taste of blood, they attached themselves and began to feed.

34. Writing in Blood

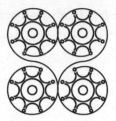

Tegen was surprised when Angor came to the King's door and offered to take the leeches away, but she was glad not to have to do it herself. 'The potter wants his jar back,' he said. 'I think his woman is pickling eggs.'

Tegen's stomach churned at the thought of leech-flavoured eggs, but she handed the pot over.

A few moments later, Angor was at Admidios's lodging. As the Shadow Walker was neither significant royalty nor a druid, he had been given sleeping space in a tiny oblong wattle-and-daub hut. There was just enough room for a bed and a table. Under the thatched eaves swung a large wicker cage that housed a malicious-looking raven.

The young man was given a silver piece. Then he left, glad to be out of the sight of the bird. It stared after him with hungry eyes.

Admidios stood by the door and considered the leeches. A slow smile spread across his clean-shaven face.

Krake also eyed the freshly gorged creatures and screeched. Admidios kicked the cage and his familiar fluttered and almost fell from her perch. 'You'll get fed if there's anything left,' Admidios snapped. Then he put the bird and her cage in the rain so he could work in peace. He had ready a marble pestle and mortar. Into this he placed two of the fattest leeches. Licking his lips he raised the pestle and smashed it down hard, forcing blood to squirt from each end of the twitching corpses. One by one he added them all, pounded them into a bleeding, black, messy paste, then drained the blood into another bowl. He took the remains outside and held it above Krake's cage.

'Open!' he demanded. The bird jumped to a higher perch and stretched her beak wide as Admidios rolled the biggest pieces into a ball. 'Swallow with hate, my pretty!' he said softly. 'May it churn in your gut so you learn to loathe Eiser as much as I do.'

Admidios pushed the food down inside Krake's throat, allowing the bird to hang on to his finger with bloody delight. Then he shook her off, sending her sprawling, and went back inside.

Taking a quill pen cut from one of Krake's tail feathers, Admidios dipped the nib in the blood and began to write on a tiny piece of parchment. At last he sat back on his bed and knitted his fingers over his belly.

When the writing was dry, Admidios rolled it tightly, then curled bulrush leaves around it and hid it under his pillow. 'Time to go, I think,' he said. He tied on his Roman boots, changed his blood-spattered shirt for a clean one and set off down the hill with Krake on his shoulder.

It took Admidios longer than he had hoped to find the salt traders. He trudged round and round the waterlogged meadow until he had almost convinced himself that finding Kieran's family was a pointless quest. The perpetual splash of the rain was a nightmare as he slopped through the quagmire between the muddle of carts and wagons, booths and shelters. Carefully he searched through the discarded refuse until he stood by a sagging oiled-linen tent tied against the side of a cart.

Inside, Caja was sulking. She had always despised Kieran, but she missed his usefulness. They had done well at the fair – they would return to their village wealthy – but she would have to pay for help in future. Caja was kicking herself for not handing over the silver pieces due to the King. Eiser had not asked overmuch for his warriors' protection – but she had tried to be too clever.

Wynne sat in poisonous silence, hating her sister.

Caja threw her a spindle and wool. 'At least get some

work done while you are blaming me for what I couldn't help!' she snapped. 'You're worse than useless!'

Admidios smiled when he heard Caja's searing tones. He stood next to the tent and coughed politely. 'Madam,' he said, 'are you the salt trader whose dear boy was so unjustly *taken*?'

Caja flung back the linen flap and glared up at the visitor. Her face was hot and red, her hair like a bramble thicket. 'Who the blazes are you?' She looked him up and down and curled her lip.

He bowed. 'I am Admidios, druid – er, *chief* druid of the Catuvellauni. I saw the *miscarriage of justice* you all suffered at the hands of King Eiser. I was horrified, mortified, *disgusted.*' He wrung his hands.

Caja, sensing she might have an ally, began to dab at her eyes. 'Indeed, sir, they have my precious little nephew, scarcely out of his cradle, not knowing anything about the world, and the poor little mite is fatherless, so he needs his Mam more than most. We're fretting for him – look at us, it's like a funeral in here, sir,' she whined.

Admidios lowered his head to peer at the squalid, sour mess inside the tent. At the back, a pale woman stared at him from dark-rimmed eyes. Between them lay a tangle of half-spun wool trailed in a mess of muddy sheepskins.

Admidios squatted down and hoped he looked concerned.

'Ladies –' he bowed his head slightly – 'unfortunately at

the time of the tax collection I was powerless to help as I am not of your tribe so my words held no sway in King Eiser's ears. However . . .' he tried to shift to avoid the rain that was pouring from the tent and cascading down the back of his neck, 'I have tried *diligently* to find your dear family since that day. At first I simply wanted to offer money and any other assistance I could to ease your plight. *I* could see you weren't lying about your circumstances. You have been tortured with suffering . . .'

Caja's ears pricked at the mention of money. 'Oh, it is true,' she whispered plaintively.

He went on. 'But I have since learned that things are worse than even I had guessed. The cruel king is so incensed at your inability to pay taxes this year that he has ordered his ruffians to come and arrest you two as well.'

Even Caja was shocked at this news.

'No! He wouldn't!' Wynne leaned forward, ashen-faced.

'I'm afraid he would.' Admidios shook his head.

'You cheating bitch!' Wynne screamed, thumping her sister on the chin. 'We'll all end up as slaves now, and it's all your fault!' Blood seeped from a cut lip as Caja picked up a cooking pot and flung it as hard as she could at Wynne's head, spilling cold stew everywhere.

This was not the response Admidios wanted. 'Please, please, calm yourselves. I have managed to bring your boy into the care of my own household to protect him from the worst evils of slavery. Furthermore, I have managed to distract the King's men with a little misleading information and a few coins. I think I can steer them awry long enough for you to get away. Believe me, it is your only chance. Pack and go *now*, before you all are captured and made slaves by this wicked tyrant!' With that he looked nervously over his shoulder and said, 'I must go. Hurry. Save yourselves!'

Then he strode away between the carts, tents and benders, smiling as he stroked Krake's breast feathers with a forefinger.

Within moments Wynne had folded the sodden tent and Caja had checked that all their money was safely hidden in secret places.

When everything was ready Wynne hitched the horses to the cart and, with much swearing, kicking and hauling, she coaxed them out of the mud-soup field and on to the road. As Sinodun faded from view in the veil of mist and rain, Caja took a goose bone and spat on it. 'Eiser, so-called King of the Dobunni, my curse stays with you as I go.' And with that she snapped it in two, tossed it aside and the iron-shod wheels crushed it into the road.

At his lodgings within the palisade, Admidios put Krake in her cage. 'I'll soon be out of this hovel!' he promised. 'By Samhain I'll be living like a Roman governor.'

From one of his panniers he drew a small silk-wrapped parcel. Inside was a human finger bone. Twisted around its pale shank were a few black and grey hairs from Eiser's comb, sealed in place with wax. He retrieved the bulrush-wrapped scroll from under his pillow. 'Now,' he whispered, 'something to tie these securely . . .' He cursed as he tugged threads from the edge of his cloak but they broke. 'This will never be strong enough. Nothing must drop off, or it won't work!'

Rummaging around, he found his Roman toga. Drawing his knife, he hacked a thin strip from the edge of the white wool. He tugged it between his hands. Much better – it was properly made.

Once he had tied the bone, the hair and the scroll together, he dripped some of the remaining blood over the bundle and pushed it through the wicker bars to Krake. She began to nibble at the bloodied knuckle.

'Don't eat it, *use* it!' he hissed. 'Now, show me how well you learned your lessons.' Admidios lay on his bed, and as he did so Krake remembered her cue and repeated the words he had taught her so carefully.

'Excellent,' Admidios said and rewarded her with a fresh shrew. 'When this is over, I promise you will have the King's eyeballs as a treat.'

But it was not *Eiser's* eyeballs Krake was considering as her black tongue flickered inside her beak.

*

Admidios's next visit was to Eiser's roundhouse. There were no guards outside, as the King had gone to watch the collection of taxes in the hall, so Admidios, who could be patient when it suited him, reclined on the King's bed and waited.

He woke at the sound of Eiser's voice talking to Dallel. The old druid was the last person Admidios wanted to see. Twm was a fool and could be manipulated, but Dallel was different.

For a moment he felt nervous.

But the King entered alone. He looked startled to see his visitor, but calmly poured himself a cup of wine. He swirled the drink and smelled the rich red liquor. 'I suppose it isn't poisoned?'

Admidios laughed. 'No. I'll drink some myself if it makes you feel more comfortable.' He reached out his hand for the cup.

Eiser ignored the gesture. 'What do you want? Owein is no longer under my care or control.'

'I noticed.' Admidios took another cup and poured a drink, then made himself comfortable again on the bed. 'Your health, sir. Things might have gone more easily for you if you'd kept the boy by your side.'

'And just what do you mean by that?' Eiser demanded, his thick moustache twitching with annoyance.

'I mean, dear friend, that you could have legally kept the money you have been embezzling slowly over the years as your fee for caring for the boy. You needn't have found the Romans to be bad masters; you could have become king of a whole province, not just your own lands. You would be strong and rich, with all your sons still standing proudly by your side. You could have married Sabrina to a fine man . . .'

'She and Owein aren't suited – even I can see that!' Eiser snapped, refilling his cup.

'I was thinking of myself actually . . .' Admidios said demurely, examining his fingernails. 'Our families have always been . . . close.'

Eiser went quite white. 'I will pretend I didn't hear you say that,' he said quietly.

'Which bit?' Admidios sneered, refilling his own cup.

'All of it,' the King replied, slapping the table. 'Now leave!'

Admidios drained his wine and gave a mock bow. 'Very well, I am going . . . but I had hoped to ask a favour.'

'I said, *GET OUT!*' Eiser roared.

'Please . . .' Admidios raised his hands, 'just listen. You *owe* me a favour – several in fact – if you don't want everyone to know how you betrayed *Britain*!'

Eiser flung his wine in Admidios's face. '*You* betrayed Britain!'

'Have it your own way,' he replied, calmly wiping the mess with his sleeve. 'But before you call your guards and have me roasted for Samhain, just listen, *please*.'

Eiser narrowed his eyes as he leaned against a roof support. 'If I hear you out, will you go?'

'Immediately, I promise. It's two very simple things – firstly, I have no servants here. I want to buy the new slave-boy. I'll give you half an amphora of wine for him. I know slaves are usually a whole amphora, but he is rather young and scrawny, so I think this is a fair price.'

Eiser sighed. 'Very well, and the second thing?'

'Also very simple. I need you to look after my raven.'

'*What?*' Eiser could scarcely believe his ears. 'I am a king in a time of war – I have a people to lead!'

Admidios walked towards the open door and looked out. The rain had stopped, leaving the mud a warm brown colour. A remnant of a rainbow painted the eastern sky. 'I must go away for a few days, to make sacrifices at an ancient shrine not far from here. I want to pray that we will have peace at last.'

Eiser folded his arms and looked at Admidios suspiciously. 'I don't believe you.'

'I swear it.'

'So let your new slave care for your bloody bird!'

Admidios spoke slowly and carefully. 'If you don't do it, I will tell the druids about why you threw poor little Owein Sextus out with only that fat pony and the shirt on his back. No one believes your tale he went to study druidry willingly . . . They would like to know what happened to all the gold and silver that was supposed to pay for setting him up

☀ 277 ☀

as a British king . . . I am sure the bards will make a very pretty song out of that tale. On top of that, the Romans have a very good court system – one that you might be finding out about, if you aren't *very* careful . . . So why don't you just take my bird for one, two days at the most?'

Eiser reached for the dagger at his belt, his cheeks flushed. 'I have done nothing to be ashamed of. You don't *know* the real reason I sent Owein away . . . and that money was put to good use with Owein's consent. It paid warriors to get rid of the Romans from the sacred lands of the Dobunni.'

'But it didn't work, did it?' Admidios sneered, his words snaking venomously. 'How many sons did you lose in that campaign? As you know, I can be *very* persuasive. Whether I tell the druids or the Romans or both, it will make no odds. No one will believe you.' Admidios raised an eyebrow.

Eiser strode backwards and forwards for a few moments. 'Very well,' he said. 'I will look after your bird. What does it eat?'

'Flesh,' Admidios replied, sauntering out the door.

35. A Distant Scream

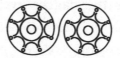

When Admidios left just after dawn, he woke the entire stronghold with his shouts and demands. As the sun rose, he rode out of the main gate driving a borrowed cart. Kieran dragged miserably behind with his head down. In the back lay a trussed-up calf, moaning for its mother. 'A sacrifice!' Admidios had said, 'to persuade the Goddess to bring us all peace!'

And peace they had, once he was gone. Tegen and Owein watched the cart disappear between the trees on the south road. 'Let's go and make our own sacrifice to the Lady.' Owein grinned. 'I will buy us a horn of cider each as a thank-offering for getting rid of him!'

'How long is he away for?' Tegen asked, shielding her eyes from the early-morning light.

'Forever, I hope! Eiser says he is going to some ancient shrine or other in the hills. Personally I suspect he is sloping off for a good soak in a Roman bath. I can't say I blame him – that's one of the few things I would make compulsory if I was king!'

In the meadows below Sinodun the hot sun was drying the churned mud. With the tax gathering over for another year, the day was devoted to the more interesting task of young, would-be warriors proving their worth with sword-play and spear-throwing contests. They were keenly watched by chieftains searching for the best recruits for their war-bands.

As evening approached, a few soldiers from the garrison across the river strayed into the fair. No one took any notice until they stopped to watch the sword fighting. The crowds parted; the shouting and betting fell silent. Then, after a few moments, a badly scarred warrior stripped off his shirt and leaped towards the soldiers. 'Come on!' he yelled. 'Let's show them how good we are, give them something to make them run away with their tails between their legs!' With a blood-curdling cry, he grabbed a sword from a contestant and gave chase. The soldiers ran like frightened goats all the way back to the river and their boat.

Tegen laughed, but Owein couldn't help frowning. 'This could get nasty. I don't want to get caught up in a fight – let's get back.' Reluctantly Tegen followed. She had never seen a real skirmish before and she wanted to watch.

As they entered the stronghold, they saw Eiser sitting on a bench by the longhouse doorway. He held a large horn of ale and was chewing at a lump of cheese. When he saw the visitors Eiser moved up so they could join him. 'I am going to have an early night. Owein, I trust you will be at the court hearings tomorrow? You know how tedious I find the people's whinging about injustices I've had nothing to do with.' He paused. 'I would be grateful if you would forgive the past and stand once more at my side.' He smiled. 'I don't know if you ever knew the real reason I sent you to Siluria. It was to free you from Admidios. That insidious voice of his drains everyone of their will and strength. He was using you for his own ends. I ordered assassins after him, but he had very powerful magic and they all perished or went mad.'

Owein stared at the ground. 'I thought you despised me because of my leg – because I couldn't rule or marry Sabrina . . .'

'I was disappointed, but I never hated you. I couldn't explain at the time. Admidios had too many friends. It was easier to make everyone – even you – think I had sent you away. I am truly sorry if I hurt you.'

Owein gripped his foster-father's hand and wrapped him in a bear hug. After a few moments Eiser turned and walked back to his roundhouse, his head bowed.

Tegen saw tears in Owein's eyes and pretended to retie her shoe. 'It's time for the evening rites.' She looked towards the sacred hill. 'I can see the others are almost at the top.'

Owein nodded, climbed on to Heather's stout back and guided her head to the northern gate.

Krake was sulking. She hated being caged. She didn't like this stranger pushing lumps of raw meat through the bars at her. She wanted to pluck out his eyes. She had been *promised* them . . .

Eiser put his face near to hers. 'Who's a pretty boy then? Do you talk? Hey?'

Krake longed to rip strips of flesh from his pale cheeks. But she was not allowed. She couldn't even pluck the thick moustaches that bristled so temptingly between the bars. She knew the emptiness would swallow and devour her if she disobeyed what her master commanded.

The emptiness had been getting closer lately.

She considered biting at the thick pink worm-shapes that offered her food. She snapped her beak at him. Why wasn't he a thin shadow like her master? This human was solid, but *hers* was insubstantial. She hated her human. She wanted *his* eyes most of all.

The bars of her cage were only made of wicker – she could break them so easily! She caught one in her beak and felt the ease with which it twisted. The human made more sounds. She guessed it meant he wanted her to stop doing that. Why should she care? She took a firmer grip and twisted again until one end cracked clean away from the bottom.

Cold fear crept and spiralled inside Krake's chest. The spirit inside her ached to leave her feathered prison, but she was trapped. It served only to increase her fear and hatred. She turned her bird shape so she needn't see the man. His thick black moustache waggled at her.

Krake preened herself. She didn't want to be here. She wanted to be in full, glorious flight, soaring in the warm air, delighting in tumbling and playing. But she was more than a bird and would never be free. The weight of the bitter soul trapped inside would always drag her back to earth – to servitude. And if she didn't obey, the emptiness was always just behind her, waiting to devour . . .

'Come on, bird, eat. That's best pork I have put in there – would you prefer it cooked? Is that it? Do you want your cage cleaned? You have all sorts of rubbish in there, old bones, bits of twig . . .' Eiser put his hand into the cage and reached to scoop up the scattered rubbish. Krake watched the five strong worms moving towards her master's treasures. She sprang forward and lowered her head, half spread her wings and bit.

Eiser jerked his hand back and sucked at the wound. 'Starve then, for all I care. I didn't want you here anyway.' Then he stormed out of the roundhouse and slammed the door.

That evening there was no fire on the hearth. Only a few

cracks of light filtered under the thatch and from a small, triangular wind-eye above the porch. Krake strode restlessly the five paces each way her prison allowed. The malicious spirit that inhabited her writhed and twisted. From amongst the twigs and rubbish at the bottom of the cage she picked up the bone. The bulrush leaves with their hidden scroll swung from the woollen strip. She gnawed at the bone, but it was too hard and dry. It tasted bitter. She dropped it and, lifting her tail, soiled it. She made a small jump to the perch above her head, closed her eyes and went to sleep.

It was almost dark when Tegen and Owein returned to eat in the longhouse. The place was packed with more druids and their followers arriving for the discussions.

Amongst the bustle, King Eiser stared at his untouched evening meal, then picked up a hard-boiled egg and left. An intense heaviness was hanging around his shoulders like a bearskin cloak. He went to his guest house, shut the door and peeled the egg. Breaking a piece of grey salt from a small slab on the top of one of his tax baskets, he ate his meagre supper.

As Owein went to bed he called out a goodnight through the roundhouse door, but there was no answer.

Tegen frowned. 'Should we see if he's all right?'

The guard stood to attention. 'He went straight to bed, sir and miss. You won't see him till morning.'

In the lonely, desolate hours of darkness, the emptiness consumed the raven at last.

The captive spirit screamed and screeched to leave the tormented little body. But no sound came from her open, gasping beak. She spread her wings and thrashed against the sides of her prison. The cage rocked and fell from the table where Admidios had left it. With a thud it landed on the bare earth floor. Incensed with terror and rage, Krake wrenched and tore at the withy bars with her beak and talons until she was free.

With a few swift strokes of her wings she flew to the little wind-eye in the thatch, where a faint hint of pre-dawn glimmered.

But thin horn strips had been nailed across the opening. Krake was still trapped, although the trap was bigger than before.

In despair she gripped a roof support and hung upside down, swinging back and forth, cursing with all her heart in words she did not understand.

As the dawn came, hunger knotted her stomach. She swooped down to feast on Eiser's eyes. She *had* been promised them . . . she *had* . . . but the emptiness forbade her. And it was *inside* her now. She gripped the wooden rail at the end of the bed and dared not move for terror.

But the night had given her joy too. The first she had really known in this miserable life.

The following day dawned pale gold with a light breeze. Tegen skipped up the sacred hill like a child. On mornings like these she couldn't wait to greet the spirits. Thank you, she called out inside her head. Thank you for helping us to live in such a wonderful world! The air was fresh and smelled clean, the birds were singing and she wanted to dance forever. Any day now she would be going to Mona to fulfil her destiny. She looked up at the rich viridian canopy of the oak grove above her head as the spirits of the West were offered fresh spring water. The world is so rich and good, she thought. The Romans are a mistake, something that will go away in time . . .

Lost in her own thoughts, she took her place in the circle of druids and had to be nudged by Owein to repeat her words of honour to the North.

> *Greetings, spirits of the North,*
> *who give rest and peace to our departed.*
> *In the still coolness of your hidden womb*
> *the earth – the seat of life and rebirth . . .*

But she managed no more, for a distant scream made her pause.

'*We offer you . . .*' She tried to go on, but then came more screams and a high-pitched ululation followed by the clattering howl of a carnyx. As one the druids turned towards the stronghold on its companion hill.

'Go and see what is wrong,' Dallel ordered a young ovate, who immediately hitched up his green robes and ran.

Hurriedly Dallel said a short prayer, begging the Goddess for her help, then he ended the ritual and closed the circle. 'Go, but be careful. If it is the Romans, don't let yourselves be seen. Flee immediately to Mona. We will meet there. Farewell, all of you.' And he raised his staff in blessing.

Tegen's heart flipped at the thought of going to the druids' island so suddenly, but first she had to know what was going on. She caught up her skirt and sprinted down the slope and up the other side to the stronghold. Puffing and panting, she fought the crowds to get to Connal's longhouse. But the commotion was not there; it was to her right.

Outside Eiser's lodgings.

Two whey-faced guards stood with their spears crossed, blocking the doorway. 'Let me in,' Tegen said. 'I'm his healer!'

'Can't, miss, due respect and all. But it's Lord Connal's orders. Until the chief druid Dallel of the White Horse gets here, no one can go in.'

'But *why?*' Tegen demanded. 'What's wrong?'

The guards exchanged glances. 'Didn't you hear?' the second one said in hushed tones. 'It's the Dobunni king, Chieftain Eiser of the Rearing River . . . He's dead.'

36. Sweating the Truth

Owein tethered his pony and pushed his way through the crowd, knocking his crutch against people's ankles to clear his path.

'Let me through!' he demanded. 'Is it true? My foster-father is dead? What happened? I must be allowed to see him.'

But the soldiers were adamant. No one was allowed through, and no further questions were being answered. The two men remained silent and grim-faced. Owein thumped his crutch on the ground in frustration. Then, elbowing his way through the crowds, he strode into the longhouse yelling for strong ale with no water in it.

Dallel arrived before Owein had finished his drink. The old man's bald head was red from exertion. 'My son,' he said, holding his arms out, 'my condolences to you. May your foster-father be born again soon.' The druid glanced at Owein's shrivelled leg. 'Did he . . . er . . . name an heir?'

'Sabrina, his daughter, will become chieftain of his tribe.'

'Will you marry her, as was promised so long ago?'

Owein laughed cynically and drained his cup. 'What use is a lame lawyer to a warrior queen?' Then he paused. 'Sabrina went to the land of the Brigantes half a moon ago. Nothing has been heard of her since.'

The old man scooped ashes from the hearth and rubbed them on to his pate. 'Then if you are not his son in blood or marriage, we must wait for your foster-sister to return and announce who the murderer is.'

'Murderer?' Owein's cup smashed on the ground.

Dallel ordered his hands. 'Well, he wasn't well, but he wasn't deathly sick, was he? Everyone knows it wasn't his time to die. Cluan himself prophesied: "And you, Eiser, will soon lie cold, your breath cut short. You will die from a blow from no man's hand . . ." If it wasn't sickness, it was murder. By a woman.'

Owein shivered. 'May I see him?'

The old man nodded and led the way. The silent crowds parted. The soldiers drew back their spears and allowed Dallel and Owein to enter, followed by several of the senior druids. A screech made everyone look up. Krake was swinging upside-down from the rafters and flapping randomly, as if she had forgotten how to fly. 'Get that bird out of here!' Dallel ordered. 'And get a servant to clear up that filthy old cage. Look at it – full of twigs and bones. It is an insult to a great man's memory.' The old druid sat on Eiser's bed and began to straighten the corpse that lay twisted, eyes and mouth wide, as if he had tried to scream. In his hand was a half-eaten egg and a few grains of salt.

Owein touched Dallel on the arm. 'Sir, if I may?'

The old man raised an eyebrow. 'What?'

'Shouldn't we examine everything before we tidy up, in case there are any clues as to who did this?'

'Nonsense!' Dallel snapped. 'There isn't anything here that the spirits can't make plain through divination. It is visions and omens we need now, not rubbish in a corner.'

Just then a slave entered and stood waiting for her orders. Dallel pointed to the cage. 'Toss that on the midden. Then return with a besom,' he added. The woman obeyed.

Owein was about to object, but the old man was already intoning the prayer for Eiser's soul to be given safe passage to the Otherworld of Tir na nÓg. Owein watched the slave and wondered how he could hint to her not to throw the cage away. But she was busy with her back to him; she would never see his signals. He would have to catch her later and find out what she had done with it.

While Dallel prayed, Owein drew his knife and shaved the front part of his hair in mourning. Then he surveyed the room to gather as much information as he could before any more clues were destroyed. Eiser's body had no marks, no sword or knife wounds apart from the tiny bloodied points where Tegen had put leeches – and there was a V-shaped cut on one finger that looked like a peck from Krake. The egg he was holding smelled fresh. There was nothing that would have killed him.

In death, Eiser looked terrified, with a blueness around the mouth, lips and hands. But there were no signs of a struggle, no wounds on his forearms from fending off an attacker. His bed was as neatly made as if he had only just lain down.

In the middle of the prayers, Twm bustled into the round-house followed by his apprentices. As the most senior doctor, it was his duty to examine the body and pronounce which spirit had killed the King. Twm whispered to his companions about the alignments of the planets and whether geese had been seen flying from west to east in the last day or so, and if so, how many.

The house was full of argument.

'I think the heavenly sign of the dragon has been a little weak in the last few nights, don't you?'

'He was born under Ceridwyn.'

'In that case, has he drunk mead from a silver vessel before noon?'

'I don't know . . .'

'Well, someone should have watched him to make sure he didn't.'

Owein rubbed the bristly hair on his shorn head in frustration. Despite the heat, the unfamiliar baldness made him feel chilly. He left the druids bickering and moved around Eiser's lodging as carefully as he could. How should he start looking if he didn't know what he needed to find? What did Cluan's prophecy mean? What was 'a blow from no man's hand'?

From high in the rafters, the forgotten raven swooped down, made a bid for the door, then screeched into the sky.

'There will be a meeting here of all druids and ovates – yes, and any bards who are training to be ovates,' Dallel added, catching sight of Tegen from the corner of his eye. 'I know it is hot, but you must wear your robes. Bring your wands, amulets, talismans and anything else that might help to find the perpetrator of this heinous crime. Return here by sun's mid-haven.'

Everyone erupted into argument once more as they drifted away to get ready.

'We should question the guards and ask what they saw,' Owein ventured.

'You can if you like,' Dallel answered, 'but I have told you already: there is nothing here that won't become plain with careful divination. Believe you me, I have heard men swear on their lives something was true – good men too. But in the end it turned out they were quite wrong. What you *think* you see isn't always what really happened. Only the spirits can be relied upon completely. Now, we have a great deal to do.' He beckoned to two of his elderly companions.

First Sean with the huge moustaches took the birch

broom and swept the stone hearth deosil – following the sun's path – then Danaan brought a silver bowl of fresh spring water and a branch of hyssop, which she used to sprinkle the floor, crooning a low chant as she worked.

Bronnen and Gwynedd washed the corpse and laid silver coins on the eyes, then tucked sprigs of yarrow and summer-solstice flower inside Eiser's robes to protect him.

By noon, the druids filed back bearing all their ritual paraphernalia. They brought gifts of eggs to signify rebirth for the dead king. Some laid honey or oatcakes by the body to feed his spirit on its long journey.

Two young bards carried oak and holly logs to the hearth, added dried grass and juniper for kindling, then struck flints until a flame burned brightly.

When as many as could be were crammed into the little roundhouse, the door was shut. It was immediately hot and unbreathably stuffy. Dallel stood by the hearth holding a branch decorated with tinkling silver bells. A white-robe with curly hair sprinkled vision-incense over the hearth edge as Cluan began a long song of mourning, extolling Eiser's virtues and bravery in battle.

Tegen chewed her nails as she sat at the back with the other bards. I'm sure Admidios is behind this, she thought, but I can't see *how*. I'm sure I could think clearly if I could dance in the open air . . .

But an adder couldn't have slithered between the packed, sweating bodies in that little space. Tegen's head began to swim. She longed for a drink, but she tried not to think about the heat and the thirst, or about the growing sense of panic and claustrophobia welling up inside her as the afternoon dragged on. The last time she had been with druids sweating into a trance was the night she was tested by floating Ogham to see whether she was, or was not, the Star Dancer.

But in the swimming haze of her consciousness, Tegen heard Twm's voice. 'Who was doctoring the King? Let that one speak.'

Owein called out, 'Tegen, that's you!'

Trying to get her balance, Tegen struggled to her feet. She swallowed hard. 'I gave the King some healing,' she said, trying to focus and stay upright at the same time. 'It was two days before he died.'

'What sort? Speak up, girl. I can't hear you!' demanded Twm from his chair in the corner.

Tegen looked around. The semi-darkness was punctuated with shafts of light from the tiny wind-eye and cracks in the thatch, but the air was chokingly thick and pungent. She took a breath. 'I danced for him, to help him know . . .' she swallowed and gasped for air, 'where he would find his hope.'

'Is that all?' Twm peered up at her from under his twisted back.

'Yesterday I gave him leeches as well, to try to purge his blood of the evil spirits of melancholy that had been plaguing him. You will see nine marks on his chest where I laid them.'

'Ah yes, good . . . very good!'

Tegen fell rather than sat down and closed her eyes as she fought giddiness. If only she could get outside for a short while.

The flames of the fire rose, making the room hotter and hotter. Tegen looked away, she dared not allow herself to see the shapes that hovered there! All around, murmurs rose to chanting, then to ecstatic cries and howling as one by one the druids slipped into trances.

Get me out, please get me out! Tegen prayed. Lady, I can't open my mind to you in here . . . I need your sky and stars . . .

She had a sudden rush of panic as she sensed an evil presence smothering the roundhouse.

Loud shouting and banging outside broke the mood. The doors were wrenched open, sunlight streamed in and fresh air swept inside.

A tall, heavy figure stood framed in the entrance. 'What in the name of all the gods is going on here?' Admidios roared.

37. Strange Words, Strange Theories

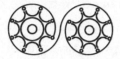

A little later, Owein brought Tegen a tisane of chamomile and honey as they sat on the grass beside the long-house. 'That'll help clear your head. Did the spirits speak to you?'

'No, it was too hot. I hate sweating rituals. Did you find any clues?'

'Not a chance. I am going to have a good look around now everyone's gone. There must be *some* sort of evidence. It's not that I don't trust the spirits, it's just that judgement ought to be based on tangible facts, not dreams made out of herbs and mushrooms.' He picked up his crutch and hobbled away.

Tegen gulped her drink. 'I'll join you when I'm finished.'

She found him face down under Eiser's bed, only the heels of his familiar, oddly sized boots sticking out.

'Have you found anything?' she asked.

He wriggled backwards and held out a large bone comb snapped in two. 'Only this.' The wide, carved spine clearly showed a muddy footprint.

'What do you want that for?'

'I'm not sure, but I'm going to keep it,' he replied, laying it carefully in a small basket by his side.

'But it's all dirty. Let me wash it at least!'

Owein spread his hands defensively. 'Don't touch it. Even the mud might be important. You never know!'

Tegen thought for a moment. 'I've seen that comb before – a couple of nights ago. I was worried about Eiser, so I came to put a protective spell on the roundhouse, although I never did it because I was distracted. Someone was leaving; there was lightning, but not enough to see who it was. I looked inside for your foster-father, but the place was empty, and that's when I saw the wet footsteps and that comb on the floor. It was broken and muddy then.'

'It's an unusual shoeprint – hobnailed. Where exactly were the footmarks?'

'They came and went from the door to over there, by the bed. Does that matter?'

'I have to notice *everything* and see what patterns emerge.'

'Like what?'

He clambered to his feet. 'So far, nothing. I've just been to the midden and looked at the birdcage. It was smashed and filled with twigs and mess. But I want to know why it was in here at all. I'm going to look for Admidios and ask him. It was his birdcage, and don't you think it was rather fishy him turning up like he did in the middle of the ritual? Coming?'

They found Admidios drinking ale in the longhouse. When Owein came in he rose to his feet, smiled and bowed. 'My Lord Sextus, or may I say *King* Sextus?'

'No, you may not!' Owein snapped, sitting opposite him. 'Now, I want a few straight answers from you, without any of that *voice* you use to persuade people. What was your raven's birdcage doing in Eiser's lodgings?'

Admidios merely raised an eyebrow. 'It's no secret. My *dear* friend Eiser knew I was going away for a few days to sacrifice to the Goddess and pray for peace. The King *insisted* that he look after my little pet raven. I told him I could get a servant to do it, but he wouldn't hear of it. He said he'd grown fond of the bird. To be honest I was rather pleased – I didn't want Krake distracting me.' He laughed. 'She can be a bit of a handful at times!'

'I don't believe you,' Owein said. 'Eiser could never be bothered with animals. He didn't even keep a dog.'

'Believe what you like,' Admidios replied. 'What interests me most is what you will be doing, now your poor foster-father is dead.'

Owein felt a familiar chill creep down his back. 'What do you mean?'

'I just wondered . . .' Admidios looked slyly across his ale pot, 'whether you had given any more thought to your true inheritance as king and governor of the southern tribes?' He smiled and opened his hands. 'I could heal your leg, you know, Sextus – the Dobunni would accept you as their lord without hesitation and the Catavellauni would be permitted to proclaim you as well. It could work out awfully well . . .'

For you maybe, Owein thought. 'I have told you before, I refuse to be your puppet, and will you stop calling me *Sextus!*'

His uncle's smile did not waver. He stood, bowed and said, 'Just as you wish, my lord. But if you don't take up the kingship, then with Sabrina still away, there might be a great deal of trouble brewing . . .'

He leaned forward on the table and glanced from Tegen to Owein. 'Listen, both of you, your options are running out. Unless Sabrina returns quickly to take up the leadership of the tribe, there will be a scramble for the crown between the high chiefs.

'Tegen, you call yourself the Star Dancer, yet you're unwilling or incapable of using your divining power so you will never discover in time where Sabrina is . . . and Owein, as you won't take up your legal kingship – not even to hold it for Sabrina until she returns – it looks like you are both choosing war.'

He lowered his voice and his eyes gleamed. 'Neither of

you is a fool. You know this won't simply be war between the tribes. I can keep the Roman invaders off your backs only for so long – unless, of course, you both choose to accept my help?'

He was met with a stony silence.

'I thought as much.' He nodded. 'Think about it. I understand the fears and inexperience of youth. My offer still stands. Good luck!' Then he sauntered out.

'What *is* he up to?' Tegen whispered.

Owein shrugged. 'Search me . . . but it's bound to be no good. Did you notice his smell?'

'His *smell*?'

'Yes,' Owein replied. 'He doesn't. His clothes are immaculately clean and he's just been shaved and had his hair cut. He has had a Roman bath. If he has been in the hills sacrificing, then I am a marsh toad. The cleaner he looks, the more convinced I am that he is neck deep in filth. He's behind Eiser's death, and I'm going to find out *how*.'

Admidios stood outside Dallel and Bronnen's roundhouse and considered its sagging thatch. He felt a surge of smug pleasure at the thought of the new villa he planned for himself just across the river. He knocked and entered. The old druid and his wife were seated on comfortable chairs either side of the hearth. Admidios was offered a little three-legged stool that he ignored.

'We are sorry we cannot provide more hospitality,' Bronnen said coolly. 'We are already accommodating three white-robes from the Silures, and today has been difficult. How may we be of service to you?'

Admidios made a show of looking around the house and out of the door. Then he stooped near to the old couple and said in a harsh whisper, 'I know who killed Eiser.'

Dallel frowned under his bristly white brows. 'Who?'

'Well,' Admidios began, sitting at last, 'do you remember the family of the boy who was enslaved in lieu of taxes?'

'The awful woman with the screeching voice?' Dallel asked. 'Why her?'

Admidios smiled smugly. 'Vengeance – for Eiser taking their child. You saw how upset they were at the time, and who can blame them? I bought the boy from Eiser and he is intelligent and hard-working. He must have been much loved . . .'

Neither of the druids spoke, so Admidios went on. 'Well, just to be certain – I am the last person to accuse people unjustly – I went down to the meadow to see what they had to say. I asked around, but *they have gone!* I was told they left very hurriedly last night, just after dark.'

'Nonsense!' Bronnen snapped. 'How could they have done it? The guards saw no one enter or leave Eiser's lodging. Furthermore, the spirits have not spoken about them.'

Admidios slapped his knees. 'Good points, my dear lady. I don't have the answer to either of those questions, but here we have two females with a strong motive. Remember the prophecy? If you ask Connal for warriors to give chase and bring the suspects back, we might begin to understand. It's up to you, but time is short, and the alliance is fragile.'

Dallel sighed. 'Very well,' he said. 'I will ask if a few men can be spared.'

38. A Sword, a Shield and a Funeral

They waited four days before laying the King on his funeral pyre, hoping that Sabrina would return to light the flames. But even the Old Ones sent to track her down could not discover her whereabouts. Despite the cooler breeze that marked the end of summer, Eiser's body had begun to swell and go blotchy. The moon was at its darkest, not an auspicious time for a funeral, but it could not be left any longer. His spirit was wandering homeless between the worlds.

At dawn on the day of the funeral Owein missed the morning rituals. Instead he rode Heather down to the river. In the grey half-light he could make out the Roman garrison with its stout jetty on the opposite bank. Two soldiers on sentry duty watched as Owein tethered his pony, then untied a willow-and-hide coracle from outside a ferryman's hut. He dragged it to the water, threw in two bundles and climbed in. He manoeuvred the little craft upstream until he disappeared around the bend. Once out of sight, he shipped his paddle and let the little boat twist and spin like a nutshell on the current, sweeping him back towards Dorcic.

Owein opened the first bundle and took out King Eiser's long sword just as the encampment came within sight on his left. He held it high so the soldiers could see the rising sun catch the gleaming bronze and scarlet enamelling on the sheath and hilt. Then he plunged it into the river on the Roman side. 'My foster-father's spirit will take this and protect the west for ever!' he shouted, shaking his fist.

The sentries exchanged glances, but seemed to think Owein was merely mad.

The river swept the little craft onward until the twin hills of Sinodun rose on his right. Owein unwrapped King Eiser's shield and laid it on the swirling brown waters. 'And with this he will defend us for eternity,' he yelled again. The heavy bronze central boss, patterned with running boars, dragged the shield down and out of sight.

Owein closed his eyes and spread his arms. 'Foster-father, guard us. Summon the spirits of our ancestors to make a spirit wall along this river. Defend your people in death as you did when you breathed, and I swear by my own life I will do all I can to bring peace.' With that he drew his dagger and pressed the point into his right palm, letting a few drops of blood drip into the water. 'I am one with the Land,' he said and sheathed his blade.

For a moment Owein permitted himself to cry. Then he grasped the paddle and worked hard to regain control, manoeuvring himself back upstream to return the coracle to its owner.

From above, the sound of a carnyx on the wooded hill told him that the morning ritual was over and that all were summoned to witness the passing of the King to Tir na nÓg.

A heavy golden torque lay around Eiser's neck, and his white hands gripped his dagger. His body was swathed in his seven-coloured cloak: the dark and light green stripes were crossed with bands of yellow, interwoven with blue, gold, red and black. Two huge bronze pins with blood-red enamelling clasped the folds together.

Owein leaned heavily on his crutch as looked at the bier laid atop the funeral pyre. 'The black is for the rocks of his home, the green is for the grass and trees, the blue is the great river that rears in spring and autumn, and the red, gold and yellow are for Bel the Sun God, who brings us life.'

Tegen stood silently by his side. She wanted to hold his hand to comfort him, but wasn't sure whether to or not. 'Will he be burned with his golden torque and his brooches?'

Owein pulled himself straight and stared, unfocused, at

Eiser's body. 'Of course. He must be dressed as a noble when he feasts in the Hall of the Blessed. More than that, his spirit must remember he is a king when he is reborn. It would not do for him to forget and come back as a slave ...' He leaned across the pyre and laid Eiser's treasured plait of Sabrina's hair on his chest. 'May her spirit comfort you on your way,' he whispered, 'and may my love and honour strengthen your soul through all your lives.' Then he bowed.

Tegen stepped back. Sending Eiser to Tir na nÓg was a sacred duty. Owein had to do it alone.

Chieftain Connal, lord of Sinodun, placed a wreath of yew leaves on Owein's partly shaved head and helped him pin a cloak in his foster-father's colours around his shoulders. Dallel handed him a tarry torch, which he laid to the kindling on all four sides of the pyre.

As he worked, Owein chanted a prayer:

May you be born again soon, Eiser,
High King of the Dobunni,
noble Lord of a thousand warriors,
none less than Chieftain in rank.

Father of Kings,
generous to heroes,
smiter of the damned,
I send you on your way.

May your next mother be a Queen of Queens,
your wife no less,
and may I be honoured to be your son again.

There was a long pause, then Owein bowed to the motion-less figure lying amongst the hungry gold and yellow flames.

Cluan began to sing a hymn to the Goddess and the other druids joined in.

Burning Eiser's body was a strange idea to Tegen, whose people always sent their dead to the inner caves below the hills so their spirits could go straight into the Otherworld through water. But, Owein explained, fire freed the spirit quickly from the body so it could fly away.

Perhaps different ways are right for different people, she mused, as holly logs spat and burned with a warrior's urgent passion. Silently Owein threw a yew bough across the body to guard his father's spirit-journey.

The sounds of wailing and keening drifted on a breeze already burdened with the stench of burning flesh.

The heavy smoke made Tegen cough. Once again, she dared not look into the flames in case she saw a Fire Dreamer's images and shapes . . . Admidios was nowhere to be seen, but she still dreaded his Shadow Magic. Instead she slipped away and found a place to sit in the shade of an oak, looking northward across the river to the Roman gar-rison that grew day by day on the opposite bank.

Later that night Tegen tossed and turned on her bed. Wolf was stretched out by her side, gnawing noisily at a bone.

The wake's singing and feasting was long over. Tegen grieved for Eiser and was worried about what Owein would do. Admidios's threats carried too much truth; war was close, but did they really need his powers to avoid it?

She was angry with herself for not protecting Eiser. A good man is dead, she thought. I don't deserve the title of Star Dancer! Lady Goddess, show me what to do, she prayed.

The answer came more quickly than she could have imagined. In the darkness, a pair of soft leather shoes shuffled between the makeshift beds and stopped. 'Tegen?' a voice whispered.

She raised her head. 'Dallel?'

The old man crouched by her side, his knees cracking as he moved. He grasped her hand with soft fingers. 'Please come. We need to talk to you.'

She pulled on an overdress and shoes, then followed the druid out of the hall and across the midnight compound until they reached the door of his home. Firelight and voices crept into the darkness from the crack between the doors as Dallel hesitated.

'Your old friend the druid Huval from the Winter Seas has arrived for our great assembly, which will start tomorrow. He tells me that if anyone can unravel the mystery of Eiser's death, it is you. Our divinations say the same. Eiser did not die naturally, of that we are certain, but we think his murder was political. Maybe someone didn't want him to attend our great discussions. Maybe his determination to fight the Romans was too powerful. The Lady has sent you to us for a purpose. Help us to divine what is going on. Eiser's warriors are baying for blood. They are blaming everyone within sight. There could even be war right here in Sinodun if justice is not seen to be done very quickly.' The old man gestured to the north. 'Only a few bowshots away the Romans are at our gates, waiting for us to turn against each other so they can walk in and take over. This is a time of deep shadows that must be held back. We need you, Star Dancer.'

Tegen suddenly felt very weary. She sighed. 'But I'm no good at anything like that. I failed Eiser. I'm thinking of going home.'

'*If you sow, you labour,*' said a second voice. 'That is the first law of being a bard. It brings responsibility – one you will never be free of, Tegen, Nessa's-child.'

Standing in the light of the doorway was Huval, firelight edging his thick beard and strong arms in red gold. He scooped Tegen up and gave her a warm hug.

She laughed and hugged him back. 'Huval, it's wonderful to see you!'

'Come inside,' he said. Then he filled her hands with a pot of honey sealed with wax and a twisted silver bracelet. 'These are from your parents. They send their best love. My apprentice is caring for your village until you return. The harvest is good and all is well.'

She slipped the bangle over her wrist and smiled at her father's love and craftsmanship. 'Are any of the other brothers from the Winter Seas here?' she asked as she licked honey from her fingers.

'Pwyll is staying with the bard Cluan, and Marc is going to try to come. But it is you who are the important one.' He took her hand and led her to a stool by the hearth. 'You were born to avert evil – I suspect you will die doing it.'

A lump caught in Tegen's throat. 'Won't there ever be peace for me? I long just to be an ordinary village druid...'

Huval smiled and shook his head. 'You will never be ordinary and these are uneasy times. The Lady sent stars at your birth to give us all hope. Now you must honour those stars as you did before. I cannot say whether this will be the last time or not. But we will all be with you to help, I promise.'

'But I am out of my depth. The King died...'

'That was prophesied. There was no escaping his fate,' Dallel put in curtly.

'You are the Star Dancer.' Huval caught her hand and squeezed it. 'That means you were given to serve the whole Land. The battle with the demon in the caves at home marked the first flowering of your power.'

'I understand,' she said quietly.

Dallel pulled his chair next to hers. His kind, wrinkled

face looked tired and his eyes were watery, with flecks of ash and soot caught around his lashes. 'Admidios has dreamed up some strange idea that the slave-boy's mother and aunt killed Eiser and he has demanded that warriors go and bring them back – apparently the women fled on the night of the murder. He reckons it was vengeance on the King for enslaving the boy.'

Tegen sucked her lips. 'Caja is a vicious woman, but I don't think she is capable of killing Eiser without a trace. Also, the boy is still here. If it was them, surely they would have taken him back.'

'I quite agree,' Dallel said. 'I pretended warriors had gone after the women to keep him quiet, but the spirits' wisdom and knowledge is all we can truly rely upon.'

'The Lady speaks to you as she speaks to no other.' Huval smiled.

Tegen rubbed her face to clear her head. 'You want me to try some divining?'

'Yes, with our help – if you want us,' Huval said.

'If I agree, can someone take me to Mona? What I want more than anything in the world is to go and be trained, to earn an ovate's robe, then to wear the white before my hair turns the same colour!'

'I promise,' Dallel said.

Tegen sighed. 'Very well. What do you want me to do?'

39. Through Fire to Tir na nÓg

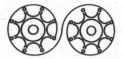

Dallel beckoned his listeners closer. His voice was scarcely above a whisper as he spoke: 'Nearly everyone feels certain that Admidios is at the bottom of the murder – even though he wasn't here when it happened. Yet Cluan's prophecy made it clear the perpetrator would not be a man . . . There are no women we really suspect, and Eiser was not seriously ill, so only the spirits can possibly know how it was done.'

Dallel poked at the hearth's dying embers with his staff, raising a few tiny flames. 'Do ever see images and patterns in the fire, Tegen?'

She held her breath. 'I . . . I don't like using fire for divining.'

Huval looked at her and she dropped her gaze. 'What happened? Do you want to talk about it?'

Tegen shook her head.

'When you were a child, I seem to remember you ran with the wind in your hair.' Huval smiled. 'You were a natural bard; air was always your medium. Now you are growing, you must not fear any of the elements. Fire is next. You must not let it better you. If you hesitate, it will destroy you.'

Tegen met his gaze, then took a deep breath and told them about the vision of the bone in the fire. 'Since then I'll have nothing to do with Admidios's magic,' she concluded. 'It is wrong.'

Huval thought for a short while. 'Have you ever met a smith,' he asked at last, 'by the name of Goban?'

Tegen sat up. 'Yes,' she said. 'He talked to me about fire once.'

'What did he tell you?' Huval asked.

Tegen allowed her gaze to rest on the red embers in the hearth. His words came back to her as clearly as if he had just spoken them:

'Iron is hard earth-blood. Fire plucks it from stone, and fire can send it back. If you ever need an answer, look for it in fire. Remember, fire protects from magic, but it also leads you into the deepest part of a mystery. Fire will lead you to your innermost soul and bring you out into the world again. Fire creates and destroys, cleanses and leaves soot. What you put into a furnace, and how long you leave it there, will determine what comes out: be it gold, charcoal or bone ash.'

Tegen hesitated, then concluded, '*But be careful – always use fire to drive shadows away, never to summon them.*'

She straightened her back and looked at Huval. 'I can see where I went wrong. Fire isn't Admidios's magic – he was using *my* Fire Dreaming for *his* ends, to summon shadows . . .' She stopped and looked across at Huval. 'How do you know Goban?'

Bronnen laughed and patted Tegen's knee. 'He comes to most of us eventually, when we need him. Now, which wood shall I put on the hearth for your visioning?'

Tegen took a deep breath and said, 'Holly.'

'A good choice,' Dallel replied. 'It is bright and gives clarity, and its Ogham name, *tinne*, also means fire itself. It speaks of a true direction – that's why our warriors love to use it for spear shafts.'

Bronnen bustled forward with a fine log and placed it carefully in the centre of the hearth, banking the crumbling red embers around it. 'Now, dear,' she said, 'let it catch, then you take your time. Don't let these men push you too fast. Just think about Eiser's death and take a good long look-see in the flames. When you are ready, you tell us what comes into your mind.'

Tegen nodded, pulled her stool closer to the hearth and raised her right hand towards the holly log. Immediately fire roared and licked around it, just as it had on the sacred hill.

Dallel and Bronnen almost fell off their chairs, but Huval

just smiled. 'I often wondered whether you would do that one day, Tegen. I only managed it once . . .'

She let the flames die back and settle to a normal blaze, hissing and spitting around the fresh log. Apart from the comforting song of the fire, all was silent. Tegen steadied her thoughts and watched, concentrating all the time on an image of Eiser lying dead. What killed him, Lady Goddess? she asked in her mind. What do we need to know?

She had no idea how long she sat gazing and praying, but she became fascinated by a long strip of bark that curled in the heat, twisting back on itself again and again.

At last Dallel could keep silent no longer. 'Well?' he whispered. 'Can you see anything, Tegen? Anything, at all? Tell us, even if it doesn't make sense, and we will help you interpret.'

Tegen shook her head. 'I see nothing, apart from a log burning.'

'Nothing?' Huval asked. 'Don't be frightened – even insignificant images might have deep meanings.'

Tegen laughed. 'All I can see is a funny piece of twisted bark making a black spiral path through the flames. But that's nothing. I'm sorry, I'll keep looking . . .'

Dallel held up his hand. 'No need, Tegen.' He exchanged glances with Huval.

Bronnen gasped, 'You can't! She's too young . . . That takes years of training . . .'

Tegen looked from one to the other. 'What are you talking about?'

'I have in mind,' the old druid replied carefully, 'that you should walk a fire spiral. What do you think, Tegen?'

She shrugged. 'What's a fire spiral?'

Bronnen wagged her finger at her man. 'I'm not letting you, Dallel – it's not safe!'

The old druid rolled his eyes. 'Keep out of this!'

Bronnen folded her arms across her ample chest and scowled.

Huval leaned towards Tegen. 'You know about following a spiral path to your innermost self?'

'Yes . . .'

'Well, in this ritual, the spiral is not metaphor; it is real. It is made of fire – just as Goban told you. As Eiser went to Tir na nÓg through the flames, you must go the same way and ask him how he died.'

The roundhouse fell silent.

'You . . . You want me to go to *Tir na nÓg* . . . through *fire* . . . ?' she whispered.

Bronnen took a deep breath to scold her man again, but Dallel glowered at her.

Huval raised his hand for peace. 'What happens is this: we lay a spiral out on the ground made out of wood shavings and chippings, then we build it up with branches and brushwood; finally we set fire to it. We'll leave a path wide enough for you to walk between the flames. The twist

☼ 317 ☼

unfolds widdershins – to the left – so as you walk it will be like drawing the sacred circle and breaking all the ties with everyday existence.

'Once you are in the centre, you will be separated from our world by several coils of fire. You will have stepped beyond your body and gone into your spiritual centre, like Goban said. You will be standing in Tir na nÓg. There you must meet with Eiser's spirit and ask him to tell us the truth.

'When he has spoken, you then walk out deosil, to the right hand, as if you were finishing a sacred circle, retying yourself to the threads of this world. We will be waiting for you at the entrance to the maze. Quite often the flames will have burned themselves out before the return journey so it is easier.'

He paused and looked hard at Tegen. 'Will you do it? Will you go through fire to Tir na nÓg for us?'

Even in the poor light, it was obvious her face was as pale as ash. 'It is not the fire that scares me; it is going right into Tir na nÓg. I have stood on the threshold in the funeral caves at home, and when I have slept in wight-barrows . . . But this is different. What if my spirit gets waylaid and cannot return?'

Huval leaned forward. 'Why should it?'

Tegen turned and looked at him with wide eyes. 'You weren't here, but Cluan the bard prophesied and the spirits possessed him. They almost took his soul. I helped him find his way back. What happens if the spirits remember me and are angry? What if they won't let me return and want to keep me in the Otherworld in exchange for Cluan?'

The older druids exchanged glances. 'We can't answer that,' Huval said.

'Furthermore,' Bronnen added, 'we cannot guarantee that Eiser will look like you remember him. He may take any form – or none – in the Otherworld.'

Tegen pushed her hair back and swallowed hard. 'So when will this fire spiral take place? Tonight?'

'No,' Dallel replied. 'Not now. The moon is at it weakest and the Shadow Walker's power is strong. We need a night when the moon is full, or as near as possible. It'll be even better if Admidios isn't here! We will wait for him to go to Dorcic to take a bath.'

'What if he doesn't go?'

'We'll think of something,' Dallel promised.

40. The Bargain

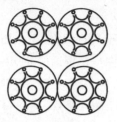

The following afternoon Admidios was making some magic of his own. He built a straw figure and dressed it in his clothes and cloak. He placed it at the entrance of his lodging and gave it a glamour of reality, so all the world would see Admidios asleep on a stool, snoring gently as he leaned against the doorpost. He did not want anyone to know he was missing from Sinodun.

When Kieran returned from his errands he crept around his sleeping master and curled up at the back of the hut for a rest. As daylight faded he wondered whether to wake Admidios for the evening meal. The boy touched an arm timidly. It rustled and was lumpy and uneven. His master looked real enough and snored loudly enough, but he wasn't there!

Kieran's heart skipped. Dare he . . . *dare he* run away? If Admidios had gone to the trouble of creating a double for himself, then he must be very busy away from the strong-hold. Once the gates were shut at sunset there would be no return. The boy knew he would have one whole night to escape. He could travel deep into the woods. He'd not be seen . . .

But where would he go? He chuckled to himself. Who cared? He'd be free! He stole an old cloak of his master's – wages, he reasoned, for the long hours of work and beatings he had endured. He wrapped it around his shoulders and made sure it covered his slave's iron collar. Someone somewhere would take pity and help him get it off.

He grabbed a small knife, pushed it into his belt and made his way to the northern watchtower.

'Where are you off to?' demanded a guard. 'A bit late to be going out.' He jerked his thumb at the heavy gates.

Kieran shrugged. 'My master left his cup by the spring and wants it for his meal tonight. I'll be back in no time.' He looked pleadingly at the guard. 'He'll beat me else!'

The man nodded. 'Run. Can't hold the gates for you though.'

There was no time to linger. At the top of the sacred hill, druids would already be standing in their evening circle. Kieran slipped between the trees and made his way down-hill towards the river. There he turned to his left and ran. Far behind, he could hear the horn blowing for sunset. Soon men would be closing the gates and pushing the heavy bar into its slots. Then night would leave Sinodun to itself.

Ignoring the rustlings and shufflings of night creatures, Kieran made his way into the forest-lands that lay ahead. He had no idea where he was going; he just wanted to be as far away from the stronghold as he could by dawn. He knew Admidios did dark magic, and he suspected he could find him if he wanted. He might even send that vicious black raven after him, but Kieran hoped he would be too busy to care. Admidios *always* seemed busy.

After a while the forest became so dark and thick the boy decided he would have to find a path, something he had wanted to avoid. There was a glimmer of a faint blue light to his left. He instinctively made his way towards it, treading as quietly as he could.

At last he saw it was not one blue light but several: shimmering and twisting like ethereal figures, dancing slowly around what looked like a man. Kieran held his breath and flattened himself against a tree. He realized with horror that he was very close – too close! The slightest movement might be heard and he'd be caught. All he could do was crouch low, hold his breath and wait for it to end.

He cursed himself for his carelessness, but when the figure in the middle spoke, his heart sank.

It was Admidios!

He seemed to be arguing with the tallest of the wraiths.

The demon's voiced coiled like an icy mist with despairing words that chilled Kieran's blood.

'I have given you every chance,' it moaned. 'Where is the raven-haired one I desired? Why have you not brought her powers to be joined to mine?'

Admidios spoke in a low, calm voice, 'My lord, I came very close to capturing her obedience . . . Next time I will make sure she does not escape me. She has no confidence in her own abilities – she is learning that she needs me. I also have something she wants to know: the whereabouts of the warrior princess Sabrina. Without that knowledge the British alliance will fail. The Fire Dreamer is no fool. She is desperate for peace. My plan is working; she will come to me. I just need a little more time.'

The blue lights flickered. 'You have until Samhain. If she is not in my thrall by that nightfall, our bargain is null and void.'

'But I need more power; your demons won't obey me. I can't do it on my own—'

'They won't obey you because you are weak!' the voice sneered.

Just then, a squall of wind gusted through the trees and a sharp shower of rain stung Kieran's eyes. Without thinking he raised his hand to rub them. There was a banshee screech as cruel talons gripped his wrist. He cried out.

The lights extinguished. The sudden storm dropped and

Admidios's heavy feet crashed through the undergrowth. 'What have you got there, Krake? A spy?'

'A spy! A spy!' squawked the bird, letting go her hold and flapping off into the night as Admidios's fierce grasp dragged Kieran forward. He clicked his fingers and a pale wyr-light shone in the palm of his hand. He held it up to Kieran's face. The boy trembled, his eyes wide with terror.

'What are you doing here?' Admidios roared.

'I was worried, sir,' he stammered. 'When I found you wasn't really there . . . I came out to see if you was all right . . .'

His master gently laid his hand over the boy's mouth. 'Then you shall be rewarded . . .' his fingers tightened cruelly, 'with *silence*, until you can learn to tell the truth.'

Kieran tried to scream, but nothing came out. He drew his knife and tried to plunge it into Admidios's heart. But his master laughed as the handle turned red-hot and Kieran dropped it.

In one swift move, Admidios had the boy by the ear. He twisted the lobe and turned back towards Sinodun, dragging the silently sobbing captive behind him. Admidios hammered on the gates. 'I've caught a runaway slave!' he yelled up to the guards, 'Been up half the night after the little bastard!'

The small porter's door swung inward, and a face with a lantern appeared. Admidios tried not to wince as the bright flame caught his eyes. Kieran, pale as a wraith, was shoved inside. Back at Admidios's lodging, he was chained by his iron collar to the back wall. He tried to beg for mercy, but his voice choked in his throat.

For a short while his master busied himself with warm wax, wood and a hair from Kieran's head. Then he climbed into bed, leaving his slave crouching in the dark, unable to stand or sit, tears streaming down his face.

41. The Assembly of Druids

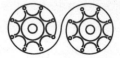

The proceedings began with pomp and circumstance and a waxing moon. Tedious rituals on the sacred hill, in full robes, made Tegen wonder whether she really wanted to be a druid at all. The only consolation was the cooler breezes of autumn's approach.

But the death of Eiser had delayed the proceedings badly and Chieftain Connal's warm hospitality of Lughnasadh was rapidly fading as his resources dwindled. Despite the generous gifts his hoard of visitors brought towards their upkeep, the chieftain was worried about winter stores for his people. The druids prayed for blessings on the stronghold, but Connal knew that blessings did not fill hungry bellies.

While the druids met and argued, the chieftain looked daily across at the Roman garrison. Sometimes emissaries were sent between Sinodun and Dorcic. Little was said. The two sides moved around each other like wrestlers sizing up their opponent. Admidios made himself useful as an interpreter, but Connal did not trust his words.

From time to time Admidios went to his officer's quarters to bathe and to pass information on to his spymasters, but the last moon before Samhain was waning. He had one more chance to hand Owein over to the Romans and to bind Tegen's power to the demon he served.

Tegen was anxious and frustrated. She nagged Huval to complete the fire spiral so she could leave for Mona. 'Be patient,' he reassured her. 'The time will come. Meanwhile, you have many of the greatest druidic minds right here,' he said. 'Use them! Spend this time studying.'

Tegen was not consoled, but until a guide was available to take her to the land of the Cymry, she could do nothing except make the best of things. Bronnen taught her herbalism, she learned astrology and surgery from Twm, singing and composition from Cluan, and as much as she could about law from listening to the assembly's interminably dull arguments.

The only bright moment was when, at the end of the talks, Owein was required to speak. They all wanted to hear the youngest son of the greatest British war leader, the High King Cara, whom the invaders called Caractacus.

Owein stood in his real father's colours, leaning on his crutch in the centre of the longhouse, surrounded by two hundred of the greatest druids and warriors in the land. He looked around at his listeners, many of them friends and loyal supporters of his family. He didn't want to let them down by telling them their sacrifices had been for nothing. What could he say to give them heart? Their pride was crushed. For thirteen years they had fought and struggled . . . and lost.

Every eye was on him. Owein pulled himself as straight as he could.

'My father believed that the Romans could be driven out of Britain. He paid with his freedom for that belief.

'If the Romans cannot come in peace for honest trade and to share learning, then we must defend ourselves. For that, we will need *unity*.' He paused and looked around. 'That means trusting each other, becoming *one* people with *one* aim: living as a single tribe in our land.

'On the way here I saw the head of King Eiser's steward impaled on a gatepost. He was a good man. I suspect his crime was to wear Dobunni colours in Atrebatian lands. While we are picking off our best warriors in petty quarrels, the Romans walk in and help themselves to everything we have. They are standing at our backs as we speak.'

He glanced around to see if Admidios was in the hall. Owein prayed he was not there. His hypnotic tones and contorted arguments might spoil this one chance to put forward a real solution.

'Have any of you studied the way the enemy fights?' Owein continued. 'They move as one man – a team, pulling together. We fight as individuals, picking off the opponent whose head we like the look of. We need to *think like Romans,* if we are to defeat them!'

'What good is that?' roared a voice at the back. A man stood, his huge frame swathed in a tartan of many greens; his fierce eyes glowered from under a mat of wild black hair. 'My name is Feagus mac Duach from the Island of the Blessed,' he bellowed. 'I came here because our people received messages requesting help – and what do I find? A beardless boy suggesting that great heroes belittle them-selves by fighting as *one*! Where is the glory in that? How will the poets know who struck the death-blow to which warrior?' He spat. 'I came to offer help to men, but I find you are being guided by children! I am leaving!' And with that he swirled his cloak and stormed out of the longhouse, yelling for his horse and his gear.

The druids and warriors murmured, a few stood and argued one way or the other, but at last Connal rose and raised his staff for silence. Then he turned to Owein. 'So you suggest we unite and retrain our armies to fight the Roman way?'

'Yes. It will take time to win back our land, but our losses will be less. We will also keep the Romans on edge; they won't expect us to change our tactics.' Then he added, 'But there is a catch . . .'

He paused and took a deep breath . . . 'We must first con-cede Britain.'

The outrage within the halls was deafening, with stamping, shouting, swearing and fights breaking out.

'*Silence!*' roared Connal. 'Hear the boy out. His father was no coward, and I don't believe he is either.'

Reluctantly the row subsided. Owein spoke as clearly as he could. This was the crux of his argument. They had to believe him . . . 'If we concede, there will be no more bloodshed. It will give us the time we need to make secret alliances and for our dead heroes to be reborn. We must send our young men – I am afraid they don't allow women in the army . . .' At this hissing and yowling came from the female warriors, but Owein kept going. 'Our youth must train with the Roman army to learn their stratagems and tactics. When our warriors come home, they must train their brothers and sisters in all their skills.'

He paused, raised his head proudly and thumped his crutch as he shouted, 'Then we *turn* on them when they least expect it! That way we will defeat the invaders with *our* courage and *their* training!'

'But that will take too long!' raged a tall chieftain from the Catuvellauni.

'We don't have much choice.' Owein's eyes burned like hot coals. 'Our young heroes are dying. We don't have more to replace them. We are losing badly. What we have to consider is how to control that loss with the least damage and fewest concessions. The Romans have much that is good to give us. We *want* their trade, ideas and skills; we *don't* want the slaughter and slavery. Our land is soaked in blood and tears, and our fields lie unploughed. No one . . .' he turned a full circle, catching the eye of as many of his audience as he could, 'No one can say that this is the will of the Goddess. The spirits of our land are dying.'

He took a deep breath. 'We need peace – at least for a while, to recover and give ourselves a chance to fight back!' Then he turned to where most of druids were standing. 'Think of it as winter,' he said. 'At Samhain we burn what is worn out and useless; then we rest for several moons awaiting rebirth . . . All I ask is that we now follow that sacred pattern!'

Once more shouts and fierce arguments filled the hall.

Dallel rose from his chair by the fire. A reluctant silence fell. 'There is one more alternative . . .' he began.

All turned to him.

'I propose that all the druids who can, go to the sacred island of Mona. There, together, in the most holy spot on earth, we will create a spell of such potency that the invaders will be flung from our shores by the force of that magic.'

For one long moment everyone held their breath in awe.

A thrill of excitement made Tegen's green eyes sparkle. Was she about to set off for Mona to take part in the greatest spell ever wrought within the land of Britain? Would *this* be her ultimate Star Dance?

Connal rose to his feet. 'Owein's words have sense in

them, but I would vote to try Dallel's solution first. The commander of the garrison at Dorcic says that if I do not surrender Sinodun before winter's birth at Samhain, they will take it by force. I do not have enough warriors to defend these hills. My people will be slaughtered.'

A dark-haired chieftainess called out, 'My stronghold has already been sacked and burned.'

'And mine . . . Mine too . . .' echoed others. All around, voices were raised with tales of destruction and looting.

Once more Connal called for silence. 'The moon is waning. Soon it will be inauspicious for travel. Do not wait. Go back now, before the dark of the moon puts you all in danger. If all the other kings and chieftains agree, I will propose Dallel leads his druids to Mona to raise the spirits of the Land against the invaders. If that solution does not work, then we must consider Owein's option . . .' Connal hesitated and glanced across at him, 'although it galls my heart to say so.' And with a heart-wrenching sigh he sat.

42. Fleas

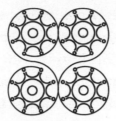

In the following days the kings and warriors left, but the chieftains of the Dobunni remained behind. They had not seen justice done by the old king's spirit, and they were already squabbling amongst themselves for the crown.

Owein summoned the Dobunni together on the sacred hill and, wearing Eiser's colours, he held high the sooty, melted remains of the King's golden torque. 'I swear, by the gods of my tribe and my foster-father's spirit, that I will seek out Sabrina to be your crowned queen and bring her to the rearing river. If the princess is dead, I will help you choose another lord. All I ask is that you take an oath of brotherhood for one year. I offer my life as forfeit if, by the autumn feast of equal day and night one year hence, I have not done as I have promised. For now, you must go home. There may be Romans at your gates even now.'

The chieftains argued, but none could think of a better plan. Grudgingly they took the oath and left.

Huval followed them. 'I will do my best to hold them to their vows until you come,' he promised.

To Tegen he said, 'When you walk the fire spiral, remember you are the Star Dancer. You will be given the power to fulfil that destiny. As you walk, wrap a cloak of cool air around yourself. That will protect you.' He kissed the top of her head and mounted his horse. 'We will meet again; I have seen it.' Then he smiled, squeezed his horse's flanks and was away.

As the druids left for Mona, Tegen longed to go too. She belonged there – what did Eiser or his murder have to do with her? But she had promised to stay.

By the time the moon was almost waned, only Connal's own druids remained, old Dallel and his wife, Bronnen, with their apprentice, Angor the ovate.

Admidios stayed as well. Connal knew he had to tread carefully. Admidios insisted Eiser had secretly betrothed him to his daughter before his death. Furthermore, he was also a friend of the invaders, and his Latin *was* useful when envoys came.

One morning Tegen dawdled after the morning circle, picking bluwits from the autumn woods. Admidios met her as she entered the northern gate. 'I have come to ask if you have reconsidered,' he said, smiling.

'Reconsidered what?' she snapped as she tried to push

past. He stepped in her way. 'Me teaching you divining. With your Fire Dreaming and my interpretation skills, between us I am sure we could find Sabrina.'

'I already know where she is,' Tegen glared as she sidestepped him and elbowed his belly.

Winded, he turned and glared at her. 'You do?'

'*You've* got her . . . haven't you?'

Before he could answer, a cart trundled past. Tegen leaped on the back and was carried across the cobbled courtyard.

Admidios and his raven watched her silently.

Suddenly she noticed what she should have seen all along. Neither the Shadow Walker nor his bird was alone. A heavy emptiness hung over them both. Tegen's heart skipped a beat. In that moment, she realized with dread that she *recognized* the aching nothingness that shivered and shimmered around her enemy, distorting his form like a deadly heat haze.

She covered her eyes and held her breath. In her mind she slipped back to the funeral of her dear friend Gilda in the caves beneath their Mendip home. Once more, the old witch Derowen's ululations spun a spell that summoned an Otherworld demon.

A demon Tegen thought she had defeated and bound.

She jumped down from the back of the cart and found Owein currying Heather's coat. He stopped and looked up. 'Are you all right?'

She told him what had happened. Her throat was tight as she said, 'It's time to *make* Admidios go to the garrison for a bath. I have to walk the spiral *now*. If we can prove who killed Eiser, the alliance might hold long enough for you to be able to rescue Sabrina and bring unity to the Dobunni.'

Owein shrugged. 'How will you get Admidios to go?'

'I will ask Kieran. He once promised me he would help us.' And she told Owein her plan.

When Tegen asked Kieran for help, he simply nodded and smiled. She thought nothing of it – he was always quiet.

The boy saw his chance while Admidios was eating, an activity he enjoyed taking his time over. Kieran combed Wolf's mud-coloured pelt for fleas. The huge dog licked Kieran's face lovingly as hundreds of leaping villains were trapped in a wad of oily fleece that the boy then hid carefully in his master's bed. Time and nature did the rest.

Next morning Admidios was covered in bites and was scratching all over. The whole stronghold could hear him swearing and cuffing Kieran around the head for letting his bed get so filthy. Within a hand-span of the sun Admidios was marching out of the north gate with Kieran following behind, struggling under a large basket strapped to his back.

Her enemy was gone. Tegen's heart sank as she realized that night was the last dark of the moon before Samhain.

Dallel shook his head when she went to see him. 'This isn't a good time; it's very inauspicious. There'll be too many beings travelling between the worlds so it'll be difficult to discern Eiser's spirit clearly . . .' He paced up and down. 'But dare we wait for another chance? Time *is* getting short!' He stroked his wispy moustaches.

Bronnen scowled at her man but bit her tongue.

Tegen smiled as she reached out and held the old woman's hand. 'I *need* to do this *now*,' she said firmly, looking towards the crackling fire in the hearth. 'I have seen a demon nearby. It's one I have met before, in the caves near my home village. I *have* to put rings of fire between me and it as soon as possible. Don't be afraid for me. Let me go with your blessing, and all shall be well.'

43. Walking the Spiral

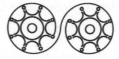

As the sun rose in the sky, Dallel went to the sacred hill top and tied a long piece of nettle twine to the highest twig of the upturned tree root. Using it as a centre point, he walked around the altar, trailing fine sand on the grass, creating a circle the length of three men in diameter. Next he placed six equally spaced white stones around the circumference. Starting at the first, he laid his splayed hand next to the stone and marked the width with more sand. At the second, he used two hand-widths, and at the third, three, and so on until at the sixth a path was clearly spiralling outward in an even sweep. Tegen watched.

Still using the sand, he followed the pattern until he had marked three wide turns of the spiral. 'Really we need seven turns or, even better, nine,' Dallel said, 'but . . .' he looked up, 'the trees hang rather low, and we mustn't risk setting them on fire. Do you think this will be enough, Tegen?'

She nodded, but wished she knew for sure. A bitter wind swept from the north-west, making her shiver. The intimation of the demon she had sensed made her even colder. Nervousness didn't help. When she had asked the others what walking the spiral was like, they had smiled and said, 'It's never the same twice,' which didn't help.

'What woods do we burn?' Tegen asked.

Bronnen was already cleansing the space with smouldering bunches of sage stalks, her long white plaits swaying as she walked. The druidess reverently laid the remnants of the smudge stick in the central tree root. 'It's your ritual. What would *you* like to guide and protect you? We use brushwood and wood chippings, not the logs – they don't burn well unless they are packed closely together.'

Servants were already laying a snake of kindling along the spiral. The wind tossed golden stalks of straw into the air. Two more men followed behind, piling thick bundles of dried gorse on top.

From the wood stores dotted amongst the trees, Tegen chose rowan for protection, holly for brightness, willow for vision, ash to link the inner and outer worlds, hazel for wisdom, yew to make the spirits of the ancestors welcome and oak to open the doorway to mysteries. Lastly she gathered several armfuls of dried ferns for truth.

Bronnen organized the servants to tie the woods into

bundles then place them around the spiral, stacked in stooks across the gorse in a twiggy harvest. Soon the twisting path was a shoulder-high hedge of firewood. As they worked, Bronnen inspected everything meticulously, poking her staff here and there to make sure nothing would tumble across Tegen's path as the lower layers of kindling disintegrated. 'No higher!' she growled. 'She's there to dream, not be burned alive. May the Goddess preserve her!'

Dallel muttered irritably, stood back, walked a little way into the spiral himself, then agreed.

The building of the spiral had taken almost all day. Now the autumn sun was getting low and the wind was rising. Tegen walked down to a stretch of the river overhung with trees. During the summer months she had bathed here. Now it was chilly and carpeted with gold. She shivered as she listened to the water lapping. Wolf came sniffing around her. She hugged him and rubbed her face against his comforting coat. Once or twice she saw birds flying overhead. She watched between the almost bare branches, wondering whether Krake was spying on her. 'One more day,' she told Wolf. 'Then we will be on our way to Mona.'

As the daylight began to fade she trudged back up to the sacred hill. Angor was there with a drum, beating a slow rhythm. For once Tegen was not sure whether she wanted music. Owein was looking nervous. 'Send Wolf away,' he said. 'You don't want him to think you are in danger and plunge after you.'

Tegen rubbed Wolf's back and beckoned to a servant. 'Take him back please . . . Go home, boy.' The dog looked crestfallen, but obeyed.

Owein handed her a shirt and neatly folded breeches. 'These are my best ones, so don't get them singed.'

Tegen took them. 'Ugh, they are all wet! What do I need these for?'

Owein laughed. 'Fire and long, dry skirts don't go together well, believe me!' Tegen grimaced and went behind one of the woodpiles to struggle into the cold, clinging clothes.

As she returned with chattering teeth to the almost dark grove, she saw Bronnen and Dallel in their white robes and coloured cloaks. Dallel approached with his silver branch decorated with tiny silver bells. He raised it in greeting. 'Welcome, Star Dancer. Are you ready?'

'Yes,' she replied, her mouth quite dry.

Night had almost fallen. Tegen looked apprehensively at the looming, sinister shadows of the spiral twisting around the grove.

Bronnen made her drink a draught of strong mead, then slipped a satchel across Tegen's shoulders. 'Take this. Inside are gifts for the spirits of the ancestors, especially Eiser: ale, honey and bean cakes. But first you need to walk the perimeter deosil four times, honouring a different element with each circuit. Begin with the West because you will need water and cool air.'

Dallel handed her a small silver bowl freshly filled from the spring and a little bundle of hyssop twigs. Taking her place, Tegen walked the perimeter, lightly splashing the spiral and blessing the spirits of rivers and rain, asking for their protection.

The old druid exchanged the bowl for a jug of mead. Tegen went to the North and trickled the sweetness on to the ground as she walked, blessing the earth and praying for a safe path.

Next Bronnen gave her a dish of hot charcoal smouldering with incense. Tegen blessed the spirits of the air and prayed she would be defended from anything airborne that might hate her, Krake in particular.

Lastly Dallel offered her a beeswax candle. Starting from the South, Tegen shielded the flame from the wind and the night as she walked the perimeter once more, creating a fiery spirit shield. When she had finished, she blew out the flame.

Suddenly everything was very dark.

'Go in low,' Dallel whispered. 'Keep as low as you can all the way. If you can't breathe, then crawl.'

She felt a squeeze on her right hand. She turned and Owein put his arms around her and gave her a light kiss on the cheek. 'May the Goddess walk with you.'

A sharp gust of rain-filled wind blew straight into her face as she spread her hands across the opening between the stacked brushwood swirl. She closed her eyes as rain coursed down her face, soaking through to her skin. Her teeth chattered uncontrollably.

Then she thought of Fire.

And Fire came.

With a hissing crackle, all the straw ignited at the same moment. Yellow flames crept from the kindling to the viciously spitting thorns of the gorse. Crackling and sparking, it caught the brushwood and fern. Steam began to rise. Blinding light swept around the spiral until it danced and glowed complete, challenging the darkness.

Red and gold and yellow against empty black.

All around, raging, flaming red tatters licked and danced.

Tegen took a hesitant step forward . . .

Everywhere was heat. Sharp and angry.

Dallel gripped her shoulder. 'Let the fire spirits vent their first rage before you walk between them . . .'

The straw at the roots of the fire hedges was now just twisted black worms of ash. The faggots of brushwood were shifting and settling as the flames devoured the lower layers. Soon the heart of the fires cooled to black as the flames moved outward, still deadly, but less angry.

'Now!' Dallel gave her a gentle push.

Tegen took a deep breath of cold air and shielded her

face. 'Spirits of the West, defend me,' she whispered as she stepped into the dark emptiness between the flames. As she did so, she whispered a charm to keep a cloak of cool air around herself as Huval had advised.

The golden tongues leaped above her head and made a canopy of glowing light. She paused and looked up.

So much heat.

What if the raging walls fell in on her? She ached to turn back.

'Keep low!' Bronnen hissed. 'Don't look the fire spirits in the eye!'

Tegen crouched and found it a little less hot, and much easier to breathe. Gusts of wind ripped black holes in the fiery walls on her left. Roaring. Searing. Her clothes steamed.

I must forget it all, she told herself. I must leave the world behind. Everything I love: Owein, Wolf, the stronghold; and everything I hate: Admidios, Krake, the demon – everything . . .

Nothing exists, nothing matters, I am leaving it all behind . . . I am going to Tir na nÓg.

As she walked on, the thick black smoke made her cough. Showers of glowing fragments flew and settled like crimson snow. The spitting, bright holly made her jump. Forwards, backwards, above, below, there was no way out. She kept walking, always a little to her left. The twisting spiral turned and now the gusting wind lashed flames from straight ahead. She kept her head down and breathed carefully. She felt dizzy and wanted to turn and run.

So much heat.

So much light.

Which way was in and which way was out?

Forwards, keep going forwards . . . urged a voice in her head.

A few more steps and the flames changed, springing towards her from the right.

Move quickly. Don't hesitate!

Then the spiral began to turn on its own . . .

She was staying still.

The hot earth tilted. The fire spun. She looked around in mounting terror. She tried to breathe, but the searing heat scorched her lungs. Coughing hurt. The wind blew again. The faggots shifted and flung a glowing red branch across her path, spilling twigs and cinders. Some landed on her clothes and hair, glowed, stung and went out.

Smoke.

Her lungs clenched as she struggled to breathe.

The arch of heat was less intense now. The flames that had replaced the night had parted and showed a dark path in the sky ahead. She raised her head to gasp for cold air, but the wind tossed an army of red ashes winking and stinging towards her face. To her left, several coils of burning light leaped and twisted. To her right, there was only one more turn of the red and gold raging serpent . . .

Let me out, Lady Goddess! Let me out!

Put your left foot forward, the voice in her head spoke again. *Keep low, keep moving.*

Heat . . . and smoke . . .

Slowly, golden coils of flame rose up from the ground, lifting, raising themselves into fiery hoops above her head. Was she floating between them? Were they setting the sky alight? Higher and higher they arched, swirling, twisting, crackling . . . now from ahead . . . then from her right . . . now behind her . . .

She was caught in the midst of a gyroscope of slowly spinning loops of fire.

Heat-incense-heat-soot-heat-wood-heat-smoke-heat-shapes-twisting-rearing-sinking-HEAT!

Dizzy and disorientated, she sank to her knees and crawled.

44. Fire Dreaming

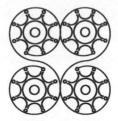

At last, a black shape reared in front of Tegen. It was squat and fat, with many arms writhing like serpents. She stumbled forward and fell into its embrace.

The skin was rough and cool, the arms solid and fixed. It was the inverted oak-tree stump – she was at the centre!

Her head spun as she sat, leaning her back against the ancient trunk and looking out across the burning spirals. They had lessened and settled but they were still undulating. As she watched, Tegen tried to count the fiery lines against the blackness of the night. She was sure there were many more twists than three . . .

The flames licked slowly – so slowly.

Rising.

Spreading.

Shredding.

Dissolving into night-borne sparks, then dying back.

Each motion took forever. Tegen looked up, but could not see the stars for smoke and light. She longed to see the cool light of the Watching Woman, the Goddess's constant reminder of her presence. *Sky-fires*, she told herself. That's all stars are. The Lady is with me here, I know she is.

Breathless and nauseous, Tegen reached into the satchel and found the honey. The waxy seal was very soft; she pushed it back with a fingernail. 'I bring greetings to the spirits of Tir na nÓg, and especially to my lord King Eiser. May your next life be sweet,' she whispered, dripping the offering on to the ground.

Close the circle, said the voice inside her head. *There are angry spirits even within the coils of flame.*

As she looked up, vermillion tongues flared where the path met the centre space. Tentatively Tegen found the bean cakes in her satchel and, crouching forward, crumbled them across the gap. With a shaking hand she spread the fingers of her right hand. Fire leaped, devouring the crumbs and the gap closed.

That is good . . . The circle of fire leaped higher. The heat became intense once more. Tegen struggled to breathe. This is too much. I will die in here, she thought. But I must complete my offerings. She unstoppered and poured the goatskin of ale. In a cracked, harsh voice she called to the spirits again: 'Drink deep of life and bless the Goddess from whom all life comes.' She gasped for air. 'May you share in the feast of the living as Samhain draws near.

Accept my gifts. In exchange, I ask to be allowed to stay here for a while and listen to your wisdom.'

What is wisdom?

Tegen hesitated, sweat trickled between her shoulder blades. Heat and light seared her skin.

'Wisdom is understanding beyond knowledge, I think.'

So what knowledge do you seek to go beyond? asked the voice, as the flames crept to shoulder height.

'The knowledge that King Eiser is dead,' Tegen replied. 'Those who loved him want to know who killed him, so justice may be done and his spirit will be at peace.'

What is justice? asked the voice again.

Smuts and soot were making Tegen's eyes water. She rubbed her face on her arm. Was this a trick? Did she need to answer these questions? Was this what she had come for? The flames were dancing so slowly all around her, she wasn't sure whether anything she saw or heard was real.

'Justice is balancing wrong with right,' she answered.

Ah, came the reply, *so if a man is murdered, the murder of his murderer brings 'balance' to the crime?*

Tegen felt so hot she could not breathe. The flames were as high as her head. 'Yes . . . no . . .' she said. 'I don't know. I do know that putting the wrong person to death for a murder doubles the wrong . . . and that if good people do nothing, evil will win.'

So, what is evil?

Tegen buried her face in the cool of the beer- and honey-smeared grass. She whispered to the earth, 'All I want to know is who killed Eiser, King of the Dobunni.' Then, thinking of what Owein would say, she managed to add, 'And *how* and *why*.'

The first answer you know; the second and third are within your own fears, replied the voice.

Just then a gust of icy air blew into the centre, carrying heavy rain. The fire hissed, sank and only the sour stench of wet ashes remained. The sudden darkness and cold were intense.

'No! Don't go yet – you haven't told me the answer . . . And I need to know where Sabrina is,' she pleaded into the night. She scrambled to her feet and looked at the smoul-dering remains. She could use her Fire Magic to keep the flames burning, but how much strength would that take from her? Would it be enough to close the circle again? Would she be able to find the way back?

The rain lashed as she huddled against the tree root.

Suddenly heat and cinders flared up behind her. Tegen jumped away. The tree root itself was on fire! She stared into the flames. 'Lady,' she prayed, 'help me! I cannot see your Watching Woman, yet I know your stars are living sky-fires behind the smoke. I am surrounded by truth I cannot understand.'

White cracked patterns like bleached bones grew along the charred roots in the fire. Roots that twisted and writhed as the flames shifted. Roots that almost had a life of their own.

Tegen shuddered. Her head was too heavy. She was so tired.

She stepped back and fought weariness as she stared at the fiery images. Figures of people she had known who had died wove their way in and out of the black and red: Gilda, Griff, then the evil Gorgans . . . They held out their arms to her and tried to speak, but they faded from one into the other as fluidly as water.

Then she saw a dark shape; the roots became a black bird flying, swooping . . . a bird that was not a bird. It had the eyes of a malevolent old woman and the hate of a demon. Tegen felt cold and sick. She knew the face that sat on the bird's neck.

It was someone she had seen die . . .

Tegen seemed to be shrinking. She became small and straight and encased. The old woman's talons snatched her up and carried her through the sky. Below, Tegen saw a man sitting in bed. The bird spoke harsh words and the man became terrified. Why? What did the words mean? They didn't make sense . . . Her dream-self screamed out, 'Say it again, more slowly this time!'

Then the bird dropped her. Tegen still couldn't move; she was being flung around. The bird had grown huge and was raging and screaming. Something smashed. Tegen was caught up again and hidden, buried somewhere that stank.

There were rotting bones, carcasses, green and slimy, the stench was unbearable.

Then nothing.

Tegen breathed deeply and opened one eye. Someone had wrapped a thick cloak around her. It was still night and she was huddled within the acrid coils of the spiral. Here and there, twisted remnants of the fire spluttered. She couldn't have been asleep for long. She had dreamed . . . What had she dreamed? She *had* to remember. The rain had stopped, but she was wet and could not control her shivering. The ashes by her feet were cold. Wolf had returned and lay with his long limbs curved around her like the old moon holding the new in its arms.

Tegen eased herself upright. Her back ached. She rubbed her eyes and stretched.

For a brief moment she thought she saw shimmering shades of Romans in full war gear beyond the spiral. From the ashes, flames leaped up in a wall of searing heat once more. Then they, and the vision of soldiers, were gone.

45. Plans

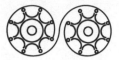

Owein's voice came from beyond the final, fading vision. 'Tegen, we can't help – you have to walk out yourself or your spirit may be left behind.'

'I understand,' she called back, getting to her feet and looking around for a way between the blackened twiggy remains. Dizzy nausea and coughing made her stagger. As she stumbled out of the entrance Owein caught her and leaned her against Heather's broad back. 'You ride,' he said. 'I can walk.'

Fussing and scolding, Bronnen helped haul Tegen into the saddle. 'Owein, take her to our roundhouse – there is a guest bed behind the screen. I will come as soon as we have greeted the spirits.'

Owein led Heather back down the muddy slope through the rain and wind. He was dying to ask questions, but he knew better. He helped her to a bed and left her.

Tegen could not sleep. Her chest and face were sore and her scalp itched. When Bronnen arrived, she sent the men outside while she fussed and bathed her patient.

With her own clothes and washed hair, Tegen felt much more herself. Dallel and Owein talked while she ate fish and barley stew.

'The fire hardly lasted any time at all,' Owein said. 'We were worried it wouldn't be long enough for you to dream. You had scarcely got to the centre when it flared up and then *poof!* It seemed to blow itself out.'

Dallel sat next to Tegen. 'Did you see Eiser?' he asked urgently.

Tegen nodded. 'I heard him, or I think I did. There was a voice in my head, then all sorts of people from my past – dead people . . .' she added. She swallowed a piece of oatcake. 'I asked who killed Eiser, and I was told I already know. And I asked how it was done, and the spirit said the answer was "in my own fears". I think that fear might be Krake – Admidios's raven. I dreamed of black wings and sharp talons carrying me, yet I wasn't me; I became something small and rigid, like a twig.' She sipped at a chamomile tisane. 'I think I saw Eiser briefly. He was frightened and sitting up in bed, there were some leaden words I couldn't understand, then I was somewhere full of death and rotting corpses.' She shuddered.

'The only explanation I can think of,' Tegen took a deep

breath, 'is that Admidios used his raven to kill the King –
but that really doesn't make sense, does it?'

Dallel tapped his fingers together. 'It does fit in a way. It
would fulfil the prophesy, it's a "blow from no man's
hand", but there were no signs of pecking or scratching . . .'
The druid leaned back in his chair and thought. 'Admidios
has many powerful friends amongst the Romans as well as
the British. We cannot accuse him on Tegen's Fire Dream
alone . . . and we still don't know *why* he would want to kill
the King. The Dobunni are so weak these days; Eiser was
no real threat to the invaders.'

He sighed. 'I hate to admit it, but Admidios's idea that
the salt trader did it out of vengeance makes more sense,
but no one came or went to Eiser's lodging all that day
except the King himself. Certainly the guards saw no one
answering her description.'

Owein's eyes widened. 'Eiser had been eating an egg
when he died. There were grains of salt on it. Could it have
been from Caja's tax? A smear of aconite on the slab would
have done the trick.'

'But there was no way she could have known *he* would
eat from it,' Bronnen added, 'and the woman didn't go near
the salt after the boy was taken.'

Tegen shook her head. 'There was nothing about the salt
traders in my dream, but Owein and I have an idea about
why Admidios wanted Eiser dead. Do you remember I told
you about the Fire Dream Admidios tricked me into, and the

vision in the burned bone? The question he made me ask was how to "achieve his ends". He had already proposed to Sabrina. We are convinced her call to battle was a trick and he has her captive somewhere. If he forces her to marry him, then, with Eiser dead, Admidios will be King of the Dobunni. He would then rule in the name of the Romans. I don't think Sabrina would live long under those circumstances.'

'And neither will I,' Owein added. 'He will never really believe I don't want to be king. As he can't control me, he'll always fear me. Absolute power is the only thing that interests him in the slightest.' Owein could hardly stay still on his chair. 'Sir,' he said, 'the spirits have spoken. Now we need to find solid *proof*. As long as Admidios is free, there will be no hope for any sort of fair negotiations with the Romans.'

Dallel sighed, 'How can we get proof?'

Owein leaned forward, his eyes bright with the light from the hearth. 'After Eiser's death I searched his roundhouse to see if I could find any clues. I also took the opportunity to search my uncle's lodging. I found very little. I need to go to the Roman garrison. Admidios must have officer's quarters there. If he has anything to hide, he won't leave it here at Sinodun.'

Bronnen was horrified. 'But how will you get *in* there? That's impossible!'

'I'll find a way,' Owein said.

*

The following day Tegen felt well enough to go for a walk to the sacred hill. She sat under the winter-bare trees, wrapped in two cloaks and staring out over the Roman garrison. After a while Owein joined her. He let Heather graze and threw himself on the damp ground. He picked up a dead stick and jabbed it into the gold and red carpet of leaves.

Together they surveyed the stone squares and oblongs of the barracks that were rapidly replacing the wooden huts.

'I've thought of a way in,' Tegen said quietly, 'but you will have to cut your hair.'

'*What?*' Owein roared. '*Why?*'

Tegen considered his long chestnut waves. All the girls at Sinodun envied them. 'Listen,' she said, 'it'll be worth it. You can always grow your lovely locks again,' she teased, lightly running her finger over a curl. 'We'll just have to be sure Admidios remains at Sinodun while we're there.'

In Dorcic, Admidios was facing Quintus Caelius once more. This time he was less of an honoured guest and closer to being on trial.

Quintus paced the officer's mess, stroking his chin. His red cloak rippled over his breastplate. He stopped, leaned on the table and glared at Admidios. He had always despised the man, and now that he was showing no sign of delivering the promised goods, the tribune could relish his disdain.

Admidios shrank into his chair and eyed a cup of wine on the table.

'I will give you until the next dark of the moon, *Briton*. If by that time the boy is not in our custody and singing to our tunes, then you will be responsible. You have had silver, gold, privilege . . . you have even shared our baths and been treated as a citizen. But for what? *Eh?'* His smelly breath made Admidios cough. 'The time has come for reckoning. We are generous masters, but we expect *results!'* He slammed his fist down on the table, making the wine cup dance and spill its contents.

Quintus folded his arms and peered down his nose. 'You have some sort of pagan festival, do you not? With bonfires and so forth? I understand unwanted criminals are put into wicker cages and sacrificed to the gods at such a time. What do you call it? *Samhain?* We will see how we can contribute to the locals' celebrations, shall we?'

And with that he turned and stormed out of the door, letting it swing in the chilly wind behind him.

Admidios jumped to his feet. '*Ave*, Quintus Caelius,' he called out. 'He'll be here, I *swear* . . .'

But the commander was gone. Swiftly Admidios swallowed the dregs of his master's wine and ran outside.

As he left the garrison he turned into the woods to the east and, cutting his thumb on his knife, dripped blood on the ground. 'Come to me, demon of hate and revenge. *Now!* I, Admidios the Shadow Walker, command you!'

A low snigger made him turn. He could see nothing except quiet woods, but the presence was close behind him.

'And why should I obey you?'

'Because you were given to serve me to achieve our Lord's ends.'

The presence drew closer and the hairs on Admidios's neck stood up. He shuddered.

'I am your Lord, and I don't care whether you live or die. Your soul is mine – now and in all your rebirths. I have better, stronger servants than you to achieve my ends. You are a mere toy, one I am almost ready to throw on to the midden.'

Admidios pulled himself to his full height. 'Then I too break my bargain with you. It is I who will see *you* cast out – you pathetic *little* spirit. Be gone!' He spat and turned on his heel, striding away through the autumn woods.

Then he spoke more quietly, 'After all, I too have power, of a different sort . . .'

Connal was delighted to be asked to take part in Tegen's plan. If it worked, he would be free of his unwelcome guest and able to deal with his own problems in peace. To achieve that, he would do almost anything. Ever since Admidios had arrived, the chieftain had longed to be rid of him, but he dared not be seen to throw out the half-brother of the hero King Cara. Neither could he order his fat throat slit. If Admidios didn't report to his Roman masters that all was well, then who knew what vengeance would be at Sinodun's gates before dawn?

These days, Roman emissaries were coming more regularly, sometimes flattering with gifts of oil and wine, sometimes threatening the sacking of the stronghold. Connal guessed his defences could not withstand the might of the invaders. He would rather abandon the settlement and escape with some sort of dignity than allow his people to be slaughtered and burned in their homes.

In recent times, he had ordered some treasures and supplies to be carefully hidden in the surrounding countryside. But he would have to make a decision soon.

And if Admidios was out of the way, so much the better.

The days dragged by for Tegen and Owein. Admidios always seemed to be following them, wanting quiet words, offering bribes, threats, hinting that he knew Sabrina's whereabouts . . . But his words no longer compelled, his powers were fading.

Tegen and Owein begged Dallel to be allowed to act, but he warned that the time was not right. He watched and waited for the most auspicious moment, and at last it came. A full moon.

*

Connal was ready. He found his nemesis drinking alone after the evening meal. He greeted Admidios cheerfully and slapped him on the back. 'Will you come boar hunting with me tomorrow? Then stay as my honoured guest at a feast in the evening? I have *Roman wine* . . .' he added.

'Is this a special occasion?' Admidios narrowed his eyes. Connal wasn't usually this friendly.

Sinodun's lord swept his arms expansively. 'Just a little private ritual I perform at the full moon before each Samhain – I thank the Green Man for the richness of the forests and I honour the spirits of the animals that feed us. Now, do say you will join me.' He leaned over and whispered conspiratorially, 'We nobles often have much to discuss that it is better not for *druid* ears to hear . . . They think they know everything, but their heads are in the stars and their backsides are warming themselves by our hearths. What do they know about anything . . . eh?'

Admidios was pleased. He had barely half a moon to deliver Sextus into Quintus's hands. Connal might prove a useful ally. 'I would like to come very much indeed. May I bring my raven to the hunt?'

'But of course,' Connal replied, gritting his teeth, for he hated the bird. 'I have been told they are lucky and lead the hunter to the prey.'

Admidios smiled. 'They do, indeed they do . . .'

46. The Other Hunt

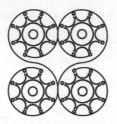

At dawn the sun rose in a clear sky. The courtyard bustled with excited chaos. Local chiefs and their retinues were mounted and ready. Servants ran to fulfil last-minute orders. Men whistled to barking dogs. Boar spears gleamed with deadly edges. At last a horn sounded and Connal rode out of the southern gate, with Admidios smugly in the place of honour at his side.

Tegen had gladly loaned Wolf to the hunt. She did not want him following her where she planned to go that day.

As soon as the gates shut Tegen found Owein seated on a stool outside Bronnen and Dallel's roundhouse. He had a cloth around his shoulders, and the old druidess was scraping at a white beard of soap lather with a knife.

'He's almost ready,' she called out. 'What about you? Have you got what you need?'

Tegen nodded and shivered at the touch of the rope and

chain in her pig-leg bag. Dressed in a dirty woollen shift and Owein's old green cloak, she had resurrected her ancient clogs that she had never had the heart to throw away. Her hair was loose and unkempt, partially covering the tattoo on her right cheek. Now she was just a village girl. Pretty, but unremarkable.

Bronnen whipped the cloth from Owein's neck. 'Go and wash, and pray you'll do.'

Owein stood and looked at Tegen. She gasped. There stood a man she had never seen before. His hair was cut Roman style, short all over, and his chin and upper lip were smooth and pink. He raised his hand in a smart salute, '*Ave!*' he said. 'Sextus Caractacus at your service, my lady. Are you ready?'

He draped a plain white toga around his shoulders. 'What do you think?' he asked as Tegen walked around him, her mouth and eyes open in disbelief. 'I stole it from Admidios's lodging just now. The hem is a bit torn, but otherwise it's just what we need.'

Tegen laughed. 'I would never have recognized you!' She unpacked the rope and chain and held out her hands. 'You'd better tie me up before we leave the camp. It'll look fishy if a sentry spots us getting ready just as we are about to cross the river!'

Owein picked up the rope. 'Are you sure you want to go through with this?' he asked.

'Absolutely. It's our only chance.'

Owein took the rope and tied her hands.

'Make it tighter,' she insisted.

'But I don't want to hurt you.'

'It's got to look convincing!'

Owein gave the rope a hefty tug and a cruel twist. The hemp bit into the skin around her wrists, making her wince. Then he took the chain and fixed it around her neck with a clip.

Dallel whistled to a servant, who brought Heather, well brushed and already saddled. 'May the Goddess protect you both – we won't be able to do anything to help you. Apart from the spirits, you are on your own. Oh, and don't forget this,' he added, holding out a dagger and scabbard on a leather belt.

'Thanks.' Owein buckled it under his toga and mounted his pony. 'Are you ready, Tegen?'

'Yes,' she whispered. Her hands were beginning to hurt and redden, and the iron around her neck was icy cruel. She prayed the sprig of dried yarrow stitched inside her dress would protect her.

Owein picked up the free end of the chain as he led her out of the northern gate and down the muddy path towards the river and Dorcic.

Owein hired a wooden boat to ferry them across. Heather was nervous on the water, and Tegen longed to calm her, but she could do nothing. From now on she was a slave. If things went wrong, the pretence would soon be a reality. She tried not to think about it.

Soon the prow knocked against the supports of the Roman jetty on the far bank. All around, brown waters swirled high, but it was hard for her to step on to the planking without the use of her hands. A sentry grabbed her elbows and hauled her up. Behind, she could hear Heather, scrabbling and kicking as Owein and the boatman struggled to get her on to the muddy bank.

'Who are you? What's your business?' demanded a rough voice in Latin. Tegen looked around. The sentry who had helped her was standing, feet apart, arms crossed, surveying Owein up and down. Would he smell a rat? She bit her lip and kept her head down while she prayed they would not be caught.

'Sextus Caractacus Catuvellaunius, with a gift for my uncle Gaius Admidios Catuvellaunius.' Owein saluted smartly.

'See the centurion by the gate,' the man replied, jerking his thumb over his shoulder. He didn't salute Brits.

Tegen's heart thumped in her mouth as she struggled to understand. 'What did he say?' she whispered as soon as they were treading the straight gravelled path towards the garrison.

Owein translated quietly, then added, 'Try not to talk. I'll find a way to explain anything you need to know when I can. You'll just have to trust me . . .'

Ahead was a row of steep-banked earthworks. The Romans had topped the ancient British defences with well-guarded palisades and a heavy-looking gate in the main gap. Owein held Tegen's chain as she shuffled behind, trying to look dejected and defeated.

The guard nodded them through to a second range of earthworks. Once more, Owein's story sufficed.

Beyond that was a sight that made Tegen's blood run cold.

To left and right rose walls of neatly dressed blocks of stone. Ahead was an oak gate surmounted by a wooden guard platform. Beyond, she could see hundreds of beardless men marching in strict rhythm, all dressed identically in short chain-mail shirts over woollen jerkins and knee-length breeches. Their faces were partly hidden by round helmets and wide cheekpieces. The uniformity was daunting.

Tegen glanced around for women and children, but there were only a few boys in plain tunics, probably servants. There was no laughter. Only barked shouts that sounded like orders. Owein repeated his story for a third time to the sentries at the main gate. One with black skin and dark eyes waved them to wait at the side of the road. He said something to a boy, who ran off.

Tegen took in as much information as she could. The smells were different – where was the midden? Why did all

the men look and act the same? How could they live without women and children?

Feet tramped this way and that along the gravelled paths.
Sometimes horses carried men in richer clothes. Some wore
togas like Owein, others had thigh-length red cloaks and
plumed helmets. A little while later a short, commanding
figure strode towards them. His chin was weak but his eyes
were stern. Tegen stared in horror. She had seen him at the
Stone Forest. Would he recognize her?

'Who are you?' he snapped in British.

'*Sextus Caractacus Catuvellaunius. I bring a gift for my uncle
Gaius Admidios Catuvellaunius . . .*' Owein replied in Latin as
he yanked on Tegen's slave-chain. She kept her head down,
trying to look sulky.

The Roman looked down at her. '*Why?*' he demanded.

'*Because I have been very stupid. My uncle has been kind to
me, and I have been rash, foolish and . . .*' he hesitated and then
he too hung his head, '*I fear I have behaved in a manner most
unbecoming in a Roman citizen. I have brought this . . .*' here he
tugged the chain again, and Tegen spat, praying it looked
convincing, '*as a peace offering, hoping that my dear uncle will
find it in his heart to forgive a very young and wayward boy such
as myself . . .*'

The man rubbed his chin. So the boy had walked right
into camp – cool as a spring breeze. Was this too good to be
true? He smiled. There was one way to find out. '*My name
is Quintus Caelius. Come inside, my son. You look as if you could*

do with a decent draught of good wine. Your uncle has often told me about you, and I have long wished to greet the son of such a great hero as the Lord Caractacus . . . No, no, don't dismount – I can see you ride out of necessity . . .'

Owein followed his host inside the gates. Tegen dragged her feet behind. From time to time she risked a glance at the endless identical rows of wooden longhouses on either side. She wanted to memorize the path they were taking . . . But the route was easy. They followed a central road to a large inner courtyard, at the head of which was a fine house in the process of being built. Stone steps led up to a magnificent door with pillars either side and a half-finished terracotta roof above it.

Quintus appeared to want them to follow him inside, but Owein seemed to be declining. Tegen wished she understood.

'My thanks, Quintus Caelius; you have been most helpful. I look forward to drinking wine with you later, but first I must fulfil my obligations. My uncle said he would meet me here this morning. It is my duty to be here waiting for him.'

'Of course.' The man nodded and took them behind the house, along another road and then turned left down a little street. At last he stopped outside a thatched wooden longhouse, with many doors at regular intervals. The Roman knocked at the fourth one along. There was no answer. He lifted the latch and pushed the door open.

Quintus shrugged. *'You can wait in here, although it's freez-*

ing. He refuses to have a brazier. He said it's something to do with your religion – is that right?'

'*Sort of,*' Owein grunted as he dismounted, tied Heather to a timber support and stepped inside. All was in darkness.

'*Ave!*' Quintus raised his hand smartly.

Owein returned the salute. Then the door shut and they were alone.

Owein listened for the man's retreating footsteps. When he was sure that no one was near, he drew his dagger and cut through Tegen's bindings. 'Ouch!' she squeaked, rubbing her sore wrists. 'And my neck chain?'

'Better not. If anyone disturbs us, we have to look at least a *bit* authentic.'

Slowly her eyes become accustomed to the poor light that filtered in around the fastened shutters. 'Do you think it would attract attention if we opened the wind-eye?' she asked.

'I think it would look odd if we *didn't*,' he said, lifting the hook fastening. 'But I'll only open it a little, so passers-by won't be able to see in.'

Tegen sat on a straw-stuffed mattress on a wooden bed frame. The room was narrow and only an arm-length longer than the bed. Under the wind-eye was a small table and Admidios's basket-panniers. She shivered as a chill wind blew in. 'He must get cold in winter.'

'That's his problem,' Owein grunted as he tipped a

wooden box of styli, pens and ink jars on to the bed and started to rake through them.

Tegen picked up a quill pen cut from a raven's feather. 'What odd ink! It's gone all crusty . . .' She tossed it back in the pile.

Owein picked it up, examined it, licked his finger and drew the nib end across the spittle. 'It's not ink . . . it's blood,' he said quietly. He slipped it into his pouch, then tipped one of the panniers out on the floor.

'Don't make such a mess – he'll know someone has been in here!' Tegen scolded.

'Help me look!' he said urgently, getting down on his hands and knees to rummage through his uncle's things. 'We'll put everything back. He won't know.'

'What am I looking for?' she asked as she spread the mixture of clothes and magical paraphernalia across the small room.

'Something that might have held blood, a small pot or . . .'

'Or this?' Tegen held up a pale marble bowl with black-brown streaks caked inside.

Owein turned it over, sniffed it, licked his finger and rubbed it on one of the blackish smears. 'Yes!' he breathed excitedly. 'This is blood too. And it's no ordinary bowl, it's a mortar – see if there is a pestle here somewhere!' He pushed piles of wax and clay figurines to one side and shook out a leather bag of human teeth.

Tegen heard voices outside, but she took no notice. The

place was full of men talking loudly. Her eyes wandered over beads and bones tied with feathers and strips of stinking uncured leather . . .

Then her fingers curled around the cool, smooth shape of a black-smeared marble pestle.

At that moment the door flew open. Quintus Caelius stood silhouetted against the chilly light, his red cloak flapping in the wind. Beside him was a tall, middle-aged man with a huge nose and cold, hard eyes.

Tegen gasped as she recognized her other captor from the Stone Forest! She kept her head down and prayed once again they would not recognize her.

Owein scrambled to his feet as Quintus raised his hand in salute. *'May I present Legate Suetonius Paulinus, a direct emissary from the Emperor himself? Is . . . Is everything all right in here?'* he asked, peering into the room.

Owein balanced himself against the table and tried to straighten his toga with his free hand. He swung his crutch towards Tegen and spat. *'She tried to escape. I was teaching her a lesson. Uncle's basket got knocked over.'*

Tegen stayed crouched on the floor. Very slowly she slid the pestle into her waist pouch. She longed to know what was being said, but she dared not respond without a signal from Owein. She shifted her balance until she was crouched like a cat ready to spring. But she could not see clearly in the poor light. She flicked her hair back and pulled her lips into a snarl.

Suetonius strode across the room, grabbed Tegen's hair and yanked her to her feet. With his other hand he caught her chin and twisted her face around. He ran his free hand down her body and Tegen bit back a scream. *'Pretty little thing, isn't she, Quintus? A bit too good for that traitorous Briton, don't you think?'*

Seeing Tegen in danger, Owein lost his head, drew his dagger and pressed it against Suetonius's throat. *'Let her go,'* he said in a low, steady voice. The Roman didn't move. Owein pressed the fine, sharp point a little further into the skin. *'NOW!'* he added.

Tegen tried to step back, but Suetonius's foot was on her neck chain. Shouts by the door made her eyes flicker past her captor. Two fully armed soldiers squeezed inside with swords drawn. Owein stumbled back against the wall.

Suetonius made a small gesture. *'Drop it!'* he ordered.

Owein let his dagger fall on the bed. Suetonius gripped Tegen's chain under her chin and pulled it until she was standing on tiptoe with her head caught on one side.

Then, to her surprise, he spoke in British: 'Will someone please tell me exactly what is going on in here?'

She kicked hard against the Roman's shin. Her heavy clogs did their work. He buckled. She grabbed his ears and tried to rip them from his head, digging in her nails as she did so. He howled and let go of her chain. She swung the free end around his neck and twisted the links.

In the same moment Owein reclaimed his dagger and

pressed it under Quintus's ear. Behind, the soldiers could not get near enough to help, for the bed and table blocked them. *'Back off,'* Owein warned. The men hesitated. Owein pressed the tip of his blade hard enough to break the Roman's skin. A crimson trickle dribbled on to his blood-coloured tunic.

'Do as he says!' Quintus barked.

The soldiers hesitated, then stepped backwards. As soon as the first man was outside, the second grabbed at Quintus's shoulder and pulled him out of Owein's reach. As he did so, he fed his sword hilt into the tribune's hand.

Quintus smiled. 'So, young Sextus, you *are* a viper . . . Just like your uncle!' Then with a sudden jump he pinned Owein against the wall, sword under his sternum.

Tegen gasped and let go of the chain that bound Suetonius. He sprang to his feet and in one quick motion hauled her over his shoulder. She screamed and began to thump hard at his cuirass.

Owein renewed his grip on his dagger and found his balance, using his buttocks to support himself against the wooden wall at his back.

His opponent moved skilfully. But Owein was also Roman trained. He knew that Quintus would attack with a direct stabbing motion. He also knew that, if he kept his nerve, he might be able to twist aside and tangle the blade in his toga. He watched and waited for the attack.

At that moment Suetonius tried to squeeze past Quintus.

Tegen kicked wildly, grabbed a roof support and held on for dear life. The heavy legate lost his balance and fell against his smaller comrade. In the cramped space, they both tumbled on to the bed. Their armour clanged. Quintus still grasped his sword.

Tegen fell on top of them and the blade slid across her hip.

She felt the warmth of the blood two whole heartbeats before the pain.

As it seared up her left-hand side, she screamed.

And in fury and fear, she spread her hands and thought of fire.

Immediately, flames licked the bedding, caught the straw and began to leap and crackle, catching clothes, hair, baskets and flesh. The men thrust her off them and tried to scramble to their feet.

But Tegen was already running out of the door, straight into the arms of the nearest soldier.

At that moment, Owein sheathed his knife, swung forward on his crutch and vaulted over the thrashing men. But his crutch slipped on the debris of Admidios's things. He crashed across the room and catapulted out of the door, hitting his face against the jamb. Blood poured from his nose.

The second soldier grabbed for him, but hearing shouts for help from inside, he let him go. Smoke and flames were billowing out. Red gold licked along the thatching, light sparks and tufts of burning straw danced in the wind.

'*Fire!*' he yelled.

'*All units!*' Tegen's captor bellowed. '*Get water!*' Then he flung her aside and leaped into the room.

Tegen stumbled to her feet, untied Heather and thrust her reins into Owein's hand. 'Get up!'

Dazed, he wiped his nose on his sleeve, retrieved his crutch and heaved himself into the saddle.

The chilly autumn wind spread the flames through the thatching along the whole length of the barrack block. Tegen spread her hands once more and kindled fire on the other side of the street.

'Let's go while they're busy!' Owein shouted.

The once-ordered garrison now seethed with shouting men forming human chains for buckets of water. Others grabbed besoms and rushed to beat out the flames.

Stinging, blinding, choking smoke blew everywhere as bright tatters of straw flew in the wind, setting more and more alight.

Owein kicked Heather into the fastest trot she had ever done. Holding her mane, Tegen ran alongside, her hand pressed to her bleeding side.

The shouts for water swelled, as did the panicked rush of men. Tegen and Owein slipped between them, unnoticed. They turned to their right and ran towards the central square with the grand house. Men were running from all directions, knocking into them, shoving them aside, dashing this way and that and shouting orders.

'Take the next left, over there!' Owein yelled.

'But we'll get lost!' Tegen looked around, terrified by the mayhem.

'We won't!' Owein grabbed her arm and kicked Heather into a brisker trot. 'There'll be a gate around that corner. If we go back the way we came, we'll be trampled by men rushing to get water from the river. These garrisons are all built to a set plan. Trust me! This is our only chance.'

Tegen's side hurt too much for her to argue. She gripped the horns on Owein's saddle as they made their way along an empty lane. Suddenly it opened out into a road wide enough for a marching army. It was deserted. 'Along here!' Owein urged as he slowed Heather to a dignified walk. To their left, heavy wooden gates stood open, and the sentries saluted Owein, but exchanged hesitant glances when they saw he was leading a British girl who was bleeding badly.

Owein jerked his thumb over his shoulder. *'The tribune's slave got hurt in the fire. Got to get her out of the way.'*

The men nodded and let them through. Beyond was open ground, a few deserted roundhouses and then fields edged with sparse woodland. 'Run for all you are worth, Tegen.

You can faint later! Keep going straight ahead and we'll meet the river where it bends. We can't risk being seen!'

But Tegen could not run.

Owein hauled her across his lap as he kicked Heather again. The pony sensed the urgency, tossed her head and pressed on. Tegen was gasping for air. Heather soon had them amongst the trees, with flat water meadows ahead. At last the great earthworks and the garrison were well behind them.

Owein let Heather slow and glanced at Tegen. She was as white as linen, her hand slick with the blood that poured down her leg. He steered the pony behind a fallen willow tree and dismounted. He nicked the edge of his toga and ripped off a long, wide strip. 'Lift your skirt,' he said.

Tegen stared at him wide-eyed. *'What?'*

'I am trying to save your life!' he snapped.

She did as she was told, leaned against the tree and gnawed her lip as Owein bound her wound as tightly as he could.

'Get up!' Owein ordered, once more heaving Tegen like a sack across Heather's withers. Her head spun and she felt sick, but she was too weak to protest. Owein clambered into the saddle just as a shout went up behind them. One glance back told him to move. Fast.

Heather, unused to the extra load, was getting short-winded. Owein stroked and coaxed her until her hoofs were squelching through the thick brown ooze of the river's edge.

'Hold on!' Owein ordered as Heather launched herself into the swirling floods and began to swim.

Icy cold slapped Tegen's body. She opened her mouth to gasp, but muddy water rushed in. She coughed and spluttered as she gripped Owein around his middle. The current was lifting and tugging her away from him. Owein had one hand grasping Heather's reins, the other tightly around Tegen's waist. The flowing muscles of Heather's steady strokes rippled as the brave pony fought the might of the autumn flood. She held her head high, and her eyes stared wide and wild as her milky mane spread out around them both.

Owein's toga grew heavy and began to drag. Frantically he tried to throw it aside, but it was caught between his leg and the saddle. Slowly, too slowly, the golden-leaf carpet of the far bank came closer.

Spurred on by the sight, Heather pushed even harder.

At last her hoofs caught on stones and mud. Her shoulders rose from the river. Water poured as the pony struggled to gain higher ground. Tegen slid down and collapsed behind a bramble thicket. Owein swung himself out of the saddle and put his arms around her.

He stroked her long dark hair and kissed it gently. 'I thought I had lost you . . .'

Tegen was too scared and shaken to know what to do or

say. She just stayed where she was and rested on his shoulder. As they both regained their breath, Owein said, 'Let's go,' and helped her into the saddle. Then, using his crutch, he dragged himself up the slope behind them.

The bare trees were close and tangled, but soon they came to the cleared banks and lowest ramparts of the stronghold. A shout went up from a warrior on sentry duty, and Tegen passed out.

47. Unravelling the Spell

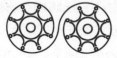

Tegen howled with pain behind the screens in Bronnen's guest bed. The old druidess gave her a piece of willow bark to chew and clicked her tongue as she sewed Tegen's flesh with a needle and thread. Tegen struggled to stay still and wept with relief when Bronnen tied a knot and cut the twine.

'It's not too bad a wound, no vitals hurt,' she said. 'You've had a narrow escape. You are to rest for a day or two and do nothing. Do you hear me?'

Tegen nodded, but looked over her shoulder to see Owein dressed in his own clothes once more. His face looked drawn and worried. As soon as Bronnen had gone he sat on the end of Tegen's bed and showed her Admidios's bedraggled raven-feather quill. 'We lost all our evidence,' he said. 'The river has washed this clean and the pestle and mortar were our only other clues. I left them behind! Everything else is burned.' He slumped against the wall and hugged his knees.

'Look in my waist pouch,' Tegen said.

The leather was dripping wet and badly slashed. Owein opened it. There was the pestle, cracked into two. 'It looks like this saved your life!' he said as he pulled out the pieces. The water had reconstituted the dark smears into red blood and lumps of something that looked like blackened worms.

'Ugh . . .' Tegen groaned, 'that looks revolting. What *is* it?'

Owein examined it in the light from the door, 'I'd say it was . . . squashed-up *leeches*. What do you think, Bronnen?'

The old druidess came and turned the broken marble pieces in the light. 'These are a couple of their biting mouths here, for sure,' she said, handing them back. Owein put the pieces carefully on the table, then walked up and down the room thumping his crutch hard and rubbing his clean-shaven face. At last he stopped, then swung around grinning.

'Got it,' he said.

'Got what?' asked Tegen.

'I know how Admidios killed Eiscr. He made a spell using Eiser's own blood. What did you do with the leeches you used on the King?'

Tegen wrinkled her nose, then said, 'Angor took them. He said he wanted the pot back. When I'd finished with them he offered to take them to the pond for me.'

'Something's wrong there – Angor's a lazy brat,' Bronnen said. 'I'll send a boy for him.'

A little later the young ovate shuffled in looking nervously from side to side. Dallel arrived at the same time. He folded his arms and scowled as he blocked the doorway.

'What do you know about leeches?' Owein asked as Angor warmed himself by the fire.

The boy made a face. 'Horrid things. Did you bring me here to ask me that? You look like a bloody Roman,' he sneered. 'You gone like your Da and your uncle?'

Owein ignored the insult. 'You gave Tegen the leeches to treat Eiser before he died.'

'What of it?'

'Why did you give them to her?'

'She won them in a game.'

'An odd sort of a prize.'

Angor shrugged. 'She does healing. I thought they'd be useful.'

'Was it your idea?'

The young man said nothing. Owein scrutinized him. 'What did you do with them afterwards?'

Angor shrugged and jerked his thumb over his shoulder. 'I caught them in the pond, down there at the bottom. I would have put them back, but Admidios wanted them. No harm in that.' Angor fiddled with a spot on his face.

Tegen swung her legs around and winced as she sat. 'Where did *you* get the idea from?' she asked.

Angor looked from one to the other of his questioners. He crossed his arms and stared back at Owein. 'Admidios told me to do it. He said leeches would help King Eiser.'

'Did he pay you?' Owein pressed.

'None of your bloody business.'

'You mean "yes"?'

Angor scowled. 'Even druids have to make a living, or does being the son of the great Caractacus shield you from such facts of life?'

Owein was tempted to punch Angor, but he took a deep breath and controlled himself. 'So Admidios paid you to make sure Tegen used leeches on Eiser?'

'Yes.' He raised his chin and stared at Owein defiantly.

Owein raised an eyebrow at Dallel. The old druid nodded. 'Angor suffers from lack of money rather than lack of morals.' He turned to his apprentice. 'Go away – we'll talk about your future here later.'

The young ovate turned on his heel and stalked out.

Bronnen watched him go. 'What have leeches got to do with Eiser's death?'

Owein drew up his chair. 'Tegen's fire spiral showed her that Krake, Admidios's raven, was used to kill Eiser. It would fit with Cluan's prophecy that he would die "from a blow from no man's hand", but it doesn't make sense, in that there were no attack marks on his body.' He opened his waist pouch and pulled out the pieces of broken comb. 'After my foster-father died, I found these on the floor. Do

you see the muddy marks? They are from a Roman boot –
like Admidios wears. If my uncle went into Eiser's roundhouse and managed to get hold of some of his hair from his
comb, and later some of his blood . . .'

'From the leeches!' Tegen added.

'. . . then you have the perfect core for a very powerful
shadow spell,' Dallel finished. 'But how could the *bird* cast
it?'

Owen pulled the bent quill pen from his pouch and
handed it across. 'When we found this in Admidios's room,
it was crusted with dried blood. My guess is that Admidios
wrote the spell in Eiser's own blood, wound it round with
his hair, then all Krake had to do was deliver it.'

'Of *course!*' Tegen said. 'The bird cage was in the room.
Admidios said that Eiser had insisted on looking after the
bird, but I bet it was the other way around; Admidios somehow blackmailed him into having it. Where is the cage
now?'

'It was thrown out on to the midden. I searched it at the
time, but didn't find anything helpful,' Owein replied.

'Did you know what you were looking for?' Bronnen
asked.

Dallel stroked his beard for a few moments, then said,
'You'd need bone, preferably human . . . and it would have
to be tied together somehow—'

Before he could finish Tegen had thrown off her bed
covers. 'The midden!' she exclaimed. 'In my fire spiral I

dreamed I was in a stinking place of rotten carcasses and I was light enough to be carried. It was as if I had become a twig or . . .'

'A scroll . . .' Owein said, 'a very tiny one, rolled as small as a stick so the bird could carry it unnoticed!' He was already half way out of the door and Tegen was hobbling behind him. Bronnen tried to call her back, but the old druidess was wasting her breath.

The friends ran as best they could out of the northern gate. 'Down there,' Owein said, pointing to where rubbish was heaped between the steep walls of the ramparts. 'That's where the cage was dumped.' And he began the slow, slippery descent.

Tegen tried to follow, but her hip seared with pain and started to bleed again, so she leaned over the earth bank and watched as he slid and slithered his way down. At the bottom he picked his way warily between rubbish and viciously pointed wooden stakes arranged to deter any would-be attackers. 'Be careful!' she called.

He ignored her and used his crutch to push decaying cabbage and broken pots aside.

'Look for a corpse,' she yelled out.

'What?'

'That's what I saw in the spiral. The spell has fallen inside a rotting body of some kind.'

At that moment the sound of hunting horns and barking dogs made Owein jump. 'Admidios! He's back!' he shouted. As he did so, something gave way under his foot and he fell. He landed on his back and the stench of decay exploded in his nose. He tried to stand, but as he struggled a screeching raven swooped, flapping viciously at his head. Owein lashed out at it, but the bird rushed past him, grabbed something in its talons and soared off into the sky. Owein righted himself, but his good leg was caught in the ribcage of a dog.

He shook himself free and pulled himself back up the slope, trailing the stench as he climbed. At last, hot and breathless, he reached the top.

'That was Krake, wasn't it?' he asked as they walked through the gate. 'Did you see what she took?'

'It looked like a couple of sticks tied together.'

'If it's the spell, she'll have hidden it. Ravens cache food and precious things all the time.'

'Look.' Tegen pointed. 'She's on the roof of that hut on the far side of the enclosure.'

'That's Admidios's lodging!' Owein said. 'We must get to it before he does. The hunt will arrive any moment. I'll distract him; you go and see what you can find.'

Tegen shivered at the thought of going into the Shadow Walker's room. Her hip hurt and blood was seeping through the bandages. Pressing her hand to her side, she imagined herself dancing under the Watching Woman's stars, the evil times long past.

*

When she arrived at Admidios's hut Krake was still perched on the thatched roof. The bird blinked her white inner eyelids and glared at Tegen maliciously. *When my master has finished with you, then your pretty green eyes will be mine*, she promised herself. Then, spreading her coal-black wings, the raven flapped twice, launched herself into the air and flew away.

There was nothing in her talons.

Tegen glanced towards Connal's great longhouse. Beyond it, the courtyard was bustling with people talking and laughing. The hunt had gone well, but she had to hurry. She lifted the door latch of Admidios' lodging and slipped inside. It was dark and cold. Dried rushes crunched underfoot. On the left, she could feel a wooden bed frame pressing into her leg. She blinked and tried to adjust her eyes to the shadows. Then she realized the bird couldn't have got *inside*. Whatever she had hidden would be in the *thatch* . . .

Just then the door opened. Tegen gasped. There was nowhere she could hide.

48. Animae Umbrosae

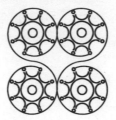

The figure that entered was slim and lithe. It wasn't Admidios. Tegen breathed again.

Kieran stiffened and took a step backwards.

'It's only me,' Tegen said. 'I'm looking for something.'

Kieran opened his mouth as if to speak, his eyes pleading urgency.

'What's the matter?' she asked.

The boy tried to make signs. Then he rummaged in a basket under the table and pulled out a small shape, which he thrust into Tegen's hands. She held it up to the light from the door. It was a wax doll and, instead of a mouth, a rough plug of wood was pushed into the face. Tegen looked at the doll and at Kieran's frantic signs.

'Is this a spell to keep you silent?'

He nodded.

'This might take some time to undo. I can't just pull the stick out – it might hurt you. I need to know how the spell has been made, but I will take it with me and ask Bronnen, I promise. Can you still hear?'

The boy nodded again as he laid a clean shirt and breeches on the bed. Suddenly he straightened and made frantic signs to Tegen. Outside swift, heavy footsteps were approaching. She dived under the bed. She felt the stitches rip her skin. She wanted to cry out in pain, but didn't dare. She forced herself to lie still, not breathing. Dust and dried rushes tickled her nose as she stared at the dark outline of her enemy's boots, only a hand-span from her face. Admidios yelled at Kieran and slapped him. He changed his clothes, tossed his muddy breeches and jerkin on the floor, then stormed out, leaving the door wide open.

Kieran watched him go, then beckoned to Tegen.

She slithered out, biting her lip as more pain seared through her side. Kieran frowned as she buckled and sat heavily on the bed. 'Don't worry, I will be all right,' she said. Then a thought struck her. 'Can you climb?'

Kieran reached up to the roof beam and swung on it, grinning.

'If you do something for me, I will tell Connal you deserve your freedom. I can't promise he'll grant it, but I will ask.'

The boy's eyes widened.

'I need you to go up into the thatch of this hut and find

something. It won't look like much, just a small bundle, maybe a bone and a hollow stick or something like that. And it'll all be tied together somehow . . .'

He frowned and shrugged.

'Please – it's really important,' she went on. 'It's something Krake has hidden.'

Kieran glanced out of the door. He looked left and right to make sure his master was out of sight. Then he pushed Tegen outside, signing to her to go.

'Thank you,' she said. 'Please bring whatever you find to Dallel and Bronnen's house as soon as you can.'

Kieran arrived just as the night brought more rain and wind. His shirt bulged with gleanings from the straw. Bronnen cleared the table and he poured out his prizes. Spoons, trinkets, a silver brooch, a ribbon of Tegen's, coins, then a twig and bell from Dallel's silver branch.

But amongst them all was a small bundle with a human finger bone wound with dark, curly hair. A strip of woollen cloth tied the bone to a piece of bulrush. Owein pounced. 'That's *it*!' he exclaimed in delight, untying the cloth and unfurling the leaves. Inside was a tightly rolled scroll of parchment. Gingerly he spread it flat. His hands were shaking as Dallel brought a tallow candle.

Owein cleared his throat and began to read:

Animae umbrosae metusque noctisque,
visu mortali apparete;
sistite cordem et mentem corripite,
ne hic diutius spirare possit.

The room fell silent apart from the popping and crackling of the fire. 'I heard those words in my fire spiral,' Tegen said quietly. 'What do they mean?'

Owein stared at the writing for a few moments, then said, 'Something like this:

Spirits of shadow and fear and night,
show yourselves to human sight;
stop the heart and seize the brain,
so this man won't breathe again.'

Then he licked his finger and rubbed it across the final word. The smudge was red. 'It *is* written in blood!' he said.

Dallel scratched his head. 'But it's in Latin, so how could it work on Eiser? For a spell like that to be effective, the victim has to understand what is said.'

'Eiser spoke Latin,' Owein replied. 'He collaborated for a while. But this scroll was so tightly tied I suspect he hadn't even opened it. Surely he'd have died with it in his hand if he had read it?'

Kieran coughed loudly. All turned to him. He pointed to his mouth frantically.

'I'm sorry . . . of course . . . the doll.' Tegen pulled the wax effigy from her waist pouch. 'Look, Admidios made Kieran dumb with this.'

Bronnen picked it up and examined it. 'It's good you didn't just pull the plug, Tegen – that might have ripped his teeth out.' She put the doll into a small iron pot and placed it at the edge of the fire. 'You might feel rather warm for a little while,' she said to Kieran, 'but it will be all right, I promise.'

Kieran began to sweat, but soon the wooden plug was floating on the surface of a pool of wax. Around the end was twisted a dun-coloured hair. Carefully Bronnen unwound it and held it out to Kieran. 'This is from your head, isn't it?'

He nodded.

'That was how he tied the spell to you. You can do what you like with it now. I'd recommend you burn it – then all connection with Admidios will be broken.'

Kieran tossed the hair into the hottest part of the fire, and Bronnen threw the wax and the wooden plug after it. The flames leaped and hissed, then died back.

'Let's have a look in your mouth,' Bronnen said, spitting on her fingers and rubbing them on his tongue. 'Try and say something.'

The boy took a deep breath and said, 'Thank you . . .' He looked around nervously. 'I've heard those Latin words before too.'

'When?' Dallel asked.

'My master taught the raven to say them.'

Owein stroked his chin. 'So all Admidios had to do was to get the bird and my foster-father alone . . . and then make sure that everyone knew that *he* was well away from Sinodun.' Owein went to where he had left Admidios's toga in a wet heap. He searched the hem; the tie matched the tear. He brought it to the light for all to see.

Dallel sighed. 'You were right, my boy – we did need hard evidence as well as the voices of the spirits. My apologies to you.' Then he raised his hands and began to chant a prayer of thanks to the Goddess and the spirits of truth. Bronnen picked up a small drum and joined in. Tegen longed to dance, but her hip hurt too much.

When the prayer was finished, Dallel said, 'Connal must be told immediately. I will ask for your freedom as a reward, Kieran. Meanwhile, can you go back and pretend nothing has happened?'

'I can,' he said, and ran back to tidy his master's lodging.

The feasting hall was bright with music and laughter. Admidios leaned back in the stout wooden chair next to Connal. Both men were so full of roast boar they could hardly move. A servant came and whispered in the chieftain's ear. Connal excused himself, went outside, spoke briefly with Dallel and then returned. As he sat, he clapped his hands and demanded more wine for his noble friend Admidios, the hero of the hunt.

When Admidios woke the following morning, his head was throbbing and his face lay in a pool of vomit. He tried to roll over and yell for Kieran. But he couldn't move. He opened his eyes. Why was he on the floor?

A pair of boots came into sight. Warrior's boots. He could also see a spear handle, breeches, a jerkin, a three-coloured cloak and, above it all, a wild mop of dark hair. The guard leaned over. 'Did you sleep well, my lord?' he jeered and kicked the prisoner in the beer gut. Admidios threw up again.

As he recovered, he realized he was chained by the neck and wrists to a heavy metal stake driven into the ground. He was in the guardhouse beside the northern gate. He managed to sit. What was he doing here? Had he drunk too much or had he been drugged? He had to speak with Owein Sextus as soon as possible. Didn't the boy realize the Romans would be on Sinodun in a flash if he didn't report back on time? He tried to think clearly enough to compose a spell to release his chains, but his demon had deserted him.

*

Suetonius and Quintus knew exactly why their least favourite spy had not reported in.

Owein had asked for two smoothly planed squares of wood. On the first he wrote a brief outline of the murder charge. On the second he penned a request that Connal, chieftain of the last outpost of the Atrebates tribe, should surrender Sinodun without bloodshed at the dark of the moon – the feast of Samhain.

A servant handed these letters to the sentry at the jetty, then turned his boat and paddled as fast as he could, back to the relative safety of the stronghold.

The people of Sinodun began to pack their things. The site Connal had chosen for the new village was not far away. Quintus sent an emissary to agree to Connal's proposal. He insisted the Roman army bore no ill will to the British people; they simply did not want them to inhabit 'seats of rebellion', by which, Owein explained to Tegen, they meant fortified strongholds that might be able to resist with military might in the future.

'The Romans like people to live in unfortified towns they can control. They'll burn Sinodun so no one will come back, like the places we passed on the way.'

She shuddered at the memory. 'Because Connal is surrendering, does that mean there will be no killing?'

'Unless someone does something stupid,' Owein said,

glancing towards Connal, who was deep in conversation with his warriors. Then he turned to Tegen. 'I need your advice.'

She sat up straight. It was unlike Owein to be at a loss. 'What's the matter?'

He drew patterns on the table with spilled ale. 'It's Sabrina. Admidios keeps sending messages saying he will tell me where she is if I have him set free.'

'And if you don't?'

He shrugged. 'Goodness knows. Perhaps she's dead already. I am certain he will try to kill *me* if he does get free.'

'Why you?'

'Because I haven't played his game. You've seen how bitter and vengeful he can be. But without knowing where she is, I cannot fulfil my pledge to the Dobunni chieftains. Either way, I am a dead man.'

Tegen stared into the fire that blazed on the central hearth. 'Are you asking me whether it is worth risking your life to find out where Sabrina is, or if I can scry the flames and find her whereabouts myself?'

'Both,' he replied quietly.

Tegen sighed. 'I have tried and tried Fire Dreaming for Sabrina, but nothing comes. If it's any comfort, I am certain she is alive, but that is all I can tell. As to the other part of your question, I would say no, don't bargain with him. I am sure that together we can find her somehow.' And she reached out and squeezed his hand.

Owein managed a half-smile. 'What worries me even more is that the messenger Admidios sends is Kieran. Admidios knows he can speak again.'

'So?'

'Well . . .' Owein began, 'I'm not entirely sure whose side the boy is on. He talks as if he is *convinced* that Admidios is sorry for having captured her and wants to set her free. I think Admidios has managed to use his smooth tongue and Kieran is working for him willingly.'

'Have you been to see your uncle?'

Owein shook his head. 'What's the point? Everything he says is poisoned. I'm done with him!'

For the next twelve days the people of Sinodun carried all their possessions down the hill to their new home on a meadow to the south. All that was rubbish or unwanted was tossed into the midden. At the new site, everyone worked together to build a couple of roundhouses and some simple shelters. The stronghold grain pits were emptied and the contents transferred to new ones. Tegen helped Dallel and Bronnen bless the stores and make sure that the new ground was protected with the best spells they knew.

But all the while, Admidios lay chained on the cold floor of the guardhouse, eating what scraps were flung his way and seething with hate.

Perched on the ledge of the wind-eye, Krake watched him and knew that the time she would feast on his eyes was drawing near.

49. Admidios's Escape

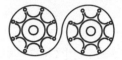

O n the morning of the Samhain feast, Tribune Quintus stood on the jetty with Suetonius Paulinus, who had just been appointed Imperial Governor of the Britannic Isles. Quintus was pleased. His new lord had seen how well his patience and good negotiating had won Rome this outpost of rebellion without a single life being lost.

Suetonius had been all for siege and slaughter. But Quintus, who ruled Dorcic, had been proved right. When the stronghold was empty and the villagers moved, the British would be weak and compliant for a few years, long enough for them to become used to Roman ways. As with all the other conquered peoples across the Celtic lands, they would soon forget their old lives.

*

But in his new roundhouse, Connal was not so easily quashed. He had his own agenda. The surprise he had left for the invaders would leave them with a few smarting scars for a while.

Towards nightfall Kieran, Connal's newly freed manservant, slipped away for one more visit to his old master.

The boy carried a pot of stew with him. He had prepared it himself. He also carried a few tools that he hoped might be strong enough to spring Admidios's iron collar.

Connal had left the prisoner chained to the floor for the Romans to find and deal with in their own way. He didn't relish the prospect of the shadow spirits Admidios served coming to wreak vengeance on the new settlement. Connal preferred that the Romans had *that* pleasure for themselves.

But Kieran did not think that was right.

He made his way across the open ground between the new village and the old stronghold. No voices challenged him as he pushed the main gates apart. The place was empty and desolate. He opened the guardhouse door. There, on the floor, was Admidios, urine-soaked and covered in faeces. He was pathetic.

'My dear boy . . .' Admidios sat up and beamed with delight, 'I am so pleased to see you. I knew you wouldn't let me down. I will reward you for setting me free. Oh yes, I will reward you *richly* . . .'

Kieran said nothing, but put the pot of food down. Trying not to breathe in the stench, he worked at the iron collar and manacles. Using a rasp, he had soon cut the bolts that held them in place.

Admidios tried to stand, but he was weak. Kieran handed him the stew and a spoon. 'You'll feel stronger if you eat. Then you must fly – quickly!' He turned and left.

As he ate, Admidios did feel stronger. Much stronger. In fact, he felt as if the world was holding its arms open to him. As soon as he was free he would become the next governor – maybe even emperor. Nothing . . . *nothing* was impossible for a man like him. He staggered to his feet. What had the boy said? He must fly? Of course he should!

He held out his hand for Krake, who was perched watching him from the wind-eye. The bird flew down and Admidios grasped her jesses tightly. 'Come now, my pretty, we are going to fly away from here together . . . you and me. We will *both* fly . . .' he staggered out of the guardhouse and struggled to make his way up the ladder to the walkway at the top of the palisade.

Krake flapped her wings in delight at the prospect of freedom. My time has come at last, she thought. There is no way this fool can fly. He will fall and break his neck, and when he dies I will devour his eyes. Then I will go so far away, the emptiness will never find me . . .

*

Then, like waking from a dream, Krake remembered who she was.

All her human memories surged back to her. She squawked with delight. At last her tongue was her own as she screamed at the heavy pall of clouds above. 'I, Derowen, wise woman of the Winter Seas, will find a human mother and be reborn, as is my right . . . !'

Admidios ignored her cawing and struggling and tightened his hold on her jesses. He swayed as he looked across the river to the Roman garrison in the fading light. His heart was pounding with dread and excitement. From all around he was buffeted and taunted with fear and hate; lust and greed slithered inside his stomach. Vindictiveness surged through him as he spread his free hand and cursed everyone he had ever known.

A gust of icy wind at his back made him shiver. Below, the silvery sliding snake of the river slipped eastward between the bare trees, towards the next day's sunrise. But he would be well away before then. He breathed deeply, threw back his head and declaimed to the skies: 'I, Admidios, Shadow Walker, am going to fly away!'

Suddenly Krake realized he was still gripping her. She gnawed at his fingers. 'Let me go!' she screeched, flapping desperately. 'Let me go. I will help you fly, but I can't if you are holding me . . . !'

Admidios pulled the bird close to his face. He gripped her neck with his right hand. 'Oh yes, my pretty, you will help me fly – but I don't trust you.' Using his teeth, he tied the jesses to his wrist. 'You *will* share your magic with me. *We will soar the skies together* . . .'

And with that, he launched himself into the air.

He landed, impaled on three wooden spikes in the midden. His dying eyes' last sight was the wrecked cage he had used to imprison Krake.

The raven fluttered and tried to get free, but her jesses held. She struggled as she cursed Admidios with every curse she had ever known when she had been a human witch, but there was nothing she could do except watch as a common crow came circling down and began to feast on the eyes that should have been *hers* . . .

As darkness gathered like a heavy cloak and the Samhain doors between the worlds opened once again, the witch's spirit within Krake imagined Tegen's face and chanted:

> *Animae umbrosae metusque noctisque,*
> *visu mortali apparete;*

sistite cordem et mentem corripite,
ne hic diutius spirare possit.

In the new village, Tegen and Wolf found Owein sitting in a stick-and-moss shelter, rubbing his withered leg with an ointment of birch leaves steeped in goose fat. He looked miserable.

'Does it hurt a lot today?' she asked.

'It always bloody hurts!' he snapped. 'Especially when the weather turns cold. Twm says that it will get worse as I get older.'

Wolf smelled the ointment and began to lick the pale, twisted ankle with his warm tongue. Tegen sat next to Owein on his bed of dried ferns.

She wanted to lay her hands on his leg and try to heal it. Twm had told her about such things. But perhaps Owein needed to let his anger out first, lest it prevent his healing.

'I wanted to thank you,' she said.

He wiped his fingers inside the grey grease pot. 'What for?'

'Saving my life, back there in the garrison, then again in the river.'

She risked reaching out and squeezing his hand. 'You have been a really good friend.'

He pulled himself free and rubbed more ointment where Wolf had licked it clean.

'You said you might be coming with me?' Tegen ventured again.

He sighed, slammed the pot down and looked at her. His moustache was beginning to smudge his top lip again and a light beard was thickening on his chin. Framed by his severe haircut, his dark eyes were sad.

'No. Better not.'

'Why?'

There was a long pause.

'Tegen, haven't you realized that I'm in love with you?' he blurted out suddenly. 'I have been since the day I saw you dancing in the rain on that hill in Sul's Land . . . I've still kept the hair you gave me by the wight-barrow. But what good is a cripple to you?' He flapped her away. 'You have a land to save, evil to turn aside; you are destined to be a hero. I am just . . . well . . .'

'A hero too,' she said gently, squeezing his greasy fingers. 'But you are right – I can't be your woman. But it's not because of your leg.'

'What is it then?' he asked, glaring miserably out of the doorway at the swirls of damp leaves that whirled in the autumn winds. 'Has the Goddess told you to desert me?'

'Don't be like that – listen. It's not *me* you should love, it's Sabrina . . .'

'Oh, for *goodness sake*!' He slapped his good leg and leaned back on Wolf, who had curled up behind him.

Tegen took a deep breath. 'Listen, Admidios was right about one thing. Her destiny – and yours – is to give rebirth to our heroes, so there will be chieftains, kings and queens to lead us when we are gone. You owe it to both your fathers. You owe it to your ancestors' spirits and to all who have died in this fight. Listen to them . . . it's Samhain tonight – the spirits are everywhere! What do they tell you?'

'Nothing. They've never spoken to me, and I suspect they never will. All my life it's been "duty, duty, duty", and now *you* are starting the same tune! I thought you were different and might love me for my own sake. But you're just like the rest!' He struggled to get to his feet, but Tegen whipped his crutch away.

'No! Stay and listen! Just for once, you *don't* know best! You're being unfair and you *know* it! Sabrina adores you, and deep down you love her too, but you think you aren't good enough because of that leg. You're running away from her, and she respects you too much to give chase – or she would, if she was here.' Tegen pushed his crutch back into his chest. 'Go on then, keep on your travels if that's what you want. But Sabrina needs you. For what it's worth, I'm still convinced she's alive – and in trouble.'

Owein tried to interrupt, but she didn't give him a chance. 'I will go to Mona alone. *Your* job is to find Sabrina and marry her. And you *are* good enough. *You* don't have to be a king. Crown Sabrina queen, be her druid, but for the sake of every good spirit, be true to your own destiny!'

Then she stood and looked down at him, crumpled in the shadows. 'As a matter of fact, I do love you – very much – but it's a friend's love. Listen to your own heart and you'll know it's true, but we must take different roads, Owein.' And with that she walked away, Wolf loping behind her.

As night fell over the new village, a tangled bonfire rose in the central space between the shacks and huts. Everyone had brought some token of their old home: roof posts, thatching, furniture, household rubbish, even some broken shields and spears. In the dark the huge pile of wood and straw took on the shape and aspect of a desolate creature, abandoned, lonely and empty.

Mournful pipes, horns and drums began to strike up sombre music. The crowds took their places. Holding hands in several rings, they walked widdershins, moving against the Sun God's path around the smashed symbolic remains of Sinodun as they unravelled its soul.

The music stopped. Suddenly the people stamped, waved their arms, spat and shouted at the unlit fire.

Dallel raised his staff for silence. Bronnen lit a torch from a brazier and made her way through the crowds to stand before the remnants of so many years and so many people's lives. She gave the torch to her man. He held the flames above the wood, speaking in a loud voice so all present could hear.

'We greet you, spirits of the West. Be welcome here at this time of remembrance. Take all our pasts and wash them away in your healing waters.' Then he turned to the crowds. 'Let your land and bodies rest as the Sun God takes his repose in this dark time of the year. Let the waters of memory flow over the stones of sleep and death. Be at peace, for as the year turns and the Mabon is born again, all shall be well.'

Then he plunged the torch into the kindling and said, 'Welcome your ancestors to their new hearths with this new fire in a new place. Show them where their children now remember them.'

At that, the musicians bashed and blew their instruments as loudly as they could to scare away all evil spirits. The crowd joined in with clapping and singing. The pale yellow flames licked the hay and shavings, then ran and leaped, devouring wood and cloth, crackling and hissing as they burned.

Bronnen picked up a bodhran and began to beat a steady rhythm. She skipped around the fire with her grey hair flowing down her back. The crowd's noise subsided as she started to sing:

> *The end of the year has come.*
> *Throw all evil away,*
> *Destroy the shadows,*
> *Welcome the new day.*

Give gifts to the ancients,
Celebrate their names,
Bless them with honey,
Welcome them home.'

As she passed by, people came forward and threw more unwanted memories into the flames, shouting tales of their bad luck and the loss of their homes into the golden heart of the fire.

The musicians played again, this time a brighter tune. Once more the people joined hands and they danced deosil around the fire, following the Sun God's own trackway across the skies.

But no one could really be merry with the firelight catching on the desolate shape of Sinodun behind them.

Tegen's side was almost healed. She ran and joined in the ring of dancers, where she found herself hand in hand with Kieran, resplendent with a freeman's belt and dagger at his waist. 'I went to see Admidios this afternoon,' he shouted over the noise.

'How was he?' Tegen yelled back, nervous as she recalled Owein's fears.

'Hungry. I made him some stew and took his iron chains off. I set him free.'

Tegen stopped dead, almost sending the other dancers into a heap. She grabbed Kieran's hand and dragged him out of the way. 'You did *what*? How could you?' She glared at him in disbelief. So Owein had been right about the boy's change of loyalty.

A slow smile crept across his face. 'You ought to ask me what I put in his dinner before you get angry . . .' His eyes were full of mischief.

Warily Tegen asked, 'Very well, what *did* you cook for him?'

'Fly agaric, those red toadstools with white spots that make you go weird. I think he thought he could fly. Last I saw, he was impaled on three wooden stakes at the bottom of the midden. I'm quite a good cook actually,' he added cheerfully as he spun off back into the dance.

Tegan was horrified by Kieran's trick. The Shadow Walker's spirit would now be free to wander in this night of ghosts and spirits, but she was pleased he was dead. The world would at least have respite from his cruelty.

The flames rose higher, sending golden, joyous sparks into the soft indigo sky. Tegen wished she could feel really happy, but a heaviness around her heart told her that the people of Sinodun were a long way from being able to live at peace with their new neighbours.

Suddenly the sound of shouting came from behind her. She turned. Sinodun was alight and the midden aflame as well.

Connal came and stood next to Tegen and stroked his long moustaches. 'A little welcome gift from me,' he said. 'I had men waiting. As soon as the Romans were inside, my warriors slammed the gates and set fire to the walls and ditches.'

Tegen looked at the chieftain in disbelief. 'But that's terrible,' she said. 'Your men will never get out!'

Connal bowed his head in respect. 'They understood the cost. May they be born again soon.'

'But there will be reprisals,' Tegen gasped. 'The Romans will destroy you and your people! There has to be a chance for peace and forgiveness or things will get worse and worse . . . You have to break the chain of hate – can't you *understand*?'

But her protests fell on deaf ears. Connal was drinking from his best mead horn as the dancing flames reflected the delight in his eyes.

Tegen's heart thumped. This isn't just fire; it's mass murder! I must put a stop to it. Maybe if I can light fires, I can also put them out. She whistled for Wolf, and together they ran as fast as her wound would let her. The flames in the midden rose to the top of the palisade as men jumped from fire to more fire. The screams of the dying made her freeze in her steps.

It was too late.

A harsh cry made Tegen stare. *Krake!* So you have escaped, have you? On this night when all evil should be put away, it seems to be pouring out of the pit faster than ever . . . *'Lady, help us!'*

In that moment, she saw the raven's silhouette flying

with outstretched wings through the flames. She tried to gain height, then twisted and fell, plummeting into the inferno. From out of the fire came an agonized howl of fury and loathing: *'Tegen!'*

Tegen kept her heart's pace steady as she stood straight, raised her hands and said aloud, 'Derowen, return to the demon who bought your soul. Be gone, both of you!'

A sigh of despair blew through the leafless trees and a jet of belching flames roared high into the night as Tegen spat and guarded herself with a spirit shield.

A figure standing nearby spoke softly. 'Your words sounded very heartfelt.'

She spun around. The firelight flickered on a tall, broad-shouldered man, but his face was in shadows. She nodded. 'That bird was evil. The spirit of someone I once knew possessed its body. Someone who brought hate and destruction everywhere she went.' Tegen paused, 'And there was a demon too . . .'

The man stared at the all-consuming flames. The palisade at the top of the hill was buckling and falling. The twisted, blackened memories of Sinodun shimmered in the heat.

Tegen turn to the man. 'Excuse me, I must go; I might be able to lessen the fire and help some of the poor wretches trapped there.'

He touched her arm gently. 'You can't help. Some fires have to burn themselves out before there can be coolness.

Save your magic for what *can* be achieved. Come back to the celebration. Bring your dog.'

Reluctantly she followed him, her heart heavy. Surely this was an evil she might have been able to avert – at least a little? But she knew he was right.

In the light of the bonfire, people were drinking and singing. A trestle table of wine and cakes had been set out, but no one had eaten any: for these were soul-cakes – sweets for the ancestors, ready to be dedicated.

'Do you think our dead come back and share the feast?' Tegen asked.

'Certain of it. Come.' And the man led the way to the table. She took three cakes and poured a beaker of mead.

'Who are those for?' he asked.

'Griff, my foster-brother; Gilda, my best friend; and a man I once met – a blacksmith. He was very wise,' she said as she walked across to a cluster of bare trees. She laid the cakes between the roots and poured the mead over them. 'May you all be born again soon,' she whispered.

51. Epona

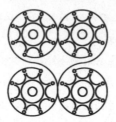

'The Romans are coming!' Shouts and screams swelled in the night.

Tegen turned. Not only was the whole of the stronghold alight, but now the trees on the sacred hill were aflame as well.

People screamed and ran hither and thither. No one knew where to go, or why. Panic spread faster than the flames in the night.

At the bottom of the stronghold hill, a line of shining helmets betrayed an army marching forward in a steady formation across the meadow. It was just as she had seen at the end of the fire spiral!

An order was barked. The pattern of gleaming changed. Raised iron spear tips shone red, as did the drawn swords between the tight shield formation. The thud, thud of hundreds of booted feet made the ground tremble.

Tegen felt a strong hand on her arm. 'Hurry! Follow me.'

The man's dark figure disappeared into the even darker night. Tegen followed, groping her way between the trees. The comforting rub of Wolf's hide pushed against her as she ran, guiding her towards a tall, pale shape.

'Epona!' she gasped.

The man caught Tegen by the waist and swung her up, then gave her a bundle. 'Strap it to your back,' he said. She stared down at the scarcely lit face at her side. 'You . . . You're *Goban – the smith*?' she whispered.

In the faint flickering light he bowed.

'But I . . . Didn't I . . . ?'

'You did,' he said. 'But as the old song says, I, like the barleycorn, have sprung up again to bring life to the land. Now go. You can do no more here. Your path lies north-west until you come to the mountains. Go through them to the sea, and then turn due north. You will find help on the way. Remember, you must never be afraid. It is fear itself that destroys – not that which is feared.'

Tegen swallowed hard. She glanced around. The shouting and screaming were getting closer. 'But what about Owein and Sabrina and all these people? I'll be needed to help!'

'If you stay, you will never fulfil your destiny. I will do what I can here. Trust me, you *must* leave.' Then Goban pushed a cool ring on to her middle finger. 'Take this back; you'll need it. And always trust a smith.'

Just then, someone came crashing through the trees.

'*Go!*'

Tegen leaned down and kissed his bearded cheek. 'Thank you!'

Goban smacked Epona lightly on the rump.

As the horse gathered speed a sobbing voice called out of the darkness, 'Tegen . . . Tegen . . .' A hand snatched at the reins. 'Take me with you!' Kieran begged. 'I'll do anything, but take me, *please* . . . !'

Tegen gripped his arm as he sprang up behind and together they cantered into the night, with Wolf's steady stride alongside.

SAMHAIN

When the new year begins
All that is diseased and evil burns.
The ancestors' spirits visit their old hearths
and are reconciled to change.
The world appears dead . . .
. . . but it only sleeps, waiting for new birth.

Dawn

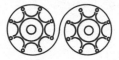

When Tegen awoke, it was dawn. A light frost and a pale mist made the world look white. She was shivering, for the rock she had sheltered under gave little protection from the cold.

Curled up next to her, sharing her cloak, was Kieran, still asleep. She glanced down at him. She didn't want to take a new companion. As soon as they reached a village he would have to find someone to take him in.

She opened Goban's bundle and spread the contents out. There was bread and cheese but, most importantly of all, another cloak, wrapped around an ovate's dress as green as the mossy turf.

She tucked her old cloak around the boy and, without waking him, pulled her new clothes on over her old. Then she led Epona to a stream to drink. The horse lowered her head to the water while Wolf splashed playfully. Tegen looked around for the sun. Which way was west? The hazy sky spread an even light across the wild open countryside as far as she could see.

Then she spotted a thick pall of smoke hanging heavy in the distance behind her. She went back to the rock and woke Kieran. 'Time to go,' she said.

There was no sign of Owein, and she didn't even have Griff's staff to comfort her. All she had in the world was a dog, an iron ring, a white horse and a green dress.

But for now, that was enough.